THE PERFECT FAMILY

Jacquie Underdown

ISBN: 9781687456762

The Perfect Family

***Three everyday couples, from one ordinary family …
and an astonishing murder plot.***

Outwardly, The Radcliffes are a typical suburban family. But anyone close enough to them will know that it's all for show.

Matt and Nikki's life is perfect. They're happily married, work great jobs, and are raising two loveable teenage sons.

Anthony and Belinda have it all—the looks, the big house by the water, and a successful business.

Vaughn and Paige couldn't be more in love; they can't wait to start a family of their own.

But underneath, each couple is in crisis and there is one root cause. Out of options and their backs against the wall, they discover that murder isn't a tool reserved only for criminals.

Table of Contents

About the author

Jacquie in an Australian author who lives in Central Queensland, Australia, where it's always hot and humidity coats the skin, summer or winter. After writing her first story over a decade ago, it didn't take long for the writing bug to take her over completely, and she happily did away with her business career. Now she spends her days wrapped up in her imagination, creating characters, exploring alternative realities, and meeting a host of characters who occupy her mind at first, then eventually her books.

Her novels, *Bittersweet* and *One Hot Christmas*, were finalists in multiple categories in the Australian Romance Readers Association awards in 2019 and 2020. Bittersweet was also a finalist in the Romance Writers of Australia RUBY Awards in 2019. Jacquie has a business degree, studied post-graduate writing, editing and publishing at The University of Queensland, and earned a Master of Letters (Creative Writing) from Central Queensland University. But all that means is that she's super-dedicated to writing the best books she can for readers to enjoy.

With well over a million words published, be sure to check out her many published novels, novellas and short stories that will hit you in the heart with deep emotion and fill you with love. You can find out more about Jacquie on her website: https://www.jacquieunderdown.com/

Acknowledgements

Being an author is a solitary career, but no book is ever created without help from others. This book was no different.

Liz McKewin, thank you for reviewing the original draft and offering suggestions that helped improve this story immensely.

Thank you, Lea Darragh, for speed reading this story when I thought all hope was lost. You gave me the confidence I needed to push through. And your notes surrounding a major conflict helped shape this story in a positive way.

Sue-Ellen Pashley, much thanks to you for reviewing my psychologist scenes. I appreciate your guidance.

Thanks, Nicola Beshaw, my patient sister, who puts up with all my medical-related questions. I appreciate you pointing me towards the right resources regarding asthma treatment.

And to the daughters-in-law who shared their stories with me, thank you. You may note a few of them have made it into this novel (but don't worry, I won't say who you are).

Dedication

For kind-hearted mothers and mothers-in-law.

Prologue

I usually hated death. But there was something different about this death. As I watched the lacquered timber coffin being lowered deep into the grave, instead of stifling sobs or my heart sitting like a lump of smouldering coal in my chest, I was comforted.

That weight I had worn across my shoulders was gone and my muscles were left limber and buoyant. The blue sky suspended above this small assemblage of mourners was expansive, the sun warm. I ached to turn my face to the balmy glow and smile.

Emerald leaves hanging from overarching tree branches waved and rustled in the breeze. A breeze that didn't carry the scent of death, but life, new beginnings and moving forward with freedom.

Sniffles and tears sounded beside me and snapped me from my contemplation. I had to remember where I was. A funeral. Funerals were sad. Death was bad.

Murder was abhorrent.

Maybe. I didn't know for certain anymore. I saw murder differently now. Too many grey areas. Too many details and factors and consequences.

I know you are wondering how I could possibly feel this way about something so despicable, but, please, give me a moment to explain.

If a snarling wolf, fangs bared, backed a flock of bleating, stumbling sheep to the edge of a sheer cliff, and there was no one to usher the sheep back to safety because the wolf expertly concealed its maliciousness from others, then didn't it make sense, if you had the opportunity, to eliminate the wolf and save the sheep?

Or did you, day after day, allow the wolf to brutalise the sheep until, with a nudge of its snout, it tossed them, one by one, over the edge to plummet and splatter on the rocks hundreds of metres below?

Survival of the fittest. The wolf was stronger, right? That's what we're conditioned to believe. But we can all agree that today's survival of the fittest is distorted by laws and regulations and affords all the power to the wolf while the sheep are censored, shackled or sent to jail if they dare fight back.

Well, I fought back. And I don't feel guilty. The wolf had to die. I won't apologise. I won't because I had no other choice. None I could live with.

I'm only sad that death didn't come sooner because the damage caused wouldn't have been so extensive. But that was my error of judgement, you see, because this wolf wore sheep's clothing, and it took me too long to see what was lurking underneath.

Chapter 1

Nikki

Nikki gripped the steering wheel, knuckles white, and stared out the windscreen at the damp, winding road ahead. On one side were tall she-oaks, turpentine trees and a carpet of ferns, and on the other side was a sharp plunge hundreds of metres down the side of the Blackall Ranges to the valley below.

Her breathing was short and shallow. A dull buzzing in her ears. Her heart thumped, each pound hard and insistent, convincing her she was about to die. But Nikki wasn't about to die, merely driving to work.

She couldn't deal with another day at work. Not the fluorescent lighting. Not her small cubicle and lone computer. Not the aroma of cheap coffee that tainted the stale air blasting from the air conditioner.

Of late, her nervous system had been rioting. The slightest incident, even something as petty as a tax interview with a client, would dump adrenalin into her bloodstream and make her hands shake. Attempting to hide her nerves as her fingers tapped on her keyboard with the client barely a metre across the desk only made matters worse.

No, she couldn't do that today. She couldn't be there.

Nikki pressed her foot flat to the accelerator and yanked the steering wheel hard to the right. The car thrust forward, tyres skidding against the soggy bitumen, crossed the road and thundered through a wall of ground trees before colliding into the thick trunk of a pine.

The car crunched and buckled—a cacophony of steel, glass and wood. She slammed forward, breastplate whacking against her seatbelt, and face-butted the exploding airbag before being flung back hard in her seat.

All went silent bar the *tink, tink* as crumpled metal adjusted under the residual heat from the engine. The heavy scent of petrol curled through the car's cab.

Nikki's breaths came harder. Ears rang with an eerie high-pitched squeal. Warm fluid trailed from her nose. She wiped at it with her arm, leaving a bloody swatch along the sleeve of her white blouse. Her nose throbbed and chest ached, yet, beneath that, relief ballooned.

With trembling hands, she unbuckled her seatbelt. She groaned, pain igniting in her lungs as she stretched for her handbag that had fallen from the passenger seat onto the floor. She rummaged for her phone; finally found it.

The rumble of a car. Pops and crackles of sticks and rocks as it pulled onto the side of the road and stopped. A man raced out. Nikki let her phone fall onto her lap, and she rested back against her seat. A long sigh rushed from between her lips.

The man was jittery but spoke in a calm manner. His features were blurred. Each word he said sounded far away, gluey. He checked her over. Asked questions. She couldn't determine if she answered them well.

Within minutes, an ambulance, a police car and a tow truck arrived. More questions. More checks. And then she was assisted onto a gurney and wheeled into the back of an ambulance. She closed her eyes and sank into her relief as she was driven away.

At the hospital, Nikki waited in a curtained room in the Emergency Department. A doctor would be by soon to assess her injuries. Her husband, Matt, had been phoned.

By the time Matt arrived, she had already been treated. He stood beside her bed, his big comforting energy taking up all of the remaining room. Her injuries were twofold—a broken nose and a bruised breastplate—but nothing she needed to be admitted for. So, at twenty-two minutes past twelve, Nikki was allowed to go home.

Matt held her with a strong arm around her back and assisted her inside their Flaxton home. A functional house set on a peaceful plot of land situated beside a tropical rainforest reserve. The three-bedroom, double-storey house had enough space for their family of four.

Sweet, sweet home. This consoling feeling of coming home was everything. All else, all other aspects of life, were moments to be endured until she could come back here again and be herself. This place was her refuge.

She looked at her husband's face and her shoulders relaxed. He was another refuge. Tall, reassuring, unfaltering. He wore his work uniform—a high-vis shirt tucked into navy-blue pants. Pens and a small notepad filled his breast pocket. He smelled subtly of hot steel and fuel.

Their relationship was no longer normal. Somewhere along the line, it had morphed from an equal partnership into one of dependence. Not dependency in a financial or even an emotional sense, but more that Nikki depended on Matt for her sanity. She depended on him to function from day to day and discreetly disguised her crumbling autonomy behind his strength.

His blue eyes blazed with concern. "How are you feeling?"

"Not great." The hospital had given her an anaesthetic spray in her nostrils, so they could assess and clean her nose painlessly, but it was wearing off, replaced by a dull throb.

Her gaze fluttered away from him. Sitting in the back of her throat was a confession. She ached to tell him the truth that she had purposefully driven her car into a tree, all because this anxiety that sat millimetres under her skin and raced through her blood, made working impossible.

But Matt didn't believe in mental afflictions. As an engineer, he was logical, binary. That's what she loved about him—she knew where she stood. Order. Structure. Black and white. But now, she needed a little shadow in his outlook, enough to ask for help. After fifteen years of marriage, though, she didn't expect to find it; he would hunt for a definitive solution and apply it.

"Come sit on the couch. I'll grab some pillows off our bed. Do you want a cup of coffee?"

She nodded and followed him into the living room. "You're not going to get in trouble for leaving work?"

He smiled. "I'm pretty sure my wife having a car accident is an adequate excuse to have the day off."

Nikki managed a smile back. When he left the room, she eased onto the couch and held her hands up in front of her. They weren't shaking anymore.

The full force of what she had done solidified in her mind. She had, with these hands, pulled the steering wheel until her car careered off the road into a tree, so she didn't have to go to work.

Maybe she should have called her boss and pretended she was sick. But that phone call seemed more difficult than everything else she had endured today and much too temporary.

She lifted a hand to her head, squeezed her eyes closed. What a broken piece of equipment this brain was.

Matt's footsteps clunked down the stairs. He appeared with two bed pillows and placed them on the end of the couch. "Here you go. Make yourself as comfortable as you can. Do you need help resting back?"

"I should be okay."

"I'll go make that coffee."

He started to leave, but she called to him. “Um, I…” *Today wasn’t an accident. Today wasn’t an accident. Today wasn’t an accident.* The words clanged around in her head, but she couldn’t draw them out into shapes and sounds.

She didn’t want to be that person who did silly things like this. Not for Matt. Not for her two sons. “I’m sorry about all this fuss today. I feel like such an idiot.”

He shook his head, forehead creasing. “You don’t have any reason to feel like that. It’s fine. You’re okay. We’ve got insurance for the car. No harm done. I’m just glad you didn’t head down the side of the range.”

Nikki shuddered at the thought. “Me too.”

“It must have given you one hell of a fright.”

A sharp nod. “It did.” Tears pricked the back of her eyes, heat flushed her cheeks. What kind of mother would do this? What if she had lost control and spun out down the range, leaving Matt and her sons alone? Was work really so bad?

“It’s okay,” Matt said as he took a seat beside her again. He rested his hand on her lower back and rubbed gently in large circles. “It’s over now. You’re safe.”

“I know.”

Outwardly, she was a little worse for wear but otherwise okay. It was inside her head that she worried about.

When Matt left the room for the kitchen, she slipped her shoes off and slowly leaned back, resting her head against the pillows.

She had to see the silver lining here—the whole purpose of today—for the next two weeks, thanks to a doctor’s certificate, she didn’t have to face work. For the next two weeks, she could let this broken brain recuperate.

By the time Matt came back with her coffee, she had convinced herself it was better he didn’t know the real reason behind her accident.

Chapter 2

Belinda

Belinda shoved her shoulder against the door leading from her dark garage into the main house. She juggled a tray of leftover lasagne in one hand and her handbag in the other.

Her muscles ached under the weight of her day. Yet another phone call from a debt collector about yet more money she owed. She flexed her fingers around the plate and swallowed hard.

"Anthony?" she called.

"In the kitchen." His deep voice was medicinal. In those three small words, she heard all she needed—they were in this together, and she didn't have to shoulder their financial woes on her own. In her next breath, reality sank back in. Her stomach lurched. They may be in this together, but she sure as hell felt responsible for getting them into this mess.

"So, I got a call from the ATO…" She rounded the corner to the kitchen and stopped mid-stride when the first person who came into sight was the back of her mother-in-law, Claire. Her questioning gaze sought Anthony's.

He smiled a big welcome-home smile. "Hey, gorgeous."

"Hi." She looked at the back of Claire's head of shoulder-length blonde hair. "Um, hi, Claire, I wasn't expecting you."

Claire turned in the chair and smiled when their eyes met. She was a tall woman—height that all three of her sons inherited. Her shoulders were broad, accentuated by the square-cut shirts and dresses she wore. On her lips, in contrast to her pale skin, was bright red lipstick.

"Lovely to see you, Belinda. Oh, and what do you have there?"

Belinda lowered the plate so Claire could see. "Lasagne. Made from all organic ingredients. Leftovers from the shop." Belinda had owned an organic store for the past seven years. Handy when the last thing she felt like doing was cooking and the last thing she could afford was food.

"I remember the pressure to get dinner on the table," Claire said. "I worked full-time while raising the three boys. I always felt like I was sprinting, especially when I got home from work."

Belinda's neck tightened and her teeth clamped hard together when *children* were mentioned. She would give anything to hear small, scampering feet in this house. But in eight years, she and Anthony hadn't managed to conceive.

"Here, let me help with that," Anthony said, taking her handbag and the plate. "You staying for dinner, Mum?"

Claire set her darkest brown eyes on Belinda's.

"Stay," Belinda said. Having a conversation about anything other than her finances for a couple of hours would be a pleasant change.

"I'd love to."

Belinda reheated the lasagne and put together a simple salad—very simple as they didn't have a lot in the fridge. They sat together around the dining table that was long enough for twelve guests, their voices echoing off the high ceiling.

Never was it more apparent that they had overstretched themselves with this house. Their waterfront dream home, meticulously planned, built by a renowned builder and decorated from scratch. Everything brand new. Adjacent the Maroochy River. Five bedrooms, a designer pool, a home office and Italian decorative tiles.

How were they to know that the income from Anthony's once-booming heavy-fabrication shop would shrink by forty per cent? How were they to know that the house they paid over one million dollars to build would halve in value in a matter of eighteen short months? How were they to know that customers would tighten their purse strings and do away with such indulgences as *organic* products?

She should have listened to her sister-in-law, Nikki. She had said the first thing her clients did when they started making cash was get into debt: buy a car, go on an overseas holiday, or in Belinda and Anthony's case, build their dream home at the top of the housing market right before a crash. Now they couldn't even sell this place.

"So, did you hear about the car accident?" Claire asked.

Belinda and Anthony looked wide-eyed as they shook their heads.

"Who?" Anthony asked.

"Nikki."

Belinda gasped. "Is she okay?"

"She's fine." Claire gave a dismissive wave of her hand. "A broken nose and some bruising, but she'll live."

Anthony frowned. "I thought Matt would have phoned to tell me."

Claire speared a cherry tomato with her fork. "They were busy with calls to their insurance company, and they were at the hospital most of the day."

"He managed to call you," Anthony pointed out.

Claire shrugged. "Don't make a big deal out of it. They needed my help. That's probably the only reason they called me. After today, I'd much rather I didn't know."

"Why's that?"

"I've been cleaning all day to give Nikki a hand. She can't do it in her state. Her house was…" She shook her head. "She could use the help of a house cleaner. They're so busy and all."

Belinda may not be great with finances, but she was house proud. She knew too well the state of Nikki and Matt's home. How could intelligent, organised people be so hopeless at housework? They've only got the two teenage boys. Surely it can't be that hard.

"Each to their own," Anthony said. "I'm just glad to hear Nikki wasn't seriously hurt."

"Me too," said Claire. "Although, I am worried about her."

Belinda's head cocked and her brow arched. "How so?"

"I'm not sure exactly. Maybe I'm… I don't know…" Claire lowered her eyes to the food on her plate.

"What, Mum?" Anthony asked.

"My friend from my art class—Julie—she's the mother of the man who was first to the scene. He was driving over the hill behind her when she skidded off the road. He said there was no reasonable cause for her to have had the accident. He said it was like she almost did it on purpose."

Belinda gasped. "Surely not. Why would she have any reason to do that? She has those two boys to look after."

Claire grimaced. "That's what I told Julie. There must have been oil on the road, or it was still wet from the rain overnight."

Belinda shared a curious glance with her husband.

"I'm sure it's nothing. Small town gossip."

"Maybe I should give Matt a call," Anthony suggested.

"Keep it to yourself," Claire said. "No use shoving your nose in, especially if it's unfounded. Could cause more harm than good."

They continued to eat their meals, but the chatter melted into the background of Belinda's mind. She was lost to her worries—mainly the phone call from The Australian Taxation Office demanding twenty thousand dollars before the end of the month to cover outstanding withholding tax.

The gravity of this existence was too much at this time of night. Belinda's eyes stung. She rolled her neck from side to side, allowing little pops and cracks to ease the tension. She ached to jab her fingers into the hard muscle of her shoulders and knead it like dough.

"I probably should get home," Claire said. "You look tired, Belinda."

"Oh, no. No, that's fine. Just a little tight in my neck. I haven't been taking care of myself enough lately." Unable to afford a physiotherapist or masseuse was more like it.

"And here I am taking up your time." Claire stood and piled their empty plates on top of each other.

"Mum," Anthony said, but Claire kept on.

Belinda parted her lips but found she couldn't object to Claire leaving. She was utterly exhausted, needed to vent to Anthony about the phone call, have a cry in the shower afterwards, and then head to bed.

Claire helped load the dirty plates and cutlery into the dishwasher and cleaned down the benches.

Much like a socially aware robot, Belinda maintained a polite disposition as they walked Claire outside to her car. The September evening remained cool from the salt-laced ocean breeze.

When Claire drove away with a beep of her car horn, Belinda turned to Anthony and tears sprung to her eyes. Every last ounce of strength in her muscles dissolved, and she was no longer capable of holding her body upright. Her shoulders sagged, head drooped.

Anthony took her in his arms, held her against him. "It's going to be okay, Bel. I promise."

Tears ran down her cheeks and wet his shirt as she rested her face on his chest. "You can't say that. I don't think it is. I had a call from the Tax Office—"

"I borrowed twenty grand from Mum."

She jerked her head upward and looked at him, lips parted, eyes wide. "You what?"

"We had no choice. If I didn't bite down my pride and ask for help, we would soon drown. You know it, and I know it."

Belinda unravelled her arms from around him and took a step back. "But from your mother? It doesn't feel right."

"She was fine. She actually seemed happy to help. We should have the money in the bank in the next day or two."

A part of her tingled with the relief, and yet it didn't feel like something Anthony should have done without a conversation first. "You should have consulted with me," she whispered, voice hoarse.

"I didn't want to burden you with it. I called Mum on the way home from work, invited her over and asked outright." His attention wandered to the imposing houses in the darkened street, their lights glowing through the windows. "Come on, let's not talk about this out here." With an arm around her back, he piloted her into the house.

Belinda sank onto the couch in the living room beside Anthony and lowered her face into her hands. "What if she tells people about this?" She gave a long-suffering sigh. "They will know we're in trouble."

"I asked her not to."

She lifted her head, met his eyes. Blue eyes like his late father's. "She'll tell your brothers. I won't be able to face them again if they know we've borrowed twenty thousand dollars."

"Mum promised me." He rubbed her back with a soothing hand. "Trust me. It'll be fine."

"You promise?"

"I do. And besides, we don't have a choice. That ATO debt is the final nail in the coffin. I had to ask Mum, or we'd sink."

Tears welled, but she wiped them away with the heel of her hand.

"Hey, come-on. It'll be okay. We don't have to pay her back until we're on our feet again. This gives us some time."

"She said that?"

He nodded, a small smile curling his lips.

She sat up taller. "It will give us some breathing room."

"Exactly." His smile grew. "See, it's not all bad."

She leaned forward and kissed his stubbled cheek. He smelled like salt and man and subtle cologne. Even after nine years of marriage, she loved everything about him. His bear-sized height and build. His kind, gentle nature. His promise to always remain by her side. So far, he had stuck to that one hundred per cent.

"Thank you," she whispered. "I love you so much."

"I love you too, gorgeous."

Chapter 3

Paige

Paige checked the slab of pork belly roasting in the oven. The top layer of golden crackle was bubbling and crisping. She closed the oven door and breathed in the delicious, meaty aromas that escaped.

Kneeling on a stool at the sink, her three-year-old daughter played with carrots under the water streaming from the tap. Paige often allowed Evie to *help* her in the kitchen—a great way to keep her occupied while she was cooking.

She tickled Evie's ribcage. "Smells good, hey?"

Evie giggled as she nodded.

"You getting hungry?"

"Yes," Evie said, climbing off the stool.

"You finished there?"

Evie nodded.

"Would you like me to put cartoons on while I finish up here?"

Again, the nod as she ran barefooted out of the kitchen towards the living room, her little blonde curls bouncing. Paige made her a drink of milk and grabbed a few biscuits to tide her over until dinner was ready.

Little rumblings of nerves filled Paige's belly every time she remembered that tonight she was meeting Claire Radcliffe. For the past six months, she had been in a relationship with Vaughn, but, during that time, she hadn't met any of his family. Since taking the next big step and moving in with him a fortnight ago, their relationship was officially *serious,* so there were no more excuses to put off meeting his mother.

Today, in between planning and preparing tonight's meal and cleaning the house, Paige had rushed to sew the finishing touches of her client's outfit—a black dolman sleeve knee-length cocktail dress.

A knock at the front door announced her client had arrived for her appointment. Paige hurried to the door to let Marie in and led her through to her sewing and fitting rooms—formerly Vaughn's garage. It was a roomy space, much bigger than the single bedroom she had used at her former two-bedroom place in Mooloolaba.

A big cutting table edged with rulers sat in the centre of the room, multiple clotheshorses were off to the side, and cordoning the garage from the small kid's room she kept for Evie were open shelves filled with small baskets overflowing with cotton spools, lace, thread, zippers, clips and buttons in a rainbow of colours. The sidewall was floor-to-ceiling cupboards stuffed with materials.

Marie squealed when she spotted her finished dress hanging on a clotheshorse. She ducked in behind the curtain, changed into the dress and when she came back out, she spun a circle for Paige. The dress was stunning—a flowing design with a cinched waist that flattered Marie's frame—but it needed a couple of last-minute stitches.

Paige made the few small adjustments to the dress while it was on Marie, in between stories about multi-million-dollar fundraisers and trips to Maui, well outside the scope of Paige's modest means.

Realistically, she could have taken the dress in at the waist another half-centimetre, but time had run out. Had this woman not eaten for the last fortnight? For someone who had been size eighteen since she was sixteen, Paige couldn't understand how anyone could drop weight as quickly as she could gain it.

A little flushed in the cheeks, Paige was finally happy with the dress and organised the final payment. Paige saw Marie out and rested back against the front door, eyes closed. She sucked her sore thumb, which was throbbing from a couple of deep pin pricks.

A pungent smoky scent filled her awareness and her eyes flung open.

"Shit. The pork," she hissed and raced into the kitchen, skidding to a stop in front of the oven.

A plume of smoke puffed from the oven door when she opened it. Tea towel in hand, she slid out the tray, revealing charred meat, too dry and shrunken to be considered palatable even for a dog.

"Shit, shit, shit," she growled as she dumped the tray into the sink. It hissed and sizzled. Dinner was ruined. Hands on hips, she stared at the pork, breaths heavy in her chest, tears pricking the back of her eyes.

"What the matter, Mummy?" came Evie's precious voice as she ran into the room.

"I burnt dinner."

"But I hungry."

She sighed. "Yep, well, I'll have to think of something else." She checked her watch. Six pm. Vaughn was late, Paige still hadn't showered and changed, and Claire would be here in thirty minutes.

The front door swung open, Vaughn strode in. He met her gaze from the foyer, dropped his bag and hurried to the kitchen. "What's the matter?"

She pointed to the scorched, steaming pork in the sink.

The corners of his mouth quirked when he looked at the blackened mess.

She narrowed her eyes, lowered her brows.

The smirk grew into a full-blown grin and Vaughn burst into laughter.

"It's not funny," she hissed, though her own lips were twitching with the need to grin. "Your mother will be here soon. What the hell do we eat?" There were no alternatives in the fridge—she was at the tail-end of her weekly shop. It would have to be takeaway. Wonderful, that would make a brilliant first impression.

"It's funny to me because I know Mum just called me to cancel."

Paige shoved her hands on her hips, leaned in closer in case she hadn't heard right. "What?"

"Nikki had a car accident today, so Mum's been over there cleaning all afternoon to help out. She's exhausted."

Her pulse thrummed. "A car accident? Is Nikki okay?"

Vaughn nodded. "A broken nose. Otherwise fine."

Paige's shoulders relaxed. She glanced at the pork again. "I don't mean to sound rude, but that's the best news I've heard all day."

Vaughn grinned as he drew her into his arms, enclosing her in his big, protective embrace. Warmth and strength. He kissed the top of her head. "How about we organise dinner out next time? That way my brothers and their families can join us too. Kill two birds with one stone. And no cooking involved."

She looked up into his hazel eyes. "That sounds much better."

"So, I guess we're having takeaway?"

Paige laughed. "Looks like it."

Chapter 4

Nikki

Nikki handed Flynn his lunchbox and he jammed it into his overfull school bag. She squeezed her lips together, so she didn't lecture him, yet again, about only taking the textbooks he would need for classes that day.

Ryan's lunchbox fared better but only because he was in grade seven and didn't require so many textbooks at this stage.

Ryan and Flynn were smaller versions of Matt. Both boys were tall but without the full force of puberty, they were yet to stack on the bulk, so were deep into the gangly stage—big knees and elbows set between long thin thighs and forearms.

With their bags on their backs, she ushered them out the front door. They would walk together to the bus stop a little way up the road. With both kids in high school, this was the first time in ten years that Nikki hadn't had to do the school run. Small mercies.

Nikki closed the door behind them and trudged up the staircase to her bedroom. Two days since her accident and her nose was swollen and full of pressure like wet cotton wool was jammed up her nostrils.

All night she moved and wriggled around in bed but sleep only came in small bursts. She had to breathe through her mouth because it was impossible to draw air past her nose, which only made her thirsty, and, with all the water she then drank, she was up all night peeing.

Nikki wasn't someone who coped without sleep. She was a horrendous sleeper as it was, her nights full of strange dreams, sometimes nightmares, tossing and shifting. Meanwhile, no matter how many times she got up to pee or rolled from side to side, Matt would be softly snoring beside her.

How she coveted his brain, full of peace. He could find deep slumber usually within seconds of his head hitting the pillow.

Matt left for work a little after five am. That had been his routine since they first met. Ten-hour workdays were the standard in the heavy engineering industry. She was well-accustomed to taking care of the kids in any condition. She had done the drop-offs and pick-ups with migraines, diarrhoea, the flu, you name it. Her life didn't stop for an injury or illness.

Occasionally, resentment for Matt's schedule, which precluded him from nearly all home duties, would fill her with angry heat. Most of the time, though, she got on with it, knowing that that's how it was. But not this morning when she had barely been able to drag her aching body from bed to help Flynn and Ryan off to school.

While she signed last-minute school forms pulled crumpled from the bottom of backpacks and helped answer the usual questions like 'where are my sneakers?' and 'where is my hat?', she quietly seethed.

Matt had never assisted with the school drop-off and pick-up, but he also didn't help with most other domestic chores. He always earned three times more, which justified the arrangement. And she was the mother and the wife, so culturally, despite what she had heard about feminism, it all fell to her.

Her work life had been patchy. In between taking leave to have children, she was easily burnt out. A few times she had to change roles or reduce her work hours, so she could cope with motherhood, home management and work.

She was always jealous of those mothers who *did it all* because that was not her reality—she had it all, but she could not cope with all of it.

When Nikki woke again, it was almost eleven-thirty—three hours of unbroken slumber. She crept downstairs to the kitchen for a strong cup of coffee, but when she made it to the entry, she stopped.

The dirty dishes that had been strewn across the benches and in the sink when she had seen the boys off to school were no longer there. The countertops were clean. The sink sparkled. The fresh, piney scent of disinfectant filled the air. The rubbish bin was empty and lined with a fresh bag. The floor mopped.

Blisters of anger ran down the back of her neck. She spun and marched to the living room, hands on her hips as she surveyed the carpet with its fresh lines left from a vacuum. The couch cushions were straight. No empty cups or magazines were on the coffee table.

Claire must have stopped in while Nikki was asleep.

This wasn't unlike her mother-in-law. She was the type of woman who had stayed with her for three weeks after each of the boys were born. The type of woman who lent a hand with the housework, cooked meals—an all-round diligent helper.

Had Matt asked his mother to come over? No, he wouldn't even think of such a thing. Not only was his participation in domestic duties limited, so was thinking about them.

Nikki rolled her eyes, headed back to the kitchen. *Aren't I in a mood today*? She was crucifying poor Matt. He didn't deserve it. Not entirely. But this was her brain; it didn't stop. Not even when she slept. Always thinking, talking, calculating, worrying, having imaginary conversations and confrontations and reliving everything. Even scrutinising encounters and exchanges from thirty years ago.

She made a coffee and carried it to the living room, so she could relax with it on the lounge in front of the television. Halfway through the milky flat white, life returned to her veins.

The clothes dryer beeped. *Claire has done the bloody washing.* A full shiver of anger shot through the muscles on either side of Nikki's spine and embedded in her jaw, clamping her teeth hard together. But without the ability to breathe through her nose, she had to soon unclench the tight muscles and inhale.

She should be grateful to have a mother-in-law who did things like this, but one thing Claire was incapable of doing was washing. Although, she managed to keep her own clothes in impeccable order.

Nikki was no domestic goddess by any stretch of the imagination, but didn't the most domestically challenged know that you didn't put worksite-dirty uniforms in with towels, or whites in with colours, or silk shirts in extra-hot drying cycles, or dry good black work jackets with white, fluffy towels?

She marched to the laundry and held her breath as she lifted the washing machine's lid. Inside were spun-dry towels and her expensive lace bra, now stretched and one underwire hanging loose. Nikki gritted her teeth as she slammed the lid shut.

Should she even dare check the dryer? She couldn't help herself. She pulled the warm, detergent-scented contents into an empty basket and glared at her expensive white blouses she wore to work, which were now grey thanks to being washed with Matt's filthy work uniforms. Like her bra, they would be tossed in the bin.

"No one can be this bloody stupid," she hissed.

She closed her eyes and tried to calm the boiling frustration. She imagined what her own mother would say if she called her and whinged about this. "Let me get this straight, you're upset because Claire came over, cleaned your house from top to bottom but didn't do the washing to your standard?"

Perspective. That's what her mother always gave her. Mum was right. A couple of ruined clothes was not the end of the world. Claire was only trying to help.

She pulled her mobile out of her pocket and typed out a quick text.

NIKKI: Thank you so much, Claire. It was a lovely surprise to wake up to a clean house. You really shouldn't have gone to the trouble. I'm going to be home for a fortnight at least, and I'm feeling much better, so please don't feel obliged to clean for me. I know you have a very full schedule. And don't worry about doing our washing—it's easy peasy for me to throw it in the machine and transfer to the dryer. But thank you so much again.

Nikki read and re-read the message at least five times, changing words here and there, hoping that she didn't offend. She did like having a clean house, because, truthfully, she wasn't feeling better, but this arrangement did not sit right.

It had never felt right. Yes, Claire was Matt's mother, but this was Nikki and Matt's home. To have someone letting themselves in, unannounced and unasked, and cleaning her things was intrusive.

Would she feel the same way if her own mother came to help? Nikki frowned and rolled her eyes. That was laughable. Her mother couldn't even visit, let alone bloody clean.

And her own mother would never have helped with her children like Claire did—always perfectly willing to take the kids for a weekend if Nikki and Matt wanted to go away for a few nights.

Her anger cooled somewhat. *Go sit down. Claire has given you a gift.*

At three forty-five pm, Flynn and Ryan rushed through the door, smelling of summer sweat, and announced in their cracking voices, how hungry they were. Nikki smiled to herself. Usually, without her or Matt at home when they finished school, the boys let themselves in and organised a snack, which meant as many sweet biscuits or chips as they could get their hands on.

With two extra-tall teenagers and a one-hundred-and-ninety-centimetre tall husband, the grocery budget was enormous. When hearing how other families could get away with less than three hundred dollars a week for groceries, Nikki was flabbergasted and left questioning her shopping abilities.

Nikki dragged herself from the couch to help her sons in the kitchen with afternoon tea. Seeing their bags dumped on the floor along with their shoes and sweaty socks, she yelled at them to clean them up.

"Your grandmother has just cleaned this place. She'll be upset if you undo all her good work in five minutes."

Moreover, she was worried about what Claire would say—not to Nikki but to everyone else in the town—if she arrived here tomorrow to find that, already, the house was back to its pre-Claire cleaning condition.

She wouldn't put it past her mother-in-law to turn up despite Nikki's text not to. A text, Claire had not responded to yet.

Nikki pressed her palms to the benchtop and closed her eyes. Her heart was thudding hard. Was she seriously getting worked up, yet again, about this? She could name a hundred other women who would beg for their mother-in-law to stop in like a magical cleaning fairy and get their house in order.

"What's the matter, Mum? Is your nose hurting?" Ryan asked. He was twelve, at that awkward in-between man and boy stage, still young enough that he would happily accept a cuddle and indulge in childish cartoons and videogames, yet his body betrayed his youthful mind.

She managed a smile, leaned over and kissed his cheek. "No more than usual. Now, do you have homework?"

He shook his head.

"Do you have homework, Flynn?" she called out, unsure of his whereabouts.

"No," came a deep voice from upstairs.

"You guys never have homework."

"We do it at school."

She threw her hands up. "If you say so. Who wants a salami and cheese toasted sandwich?"

Ryan grinned. "Yes, please."

"Me, please," came Flynn's voice as he skidded into the kitchen. Flynn was a head taller than Ryan and his voice was already a half-octave deeper. "Remember we have football training tonight?"

Nikki nodded. "I know. Dad's going to knock-off early, so he can take you." She was unable to drive yet, and her car was still at the panel beater's.

Flynn lifted his eyes to hers. "Dad's going to take us?"

Nikki laughed. "Don't sound so shocked."

Matt arrived home with the kids when Nikki was on the phone, partway through a takeaway order of fish and chips. The boys kicked their boots and socks off in the lounge, not before trudging grass and dirt up the hall. She rolled her eyes, but, by this time of the evening, she hadn't the energy to get on their backs about it.

And that was her problem. If she had the time to be more consistent with them, perhaps she could have two kids who helped without needing to be told.

Matt was partway through a phone conversation too. He winked at her as he made it to the living room and gave her a thumbs up when he heard her place an order of battered fish.

He pointed to his phone and mouthed 'Anthony' then he strode off. She finished her order and caught the tail-end of Matt's conversation. Something about a house cleaner.

When he ended the call, he joined her on the couch and kissed her cheek. "How are you feeling?"

"A little better. The swelling has gone down some."

He inspected her nose and nodded. "It looks smaller."

"So, what did Anthony want?"

Matt shook his head. "Not a lot. He was recommending a house cleaner he used to have."

Nikki squeezed her lips together. "A house cleaner? Why would he do that?"

"Mum mentioned to him that our house was pretty bad when she cleaned it the other afternoon. Ant thought we might have been interested."

Nikki drew a sharp breath inward. "She what?"

Matt sighed. "I don't know exactly."

"How dare she say that?" She pressed her finger and thumb to her forehead and groaned. Heat filled her cheeks. "How bloody embarrassing. So, what, they think the place is a dirty dump, do they?" Sure, during the workweek, the house was eternally untidy, but it was always clean. Every single weekend, Nikki scrubbed this place from top to bottom—showers, toilets, floors, furniture, washing.

"He was just trying to help."

"Well, I'd rather he didn't. And I'd rather your bloody mother butted out. I didn't ask her to come over and clean. I would have sent her home if I knew the whole neighbourhood was going to hear about how dirty my house was."

"Anthony isn't the whole neighbourhood."

"Really? Want to make a bet about that. God, it's hard enough living in a small town, let alone everyone believing I live in squalor. I sent your mother a text today telling her not to come over. If the house is too much for her that she has to whine to people about it, then it's best she doesn't bother."

"I think it was more that she was worried about mould in the bathroom. You know how she's petrified of mould."

Nikki rolled her eyes. A pedantic freak, more like it. Yes, everyone who knew Claire was aware she was infected by toxic black mould as a child, which nearly killed her. On top of her asthma, it's all anyone ever heard about.

"I have no mould in my bathroom. At all. It's a four-year-old house, Matt. Fully waterproofed. Mould killer is used each and every week. There is no mould!" She was screaming. Her hands were shaking.

He lifted his palms to say, 'okay, calm down', knowing too well not to speak those words aloud. "She's just worried about re-exposure."

"All the more reason for her not to come over anymore. I'll cope. I'll get the boys to help."

"She wants to help. She likes to feel useful."

"I know her intentions are *kind*, but she is not useful. I don't find this helpful at all. It stresses me out." Tears pricked her eyes. She blinked fast, but it was too late, and tears rolled down her cheeks.

Matt's brows lowered. He shifted closer. "What's the matter? Truly the matter?"

She closed her eyes, rested her head in her hands. She couldn't hide this anymore. "I crashed the car on purpose," she blurted before she could stop herself. "I'm not coping with anything at the moment. I think there is something really wrong with me."

Chapter 5

Anthony

One year ago…

Anthony rolled over, turning away from Belinda. How he even managed to make it through to completion anymore was beyond him. Repulsive, the way he would swamp with blood until he was hard and ready the moment she tapped him on the shoulder and said, 'I'm ovulating. Now is our best chance. Come on, let's go try again'.

He would caress her body, revere her as he had earlier in their marriage, where each lovemaking session was exploratory, passionate, when he had never wanted it to end. But now she would turn and twist away, hand him a bottle of lube and tell him in one way or another to go at it.

It. That wasn't the wrong word choice. That's what she had become—an object less than his wife. A receptacle, and he a fertile mule. Yet, there he was, hard and aching, ready to go. Any chance he got, his body made sure he took it.

Biology was a joke. This constant striving for a baby was absurd. So many years of him rushing to get it the hell over with as she squeezed her eyes shut, tightened every one of her muscles, hoping, hoping, always hoping that this time would work.

As he closed his eyes and tried to calm his breathing, his dick slowly shrinking back to flaccid, he almost laughed. Who would have ever thought that having sex on tap would become absurd? His fifteen-year-old self chided him through the tunnel of time to stop being such a whinger—there was once a time he would have done anything for this.

He clamped his lips together, couldn't bear to open his eyes yet and see his wife. She would be lying there with her legs up in the air like a flesh blow-up doll on a single-minded mission.

He rolled out of bed, stepped into a pair of shorts and threw on a T-shirt. He was done. Over it. Having a baby was not worth this. What good would a child be when their marriage was barely existent? A baby would not possess the power to bleach their brains of what they'd endured these past years.

Honestly, he couldn't give a shit about having a kid. He just wanted his wife back—that magnetic pull they used to have. Her laugh. Humour. Cheekiness. When they couldn't be in the same room without desiring so much to touch one another.

He once believed he was the luckiest man alive. Now, he wondered what kind of torturous hell he'd landed in. Exasperation burned through him.

He made it to the door and turned back to Belinda, marvelling at her lean tanned legs and long hair, the colour of the Maroochydore sand, spilling over her breasts. But his resentment tainted the illusion.

"No more," he growled.

Belinda frowned, lowered her legs to the bed. "What?" Fear flamed in her green eyes.

"This ends now. I don't want a kid. It's not worth it. Don't pressure me again. The decision is made."

She pushed up onto her elbows. "You can't mean that."

"I mean it. More than I've meant anything in my life. This is no longer a marriage. I don't even know what we could call it anymore."

Her eyes watered, bottom lip trembled. "But…"

"Enough!" he yelled. Eight years they had been trying. Eight long years. They were broke from the countless IVF cycles they were never able to afford. The moment they had to borrow money, he should have stopped it all.

Obviously, they were unable to have kids. And now they were no longer financially capable of supporting a child. How long would it take for Belinda to accept it? How much more of a hole did she expect them to dig? "It's done."

Ignoring her whimpers of resistance, he walked away, shoulders slumping, through their big, silent house and out onto the balcony. He glared left and right at the endless suburban rooftops lining the canal like oversized blingy dollhouses. God knows how long he stayed there as his wife sobbed and cried and slammed doors.

Then Belinda's trips to the bin began—all the accumulated baby clothes, toys and blankets that filled an entire cupboard and all the space under the spare bed.

His throat pinched and his next swallow was like guzzling gritty sand. Tears welled and rolled down his cheeks. He swiped them away with his palm and sniffled, but they wouldn't stop coming.

He should have put an end to this a long time ago. He should never have let it come to this. Too much of 'them' had been eroded, and he wondered if they could ever claw back what they once had.

Chapter 6

Belinda

Belinda lifted her shirt over her head and threw it on the bathroom floor.

Anthony was sitting on the end of their bed, scrolling through his phone. She glared at him. "I really wish there was a way we could get out of this."

"We can't get out of this."

Along with the extended family, she was meeting Vaughn's new girlfriend tonight. The restaurant chosen couldn't be more expensive.

She unclipped her bra and hung it on the door handle. "We can barely put food on our own plates, let alone spend so much on an overpriced restaurant. And you know if we say we can't have a glass of wine, they'll presume I'm pregnant. And then I'll have to deal with that too." Her voice was shaky, as much as she attempted to keep it steady.

She bit her bottom lip and turned away from Anthony as she slid down her shorts, underwear, and climbed into the shower, slamming the door behind her.

The warm water on her face allowed her a moment to suppress her rising emotions. When she opened her eyes, Anthony was standing at the shower door. He opened it.

"Don't do this, please," he said, shoulders hunched, frown solemn. "I hate that I can't give us a stress-free night out. I feel like I've let you down."

The blade of guilt twisted in her stomach. "You haven't let me down." If anyone has let anyone down, it was her. Six IVF attempts, tens of thousands of dollars, and all of them failed. Not only was she defunct, but she was solely to blame for their money problems. "Honey, I'm sorry. I'm just stressed. A little more than usual."

He nodded, but the frown remained. "We'll have the cheapest item on the menu and one drink each—the house wine."

"Fine. But I'm also pissed about your brother. He leaves a perfectly good relationship and ends up with a girl half his age—"

"Paige is nine years younger—"

"—and now we're expected to play happy families."

"Joanne left him. He has the right to move on."

She spurted a blob of shampoo onto her palm. "Yes, but with a twenty-six-year-old? Didn't your mum say her ex is an NRL football player? God, I can't deal with this and I'm not even there yet."

"He's my brother. We need to support him. He was a mess after he and Joanne divorced. I think it's great that he's finally getting on with it."

"How surprising for you to think this relationship with a younger woman is wonderful. Typical man." She aggressively scrubbed the shampoo until her scalp stung from her nails. She longed to be what this young woman represented—fertility—so much her bones ached. Vaughn's girlfriend already had a child and a long future of fertility ahead of her.

And here Belinda was thirty-five years old and hadn't been able to have an embryo do anything more than be transferred inside her womb then die and be reabsorbed by her body. All that ancient shame she held about her infertility crept up her neck and flushed her cheeks. Her throat grew tight and painful.

"Never mind," she whispered, unable to meet her husband's eye. "Shut the door, please, so I can get ready."

"Belinda, don't be like this."

"I'm fine. Let me get ready or we're never going to get there."

Chapter 7

Claire

The past…

After school, Claire charged through the front door and called for her mother. The house was silent. Her little sisters' giggles and childish chatter floated further behind her. They had stopped in the front yard, backpacks thrown to the grass, to play on the monkey bars.

When Claire climbed the stairs to Mum's room, the door was closed. She opened it quietly and stuck her head inside. The curtains were drawn, and the room was thick with shadows. Mum lay cloaked in darkness on the bed. Claire backed out, didn't open her mouth, and she didn't breathe—knew well enough not to make a noise if Mum had a headache.

This was the third headache this week, which meant tonight Claire would be scrounging for something to feed her sisters and herself. Her stomach growled thinking about it.

No use counting on her father for anything; he wouldn't be home until Sunday night. She'd overheard Mum fighting with him yesterday—though, the whole neighbourhood would have heard them—to not leave the house with his full pay cheque. To please, for God's sake, leave them something to buy food with. Whenever they had that fight,

Dad would leave the house, self-righteously incensed, and head to the horse track and not come home until he was broke. After one such fight, he didn't come home for three weeks.

Claire tiptoed down the stairs to the kitchen. She opened the fridge. Inside was the usual pot of drippings, a quarter bottle of milk, some cheese and butter. If there was bread in the bread bin, there was at least a dinner to be had. She shut the fridge and slid the bread bin open—a third of a loaf sat in the bottom. The stale, yeasty scent wafted, and her stomach growled again.

But she wouldn't eat now. No, she'd wait until later, so when she finally went to bed, her belly wouldn't be so empty it hurt. Easier to find sleep that way. And her sisters wouldn't whimper all night as their echoing stomachs groaned in the silent darkness.

Instead, she put the kettle on the stovetop, found a tea bag in the cupboard and made herself and her sisters a cup of tea using the one teabag for all three cups. It worked well because she liked the stronger tea and then Maggie the second strongest because she was three years younger, followed by the weakest cup for Sue because she was only seven. She splashed the tiniest bit of milk in each and called her sisters in.

They sat at the kitchen table together and sipped at the weak brew. It would provide satisfying warmth for their bellies, just like food. And it may mean that her sisters would not start whinging quite so soon for dinner.

"Come on, upstairs and have your bath," she said when they were done. "It's going to be cold tonight, so it's best to get it out the way while there's a bit of sun still around." They raced out of the kitchen, giggling. "And be quiet running up those stairs. Mum's got a headache."

Claire washed the teacups and spoons, dried them and put them away in the kitchen cabinet. She collected the girls' bags from the front lawn and carried all three bags up to their room. A small room fitted with three single beds squashed close together to allow enough space for the cupboard door to open fully.

She hung their uniforms up, so they would be good enough to wear again tomorrow, then sat on her bed and looked out the window. Claire had a direct view into Marie's bedroom next door. Marie went to the same school as Claire but was two years older.

Next door's house was spacious. Mrs Andrews was always cleaning it. Always making little cakes and fresh loaves of bread. The scent would drift over and tease Claire.

They had a beehive in their backyard where they got honeycomb. Claire would imagine spreading it on fresh crusty bread, letting the drips of amber sweetness leak onto her fingers and she would lick it off.

Marie's room was enormous. As big as Mum and Dad's. She had a double bed with a patchwork quilt. Right now, she was sitting at her desk in front of a long mirror, singing while she brushed her hair. She had long blonde hair that hung down to the middle of her back. Never a day passed that it wasn't clean and silky. On sunny days, it shone like a glistening lake.

Claire patted a hand down her own hair—limp and oily. They had run out of shampoo last week, so she had to wash her hair with Pears soap. But that was many days ago now. She would have to remember to wash her hair tonight.

Marie ran her fingers through her blonde strands, gathered it up and tied a band around the ponytail. When she brought a thick blue ribbon to her hair and fastened it around the band in a curling bow, Claire was fixated.

A well of envy spiralled up the length of Claire's spine and pulled at her hollow, hungry insides. She recalled a dress of Sue's that had a ribbon threaded through the hem. A beautiful red ribbon.

Claire rolled off the bed and scurried to their small timber cupboard. Hanging inside was the dress, the red ribbon indulgently bright.

She dashed downstairs for the sewing scissors and raced back up to her room, ensuring each step on the stairs was soft against the carpet. She snipped the ribbon, gently pulled it from its weave, shoved it into her pocket, and hung the dress back in the cupboard.

The dress was getting too small for Sue anyway. Much better that Claire made good use of the ribbon.

The next morning, Claire stood before the bathroom mirror that was marred with black splotches around its edges. She tied the red ribbon in her hair, and, turning her head from left to right, appraised the neat bow. She indulged in a smug grin.

While they drank a cup of tea for breakfast, Claire fended off her sisters' questions about the ribbon."

"I found it at school," she finally lied when their questioning wouldn't let up.

Mum still wasn't out of bed. Claire was glad because Mum would know that the ribbon had come from Sue's dress. She would probably even smack her bum for ruining the one Sunday dress Sue wore to church.

Bags packed, Claire waited at the front door until the familiar snap of next door's screen door sounded. She raced outside, heralding her sisters to follow.

She skipped to the end of the driveway just as Marie was walking past their front yard.

"Hi, Marie," Claire said as she stroked a hand down her ponytail to draw attention to her ribbon.

"Hi, Claire." Marie's eyes flicked towards Claire's ponytail. "I really like your ribbon."

Claire grew taller, her chin tilting upwards. Warmth spread through her chest, and she beamed. "Thank you."

Chapter 8

Paige

Paige squeezed Vaughn's hand as they strode across the dimly lit Spanish restaurant to a table along the back wall where Claire waited with a dozen empty chairs surrounding her.

Evie held tight to Paige's other hand and kept pace beside her, each short step double-timed to keep up. She had dressed Evie in an adorable navy-blue pantsuit with capped sleeves that she had sewn for her yesterday.

Nerves gripped Paige's stomach when Claire stood and smiled as they neared. She hadn't anticipated Claire's height, and she faltered a fraction before mustering a smile back.

"So, this must be Paige," Claire said.

Paige nodded, taking in Claire's rectangular-shaped, button-up blouse and white slacks. She wore a colourful chunky necklace and the most striking shade of red lipstick. "I am. Lovely to meet you, Claire. It's wonderful to finally meet Vaughn's family after hearing so many great things."

"And it's lovely to meet you too." With blonde curls, lips that had obviously seen fillers, and a youthful style of makeup, Paige would have placed Claire five to ten years younger than sixty-five.

"And this is my daughter, Evie."

Evie came out from behind Paige's legs. "Hello."

“Hi, Evie. It’s great to meet you.” Claire’s voice took on the tones of a cooing grandmother.

Evie’s smile was shy.

Claire was open and friendly, with a wide grin, but she maintained three feet of distance between Paige and herself.

“Hi, darling,” Claire said, kissing Vaughn’s cheek. “It feels like ages since I’ve seen you. But, of course, you’ve been busy.” She winked at Paige.

Paige’s cheeks flushed with heat. Vaughn laughed and cast a cheeky sidelong glance at her, which made her cheeks burn even more.

“Let’s take a seat, shall we?” Claire said.

Before they could get settled, from across the room strode Belinda and Anthony.

After introductions, Anthony kissed Paige’s cheek. “Nice to meet you.” Then he shook Evie’s hand. “And lovely to meet you too.”

Paige was shocked by how similar and yet different Vaughn looked next to his brother. Vaughn’s hair was a dirty blonde while Anthony’s was dark. Vaughn’s eyes were hazel, yet Anthony’s were a piercing pale blue.

Vaughn and his brother both had height and broad shoulders, but Vaughn was younger and more attractive in Paige’s eyes—maybe it was his clean-cut, professional vibe.

“Nice to meet you, Belinda,” Paige said and leaned in to kiss her cheek.

But Belinda crossed her arms and took a step back avoiding the intimate greeting. “You too.”

Paige stalled, hesitated a moment before she drew back and managed a strained smile that might pass as genuine around people who didn’t know her well. She rested her hand on the back of Evie’s head. “This is my daughter, Evie.”

Belinda crouched and looked Evie in the eye. She smiled so broadly, Paige convinced herself that the coolness she felt a moment ago was an awkward miscommunication. “Hello, Evie. I’m Belinda.”

Evie smiled. “Hello.”

“So lovely to meet you. Have you moved into a new house with Mummy and Vaughn?”

Evie nodded. “I got a pink bedroom. Mummy and Vaughn paint it.”

“I love pink bedrooms. You must feel like a princess.”

“Yep. And I got a unicorn pillow.”

Belinda laughed. “Perfect. You’re a very lucky girl.” She rose up tall again and followed Anthony to a seat.

Before Paige was able to sit down, Vaughn’s eldest brother, Matt, arrived with Nikki and their sons. If she hadn’t been hearing all these names for the past six months, they would have flittered from her memory the moment they were introduced.

Nikki was a muscularly fit woman, only half a head shorter than Matt. She wore black and green bruising under both eyes, which she had attempted to hide behind a light touch of concealer.

“I heard you were in a car accident. I hope you’re feeling better,” Paige said once introductions had been made.

Nikki’s smile was bashful. “I look worse than I feel.”

“I’m glad you weren’t seriously hurt.”

“You and me both,” Matt said, placing a protective hand on Nikki’s lower back.

They all found their seats. Hidden by the tabletop, Vaughn placed a hand on Paige’s thigh and gave her an *I’m here for you tonight* look. His intuition about her needs was one of the many things she loved about him.

“I love your dress, Paige,” Nikki said.

She glanced down at the fitted bodice of her most recent vintage replica creation and brushed her hand along the full skirt. “Thank you.” There was so much about the ‘50s-inspired silhouette and design that flattered Paige’s figure—an internal corselet with bust shaping, raglan sleeves, and shapely darts and seaming. The matte red satin fabric was what she loved the most.

Vaughn extended his arm across her shoulders and smiled with pride. “Paige made it herself. Everything she and Evie wear is handmade.”

Nikki’s eyes widened. “Wow. I would have thought you pulled it off a rack in an expensive shop.”

Pride filled Paige’s chest with heat. “Thank you.”

“Paige is a fashion designer,” Vaughn said.

Belinda arched a brow and tugged on the frill of her sleeve. Belinda’s off-the-shoulder dress was designer but a few seasons out of date, as was Anthony’s shirt. “Really? Like, you actually make money from it?”

Paige smiled. “I do okay. Still operating out of home at this stage, though.”

Belinda nodded, and a tiny flicker of a brow-raise let Paige know that working from home somehow reduced her credibility.

“Vaughn was saying you both run your own businesses too?”

Belinda shifted in her chair, lowered her eyes.

Anthony cleared his throat. “I run a steel fabrication workshop in Maroochydore. We construct all sorts of steel structures—frames for new construction, equipment for mines and industry, that sort of thing.”

“Sounds interesting.”

He shrugged. “I’m not sure *interesting* would be the right word. It keeps me on my toes.”

After a beat of silence, Belinda said, “And I own an organic shop—groceries, skincare, herbal remedies...”

Looking at Belinda’s lean, strong body, tanned skin and blonde hair, she could see how perfectly that fit with her appearance. "Well, it obviously ensures you keep a healthy glow."

Belinda's smile came a little more naturally. "I guess so."

"Now, I want everyone to enjoy themselves tonight," Claire said over the conversation. "Order what you want from the menu and bar, because I want tonight to be my treat."

"You don't have to do that, Mum," Matt said. "Let me get half, at least."

"I insist. And there will be no more conversation about it."

Matt held his hands up, palms out. "Fine."

"That's lovely, Claire. Thank you," Paige said and lowered her focus to the tablecloth to hide that her eyes were glossing. This simple show of generosity from Claire moved her with a ferocity she hadn't anticipated. It spoke to her yearning to fit in and become a loved member of Vaughn's family.

When Paige was seventeen, she had lost her mother to breast cancer. Her mum's death tore her in half with a breath-stealing force, leaving her devastated to her core. She had been parentless for so long she had forgotten what it felt like to be taken care of.

Claire ordered a bottle of champagne and when each of their glasses was filled, she raised hers in the air. "To Vaughn and Paige."

The adults chimed their glasses filled with fruity bubbly, while the kids drank lemonade. "To Vaughn and Paige."

Claire sipped her champagne. "I'm so glad you're finally moving on, Vaughn. I, honestly, never thought you'd ever get over Joanne leaving."

Paige stiffened to hear Vaughn's ex openly spoken about. It was easy to forget that Joanne was not merely a name in Vaughn's history but his wife, Claire's daughter-in-law, and sister-in-law to all the others at this table.

"Mum, do you think that's appropriate?" Vaughn asked.

Claire cupped a hand over her mouth and gasped. "I'm so sorry. I didn't mean to be rude. I was trying to share how happy I am for you." She looked at Paige and frowned. "I apologise, I didn't mean any offence."

Paige waved her apology away. "None taken."

Claire turned back to Vaughn. "See, Paige is mature enough to know I didn't mean any harm."

Vaughn scowled, parted his lips to retaliate.

"So, what's everyone ordering?" Matt asked.

The change in topic gave way to a discussion about what looked good on the menu: garlic prawns, paella, frittata, and various braised meats. The delicious aromas filled the restaurant as waiters rushed past carrying sizzling dishes to neighbouring tables.

Vaughn squeezed her thigh under the table and smiled apologetically. But Claire was right, there was going to be talk of Vaughn's ex-wife. Simple as that. They'd shared a decade together. And, yes, Paige would bristle about it, exactly the same way Vaughn did when he saw her ex on the TV or in the news. Especially when the topic was about her ex's latest female exploits—of which there were many.

"Seeing as we're on the topic of exes. I've got to say, I'm a big fan of Joshua Michaels. For many years. He is a talented footballer," Anthony said. "I've been following the Brisbane Rays since I was a kid."

Matt's brows rose. "Joshua Michaels is your ex?"

Paige suppressed her frown and managed a nod. It was best to get all this out the way, so they could move on. "We started dating in high school when we were sixteen."

Belinda shook her head. "I could never date a footballer. Ever. Is it as bad as I imagine it would be?"

"He was once a really sweet guy. I think, in the end, he got mixed up in the boys-will-be-boys culture." He wasn't always like that, though. When Paige's mother was dying, he had been a rock for her. But then he received attention and accolades as his playing career progressed and his head inflated. Rumour after rumour of affairs.

One night, when she could no longer ignore the news reports and whispered gossip, she confronted him about his latest affair, and he belted her. She'd fled and hadn't looked back.

Vaughn insisted she chase Joshua for child support, but Paige preferred her ex had nothing to do with Evie. No amount of child support in the world was worth Joshua being back their lives.

"And he has nothing to do with Evie?" Anthony asked.

She winced and glanced sidelong at her daughter, who was playing with the ice in her drink with her straw. She resented people who blatantly brought up this type of conversation around Evie. "Um…no."

Vaughn cut in. "Enough of this talk about exes. Please, it's our past. And we'd like it all to remain there."

Anthony nodded and lifted his glass in the air. "To the bright future."

"Speaking of the future," Claire said. "I would love everyone to have Christmas at my place this year."

Darts of excitement pulsed through Paige's limbs. It had been so many years since she had Christmas with a family. How lovely of Claire to invite her. She glanced at Vaughn with a grin, and he shrugged as if to say, 'It's totally up to you'.

"I think that sounds great," Paige said.

Claire smiled. "Wonderful."

Belinda sat up taller and rubbed the back of her neck. "We'll be there, Claire."

"As will we," said Nikki.

"Good. Looks like the whole family will be together again this year. Now, where is this waiter? I think this night deserves real celebration."

Bottles of shiraz, merlot, chardonnay and sauvignon blanc were ordered. Glasses were topped. As they ate

Spanish tapas, one dish after the other until they were almost bursting, they chatted, drank and laughed.

Paige was the designated driver, so she didn't have more than two drinks. Maybe that's why she noticed Claire slurring more and more as the night progressed.

She nudged Vaughn and whispered, "Your mum likes to put a few away."

Vaughn laughed. "Every now and then. But, tonight, she seems to be making an extra effort. It's good, I think she's enjoying herself."

"Yeah, me too."

"And I really think she likes you."

Warmth bloomed in Paige's chest. "You think so?"

His smile was broad. "Definitely. How could she not?" He brushed his lips against her ear and whispered, "You're the most incredible woman in the world. And I love you so much."

His warm breath sent tendrils of desire down her neck, lower, to between her legs. "I love you too."

"Matt was always the logical son. Always so interested in everything," Claire said, snagging Paige's attention. "If he were given a mechanical toy of some kind, within three days he'd have it broken and the insides taken apart. I would get so angry, but your father always knew it was leading to a good place."

Matt laughed. "Exactly. Piqued my interest in all things mechanical."

Nikki placed a hand on his shoulder. "And look at him now."

"Vaughn was the exact opposite. I don't know how two distinct personalities can exist within the same family. Your room was a constant pigsty. You had no time management. And, boy, did you have a temper."

"I got my act together eventually," Vaughn said.

"You did. God knows how."

Paige kissed his cheek. Vaughn owned a local bank branch and had multiple investment properties. At home, he was clean, orderly, though a little of the lack of time management Claire was speaking of was still there—especially his inability to get out the door in the morning or his always showing up ten to fifteen minutes late to appointments. Never, though, had Paige witnessed this so-called temper.

"Excuse me," Claire said, getting to her feet. She swayed a little as she strode towards the restrooms.

"So, Paige, you and Vaughn have been seeing each other for a while now?" Anthony asked.

"About six months."

"And it took you this long to introduce her to us?" Matt said with a laugh, smacking Vaughn's arm with the back of his hand. "We're not that scary, are we?"

"With kids involved, we thought it best to make sure we could see a future first," Vaughn said.

Anthony nodded. "Makes sense."

Nikki crossed her arms and leaned against the table. "So, where did you guys meet?"

Paige exchanged a look with Vaughn and grinned. "The wind blew my door open and dented his car while I was parked outside his bank. My conscience wouldn't let me drive away without saying something. So, I went into the bank and asked whose registration number it was. Turns out it was Vaughn's. He asked me out for coffee the next day. I said yes. And it steamrolled from there."

"I hope you didn't make Paige pay for repairs?" Belinda asked.

Vaughn shook his head. "Of course I didn't."

A loud crash sounded behind them. A chorus of gasps echoed, followed by a string of people lurching from their seats and rushing to the stairs.

They all turned their heads towards the ruckus to find Claire lying awkwardly on the ground at the bottom of the staircase.

All three sons were on their feet and rushed to her. Paige and the others stayed at the table, though they were all standing, watching. Evie started to whimper, so Paige lifted her into her arms and sat her on her hip. She bounced her up and down like she was a one-year-old rather than three, but the familiar movements comforted Paige.

Her breaths were coming quicker as she watched. Her heart galloped in her chest.

Matt had his phone to his ear. Anthony knelt beside Claire. She was talking, which was a good sign. After some hesitation, they slowly helped her to her feet and found a nearby chair for her sit on, though she was hunched and wincing with each small movement.

A waitress handed Claire a glass of water. Her hand shook as she brought the cup to her mouth.

Within ten minutes, an ambulance pulled up outside and two paramedics rushed in. While his mother was assessed, Matt hurried back to the table to give Nikki his keys.

"Can you follow behind us? I'll meet you at the hospital."

"I can't drive." She placed a hand over her heart. "My chest."

He closed his eyes and sighed. "Damn it. I forgot."

Anthony came striding over. "They're ready to go." His words were loud, clipped.

"I need helping getting Nikki and the boys home. How many drinks have you had?" Matt asked him.

Anthony frowned. "Many too many."

Paige looked around her. Wine glasses in various states of consumption sat at every table setting except her own and the children's. "I can drop Anthony and Vaughn at the hospital if you like. Then I'll take Belinda, Nikki and the kids home."

Vaughn placed a gentle hand on her lower back and leaned in. “You can manage that with Evie?”

Paige nodded. “She’ll probably fall asleep during the drive. I can pop her into bed when I get home.”

“I’ll order an Uber for Anthony and me. That way you only have to do one trip.” Vaughn kissed her lips. “I’ll give you a call as soon as we know what’s going on with Mum.”

“Sounds good. I’ll talk to you soon.”

Within moments, the men all rushed outside with the paramedics who were holding on to Claire as she walked slowly, stopping every now and then as pain made her flinch.

Paige slumped onto her chair and blew out a long breath, Evie perched on her lap. “Well, that didn’t end how I’d planned.”

Nikki shook her head. “Not at all.”

A waiter stopped by the table with the bill concealed within a small black folder. He handed it to Nikki with an apologetic smile and strode away.

Nikki opened the black folder and cast a glance over the receipt. “We’ll split it three ways to be fair.”

Paige nodded. “Sure.” She glanced at Belinda who hadn’t said anything. She was pale, her forehead creased. Two lines of tension sat between her brows.

“You okay, Belinda?” she asked.

Belinda nodded and offered a tight smile. “Of course. I just thought Anthony had our credit card for a second there, but I have it.”

“You sure. I can take care of your share if you need?”

Belinda shook her head hard. “Of course not.” She reached into her purse and pulled out a credit card from among a sea of them. She passed it to Nikki. “Here you go.”

Chapter 9

Matt

The past...

Her height. Her long athletic frame, that's what Matt first noticed. Yep, he'll admit it, through today's prism of political correctness, he would be crucified for confessing such a thing. But it was true.

Nikki was gorgeous, with her long brown hair that fell to her waist. The darkest, longest eyelashes rimming feline green eyes. She wore a shade of lipstick so bright and red on the fullest most delicious lips, he believed he would die if he didn't kiss her.

She was not at all perfect or even what his mates would call a stunner, but her face slid into his mind and became the object of every one of his fantasies, past and present. He realised then that she was always the star of his fantasies, but it had taken him this long to meet her.

Nikki was smart, though this he found out later. He was never one to shy from a woman with intelligence. Someone who would challenge him. Opinionated. Sure of herself in the world and all her views. He could partner with that confidence, and it also meant he didn't have to shoulder a lack thereof.

He first saw Nikki at the pub. She was sitting with a group of friends at a table, and he was standing around the bar with workmates. After signing a job offer that afternoon, he was pumped, ten-feet tall.

Matt had done the graduate-engineer time—the miniscule money, the miniscule respect, the work-hardened leading-hands and tradesmen using him as a confidence prop. He'd now moved up a rung. At twenty-four, it was a huge accomplishment. Especially when compared to what he thought his life would be like.

Most memories from childhood were of his bedroom's four walls and the firm give of his mattress beneath his back. His past was full of needle pricks, pain, medical tests and long weeks, sometimes months, beneath bedsheets reading books with medication-addled wonky vision.

He was a sickly child, and though that eroded many chances of social interaction and normal activities like sports, birthday parties and running amok on the weekends with his brothers, it now gave him perspective others didn't have.

It gave him respect for life—his life. He relished the good health he found in adulthood; he was grateful for his physical strength and intelligence. He valued opportunity.

These last few years, Matt became more and more alive and awake. He was ready to take on the world and even though he'd not said a word to Nikki yet, merely watched her surreptitiously from across the beer-sodden, smoky-scented pub, he wanted to take the world on with her.

He let the atmosphere thicken first with insobriety, laughter and recklessness. Let the few glasses of bourbon and Coke work through his muscles and sever any remaining threads of timidity. Because even with his new perspective, he sometimes slipped and believed himself to still be that bedridden boy. Especially when mustering the courage to speak to a beautiful woman. But not just any beautiful woman – *The* beautiful woman he knew he would marry.

Matt swallowed the remainder of icy amber liquid from the bottom of his glass and placed it on the sticky tabletop. He winked at Mike, a fellow engineer at Watford Engineering and Fabrication. "I'll be back. Maybe."

He didn't wait for a response and zigzagged to the table of women who were chattering and laughing like a cage of budgies. The sound was exhilarating as it worked under his skin.

They all stopped when he stood beside the table. The girls of all different shapes, hair shades and eye colours looked up at him.

He'd done all right with women up until now. Girls over the years had said it enough for him to believe it must be true that he was a decent looking man—his height and his eyes were the recipients of most compliments. He didn't care so much about that, but it did give him confidence now, especially with a table full of wide-eyed beautiful women staring at him.

He smiled as confidently as he could. "How are we all tonight?"

They gave various replies and shy smiles, some were more self-assured, and some a little snarky, but he only had eyes for one girl.

"I'm Matt," he said, only to her. Her green eyes held his and all his hopes crystallised with that first glance.

He wanted to look away, but he found he couldn't. She broke his trance by lowering her gaze to her drink. When she looked back up, she said with a warm smile, "Nikki."

"Mind if I join you, Nikki?"

The girl seated next to her scooted to the left leaving room for Matt to squeeze in. He sat, his hip and thigh pressed to Nikki's, among this group of unfamiliar girls. She was wearing a short black skirt that exposed the long creamy skin of her thighs. It was summer in the hinterland after all. Clothes were a hindrance when the weather worked to make them stick to sweat-sheened skin.

"Are you a local, Nikki?"

She nodded then shook her head. "Sort of. Mooloolaba. I've just finished my final exams at university, so we're out celebrating. Thought we'd go somewhere different."

"I'm glad you did." His eyes dipped to her lips, and he could have leaned over there and then and kissed her. "What course?"

"A Bachelor of Business."

He nodded. "What are you planning on pursuing, career-wise?"

"Accounting."

"Great." A profession that spoke to him as much as engineering had—firm rules. Numbers were predictable. Formulas were formulas, unchanging. He appreciated the stability.

"Congrats, Nikki—" he adored the sound of her name's syllables in his mouth, "—that's a worthy accomplishment deserving celebration. Let me buy you a drink. What's that you have there—a vodka and raspberry?"

She smiled and nodded. "Thank you."

He headed to the bar, his chest puffed and blood racing. When he slid into the seat beside her again with their drinks, he offered a toast. "To the new graduates, may your futures be bright."

The girls laughed and cheered as they all clinked glasses and drank deeply.

"So, what do you do, Matt?" Nikki asked, those plump red lips moving in shapes that mesmerised him.

"I'm an engineer. I'm celebrating too. Just landed a new job."

"Fantastic. Must be the night for it."

Her smile was warm, and he glanced at her lips again. "Must be."

"So, you live here?"

"Born and bred"

"It's so stunning up here. A hidden treasure right in my backyard."

She may as well have been describing herself. "Sure is."

Nikki's friends erupted with laughter over some such thing, but neither he nor Nikki noticed, not when being in their own private world was so much more appealing.

They talked and drank for hours until his mind was muzzy. Before he knew it, he was kissing her and she was kissing him back, and it was more than he could have imagined.

His blood was a boiling mass in his veins, his muscles hard and zinging. How this woman with her lips and the way she held his face brought him farther and farther away from that child he was. She made him more of a man. And that's what he wanted to be for her. That's who he was with her.

He leaned back, somewhat breathless. Even he could hear the aroused huskiness his voice had taken on when he took her hand and asked, "Let's go for a walk?"

Those green eyes held his and spoke of so much. She nodded.

Matt led her out the backdoor of the pub. A burst of fresh but humid air rushed across his skin. Gone was the acrid scent of cigarette smoke and stale grog. The backdrop of rainforest smelled of damp leaves and fertile soil.

There was a small park nearby filled with shady trees that could cloak them in shadows. She giggled as they wandered down a set of stone stairs. They arrived near a tall tree, and she pushed his back gently against the trunk. It was cool, but her body pressed to him was burning. Fire.

The way she kissed him then was beyond any kiss he'd ever had—desire and wet warmth as her tongue slid against his. He could barely breathe for the intensity of arousal filling his bones, his limbs, between his legs.

Her focus shifted to his jeans. She unzipped his fly and then pulled her underwear down until they sank to her ankles. Their wild rush of lovemaking was over as quickly as it began.

He was spent, his mouth at her ear, breaths harsh in his chest, commingling with the beautiful sound of her.

“I can be quick sometimes,” she whispered, gasping, splashes of red lipstick smudged across her mouth from their frenzied kisses.

He chuckled, but it was a breathless sound. “Me too, it seems.”

She let out one long exhalation—it sounded like contentment to him. “Now that’s out the way, we can concentrate on all the other stuff.”

He grinned and kissed her lips. “I like the way you think.”

And she was right—now that they had released some of that excited tension, they could just be. Have a conversation. Get to really know each other.

He wiped the stray smudges of lipstick from around her lips. She dressed back into her knickers and smoothed her hair while he zipped up his jeans.

They joined her friends again as though what they had experienced was so perfectly expected and necessary, it didn’t bear mentioning to anyone else.

Chapter 10

Nikki

The moment Nikki arrived home, she sent the kids up to bed. Their grandmother taking a fall at the restaurant had shaken them, but she assured them that Claire would be fine.

When downstairs, she unclipped her bra with a sigh, her shoulders rolling at the pleasure this simple act gave her. She slid the bra through her dress sleeves, threw it onto the coffee table, and plonked onto the couch. She rested her head back and closed her eyes. For a long while, she lay there, practising deep breaths.

Nikki didn't hate socialising, but she didn't exactly like it either. It exhausted her. As a social event loomed, for days, sometimes weeks beforehand, small squeezes of anxiety would swell in her belly. She would persuade herself that she would enjoy the upcoming occasion despite her lizard brain trying to convince her of the opposite. And usually, she did end up enjoying herself. Lately, though, the cost-benefit had tipped in the reverse direction.

Social activities outside of the house all had one end-goal—getting through it until she could come home, take her bra off and relax with only her family to contend with.

She opened her eyes and stared at the blank TV screen on the wall. What a night. Claire falling down the stairs had left a slight tremble in Nikki's limbs and set her heart thumping, but her slow breathing was easing the effects.

As horrible as it was to admit, and she would never say it out loud, she was grateful that she couldn't help Matt and his brothers with Claire tonight. This wasn't the first time Claire had injured herself. What Nikki dreaded, though, were the inevitable aftershocks: hospital visits; last-minute requests to pick up small grocery items, usually at night while Nikki was cooking dinner or racing to get the boys to football training; phone calls, sometimes twice a day to talk about the incident; and Claire's predictable slow recovery.

Claire drank too much, both in frequency and in quantity. First, it was a broken pinkie toe when she kicked the leg of her bed after a heavy night of drinking, then a broken arm when she slipped in the shower. Later came bruised ribs and cuts and sore backs, not to mention all the accidents she kept to herself. The word *addiction* was whispering along Nikki's tongue.

She checked her watch, hoping Matt would soon call her to let her know he was heading home. He was part of the formula for her. On top of craving to be in the comfort of her home, she needed her husband too. His presence calmed the tempest that raged inside of her. God forbid he ever died or divorced her. She shook her head, tossing that thought aside before she worried at it so much it ran through her head on a loop for days.

Nikki showered, dressed into comfy pyjamas and climbed into bed with a book. As she was settling in, the phone rang. The screen flashed with Matt's name.

"Hello, what's happening?" she asked

"Mum's fine. She's sprained her wrist and bruised her elbow, but she's otherwise okay. No broken bones. We're going to take her home now."

She sighed. "I wish I could help out. I hate that I can't drive at the moment."

"Yes, well, perhaps don't go crashing your car next time."

Vibrating heat shot through her. "That's a low blow."

A long breath. "I know. I'm sorry. I'm tired. I'm sick of hospitals. I'll be home soon, and we can chat."

They said their goodbyes and Nikki tossed her phone onto the bedside table. Matt's off-the-cuff comment had her bristling.

Since her admission about crashing the car, he had asked questions about her workplace, needing specifics, so he could wrap his head around what would have sparked her to do such a thing. She had tried to explain that there wasn't anything solid that she could blame.

He couldn't grasp it, nor the severity of how she felt, because there was no black-and-white answer. How could she explain to him what she was dealing with when she had no concrete explanation, only emotions and physical manifestations? He had eventually dropped the subject, though it had hung between them like a bruised storm cloud.

An hour later, Matt arrived home. He showered and climbed into bed beside her, smelling of soap and steam.

Nikki placed her book on the bedside table and rolled to face him. "How did it all go?"

"Mum's in bed and was out like a light before we had even left. The hospital gave her strong painkillers and a relaxant. She didn't stand a chance."

Nikki sat up against her pillows and straightened the blankets across her lap. "Do you think she might have a drinking problem?"

His nose crinkled as he shrugged. "Maybe. I don't think so."

"She worries me. Especially with her living alone. What don't we see?"

"I'm sure it's fine."

"Yeah, I'm sure it is." She crossed her arms over her chest. "I mean, she functions fine. She has no trouble coming around here to clean."

He looked sidelong at her, unsure, for good reason, if she was being sarcastic. She didn't know if she was or not. In the end, she decided she wasn't.

"And she manages throughout the day, going about all her other activities, the art classes and all that."

"Exactly. I think she doesn't know her limits. How old is she now? Sixty-three—?"

"Sixty-five—"

"Anthony's going to stay the night in the spare room, just in case she wakes and needs help. Makes sense that he's who stays with her. They don't have kids to worry about."

"Too worried about their social status to let kids drag them down, more like it. I don't understand that thinking. The kids and you are my life. My whole life and I wouldn't want it any other way."

Matt frowned. "It's not like that."

"Sure it is. Living in that big house. Just the two of them. They don't use their pool. And obviously, they pay people to clean it. What a waste of money. How hard would it be to keep a house clean when there are only two adults to clean up after?"

"That's your accountant-self talking."

She physically shuddered at being reminded of her job. She lowered her head. "Please, don't talk about work."

"I'm sorry."

"I can't do it, Matt. I physically, mentally, cannot drag myself back there."

"Then don't. If it's that bad, take a break. Reassess in a few months' time. Maybe you'll be feeling better."

Tears stung the back of her eyes, so she focused on the bedspread.

He laced his hands behind his head, elbows out wide and looked up to the ceiling. "If you're at the point where you would rather crash a car than go to work—" he met her gaze "—then it's pretty clear you should stop working."

She was quick to look away from him as guilt curled in her belly.

He lowered his arms, turned her chin with a gentle finger until she was looking at his face. The inner corners of his eyebrows were drawn in and up. His lower lip stuck out a little. "I love you. And you need to understand that there are always other options than hurting yourself."

She glanced away to hide her rising shame. "I know," she whispered. "I shouldn't have done it. I just thought, at that moment, it was all I had. I believed crashing the car was the easiest option."

He frowned.

Did Matt believe this was a failure on his part? She grimaced. "What happened was not your fault."

"Maybe."

"Not at all."

He shrugged. "Maybe you don't understand that I will support you, always, regardless of the situation."

"I know now," she whispered and leaned in closer to kiss his lips.

God, she loved this man with all her heart. All her soul. She rested her head on his chest and wrapped an arm around him.

"If I ever lost you…" he stopped, cleared his throat.

"You won't."

He tugged her closer to him and his next exhalation was long and heavy.

"I love you, Matt."

He kissed the top of her head. "I know. I love you more."

Chapter 11

Anthony

Anthony raised his hand to his throbbing skull and rolled out of bed. His childhood bedroom. His childhood bed.

Each step across the carpeted floor ignited his headache.

In the hall, he cast a glance to Mum's room at the end. The door was shut. He closed his eyes for a second as he listened. No sign she was awake yet. Good. He would find himself some painkillers first before he checked on her. Last night, the purple bruising was already blooming across her wrist and elbow. She would be worse this morning.

Anthony would be here to help his mum if she needed it, but he didn't want to come across as the son who was too hungover to be useful. No, he was the good son. The son who was always there when Mum needed him. The son who knew that after his dad died those duties were to now fall to him.

He was the second eldest, so, technically, those duties should be Matt's. But Matt had always been a sick child; it was hard to lose that reputation of frailty despite him well and truly growing out of it.

On slow, light feet, Anthony crept down the stairs. Creaks and strains sounded under every step regardless of his efforts to remain silent. He wasn't a fourteen-year-old boy anymore; he was one-hundred-and-ninety centimetres tall and a hundred kilos. No matter how light-footed he was, gravity wasn't to be stopped.

The house was dim and silent. The familiar scent of recently used bleach was a background scent to leather, books and fresh-cut roses. Birds chorused outside in the myriad she-oak and turpentine trees that grew dense and wild no more than fifty metres from the back of the house.

For three boys growing up, having a rainforest as a backyard was heaven. Especially because at the end of the rainforest was a lake. For weekends and holidays, nearly every hour of daylight was spent in the forest or on the lake in some form or another—dirt-biking, fishing, canoeing, building forts, catching rogue lizards and frogs.

Growing up in Montville was magical. He had tried to convince Belinda that they move here once they had children—to give them the childhood he was blessed to have—but it was not to be.

A hot, throbbing pain filled his chest and worked up his throat. His regret wasn't because he'd been incapable of producing children, but for the place he and Belinda were in. Their life was a relentless river of stress, and it had one source.

He should have put an end to this fruitless baby obsession years ago. What a bloody waste of life. Looking back, it was difficult to find moments where he had simply enjoyed himself. He barely laughed anymore. Between running his business, driving home to their oversized house, letting Belinda unload on him, then sleeping restlessly only to wake up and do it all over again, there wasn't anything else.

A bit hard to sit at a pub to de-stress with a couple of mates when he could barely put food on the table. He and Belinda couldn't take a vacation to unwind and rediscover one another because how could they justify the expense when there was over fifty thousand dollars of credit card debt to pay off? Hell, he couldn't even play a round of golf anymore.

He scrubbed his hands over his face and groaned.

"What's the matter with you?"

Mum. He hadn't heard her—too lost in his thoughts.

He spun to face her. "Nothing, I'm okay. Probably had a little too much to drink last night."

She smiled a smile that possessed the motherly sympathy that soothed Anthony. "There's paracetamol in the medicine cupboard. Grab a couple out. Actually, I'd like two myself."

He opened the cupboard beside the range hood. For as long as his memory would allow, the medicine was always kept in here. Neat and orderly in a long plastic container.

He found a tab and popped four paracetamols onto his palm. "How are you feeling this morning?"

"A little embarrassed, but I'm otherwise okay."

His gaze drifted to her elbow and wrist, but they were covered by the sleeves of her bright pink dressing gown. "You don't need to be embarrassed, Mum. It can happen to the best of us."

She shrugged, wrapped her dressing gown tighter around her middle. "I just feel horrible that I ruined Vaughn's night."

"I'm sure he understands it was an accident." He passed Mum two tablets. "There you go. Get them down."

He made them a glass of water from the tap, handed one to her and used his to swallow the paracetamol and quench his Sahara thirst. He poured another glass and gulped it down.

"How about I make us a coffee?" Mum offered, shuffling towards the jug.

"I'll do it. You go sit."

She did so. He set about boiling the jug and spooning teaspoons of granulated coffee into mugs. Mugs that in all the time he had been out of home still looked exactly like the ones from childhood.

Nostalgia rippled through him. How simple life was then. Even with the stress of losing his father so young, that emotional strain had remained in the background of an otherwise decent life.

Nothing he did now could drown out the worry of bad finances—especially when there seemed no hope in sight to end them. He shook off that dark blanket and poured boiling water into the mugs.

"How did you like Paige?" he asked. "She seemed like a nice woman."

"Yes, she was okay, I guess. Not sure how serious it is, really."

"They're living together. Must be pretty serious."

He turned with both mugs in his hands to find Mum waving away his comment.

"That means nothing. Vaughn's still caught up on Joanne. Paige is merely a rebound. Sure, he might think he's happy, but he's not."

He frowned as he placed the cups on the small timber dining table where Mum was seated, legs crossed. "I hope that's not the case. He deserves to find happiness again. Joanne—she did wrong by him."

"Even so, it's not a reason to grope at the next-best opportunity that comes along."

He sipped his coffee. "Let's just wait and see how it turns out. Vaughn looked happy, that counts for something." He strived to keep the defeat from his tone, but it was harder and harder to hide these days.

His phone buzzed in his pocket. He pulled it out, his stomach twisting because he knew who it was. He exhaled in a rush to see Belinda's name. A text message.

BELINDA: I had to pay a third of the restaurant bill last night. When will you be home?

He clicked out of the message and shoved the phone back in his pocket.

"Bad news?" Mum asked, a brow arched.

Elbows on the tabletop, he buried his face in his hands. "You could say that." His words were muffled by his palms. "My marriage is over."

A soft shuffle as his mum shifted in her chair, but he didn't lift his head. He couldn't—it was as heavy as a boulder.

"You looked fine last night. Why, what's happened?" Mum asked with a cautious edge to her tone.

He finally met her eyes. "I've been thinking about ending it for a while. But the finances… It makes it hard to leave."

Mum's eyes narrowed, she frowned. "I didn't realise it was that bad."

"It's complicated. It's more than just the money troubles." He thought about their almost non-existent sex life. That had fizzled out years ago, evident from their half-hearted attempt for the first time in months a few weeks ago. They went through the motions, but it was soulless, both of them using the other for a quick orgasm because it was about time they did something. "But I'm done. I'm going to talk to her this morning. We're just wasting each other's time."

Mum sighed and in that frown was the sympathy he needed. A frown that said he was not to be condemned for this decision. Recognition that this was the most difficult decision he'd ever made.

His chest ached with grief. How had it come to this? Belinda was his everything and now he no longer wanted to be near her. He couldn't shoulder this life with her anymore.

Tears pricked his eyes, but he blinked them away and stood. As he tipped his remaining coffee into the sink, he cleared his throat. "I better get going."

Mum walked him to the front door. She gripped his forearm as he stood with the door open. "I think you're making the right decision. You have to do what makes *you* happy. And I can tell you haven't been happy for a long time. There's nothing wrong with looking out for yourself."

He nodded, knowing that she meant well, but her words had the gut-twisting effect of highlighting how selfish this decision was. He promised to love Belinda forever until they died. Sickness and in health and all that. And here he was giving up because it was too hard.

But it was the right decision. Long overdue. They needed to go their separate ways and start over again.

Chapter 12

Belinda

Saturday morning, Belinda sat outside on the deck in the mid-morning sunshine. A cup of coffee rested on the tabletop next to her laptop. Cheap instant coffee; they could no longer afford beans.

After last night's blow-out at the restaurant, she had barely slept. Not because of Claire, at least, not once she had heard it was minor injuries—and honestly, it serves Claire right for getting so drunk—but because they had to pay for a third of the night's bill.

With the sound knowledge that Claire was going to be covering the evening's expenses, she and Anthony had loosened up and ordered a main meal, dessert and plenty of wine. It maxed the one credit card that had wiggle room for groceries this week. When she had got home last night, she vomited from the worry.

Anthony arrived and joined her on the deck. The subtle scent of alcohol wafting from him turned her stomach as he sat beside her.

"Hi," he said.

"How is she?"

He shrugged a shoulder. "She's a tough duck. She'll be all right."

She offered a deep sympathetic frown, hoping she had shown enough compassion for his mother before launching into what was truly worrying her. "Do you think we could ask your mum for more money?" Her shame for asking had dissipated now that they had reached desperate depths.

He raked a hand through his dark hair. His eyes were crinkled. "Jesus, Bel, she just got out of hospital last night. I didn't even want to leave her alone this morning, but I knew you would be panicking after being left with the bill." He laid his palms flat on the table and sighed. "I'm pissed about that. I'm trying not to be because Mum could have bloody broken her neck falling down those stairs, but I'm pissed. I wish she hadn't offered to pay for the night."

"Me too. Do you think we could ask her for her share, at least? We did pay for her meal."

She didn't need to see Anthony's top lip curl, baring his teeth, to know that it was a stupid request. They'd come off looking like villains.

"Do we have any money left on any card?" Anthony asked.

She shook her head. "They're all overdrawn. I had three hundred and thirty dollars on the one I used last night. The bill came to three hundred and fifty."

"Christ," he hissed.

"Maybe we can underpay some of your staff this week. Just say we had a computer glitch or something?"

The crinkle of his nose and upward curl of his lip was more pronounced with this suggestion. "I will never do such a thing. My employees are not the reason we're in financial trouble. Without them, I don't have a business. Without them, we would be six-feet under."

"I'm sorry. I just don't know what else…"

He pulled his phone from his pocket and hit dial.

"Who are you calling?"

He opened his mouth to say, but the person on the other end answered. Belinda cringed and wrapped her arms around herself wanting to shrink away to nothing.

"Hi, Mum. How are you feeling? That's good. Did the paracetamol work? Good." He blew out a long breath. "I hate to be a burden." His eyes shifted to Belinda's and scattered away again, but, in that moment, she saw all his shame so clearly. A burning lump formed in her throat and tears pricked her eyes.

"As I told you, Bel and I are in a little bit of a financial crisis at the moment. Yes, yes, I know, but that didn't quite cover all the other aspects of our finances—like the day-to-day living expenses. Well, anyway, last night, because of your accident, not that I'm blaming you in any way, but we ended up having to pay a big share of the bill. No, no, I know… It's fine… No, it's definitely not your fault and I'm not blaming you at all, but I was hoping we could, maybe, borrow some money to do the grocery shop this week. I'm still waiting on a contractor to pay an overdue invoice and it's stretching things thin. Okay, that would be great. Yeah, just transfer it into our account. That would be such a help. You're a saint, Mum, truly. I really appreciate it. We'll bring over some dinner for you tonight, so you don't have to cook, okay? We'll drop it in for you. About six. Okay, you rest up. Thanks again. Bye. Yes, I love you too. Bye."

Anthony ended the call and sagged in his seat, shoulders hunched, head arching back. "Fuck this shit, so much."

A tear rolled down Belinda's cheek. She swiped it away.

Silence sat between them for a long time before Anthony dragged himself upright. "She's going to transfer five hundred dollars into our account."

Belinda blew out a relieved sigh and nodded. "Thank god."

"It should be in there soon."

"Thank you. I know that was hard." She wished that she had someone in her life who could help them out, but her parents had no money. Her father was a professional surfer back in the seventies, but he squandered what money he did make in the early years on drugs, partying and women. And now he had emphysema and was permanently on oxygen. Her mum and dad had to survive on a disability pension.

She was so frightened to end up like them—a difficult life. Though, she wasn't sure it was any more difficult than what she and Anthony were enduring right now.

"Let me write out a shopping list, so we don't go buying anything we don't need." She jogged inside for a notepad and a pen and joined Anthony on the deck again.

She glanced at the glinting river at the base of their yard. Tranquil, deep green. Everyone along this strip had a private jetty. Big boats of all sizes were anchored to each jetty, and they bobbed and splashed, a familiar sound she barely noticed anymore. It always reminded her of a row of men, standing with their pants down, posturing their genitals to one another.

Their jetty hadn't seen a boat for a long while now, not since they sold their thirty-eight-foot Riviera. She turned away from the vacant jetty—seeing it made her chest squeeze like big arms were forcing the breath from her lungs—and focused on her notepad.

"Is there anything that you really need this week? Disposable razors? Deodorant?"

He shook his head. "I should be fine."

She wrote down the usual necessities—bread, milk, pasta shells, budget mince, chicken wings—things that didn't cost too much but were heavy lifters. She would probably need tampons, an expense she didn't care for. Maybe she could skip it this week. She opened the app on her phone that tracked her period. She counted the weeks since her last period.

Her heart thundered.

"What?" Anthony asked. "You're as white as ghost."

Tingles spread over her face, down her neck as she glanced at him then back to her app. There had to be a mistake. She scanned her memory—her last period was the week before Anthony had to travel away for work. She performed the calculations quickly in her mind and gasped when she confirmed the app was right.

After all the years of hormone treatments, planning for ovulation, and religiously filling out this calendar when her period stopped and started, it was correct, almost to the hour.

"I'm late," she whispered, throat tight.

"Late for what?" he asked.

"My period is late." Her words lacked volume. "Three weeks late. I'm never late." She stood quickly and raked fingers through her hair. Her hands were jittery. Her heart was a bullet train in her chest. "That's all I bloody need. Early menopause." She pointed to his chest. "I bet you. I bet you any money. Oh, god, or it could be something even worse?" Panic set in as the word *cancer* filled her mind.

She brushed her hands through her hair and gripped onto the strands as she shook her head. "I can't deal with this, Anthony. I can't. I can't cope with anything more."

Anthony was on his feet. A hand on her shoulder. "Hey, Bel, look at me."

She slowly turned to face him.

"Book an appointment with a doctor and go check it out. It may be nothing." He arched a brow and the smallest glimmer of a smile curled his lips. "Or it may be something."

She flinched, then stared at him, shaking her head. After everything they had been through, he actually believed she could be pregnant. Her heart was a smouldering ember. Hope no longer existed. Absolutely none. If she couldn't fall pregnant after all the expensive intervention, and the five years before that that they had tried and tried and tried, it was never going to happen, least not naturally.

"Don't look at me like that, Anthony. I can't bear to let you down again."

He closed his eyes and growled. "Don't say that. Book an appointment. Go check it out. It's probably nothing. Stress, perhaps. Doesn't that make some women late?"

She nodded and her shoulders relaxed from their hunched position. *Of course. Stress. It has to be stress.* "That's probably all it is."

He rubbed her shoulder. "No use worrying yet."

Belinda sighed. "But we can't even afford a doctor at the moment."

"Find a bulk-billing doctor."

"Fat chance of getting in."

"Worth a shot."

She slumped back into her chair and grabbed her phone. After four calls, she finally got an appointment for that afternoon at a bulk-billing doctor an hour away.

Belinda held her chin high, shoulders squared as she made it back to the counter at the GP clinic to let the receptionist know that her appointment was over. She kept it together as Anthony, who had been sitting in the waiting room for her to finish, took her hand and walked her out to the car. She kept it together as she sat in the passenger seat and buckled her seatbelt around her.

But as soon as Anthony started the car, all the heat in her chest and burning constriction in her throat, couldn't be contained. Tears pricked the back of her eyes. Her bottom lip trembled.

"What is it?" Anthony asked, a hand on her shoulder.

A sob hiccupped from her throat and tears streaked down her cheeks. She shuddered in a breath, trying to find her voice, but all she could do was cry.

"What is it?" he kept asking, but she couldn't make her mouth form words enough to answer. She sobbed as eight years of failure after failure found an outlet.

"Bel, please, I don't know how to help if I don't know what's happening. Is it cancer?"

She shook her head. Tears flooded her eyes, rolled down her cheeks and off her chin. "I'm pregnant," she howled.

"You're what?" His eyes were wide, body completely still.

"I'm pregnant."

Chapter 13

Paige

Monday morning, Paige was in her sewing room leaning over her machine. The scent of new fabrics and the warm steamy aroma from her iron filled the room. Fusible interlacing was pinned to the gathered taffeta of what would become a shimmering gold evening skirt.

A cartoon entertained Evie as she sat on her little couch in the playroom behind the curtained fitting rooms. Paige had equipped the small area with a TV, dollhouse, stuffed toys and figurines.

The presser foot bobbed up and down, needle stitching thread into the fabrics. The regular hum of her machine soothed her because it evoked a wonderful sense of nostalgia. She recalled her mother's soft singing and small smile as she spent hours in her sewing room creating all their clothes.

Paige stitched, drew the next pin out, and pressed her foot to the pedal, stitched again, on and on, as she sewed the waistband. Such peace would come over her as she watched her own hands doing so capably what her mother had taught Paige from the time she was Evie's age.

This skirt, along with two formal dresses, were to be finished by Friday afternoon, including all fittings and adjustments, so she had little downtime. She should hire an assistant dressmaker—someone she could trust to help with pattern cutting or tedious sewing, but, at this stage, while she was still earning a name for herself, she wasn't quite ready to relinquish creative control. It had taken her so long to get to where she was, she feared to expand before the business was ready.

The bulk of her highest-paying clients came from girlfriends of footballers she was still in contact with. Before glamorous events and award ceremonies, which were all happening now as the NRL and AFL seasons ended, she was swamped with orders for evening dresses.

A knock came at the front door. She eased her foot off the pedal and listened. She wasn't expecting anyone. Clients didn't stop by without an appointment—it was policy. With a business at home, it was essential she set boundaries.

She pressed her foot to the pedal and the calming chug of her sewing machine sounded again.

The doorbell rang this time. "Knock, knock. You home, Paige?"

Was that Claire?

"Door, Mummy," Evie said.

The Singer came to a silent stop. She met Evie's eyes. "Just wait there, baby, I'll go see who it is."

She opened the front door wide. Claire was standing on her doorstep. She wore beige slacks and a sheer white blouse tucked into the waistline. Big tortoiseshell coloured sunglasses rimmed her eyes. Her blonde curls were pinned up. Around her neck was a bright, funky necklace.

"Claire. What a surprise. How are you?"

Claire held out a Tupperware container. "I'm doing well. Thought I'd stop by. Those are biscuits for morning tea."

Paige took the biscuits and glanced towards her sewing room, calculating if she could fit in morning tea along with all the work she had left. That was another problem with working from home—people didn't understand that it was still work and required strict work hours.

Claire slipped her glasses onto the top of her head and set her dark brown eyes on Paige. "I'm not calling in at a bad time, am I?"

Paige managed a tight smile and gestured for Claire to come in. "No. Not at all."

Claire stepped inside and Paige closed the door behind her. "Thought I'd drop in and say hi. I'm on my way to Nikki's. I'm going to help her with a bit of housework."

"Didn't you just have a fall, though?" Paige asked, leading Claire through to the kitchen.

Claire waved her concern away. "It's okay. I like to give her a break. Matt said she's struggling at the moment."

Paige peered over her shoulder at Claire and frowned. "I'm really sorry to hear that." From the brief interactions she had with Nikki at the restaurant, she seemed like a lovely person.

Claire slid onto one of the stools that lined the bench and placed her handbag and glasses onto the countertop. "I'm not meant to know, but supposedly that car accident wasn't an accident."

Paige narrowed her gaze. "What do you mean?"

"Nikki crashed her car on purpose. She didn't want to go to work, so she had an accident to ensure she didn't have to."

Paige gasped, covered her mouth with her palm. "My goodness. That's…" she couldn't think of a polite word, so she didn't finish her sentence.

"I picked up Flynn and Ryan on Saturday afternoon and took them back to my place. To give Nikki some space. And, just between you and me, I don't think that type of environment is great for impressionable teenagers to be in."

Paige didn't know what to do with such information about Nikki. It felt invasive to hear something so personal. "I hope Nikki feels better soon. It must be rough for her if she's doing something so—" what was a word that wouldn't be misconstrued? "—*risky* as crashing her car on purpose." Paige had no idea what could be going on in a person's head to resort to something like that.

A shimmery memory intruded at that moment. A few months after her mother had died, when the grief was so painful and consuming, she was walking across a tall bridge. She had held the cold railing, looked down to the rushing river metres below, and had the brief thought that she could end this pain in a matter of seconds. Of course, her feet had remained steady on the steel path beneath her—it was just a thought.

"I hope so too," Claire said, crossing her legs. "It's quite a strain on everyone. Matt's got broad shoulders, but I've also got my own life to live. I can't be expected to clean up after a young family. Teenage boys make a hell of a mess."

"I'm sure they do. Evie makes more than enough mess and she's only three." She flicked the jug on to boil and collected Evie from the sewing room. "Say hello to Claire," she said holding Evie's shoulders.

Evie smiled shyly and said, "Hello."

"Hello, darling. You not out of your pyjama's yet?"

Evie shook her head.

Paige cringed inwardly. "I've been a bit busy with work." She looked down at her own clothes—she was in her pyjama's too. Heat burned her cheeks and up her neck.

Dressing down was a perk of working from home, but a perk she wasn't sure Claire would understand—not with the way she always immaculately presented herself. A beautiful face of makeup. Crisp, fresh clothes and bountiful accessories.

"I know what it's like with young children. It's a challenge some mornings to get anything done. Let alone work."

Paige nodded her agreement. "Cup of tea?"

"Yes, please."

She poured them both a cup and made Evie a warm mug of hot chocolate. So Evie could sit with them at the bench, Paige lifted the booster chair onto the stool.

"You obviously do quite well with your little business here?" Claire asked, then sipped her tea.

"It's kept Evie and I afloat."

"That's good to hear. Poor Anthony and Belinda don't have quite the same luck."

Paige's brows knitted together. "Luck?" She wasn't sure what luck had to do with business. In her experience, it was about around-the-clock hours, shouldering the downturns and perseverance.

"They're struggling at the moment. I don't think Belinda is too good with money. One of those keeping-up-with-the-Jones types. Why they ever thought they needed a bloody mansion to live in for just the two of them is beyond me. I had to lend them twenty thousand dollars to help pay an overdue tax bill, and then Anthony had the gall to ring and ask for my share of the bill for the restaurant on Friday."

Paige's top lip curled, her nose wrinkled. Poor Claire had fallen and nearly broken her neck—the last thing anyone was thinking about in all that commotion was the bill.

Claire sighed. "I'm disappointed, you know? I'm barely in a situation to give them money, but I couldn't say no. Since Robert died, it's been difficult."

Paige could understand to some extent with her own experiences trying to make it on her own once her mother passed away. "Vaughn has spoken about his father a lot and said he was a wonderful man. I lost my mum young too. So, I think we bonded over that."

Claire uncrossed her legs. Her spine was rigidly upright. "I'm sure your mother's death was nothing at all like what we went through as a family after Robert's accident. Our entire world was turned upside down, and I was left to raise three boys all on my own while grieving."

She studied Claire's tight-lipped expression. "Yes, I'm sure it was nothing like what you and your family went through." Paige wasn't going to argue a case for whose death was worse—that was not in her nature.

"My boys suffered. No doubt about it. I'm forever trying to make it up to them. Maybe that's why I feel obliged to help them out if there are financial problems." She patted her chest. "It feels like a personal failure on my part. Like I didn't do enough to educate Anthony about money. Not that Robert was the best father. To be honest, he wasn't a nice man." She shrugged a shoulder, barely a movement, and shook her head almost imperceptibly. "Sure, he changed his ways later on in our marriage, but in the early days, he was…horrible."

Curiosity surged under Paige's skin, but she didn't want to pry by asking for more details on why Claire's husband was horrible. Too personal a topic at this stage in her and Claire's relationship.

Beneath all that, a small glimmer of happiness flourished that Claire was comfortable enough to open up about this, but Paige wanted Vaughn to be the one to tell her such things, and, so far, he hadn't given her any indication that his dad was anything but a great father.

Claire opened the Tupperware container and pulled out a biscuit. She dunked it into her tea before taking a bite. "I was younger than Robert too. How old are you again, if you don't mind me asking?

"I'm twenty-six."

"Hmm, so that's ten years—"

"Nine," Paige said quickly.

Claire nodded. "And you've been dating Vaughn for…"

"Six months."

"Right. And your business is doing well?" She dunked her biscuit again, not looking at Paige.

"My business is doing very well."

"Thank goodness." She swallowed the biscuit she had been chewing. "I was worried you may have moved in for financial reasons. When Vaughn told me, my first thought, if I am to be completely honest with you, was that it was all too hurried." She waved her hand. "But maybe it feels so quick because I only just met you. And I don't think Vaughn even mentioned you until a month or so ago."

Paige blinked. That wasn't right. Soon after Paige had met Vaughn, she was in the same room when Vaughn was telling his mother about her over the phone. A warm gush of understanding moved through her chest, tightening her neck and shoulder muscles.

"If you're supposing I'm after your son for money, I can assure I'm not. We moved in together because we're in love."

Claire's mouth fell open as she stared at Paige. Paige's breathing came quicker in her chest as anger swamped her veins.

The corners of Claire's mouth drooped, her eyes glossed. "I did not mean any such thing." Her bottom lip trembled, but she drew herself upright and blinked quickly.

Oh, no. Paige reached across for Claire but withdrew her hand remembering she liked her distance. "I'm sorry. I didn't mean that."

Claire shook her head. "It's okay." But her crumpled expression and sagging shoulders told a different story. "I might leave. Let you get back to your patchwork."

She let the patchwork comment slide past without correction. "I didn't mean to offend you."

"No, it's fine. I'm still a little unwell, that's all. The fall. It shook me up. You see, Robert fell off scaffolding from three storeys high. That's how he died. My fall brought it all up in my memories again. I haven't been sleeping well. I figured talking about it might have helped." Her palm flattened against her forehead. "And then I'm so worried about Anthony. I just want my kids to be doing well and happy. That's all any mother wants for her children."

"Of course. Of course, you do. I'm sorry. I didn't think…"

"No."

"What the madda?" Evie asked with a deep frown as she watched Claire.

"Nothing, my darling," Claire said. "I'm fine. Your mum is busy, that's all. I better let her get back to it." She grabbed her purse and slung it over her shoulder. "I apologise for coming over at a bad time. I'll be sure to ring first next time."

"It's perfectly fine. Honestly. Any time."

"Thanks, Paige. I'll see myself out. You have a good day."

When the door closed, Paige rested her palms against the bench. Her head sagged between her shoulders on her long exhale. How the hell would she explain to Vaughn what she had just accused his mother of?

Chapter 14

Vaughn

The past...

Vaughn's cheeks were flushed as he flicked and whirled the homemade nunchucks around his body. He and his brothers had come off a week-long marathon of Bruce Lee and Jean Claude Van Damme movies. The thrill of watching choreographed Kung Fu fighting scenes sat like a coil in his twitching muscles.

When *No Retreat No Surrender* finished playing for the third time that week, he raced alongside Matt and Anthony from the living room, out to the garage where they rummaged through Dad's tools for thin chains and then ran down to the rainforest to find thick, straight sticks.

Using Dad's tools, they haphazardly combined the chains to the sticks until they had made a basic nunchuck for each of them. Their giggles, in between mimicking Bruce Lee's high-pitched fighting noises, rang out from the backyard where they practiced their moves on the lawn.

More often than not, Vaughn would clunk the sticks against his elbow, thigh or rib, and he'd bite down on his lip to stop from grunting with pain, so his brothers didn't see how much it hurt.

The faster he flicked the nunchucks around, the more skilled he looked. He was breathless, his cheeks were flushed. When he had hit his elbow painfully one too many times, he threw the nunchucks to the grass below his feet and performed a flurry of quick-footed kicks, punches and blocks.

Matt suggested they have competitions, one-on-one, to see who could deliver the best strikes. Vaughn was younger than his brothers, but he was game. Sure, he'd get his butt handed to him, but he wasn't one to back away from his big brothers' suggestions because he didn't want to look like a sooky baby.

First up, he versed Anthony. After some Kung Fu sound effects, they charged at each other, landing flying kicks and rapid punches. Anthony, who was half a head taller than Vaughn, swept Vaughn's feet out from under him, making him fall to the grass.

Matt and Anthony went for it next. A fury of hands and feet delivered body blows and kicks. Matt landed a heavy punch to Anthony's stomach. All the breath burst from his mouth as he bent over, then dropped to his knees on the grass, gasping for air. Matt ran and jumped, arms in the air, announcing that he was the champion.

Anthony pointed to Vaughn. "You verse the winner."

Vaughn eyed his brother, who was three years older, a full head taller, and swallowed hard. He would have to go in, eyes closed, and do what he could. There would be pain, of that he was sure. But if he chickened out, the pain of his brothers' teasing would be much worse.

He lined up opposite Matt. Matt indulged in a cocky grin. Vaughn attempted to recreate one himself, but his lips were trembling as adrenalin sparked. Anthony had managed to drag himself back to his feet and call a start to the fight.

Vaughn raced towards his brother with a war cry bellowing from him. Matt stretched his hand out, pressed his palm to Vaughn's head, stopping him mid-charge. Vaughn's arms flailed as he threw haymakers, but he couldn't get close enough to land a punch. Matt and

Anthony's laughter floated around him. He tried to punch harder, but he was kept at arm's distance.

"What the bloody hell is going on here?" Mum yelled.

Matt's arm was gone, and Vaughn lost his balance, falling onto his backside on the grass.

"Vaughn, I swear to God, you'll be the death of me. Get up to your room before I call your father out to deal with you."

He shook his head as he crawled to his feet. "What? I didn't do anything. We were playing."

"You were trying to punch your brother. I saw you."

He stamped his foot and growled. "We were pretending to fight. Like Bruce Lee. All of us were." He turned to his brothers, wide-eyed. "Tell her," he screamed. "Tell her what we were doing."

But they kept their eyes downcast, mouths shut.

Mum let out a longsuffering sigh. She pointed into the house. "Get to your room. You're an angry, violent little troublemaker—"

Vaughn flinched. "I'm not—"

"—I'm not going to argue."

"It was all pretend."

"Keep it up and you'll be in your room for three days."

He stamped his foot again, crossed his arms over his chest. "It's not fair. I didn't do anything wrong."

"Right, no more Kung Fu movies. They're making you an angry boy."

Tears pricked the back of his eyes, but he wouldn't cry in front of his brothers and he wouldn't give Mum the satisfaction. Instead, he stomped past her, pushed through the backdoor, slammed it behind him, and clomped up the stairs.

For hours, he sat in his room, waiting and waiting for his mother to tell him he could come downstairs. From time to time, he would poke his head out the door and hear the *thwacks* and *oomphs* of a fight scene as his brothers settled back in front of the television.

He shut the door and jumped on his bed, back to the wall, legs and arms crossed. A frown sat immovable on his mouth. What had he done that was any different from Matt and Anthony? Nothing. Nothing at all. The injustice fuelled a fire inside of him. The injustice was what did make him angry. So angry he could explode.

Chapter 15

Nikki

A car hummed as it pulled into the driveway. After preparing a resignation letter and emailing it to her employer, Nikki was on edge. So far, they hadn't called her or replied; she hoped like hell her boss hadn't decided to stop in for a personal visit.

She crept to the front window, parted the blinds to see out to the driveway.

Claire's car.

"What does she want?"

She'd only seen her yesterday when she dropped the boys back. Said she needed their help around the house with chores she was too sore to do herself. Nikki supposed she should have helped too, but she still wasn't at her finest either.

Nikki spun around and spied the state of her house. Football boots and dirty socks lay where they were flung on the floor beside the front door giving way to flecks of muddy grass along the entrance hall. In the living room, couch pillows were tossed onto the carpet. Coffee cups were left on the table. Pamphlets were discarded on the couch. The kitchen was a mess from the morning rush.

Typical Monday morning.

Sure, the kids had left for school a few hours ago now, leaving her plenty of time to clean, but she'd had a doctor's appointment first thing to check her nose, then she chose to agonise over the wording of a resignation letter after she arrived home.

Her stomach tightened like a taut band about to snap. Could she pretend she wasn't home? Hide out in her room?

But Claire was apt to come in with her key like she had done last week.

"Damn it."

Nikki was fine about her messy house. It only bothered her when she had visitors. Specifically, Claire. Thankfully, visitors were rare. Most of her friends worked and ran busy lives as she did, and when they did manage to catch-up, it was over a quick coffee at a café.

Nikki ran like a mad fly in the thirty or so seconds she had, straightening cushions and carrying cups to the kitchen. When she opened the door, she was flustered and breathless.

"Claire. How are you? I wasn't expecting you today."

Claire frowned. "Seems to be what everybody is saying."

"Come in."

Claire stepped inside and Nikki closed the door behind her while attempting to quieten her heavy breathing and dampen the jitteriness in her limbs.

"I just came from morning tea with Paige. I felt so bad about what happened on Friday night. I ruined the whole dinner, which was meant to be a fun family get-together–" Claire stopped as she gazed upon the living room.

Nikki cringed. Why couldn't she have a clean family? Why couldn't she be one of those people who loved to clean, couldn't stand even a cobweb?

Her cheeks burned even hotter "Go take a seat. I'll make us a cup of tea." That way, she could do some inconspicuous cleaning while she was in the kitchen.

"Coffee, please. I could use the caffeine before I start cleaning."

Nikki closed her eyes, drew a deep breath. "Claire, I appreciate your help, I really do, but I'm home. It doesn't make sense for you to come here and do what I'm perfectly capable of doing, especially when you've had a fall."

Claire's lips tightened. "A fall? I'm not ninety. I haven't broken a hip."

"I know…it's just…it doesn't feel right when I'm home."

"You know, when I was raising the boys, I wasn't so lucky. I didn't even have a husband to help for much of the time."

Nikki restrained a sigh. She knew well enough about how these conversations went. It was better to appease Claire and get on with it. "Very true. I'll be back in a tick."

She rushed to the kitchen and bit back a groan. How many times could you tell someone not to do something, using every *polite* excuse conceivable, before you ended up sounding like a parrot, or worse, mean?

That's one thing Nikki wasn't—mean. She hated confrontation. She didn't aggressively force her will on others. That was Matt—he lived for it. And for years, especially early in their relationship, she had tried to quell that in Matt because it made her uncomfortable.

But, as more and more people walked over her, she realised what an asset that was to have in this world. That's why Matt was so successful at work; he didn't shy away from difficult situations.

Claire was a tricky one, though, but, mother-in-law or not, Nikki should have the right to say that she didn't want help today and have it heard. Why did it always have to be about what Claire wanted?

Nikki turned on the espresso maker. As she made coffees, she loaded as many dishes as she could as quietly as possible into the dishwasher, then wiped down the benches.

Coffees made, she carried them to the living room, but Claire wasn't there. In those five short minutes, Claire had tidied the room, and, from the beeps and whooshes sounding from the laundry, she had put on a load of washing.

"Claire?" Nikki called out, trying to keep the angry edge from her tone.

Claire appeared from the laundry, smiling. "I need that coffee so bad."

Nikki placed both mugs on the coffee table and took a seat.

"See, it doesn't take long to tidy up. You didn't even realise."

Nikki forced a painfully tight smile as Claire sat next to her. "I guess not. I've been busy this morning. I had a doctor's appointment. And then I handed in my resignation at work."

Claire's eyes widened. "Really? Why is that?"

Nikki shrugged. "I obviously need more time here at home. I can't singlehandedly do everything."

"You have to do what's best for you." Claire's tone was sympathetic. "And if that's being home with the family, then that's what you do. How will you cope financially, though?"

Nikki waved her question away. "I don't earn enough for it to really matter. Not compared to Matt, anyway. And we have invested well over the years, paid extra off the mortgage and bought our cars with cash, so it's not like we're drowning in debt."

Claire leaned over to collect her mug and sat back with it between her hands. She sipped, swallowed. "At least there's one of my kids I don't have to worry about."

Nikki frowned. "What do you mean?"

"I'm not going to get into it. I'm sick with worry as it is."

Nikki shook her head, eyes narrowed. “Am I missing something?”

Claire grimaced. “Belinda and Anthony are having financial troubles.”

“I’m sorry to hear that. I didn’t even realise. It must be very stressful for them.”

“I’m not sure who it is most stressful for—them or me. I’ve given them a loan, so, I hope matters turn around.” She shook her head. “Not that I want to be burdening you with my worries. Not after the morning I’ve had with Paige. I thought I could go around there, have a nice morning tea, chat and get to know her more, but then she accused me of calling her a gold-digger.”

Nikki arched a brow. “A gold-digger? Where would she get that idea?”

“I don’t know. But she did. I was offended. I really hate how that word is thrown around these days, but I truly was offended. It was the last accusation I would make about a girl I barely bloody know.”

“So strange she would jump to that conclusion. What exactly did you say to give her that impression?”

Claire tipped her chin and glared at Nikki. “I assure you, I didn’t say anything that would give her that impression.” Her tone held an edge of warning.

“Of course,” Nikki said, ever the non-confrontational doormat she was and would always be. “I’m sorry, I didn’t mean to insinuate—”

Claire leaned forward, rested her coffee on the table and pulled her mobile out of her purse. “I know what I can do.”

“What?”

Claire lifted the phone to her ear after pressing dial on a contact. “Flowers.”

Nikki’s forehead furrowed. “For what?”

“Hi, yes, this is Claire Radcliffe.”

Nikki cringed to hear her mother-in-law’s affected phone voice. It was soft and posh. She had voices for all different occasions. Her sick voice was the worst—low and croaky and full of *give-me-sympathy*. The sick voice didn't work on Nikki, at least not anymore. When she heard it now, it made her want to slap Claire's face.

"Yes, I would like a bunch of flowers sent. Oh, I don't know, a nice hundred-dollar bunch. Paige Johnson. Yes, on the card, please write, 'I'm sorry I upset you. Love Claire.' Perfect." She gave the florist Vaughn's address and hung up.

What purpose was there to give an expensive bunch of flowers, especially when Claire was not the one who should be apologising?

A memory glimmered on the outskirts of her mind: arriving home one afternoon from juggling the shopping with a six-week-old and a toddler and finding flowers waiting on her doorstep. From Claire.

Nikki had kicked the flowers into the wall, their soft petals explosively detaching and floating to the floor. Her limbs had vibrated each time she marched past them as she dealt with the children and carried bag after bag of shopping into the house.

Her back had been aching. She'd wanted to take a nap when she put the kids down for a sleep. But now she had to ring Claire and thank her for the flowers. Thanking someone profusely for a gift was a Radcliffe imperative. Fail to do so and it was silent treatments and angry phone calls from relatives to discuss how horrible Nikki was.

Four hours later, Nikki had finally picked up her phone. She slowed her breathing as best she could and rang Claire to thank her. Every word was a lie. She wasn't grateful. She wasn't happy because Nikki knew well enough by now that any gift from Claire had an ulterior motive.

It had only been a couple of days since Claire had gone back to her own house. She had stayed with Nikki and Matt for three long weeks once Matt had returned to work after the birth of Ryan. She had done the same when Flynn was born.

All that time, Nikki walked around in a hormone-induced daze. Her body ached and she had the worst case of haemorrhoids. She craved her own space, so she could find a routine with the kids, nap during the day and not have to second-guess everything she did with her new baby.

Nikki liked her alone time. She preferred to figure things out without someone else looking over her shoulder. Feed her own baby. Let him cry if needed. Walk around the house in her pyjamas, leave the washing undone, and the dishes in the sink if she damn well pleased.

Those first weeks were meant to be Nikki's time to bond with her baby boy, but more and more, Claire would offer to do the night feeds, the day feeds, the bathing, the dressing, the burping, until Nikki craved contact with her own child because Claire was thieving all opportunities.

Nikki grew edgy, resentful. When she spoke to her friends about her suspicions that Claire was taking over, they said she was overreacting or that she should see a doctor about possible post-partum depression.

By the end of Claire's stay, Nikki could barely contain her composure or moderate her tone enough to speak civilly to her anymore. Yet, because of the flowers, Nikki was, again, having to pretend that she was grateful for Claire.

Nikki pushed that thought away. Let the past lay dead and buried. No use ploughing over that overworked minefield.

"There, that should smooth things over," Claire said with a smile when she ended the call. She got to her feet and clapped her hands. "Let's tackle this kitchen. I'm sure it's in need of a tidy."

Nikki put her coffee down and dragged herself to her feet. "Sure."

Chapter 16

Belinda

Silence settled in the spaces between the walls of Belinda's home in the two days that followed her discovery that she was pregnant. She and Anthony were too scared to speak in case talking of this baby in this house, which still bore the old energies of infertility, would make it all an illusion, some cruel trick.

But by Monday afternoon, enough time had passed to solidify this new reality—she was going to have a baby in thirty-three weeks' time. A baby.

Belinda curled up beside Anthony on the couch, a plate of leftover quiche from her shop on their laps. "No wonder I've been so exhausted lately. And overwhelmed. It was my hormones. I should have known." But how could she have? She had never been pregnant nor was she expecting to be.

"Maybe if we had been anticipating a pregnancy, we would have tied two and two together," Anthony said. "I had assumed our finances were getting on top of you."

"It was. It still is." She shifted on the couch, so she was facing him more directly. "This changes nothing on that front. If anything, it complicates it all." She frowned. "I've been thinking. I really have no choice but to sell the business. When I have the *baby*—" she could barely make her lips say the word, it had been elusive for so long and held so much gravity now, "—we can't afford to pay someone to cover the shop. And I don't make enough to pay for childcare."

The problem was, even though they lived like paupers, they did earn decent incomes. But every last cent of it went to paying off the mortgage, outstanding tax debts, and countless credit cards. Their income level also precluded them from receiving the concessions parents on lower incomes were entitled to for childcare.

Anthony shrugged. "I guess we can try."

"You never know, we might find a buyer at a good price." Wishful thinking. The retail market was beyond flat and sectors like *Organics* were frivolous in this economy. "Someone really keen on the ethos of the place, perhaps. Then I can find a job working weekends or even from home."

He cut through the quiche with his fork, his focus on his plate. "I've just put in an estimate for a really big contract. Making coal chutes for a mine up north. If we get this…it will get us out of the red. No doubt about it. I didn't want to say anything in case we don't win it, but I have a good feeling."

She dared to feel hope—if only a speck. "Please, please, please."

"But, either way, we'll make it work. We'll keep moving forward."

They had to. Their only other option was to wave the white flag and declare bankruptcy—they would both lose their businesses, their cars, their house. Everything they had worked so hard for would be taken away. She couldn't bear it. How would they come back from something so devastating?

"We have the baby to think about now," Anthony said. "Make some phone calls tomorrow to a commercial real estate agent. Maybe we can get Nikki to put together some interim financial statements, rather than paying the fortune our accountants will charge."

She nodded. “I didn’t think of her. But she could definitely do it. There’s nothing we’re hiding in the business accounts. She won’t be able to see what a mess we’re in.”

“Exactly. She’s off from work for the time being. It might be perfect timing.”

“I’ll ring her tomorrow.” She looked into Anthony’s blue eyes and his whole face softened when she placed her hand on her stomach. “Can we be happy?”

A small smile flittered at the corners of his mouth. “I already am.” Tears glossed his eyes—happy tears and they ignited her own.

“Me too,” she said, wiping her cheeks. “I still feel scared, but we’re going to have a baby, Anthony. A baby.”

His face brightened with his smile. A tear fell down his cheek. “I’m going to be a dad.”

She nodded. “You sure are. The best dad a child could ask for. And I’m going to be a mum. And I can tell you now, Anthony, I’ll do anything for this baby. Whatever it takes.”

Chapter 17

Paige

Paige was in her sewing room, still working on an evening skirt when Vaughn arrived home. The front door banged closed. His heavy footsteps echoed off the tiles as he headed to her sewing room. The needle bobbed up and down as she rushed to finish this run before she greeted him.

"You look busy," came his deep voice.

She made it to the end of the material, took her foot from the pedal and sighed as she spun to face him. He was smiling and holding a big bunch of native Australian flowers.

The stress from the day lifted from her shoulders.

"Flowers," Evie said excitedly.

"Yes, they are," he said to her.

"Wow," Paige shrieked. "They're stunning. You have made my day so much better."

"They're not from me. They were on the front doorstep."

She got to her feet, confusion furrowing her brow. "I wonder who." He passed them to her, and she looked at the letter enclosed.

"Your mother." Anxiety coiled in her belly.

His expression was blank. "My mother? Why is she sending you flowers?"

"I'm not a hundred percent sure." She handed him the card, which he read.

"She apologises to you. For what?"

"Come," she said, rolling her neck from side to side to ease the tightness. "I need wine before I tell you about my morning tea today with your mother."

In the kitchen, Vaughn poured them both a glass of wine and Evie a glass of milk.

Paige took a seat on the stool next to Evie while Vaughn stood opposite behind the bench. He was still dressed in his work clothes—long grey slacks and a crisp business shirt.

"What happened?" he asked, loosening the knot on his tie.

She told him about Claire's unexpected visit, what she had said about Belinda and Anthony's financial woes and how Claire had questioned Paige's reasons for living with Vaughn.

"The timing of her question threw me off. She brought it up right after saying that Belinda was bad with money, then questioning how well my business was doing. Not to mention a remark about our age difference. How could I not think that she assumed I was a gold-digger?"

Vaughn closed his eyes as he blew out a heavy breath. "I guess I would have felt the same."

She sipped her wine. "See, exactly. You understand why I jumped to that conclusion."

"But I really don't believe she meant it that way. It was like you said, bad timing."

"I don't know. It's not like me to misunderstand social situations."

"Honestly, Paige, I wouldn't worry about it. And besides," he said, pointing to the flowers, "she's apologised, so she must accept responsibility for the direction the conversation went."

She watched him for a moment, the way his eyebrows were higher, his eyes wider as he spoke like he was trying to convince her he was right. "I'm not wrong here. I've had all day to think about it, and the more I thought about the conversation, the more I'm convinced she implied I wanted your money."

Vaughn's fist slammed down hard on the kitchen counter. "Damn it, Paige. Don't start with all this."

Paige and Evie jumped and stared at Vaughn with wide eyes. Evie started to cry.

"I'm sorry," Vaughn said quickly.

Paige narrowed her eyes at him, grimacing, as she went to Evie and collected her into her arms before carrying her out of the room. She kissed the top of Evie's head. "Come on, darling, let's go have a bath. Mummy will hop in with you."

The warm water worked wonders at easing the pressure that had built up in Paige's muscles. When Evie's fingers were wrinkled, they climbed out of the bath and both dressed into their pyjamas.

Paige went about fixing Evie some dinner and ate it with her at the dining table, just the two of them. She ignored Vaughn when he walked past or attempted to talk to her. She was grateful when he got the message she wasn't ready to deal with him and parked himself in his office.

After Paige put Evie into her bed for the night, she stood outside her bedroom door, back against the wall, and steadied herself before she approached Vaughn.

Vaughn was at his desk in the office, flicking through paperwork. She stopped in the doorway and his head popped up to see her.

He frowned. "I'm sorry…"

She pointed her finger at him and snarled. "Don't you ever behave like that around my daughter or me again. Ever. Do you hear me? I will not put up with it."

He sighed and nodded. Remorse glinted in his eyes. "I'm so sorry. I promise I won't ever do that again."

Paige took a step into the room and closed the door behind her. “Did you know that Joshua hit me? The night I left him, he punched me so hard he broke my cheekbone. I had the wonderful coincidence of finding out I was pregnant at the same time I was being treated for domestic violence injuries.”

He was out of his chair and coming to her. “I didn’t know that. I’m so sorry.”

“I know you wouldn’t hurt me, but I will not stand for that kind of anger. Do you understand? Evie needs decent male examples in her life. And I deserve a good man.” She pointed towards the kitchen. “Not someone who beats their fists.”

“I know. I’m sorry.” He scrubbed a hand through his hair. “I forgot myself for a moment.”

“Why would you overreact like that?”

“I don’t know.”

“Was it because I said your mother was mean to me?”

He shook his head. “It’s nothing.”

“Bullshit, Vaughn. You don’t get that angry over nothing. What was it?”

He rubbed his chin, frowned. “My ex-wife hated my mum so much that she ended our marriage.” He said it like ‘There, you happy now, I admitted it’. “In the end, she couldn’t even look at me without seeing Mum. She said I repulsed her. So, she left.”

Paige gasped. “What? Why?”

“I don’t know. Mum seemed perfectly okay with me. But then Joanne would mention little things just like you did tonight. Things that I never saw.”

“Wow. Okay. I did not expect to hear that.”

His eyes were sad. “I was scared you were going to do the same.”

She shook her head. “I’m committed, Vaughn. I love you. I would never have moved in and brought my daughter into this relationship if I wasn’t.”

"I know. What you told me stirred all those old emotions. It was such a rough time in my life."

Paige frowned as she held his gaze. Such sadness was reflected in his eyes. "Is that why it took six months for you to introduce me to your mum?"

He nodded.

She blew out a long breath. "I'll try and be more mindful about what I say from now on, okay?"

He held both arms out before him, and she stepped into his embrace. He pulled her against his chest and cuddled her. "No. You can always talk to me. Don't bottle this stuff up. I would hate for you to think that I'm a violent or angry person. Because I'm not. Deep down, I know that I'm not. I won't ever act like I did tonight ever again. I promise."

Chapter 18

Vaughn

Six months ago…

Vaughn was not in the mood to be heading down the range to Maroochydore to take care of Belinda's problems. His eyes were sore and red, his muscles aching. He wanted to grab some takeaway and park himself in front of the TV until he could no longer keep his eyes open.

He had already had someone dent his car this morning. Scraped the paintwork. It pissed him off that he was going to have to hire a rental while his was booked in with a panel beater.

At least the woman had the common decency to come into the bank and ask whose car it was. Peta, Pepper, Paige or something like that was her name. A beautiful face, though she was more overweight than he usually liked.

Beggars can't be choosers. He was shocked that he had the nerve to try his luck because she was at least a decade younger than him. But when he asked her to meet him for coffee tomorrow, she had said yes without hesitation.

A little socialising with the opposite sex was an intimidating thought since Joanne left him. But enough was enough. It had been nine months; if he didn't get on with life, he never would. This young woman was a much better option than none.

He recollected the phone call from Belinda ten minutes ago. Supposedly a huntsman the size of her hand was on the front door, so she wasn't able to leave her shop. He rolled his eyes. A bloody spider. A non-venomous one at that. Fair enough if it were a coastal taipan or a king brown, but a bloody spider.

He blew out a long sigh, gripped the steering wheel harder. He had to stop being so grumpy. He wasn't really angry at Belinda. Truthfully, he was upset at Joanne. She used to hate spiders too. A genuine phobia. And he loved that he could be her knight in shining armour and remove them from the house for her.

Not that it mattered in the end—she'd still left him.

"Should have just let them bloody eat her," he grumbled.

But, of course, he wouldn't have, for the same reason he was driving down the range at twilight in winter, fog a thick layer above the road, to kill a spider for his sister-in-law.

He arrived at the shop a little after six and cursed his brother for not being here as he climbed from his car. A coastal gust of frosty air needled into his flesh.

He rushed to the front door and couldn't contain a smile as he spotted the spider. The huntsman wasn't difficult to miss, and was, indeed, the size of a hand. Thick, brown and hairy. Even he got a chill up the back of his spine at the thought of moving it.

Huntsmans were not poisonous, but they could unleash a painful bite. He'd learned that lesson as a kid when he didn't check his school shoes before sliding his foot into what had, overnight, become a new home for a spider.

He went back to the car for a notepad. If he could coax it onto that, he would avoid touching it and then be able to release it into the nearby garden.

"Hi," came Belinda's voice from deep inside the shop. He looked in; she was frowning, arms wrapped around her middle.

"Hi, Bel." He held up his notepad. "Let me see what I can do with this monster."

"I told you it was big. No way am I going near it." She shuddered, and he chuckled.

He strode closer to the spider and nudged one of its front legs with a notepad. It lifted the spindly leg, allowing him to push the pad under. After gentle prompting, the spider stepped all eight legs onto the pad. It took up over half the A4-sized book.

Belinda squealed from inside and bolted into the back room.

He laughed again as he carefully carried the spider across the carpark to the garden. He flicked the notepad and the spider flung off and landed, springy and alert, onto the mulch.

"All done," he called out as he strode inside the shop. "You can come out of hiding."

Belinda's head poked around the wall. She looked at him, then to the empty notepad, and at the door. She closed her eyes and sighed. "Thank you so, so, so much."

"No drama."

"I'm so sorry to get you down here like this. But with Anthony away in Mackay, I had no one else. And I knew you didn't mind spiders."

"It's not a problem."

"Let me make you dinner, at least, for your troubles?"

He shrugged, nodded. "Sure. Why not." Beat takeaway and a silent house.

Belinda and Anthony's house was always eerie to Vaughn. Too big. Too bright. Too many sharp surfaces and echoes. His own house was much smaller, much more homely, but now, with Joanne gone, even that space was oppressive.

This home didn't reflect his brother—that's what he didn't like the most. It must have been Belinda's choice.

Anthony was too carefree, had simple needs, for this to be his doing.

But he did know the lengths a man would go to, to keep his wife happy. Happy wife, happy life and all that. Turned out it was true, only his marriage ended up on the opposite end of that spectrum.

In his early marriage, he never thought himself capable of being happier. He and Joanne had married within six months of meeting. Why wait when he knew it was right? He settled into his rose-coloured future, anticipating children and grandchildren with her. He believed with all his heart, he would be looking into her brown eyes and loving her when they were eighty.

He sighed. A dark gloom descended over him. He should have said no to dinner. He should have gone home and dwelled on his shitty circumstances and even shittier life alone.

Belinda turned to him as they made it to the kitchen. "Everything okay, Vaughn?"

He forced a smile but found that he was too weak to make it last. So, he frowned and shook his head. "Not really."

Her eyes filled with sympathy. "Take a seat. Sounds like we need a bottle of wine with our dinner."

He sank into one of the stools, shoulders slumped, while she poured them both a glass of shiraz.

She pushed his towards him. "Drink up."

"Thanks."

"So, tell me, what's going on?"

He waved her concern away. "Same old shit, different day."

"Joanne?"

He grimaced. "Always."

"Is she giving you trouble?"

He shook his head. "Nothing like that." She had been great actually. He had paid her out for the house. Amicably split all their assets. They each took a car, closed their joint accounts and began their lives separately.

He drank deeply from the glass, though he barely tasted the wine as it hit his tongue. "I miss her. That's all."

"I can imagine it would be difficult. Married for nine years and then finding yourself on your own again."

He swallowed a mouthful of wine. "That about sums it up."

She leaned over the bench and rested her hand on top of his. "I'm really sorry, Vaughn. It must be very tough."

He glanced at her delicate hand, her clean trimmed nails, then into her green eyes. "Thanks.'

Belinda was a beautiful woman. No doubt about it. The epitome of a *surfer girl*. The type of woman you saw on ads promoting Australia—slight, tanned skin, blonde hair, pale eyes, looked hot in a bikini. Anthony was a lucky man.

Belinda lifted her hand away. "How about I start on dinner? I've got some leftover salads and bits and pieces from the shop today.

"Sounds good to me."

When Belinda had dished dinner onto two white plates, they took them into the living room to eat on the lounge.

"The dining room is too big," she said when they took a seat beside each other.

He peered up at the cavernous space above him, the high arched ceiling that hovered over the living room. "I assume it would be."

She chuckled. "So how is business going up there on the range?"

"Surprisingly well. The town is full of small-business owners, which benefits me when it comes to lending. The growing population is working out well. Getting more customers. More are refinancing mortgages or taking out personal loans." Work was the only successful part of his life at the moment.

"I'm glad."

"And how about you?"

She glanced away, then looked back to him, shoulders squaring, spine more erect. "Can't complain."

"And Matt's got a big contract in Hay Point, hey?"

She nodded. "Doing some such thing on a wharf. I never know from month to month. It's always something different."

"Sounds like he has it under control, so you don't have to worry about it."

"Exactly."

He finished the last of his wine and rested his glass on the coffee table.

"Let me fill that up for you."

He didn't object. She strode towards the kitchen, and he hated that he watched her arse shift from side to side under her dress as she went. He squeezed his eyes shut when she disappeared into the next room. God, he had it bad. One minute he was asking women too young for him out for coffee and the very next perving on his sister-in-law. This wasn't right.

He snapped his eyes open and shoved a forkful of lettuce in his mouth when he heard Belinda's footsteps. She appeared with a grin and a bottle of wine in her hand.

Yes, his brother was a lucky man.

She poured him a tall glass and topped up her own. "So, are you trying to get back in the saddle?"

He arched a brow, grinned. "Not really. May have a coffee date tomorrow with a woman I met. But I don't know."

"You should definitely do it. Get back out there, start meeting new women."

He smiled, lowered his head. "Yeah, I know." But easier said than done. Realistically, he lived in a small town. The majority of people who moved there were couples who wanted to start businesses, like bed and breakfasts or eateries, or were there for a tree change. The remainder was tourists or backpackers. No long-term options. But mostly, he was scared because heartbreak hurt like all hell. How else did it get such a brutal name for itself?

Two glasses of wine soon morphed into four. His mind was numb, his words and tongue thick. But the wine was so good, and Belinda was surprisingly easy to talk to.

She had persuaded him to stay longer after dishing him up the most delicious raw caramel slice he had ever tasted.

"And this is healthy?" he asked, biting into his third piece.

She laughed, something he noted she did often. A big, loud laugh that had a life much greater than her petite frame. "I wouldn't say it's *good* for you, but it's better than the sugary crap you'd buy from the grocery shop."

They talked about his marriage and its end. He opened up to her about things he had never told anyone—the funk he had fallen into, the pain he had suffered these past nine months.

"It would have been easier if Joanne had died. People can understand your grief then."

Her sympathetic frown coaxed him on, opened him up further.

"But it's time to move on," he said determinately. And with the backing of too much wine and sugar, he almost believed what he was saying.

She nodded like a soldier. "Exactly right. And drink more wine. Another bottle?"

He shrugged. "Sure. I'm game."

She skipped to the kitchen, so he took the moment to make use of the bathroom. When he got back, two big glasses of wine sat on the coffee table. He sank into the lounge beside her, leg curled up under him. She had purple-stained lips and it was the most adorable thing he'd seen in a long time.

The next two glasses went down like opiate and before he blinked, he was draining the last drop of the second bottle into his glass.

Belinda ran her finger along the rim of her glass as she spoke. "Ant and I had been trying to have a baby."

"Oh?" Ant hadn't mentioned it to him.

"For years. And still no luck."

"I'm so sorry to hear that, Bel."

When she met his gaze again, her eyes were filled with tears. Her crumpled expression reflected the raw grief he felt inside of himself. "Anthony no longer wants to try. It's too much for him."

His brow furrowed. How hard was it to try? Surely, they were having sex anyway. After nine months of an empty bed, he'd jump at the chance.

Belinda's bottom lip drooped, and she started to cry. He rested his glass down and shifted closer. "Shit, Bel. That's no good." He wrapped an arm around her. "I'm really sorry to hear that. I guess, sometimes, these things don't work out."

He didn't know what happened then, whether she instigated it, or he did, but her lips were pressed to his, and he was kissing her. His hands fell to her waist, her thigh, her arse.

The next thing he was aware of was lifting her from the couch into his arms, her legs spread around his waist and walking her to the kitchen bench. They didn't relieve themselves of clothes, he merely pulled her knickers aside and pulled his trousers down just enough before pushing inside her.

The relief of connection, the familiar snug warmth of being inside a woman, was more than he could bear. Nine months of nothing made this moment feel like everything.

Soon enough, she cried out as she shuddered. Seeing that pleasure all over her face, swiftly triggered his own release. For a long moment, he stood there, still very much inside her, her legs wide but limp and hanging over the bench, trying to gather his breath.

"Holy hell," he panted.

Her lips lifted at the corners as she looked into his eyes. "I guess this means you're staying the night?"

He should have said no. He should have. But he didn't.

Chapter 19

Nikki

Wednesday morning, Nikki sat in driver's seat of her car, fingers gripping the steering wheel. This would be the first time she had driven since her accident. The doctor had given her permission to get behind the wheel at her appointment on Monday, but her car only arrived back from the panel beater's yesterday.

Her chest plate was still tender when she stretched the seatbelt across her body. She pressed the ignition button and waited in neutral for a long moment, breathing deeply. The still-new scent of the interior filled the air, combined now with the residual pungency of grease the mechanics had left.

She would not get worked up about diving today. She had handled a car many times before, she could do this again. The act of driving wasn't what was frightening her, but, rather, what her mind might suggest she do while driving.

Belinda had asked her to stop by her shop to prepare some interim financial statements for the sale of her business. She had said yes without a second thought because helping Belinda didn't hold the same weight that working did. Nikki had the luxury of time and no one looking over her shoulder while she prepared the statements.

No more hesitating. She shifted the car into drive and began her descent out of town and down the Blackall Ranges towards Maroochydore. Without incident, she arrived at Organic Living a half-hour later.

The shop was empty of customers. She checked her watch—eleven am. Maybe more of a rush would occur around lunchtime.

Belinda stepped out from the backroom and smiled. "Hi, Nikki, thanks so much for coming down." The lines around Belinda's eyes were more visible and the downwards sag of her lips were prominent like her usual radiance had dimmed.

"Not a problem."

Belinda led her out the back to a small office set up with a desk, computer and filing cabinets. "I really appreciate your help with this. I hope it's not too much drama for you."

Nikki sidled into the seat in front of the computer. "Not at all."

"I rang a sales agent yesterday, and he told me to have the past three years of financial statements completed as well as this year-to-date to have on hand for potential buyers."

"Are all your statements up-to-date?"

Belinda nodded too quickly. "My regular accountant does all my activity statements every month and my tax return as soon as possible after the end of the financial year."

"A good indication it's all accurate too, so I really shouldn't have much to do." She'll just need to add back personal expenses like car loans, any wages Belinda might draw for herself and the like, so the accounts reflected the true business operations.

Belinda leaned over Nikki's shoulder, logged into her accounting program and entered the password. "There you go. I'll go make you a coffee, but if you need anything at all, please let me know."

"I will."

Belinda left and Nikki relaxed now that she was alone—her preference while working. She liked space and time to get her head around a business she wasn't acquainted with and understand how they accounted for their sales and expenses, assets and liabilities.

She pulled up a year-to-date Profit and Loss Statement and scanned the figures, familiarising herself with the specific goings-on with this business and looking for any kind of irregularities—an expense that was too high in proportion to the others, or obvious expenses or sales items that were missing, or items entered into the wrong account.

She noted that the shop was turning a profit, though small, which was a good sign for potential buyers. After a few quick calculations, Belinda's sales were a consistent percentage of her stock purchases. The expenses like insurance, bank charges, utilities and lease fees were standard for the size of the business.

But what stood out like red paint on a white canvas were the accounting fees. Almost fifteen thousand dollars already, and it was only four months into the new financial year.

She clicked on the account, opening up the line-by-line transactions. Monthly invoices were input for month-end preparation of activity statements along with a large year-end fee for the preparation of financial statements and a tax return.

Nikki shook her head—the fee was outrageous for such a small, uncomplicated business. Belinda's business structure wasn't unusual, only one company with no related trusts or other such entities, not even a car loan attached to the business. No wages, only some labour-hire fees for a temporary employee.

Nikki pushed to her feet, heart racing. If what Claire had said was true about Belinda and Anthony being in financial trouble, their accountant wasn't helping their cause.

She poked her head out of the office door. There were no customers in the store, so she called Belinda over.

"What is it?" Lines of stress sat between Belinda's brows as she twisted a cap on a coffee cup and carried it over.

"You might want to look at this."

Nikki took the cup of coffee from Belinda and sipped deeply at the hot brew. When seated, she pointed to the screen. "See here."

Belinda nodded.

"Your business is charged one thousand dollars every time your accountant prepares a monthly activity statement."

Belinda's expression was blank.

"It's too high. Your business doesn't even make enough to warrant monthly statements. You should be on a quarterly schedule."

Belinda covered her mouth with her hand. "I didn't know that."

"And eight thousand dollars to complete your year-end financial statements and tax return is a joke. Much too high. This is not a complicated business."

Belinda pulled a chair over and slumped down onto it. "Really? We only use these accountants because friends of ours recommended them. I knew the costs were high, but I presumed that was the industry standard."

"A Brisbane City accounting firm may get away with that kind of fee. But not here in Maroochydore. Not with a business like this. If these were prepared at my workplace, we would have charged a quarter of this."

Belinda's shoulders sagged and tears sprang to her eyes. "I feel like such an idiot. All that money wasted."

Nikki smiled sympathetically, but in the back of her mind, she wondered how people could be so stupid to not realise they were being thieved from. Because that's what this was—theft disguised as service. "Does Anthony use the same accountants?"

Belinda nodded; tears were leaving damp traces down her cheeks.

Nikki forced her voice to sound low and calm. "I'm about to save you guys thousands of dollars a year." She pulled out a business card from her old workplace and handed it to Belinda.

No, she wasn't an employee there anymore, but she knew with all her professional wits that they were a good accounting firm. Thorough, educated, despite operating in a small town. "Ring Roger Bramston. Tell him I referred you. Explain that you're leaving your current accountant because the fees are too high. He'll take care of you."

Belinda stared at the card—eyes wide and frightened.

"I promise they'll do a great job. I know they are a small firm, but, honestly, every accountant there knows what they're doing."

Belinda shook her head. "It just seems like such a fuss to change now."

"We're talking tens of thousands of dollars in savings."

"I know… but… it's a pain to move everything over."

Why the hesitation? "I don't work there anymore, so I won't be preparing your accounts. This is an honest recommendation that will help you and Anthony a lot."

Belinda's eyes flicked to hers. "You don't work there anymore?"

Nikki shifted on her seat. "I resigned. I want to spend more time at home with the boys."

"I didn't realise."

"It was off-the-cuff."

"Good for you. It must feel great to be home with the family."

"It does. A relief, really."

Belinda took the card. "I guess I should check it out."

"You definitely should."

The front doorbell chimed alerting them to a customer. Belinda sprang to her feet. "I better get back out there. Thanks for this," she said holding the card up, then slipped it into her dress pocket.

It didn't take long for Nikki to complete the adjusted statements and make similar adjustments in the prior years. She presented them all on the desk in year order, then scanned copies onto the computer, so Belinda could email them to her agent.

She performed some statistical calculations to determine what the sale price should be and compared the results to similar businesses. Belinda and her real estate agent would now have clear evidence and notes showing what would be a fair sale price.

"You're a godsend," Belinda said after Nikki ran her through all the reports.

Nikki flushed. "I wouldn't go that far. Just doing what I know how to do."

"I mean it, Nikki, this has been so much help. I don't think you realise."

"If you need anything else, I have a lot of free time now. I'm excellent at budgeting if you, maybe, I don't know, want some help in that department."

Belinda's back went rigid and her mouth was a straight line. "No, we're fine. That won't be necessary." Her words were curt, pushed past tight lips.

"I was just asking, in case. I love spreadsheets and numbers. It's a pleasure for me."

Belinda crossed her arms over her chest. "Has someone said something?"

Nikki looked away. She wanted to lie, but she had never mastered the art. She always sounded and looked guilty. "Claire may have mentioned you were having trouble."

Belinda mumbled a few choice swear words under her breath. "Well, she's wrong."

"I thought because you're selling the business and all—"

"I'm pregnant," Belinda blurted.

Nikki's eyes widened.

"I didn't want to say anything until the three-month mark, once we're out of the danger period. I'm selling the business because I won't be able to run it while raising a child."

Warmth filled Nikki's heart and a grin spread across her face. "Wow. That's fantastic news. I always assumed you didn't want children."

"I've always wanted children. Always." Much emphasis was placed on *always*. "Now was the right time to make it happen. I'm not getting any younger."

True. With Nikki approaching forty, and her own childbearing days long over, she couldn't imagine her body going through the rigour of pregnancy or childbirth now.

"I'm going to be an auntie," Nikki squealed. "How exciting. Congratulations. This is such wonderful news. I'm really happy for you and Anthony."

For the first time today, Belinda smiled. Her hand fell to her stomach and rubbed across the still-flat surface. Her usual radiance glowed in her eyes. "Ant and I are over the moon. Once I sell this damned business, we can start fresh."

"Sounds like a perfect plan. I hope it all goes well for you."

Nikki didn't stay for afternoon tea, preferring to sneak away before the boys arrived home from school, so she could revel in solitude for an hour or so.

As she drove up the winding range, damp, dense rainforest flanked either side of the road. The tall canopy filtered the sun and flickered shadows and light over the car. For most of the drive, she thought about Belinda and

Anthony's baby. How she would soon be an auntie. It had stirred little darts of energy under her skin.

But then another thought flittered into her mind: *Did I have the dates correct on Belinda's accounts?* She scanned her memories and confirmed that she had. But then another question struck her: *Have I missed any other personal expenses when preparing the accounts?* She tried to recollect all the accounts and figures she had studied that morning. No, it was straightforward. She had done everything right.

But it was an important set of accounts—it could mean the difference between selling and not selling the business. What if the buyer's accountants examined her figures and discovered a huge error? Belinda would think she was a dimwit.

Her fingers tightened around the steering wheel. Her heart hammered hard like it was trying to break its way through her ribcage.

She shouldn't have gone there. She should have referred Belinda to someone else instead. The road rushed ahead of her, snaking through the mossy rainforest.

Her breaths were rushed, thin, and the outskirts of her vision blurred. Nikki quickly pulled the car off to the side of the road. A loud, long beep sounded. She jumped in her seat, heart slamming. The car behind her veered and sped past, the driver's middle finger pointed up at her.

"Bloody hell," she said, trying to gather her breath. "Just calm down. Everything's fine. You didn't do anything wrong," she said in a self-soothing tone. "The figures are right. They're right. And maybe no one will even look at them anyway." Her belly was cramped with nerves. She hated herself so much right now.

After a long moment, her breathing finally calmed. Her anxiety ebbed. When confident she could make it home without causing herself an injury, she pulled out and carefully made the trip back to town.

As soon as she was home, she marched inside, shoulders hunched with self-defeat. She looked around at the fresh-scented, clean home. Claire had been here again.

Her back muscles tightened. Gone was her anxiety, replaced with a vibrating fire all through her body. She rushed into the laundry and pulled out the hot, half-wet clothes that were tumbling in her dryer. On the floor at her feet were the kids' expensive, white, formal school shirts, now grey from being washed with Matt's dirty work uniform.

"You've got to be kidding me!" She inclined her head back and screamed so loud her throat was raw and her chest hurt.

When Matt arrived home later that afternoon, Nikki sent the boys to their rooms to complete their homework despite their assurances they didn't have any. But she was in no mood to listen. She needed to vent to her husband about his mother and that had to be done outside of the boys' hearing range.

"What is it?" Matt asked when she dragged him into the laundry.

She threw the school shirts at him and they hit his chest before he caught them.

His forehead furrowed as he looked at the clothes in his hand and back to her scowling face. "The kids' uniforms?"

"What colour are they?"

"Oh," he said in a deep baritone.

"While I was at the Coast helping Belinda, your bloody mother, despite my repeated requests for her not to bother, came into our home and thought she'd throw the kids' good uniforms in with your filthy work clothes. I mean, seriously, Matt, what the hell? She can't be that stupid." She shook her head. "I swear she is doing this on purpose. She has to be."

"She's not doing it on purpose. For Christ sake, Nikki, stop blowing it up into something it isn't."

She wanted to scream at him and repeat every single incident his mother inflicted upon them, like the time she helped them move into this home and gave the floor rug to their dog to sleep on. Nikki's grandmother had gifted her the rug mere months before she passed away. Their dog was eleven at the time, incontinent and smelled every one of her years.

Nikki was guilt-stricken for days because she presumed she had lost the rug in the move or one of the removalists had knocked it off. But a week later, she found it folded neatly in the dog's kennel. When she confronted Claire about it, Claire had shrugged and said, "I thought it was the dog's. She really needs a blanket to be sleeping on at her age, don't you think?"

And then there was the expensive Japanese hand-painted vase Nikki had coveted for so long, but it was too expensive to justify purchasing, especially with young kids. Matt finally bought it for her birthday last year, only for Claire to *accidentally* knock it over and smash it into a billion pieces.

But if Nikki started to recount every little annoying thing his mother had done in an attempt to prove herself right, they would be occupied all night long. And the problem was, she didn't have solid proof. Every single incident could be fobbed off as an accident, an attempt to help, or a simple misunderstanding. Every incident was unassuming and petty but when accumulated, they painted a more sinister picture.

Nikki rubbed her face with her hands and groaned. Maybe she was blowing this out of proportion. It wasn't like she was well-adjusted at the moment, especially after her panic attack on the side of the road this afternoon.

"Please," she pleaded. "Please, please, please ring your mother and tell her not to do my washing anymore."

Matt stared at her, lips slanting into a deep frown. "You're serious?"

She nodded. "She won't listen to me. I've tried again and again. *You* have to do it."

"It's two school shirts, Nikki. It's not a big deal in the grand scheme of things."

She gritted her teeth. "It's not just shirts. It was my bra last week. My work jackets. Our towels. My white blouses. It's endless. And I'm sick of it."

He blew out an exasperated breath and strode out of the room.

She paced after him. "You don't have to be mean about. A simple request. I need you to back me up."

He stopped and spun to face her. "Back you up about the washing?"

She winced, pressed her palm to her forehead. "I know it sounds minor, but it's a big deal to me. I want my house back. I don't want to be walking on eggshells wondering if she's going to stop in to clean it."

He exhaled with a huff. "Fine. I'll call her after dinner."

"No, now. I want it done." She craved relaxation in her own home. She was exhausted. And she knew what Matt was like—by dinner, he would have forgotten, and she would have to ask again and look like a nag.

He pulled out his phone, dialled Claire's number and walked away. She managed to catch words here and there.

"We would appreciate it if you didn't do the washing. With Nikki home full-time now, there is really no need."

Shame burned her cheeks. The entire conversation sounded so ridiculous, yet, to her, it was a big deal. A massive deal. Why did she feel like she could never communicate that effectively? She always came off sounding petulant.

Maybe she was petulant. Maybe she was the problem—one of those ungrateful, princess daughters-in-law, who, no matter the situation, would never get on with their husband's mother.

Maybe she was losing her mind.

Chapter 20

Belinda

Belinda turned to Anthony as they walked, hand in hand, past the small arcade of businesses back to their car.

"Our sister-in-law is a genius," she said. "Maybe we should have asked for some help years ago."

She adored Anthony's smug smile, which hadn't moved from his mouth since leaving the accountant's office. It still hadn't sunk in that with one sixty-minute meeting, they had saved themselves at least fifteen thousand dollars a year. Their new accountant would perform the same functions but charge one-third of the price.

"It feels like such a weight off our shoulders. We are already up a thousand dollars this month. We can pay your mum back the grocery money for a start. I'm so scared to feel positive, but I can't help it. I'm tingling. We should send Nikki a hamper or a gift card as a thank you."

Anthony looked sidelong at her. "Let's not get ahead of ourselves. We're not out of trouble by any measure. Frivolous spending is a long way in the future. We've got cots and prams and baby clothes to think about."

A full bodily thrill. For so many years, buying baby gear was a magical dream. So much that in the early days, she would walk through the baby sections in department stores and buy a slim singlet or a plush toy. Over the years, she accumulated boxes under their spare bed, stuffed full of all kinds of baby apparel.

She wished that she hadn't thrown them away during one of her fits of despair. It would have saved them much-needed money.

They reached their car, and Belinda climbed into the passenger seat beside Anthony.

As they drove back towards the coast, Belinda placed her hand on his thigh. "This is the first glimmer of hope I've felt in such a long time. I don't know if I can trust it."

"Enjoy it while you can because it may not happen again."

She touched her free hand to her stomach. "I can think of one small reason right here that it will."

Anthony drew his eyes from the road, glanced at her hand cradling her stomach, and smiled. "For sure."

"Let's turn the car around and go out for lunch. We haven't done anything like that in so long. I've still got a little money left over from what your Mum lent us. We don't have to be extravagant."

His nose wrinkled. "You think we could?"

"Come on. Just this once. Let's blow off all this stress and relax for an hour."

Anthony pulled over to the elbow of the road, flicked on his indicator and swung a U-turn. They headed back towards the small CBD, which, in a town like Montville, existed merely for tourists and was made up of gift shops, arty-type stores and eateries that took advantage of the spectacular views.

Belinda's mind was buoyant, her steps light, as they strolled up the short hill towards a café that offered an outlook to the valley—green undulating hills watched over by a cloudless blue sky stretching all the way to the Pacific Ocean. The high mountainous air was humid and held the scent of moist detritus rather than the gusty brine they were used to in Maroochydore.

Belinda rolled her neck. All the tension she usually held in those hard, snarled muscles had fluttered off into the atmosphere like steam from a warm puddle. The relief that accompanied knowing they had fifteen thousand dollars extra to play with a year by simply changing their accountant, overshadowed her shame for not working this out sooner.

They took a seat outside on the big timber deck. Belinda couldn't keep her gaze from the picture of beauty extending from her eye line. She smiled as joy swelled in her chest.

When the waiter arrived, they ordered entrees followed by mains—each reasonably priced. Anthony splashed out and ordered a boutique beer. Belinda would have loved a glass of champagne, but her baby's health came first. She would happily do away with champagne for the rest of her life rather than give up this small cell of a child growing in her womb.

When the waiter left them alone, Belinda grinned at her husband. What a handsome man Anthony was, something she had noticed more and more as her pregnancy progressed. She couldn't imagine a better dad for her child.

She rested her elbows on the table and leaned forward. "Any word on that new job you put a bid in for?"

He shook his head. "Probably won't hear for another month. The tender process hasn't closed yet."

"Damn. I was hoping for triple good news."

"You and me both."

"But let's not spoil the mood. We're here to celebrate."

When a waitress carried their drinks to the table, Anthony lifted his glass of beer in the air. "To baby blessings."

Her smile was strong, proud and unstoppable. "To baby blessings. At long last."

"You do realise now that since Nikki knows you're pregnant, we're going to have to tell the rest of the family. I don't want to upset anyone."

Belinda's brow furrowed. "Upset? Why would they be upset?"

"Because it's important news. No one will want to be told last. Especially Mum."

Belinda winced. "I didn't think about that. I only told Nikki to stop her from thinking that we were selling the business for financial reasons." She crossed her arms over her chest. "I'm still not happy your mother blabbed about our personal business. Maybe we should tell her last to teach her a lesson about keeping her big mouth closed."

The moment Anthony had admitted to borrowing twenty thousand dollars from Claire, Belinda knew it wouldn't be long before his mother told everyone she knew. If you wanted something kept secret, you didn't tell Claire.

It confounded her that despite Claire being incapable of holding secrets in confidence, she ended up with so many in her possession. People must not have come to the logical conclusion Belinda had: If Claire was telling Belinda the secrets of others, it was highly likely Claire was spilling Belinda's secrets too.

Anthony frowned. "I know I promised she wouldn't say anything. I honestly believed she wouldn't."

Point proven. Anthony assumed that because he was Claire's son, he got some kind of special treatment. He didn't. He never had. The only person that was treated with any kind of genuine respect was Matt. He was the golden child—smart, financially sound, and had given Claire grandsons.

Belinda swallowed down her resentment, letting it fester in her stomach acid like she always did, because, at the end of the day, Claire was Anthony's mother. Family. Blood. She had no right to break that bond.

Belinda would flip if Anthony ever badmouthed her own mother—not that her parents didn't deserve it from time to time.

Over the years, her parents had hounded them for small loans, and, stupidly, Belinda would give it to them. But, when her own finances tightened up, and she was no longer able to help her parents anymore, their true personalities were illuminated: selfish, nasty, and unforgiving.

And yet, despite all this, Anthony never said anything against them. He knew, despite all their misgivings, underneath it all, Belinda loved her parents as any child did and should. It was only right that Belinda afforded her husband the same courtesy he extended her.

She reached across the table and rested her hand on his. "I'm sorry. I was too harsh. Maybe Claire had to get it off her chest. I'm sure she's worried for us."

"Of course she would be."

She sighed and sipped at her lemonade. "I better tell my parents about this baby too at some point."

His jaw and neck tightened. "I guess so."

But then her parents would want to visit. She recalled the last time they came to stay for a week over Easter last year. After they had left, her iPad and cash from her purse departed too. She lied to Anthony—said she had lost them.

"Or maybe not."

He arched a brow. "But they're your parents."

"I know. And I love them dearly. With all my heart." She lowered her voice to a whisper. "I just don't trust them." She sat back against the chair, bemused at how easily those words had come from her mouth. Already, she could see there was no negotiation when it came to the safety and well-being of her baby.

He nodded. "I support your decision."

She grinned, opened her mouth to speak, but a waiter stopped by with their entrees. Her grilled baby octopus, swimming in lemon and garlic oil, was placed in front of her. She inhaled the citrus and garlic aromas deeply. Anthony eyed his plate of prawns. It had been so long since they'd had seafood.

"We're going to have to start considering names."

He smiled. "What do you think? Should we find out if we're having a boy or girl?"

She shook her head hard. "I want a surprise."

"Me too."

"We should write a list of all the clothes and equipment we'll need too." She tried not to think about the gear she threw away, and Anthony was wise enough not to mention it.

"I thought we could check buy, swap and sell sites—there's some great second-hand stuff—"

"No way," she said. "It's not the baby's fault we have no money."

"I thought it made sense—"

"No, Anthony. I draw the line at second-hand baby gear." She shuddered. Her childhood had been a parade of hand-me-downs, ratty school uniforms, holey shoes and furniture collected from others' yards during roadside collection week.

Her marked and mouldy bed mattress had been hauled from a house three streets over, dressed in piss-stained second-hand sheets and she'd had to sleep on them amidst the stench. She would not subject her child to the same.

"We've waited so long for this; I want to enjoy it," she said. "Not scrimping and saving as we do in every other aspect of our lives."

"It was just a suggestion. We've got months ahead of us, so we can keep an eye on sales."

She nodded, much preferring that idea.

Anthony ordered another beer as they waited for their main. When it arrived, it was like receiving a Christmas present. Grilled reef-caught barramundi with chips and salad, while Anthony had steak.

She cut into her fish and had a mouthful, her eyes closing as she chewed. "I needed this so much. Maybe it's the baby telling me to eat good oils from the seafood."

"Could very well be." He patted his own stomach. "Not sure what my excuse is."

She laughed and he chuckled, but then Belinda looked up and met Claire's eyes as she entered the café with about eight or so people from her art class.

Her heart stuttered. "Your mum's here," she said through gritted teeth but maintained the forced smile on her lips.

Anthony flicked his head around and waved when Claire noticed him and started a direct route across the crowded café towards them.

"Damn it. Of all the days we choose to have lunch," he grumbled before Claire was standing next to the table looking down at them. "Hi, Mum."

"Hi, darling," she said, leaning down and kissing his cheek. "Hi, Belinda, you're looking well."

"Thanks."

"Out catching a spot of lunch, I see."

Belinda smiled, though her lips were tight across her teeth. How must they look—having asked Claire to pay for her share of the restaurant bill and now they were here eating out?

"Yes", Anthony said. "We're celebrating. Something we don't do too much anymore, but this news is worth the splurge."

Claire arched a brow. "I see." She tilted her head to the side. "And what are you celebrating?"

Anthony looked to Belinda and Belinda wanted to run away. Why was he leaving this for her? Claire was *his* mother. "Um…I'm pregnant."

Both of Claire's brows shot up an almost imperceptible fraction. "I beg your pardon?"

Anthony sat more erect, cleared his throat. When he met his mother's gaze, he grinned and said, "We're going to have a baby."

Claire's brows lowered and her eyes narrowed at Anthony. "Considering your current situation, that is the most irresponsible news I've ever heard."

"Mum, that's not fair," Anthony said gruffly.

She leaned closer to his ear. "No, what's not fair is you calling me and asking me for my share of the restaurant bill, and then I find you both out eating seafood and steak, no less. And then you cry to me that you're in such financial trouble that I lend you twenty thousand dollars. Money I don't have. I had to sell shares to get that cash. Not to mention our conversation not so long ago, which I won't go into—"

Belinda's curiosity piqued when she noticed Anthony's jaw tighten. *What conversation*? The pulse in his throat was pronounced. He glanced to Belinda then back to his mother.

"—and then you tell me you're having a baby. Don't talk to me about what's fair, Anthony."

Belinda and Anthony stared, dumbfounded. They had no reply because Claire was right. Technically. Sure, there were countless reasonable justifications they could use to explain themselves, but Claire didn't know about any of those. She only knew what she saw in front of her—two financially irresponsible people.

Claire stood tall again and straightened the pearls around her neck. "Anyway, I have company, so I best leave you two to it." And she strode away.

Belinda pushed her chair back and bumped her leg against the table as she stood. Pain throbbed. "Pay the bill. I'll meet you in the car."

She managed to keep her composure until she escaped outside into the daytime air before she burst into tears.

Chapter 21

Anthony

Soon after Anthony arrived home from lunch, Belinda stamped her feet up the stairs to their bedroom. He hoped a long nap might snap her out of the sulky mood his mother had heartlessly shoved her into.

Anthony took full advantage of the time he had to himself. He headed outside onto the balcony, making sure he pulled the glass doors shut. Anger still raged for how his mother had reacted to their news.

He recalled when Matt had told Mum that Nikki was pregnant all those years ago. Mum was so overjoyed, she had cried happy tears and took countless photos of the moment.

Sure, on a level, he understood Mum's reaction. They couldn't afford this baby, but neither could many parents out there, yet they made it work. Necessity meant they dug deep to give their children a good life. He and Belinda would do the same.

But what niggled at him more, and what he intuited his mother's true problem was, was that he had admitted he was going to leave Belinda. He shook his head, incredulous that Mum attempted to bring it up today right in front of Belinda.

A twinge of fear pulsed through his veins. Belinda had been right to say that his mother couldn't keep her big mouth shut. He had to speak to her now before her loose lips ruined his marriage.

If what he had said ever got back to Belinda, it would be the end of them. Whatever fine threads they had left would irreparably snap.

He looked back inside to make sure Bel was out of sight, then dialled his mother.

"Hi, Anthony. I'm still at lunch, so make it quick please."

"You can't tell anyone what I said to you last week. I've obviously changed my mind. I love Belinda. Since the news of this baby, it's like I've got my wife back. I want to make this work."

"And why would you think I'd say anything about that?"

"Because you almost did today. In front of Bel."

"Don't be silly. What do you take me for?"

His brow crinkled. "Anyway, if that got out, it would destroy my marriage. And this baby would be the victim in all this."

A long sigh. "As long as you think you're making the right decision. You were adamant a mere seven days ago that a destroyed marriage was what you intended."

"Things have changed."

"Indeed, they have. And just how do you plan to support this baby?"

"I'll make it work." His heart warmed with the truth of that. He would make it work. He would do all he could to ensure his family was taken care of. No way was he going to desert this child. He knew the pain of losing a father as a ten-year-old boy. He would not subject his own kid to that. Not a chance.

Chapter 22

Paige

Since the altercation with Claire, Paige insisted on repairing their blemished relationship—for her sake—but also for Vaughn's. So, she invited all the family over on Saturday afternoon for a barbeque.

Paige had grown up without siblings. To have a loving relationship with Claire, Vaughn's brothers and the extended family, where they could chat on the phone, stop in at each other's place for coffee, meet in town on weekends for dinner, and spend Christmas and other holidays together, would be bliss.

"We don't usually hang out," Vaughn had said as they cleaned the back deck and decorated it with table runners and fairy lights.

"But you're family. I assumed families always saw each other."

"We all have our own lives. We don't live out of each other's pockets. I don't know, maybe it's us, maybe other families are different. But it works."

Paige placed her hands on her hips. "Well, I hope I can change that." She didn't want Evie to have the same lonely childhood she had had. She wanted to give her daughter a life full of familial memories and role models.

Belinda and Anthony were first to arrive, a little after lunchtime.

"Hi," Paige said, grinning when she greeted them at the door. "Come on in."

Anthony handed her a bottle of wine.

She looked at the label of sauvignon blanc. "Beautiful, thank you. We can crack it open during lunch."

"I hope you don't mind that we're a little early," Belinda said with a bubbly voice. Her eyes were bright, and she was smiling.

"Not at all."

"We have some news we want to share with you before the others arrive."

"News?" Paige's grin widened. "Exciting. Well, head on out the back. Vaughn is there. I'll put this wine in the fridge and come join you."

She quickly dealt with the wine, grabbed a tray of nibbles from the fridge—soft cheeses, crackers, and dips—and joined the others at the outdoor setting.

Evie was dressed in her bright pink swimmers and was playing on the grass under the sprinkler. That would keep her occupied for some time and tire her out, so she would go down for a nap later, giving Paige an hour or so to relax with the adults.

She waved at Evie and Evie grinned back as she dashed through the sprays of water, skipping over the sprinkler to the other side. Paige clapped her hands and laughed. Evie's smile was triumphant as she lined up again, ready to power through the mist of water. This little girl was the most adorable in the world.

Paige sank into the seat next to Vaughn on the side overlooking the backyard, so she could keep an eye on Evie. Belinda and Anthony were opposite. Something was different about them—Belinda's smile was big and genuine. Her arms were open, her eye contact much more direct than when they had met at the restaurant. Anthony was more upright. Proud, perhaps?

Paige placed her hand on Vaughn's thigh. "Belinda and Anthony said they had some news to share."

Vaughn turned to his brother and sister-in-law, brow arched. "Oh? News, hey?"

A slow smile grew on Belinda's lips. She didn't suppress it as she shared a glance with Anthony, then turned back to Paige and Vaughn. "Anthony and I are going to have a baby."

Paige squealed and threw her hands in the air. "How wonderful. What fantastic news." She jumped out of her seat and raced around the table to kiss Belinda's cheek.

"Congratulations." She went to Anthony, giving him a cuddle and a kiss on the cheek. "Wonderful news. Congrats."

Vaughn reached over the table and shook Anthony's hand. "Congrats, mate. I was starting to think you were never going to have any kids."

Anthony laughed. "I could say the same about you."

Vaughn went to Belinda's side and kissed her cheek. "Congrats."

"Thanks. We're so happy."

When they were all seated again, Belinda said, "I'm due April next year."

Paige nodded. "Perfect. Just before winter. Makes feeding time much more comfortable." Rather than sweaty bodies pressed together and the sickly scent of milk that she remembered when Evie was born in February during one hell of a hot and sticky summer. Finances were tight back then, so air conditioning had been a luxury she couldn't afford.

She would turn the pedestal fan on high and have it facing her as she sat in the poky living room, warm humid air working overtime to cool her down. A deep thrumming pulse of remembered loneliness filled her heart—it had been a long time since she had recalled that loud emotion.

"Do the others know?" Vaughn asked.

Anthony and Belinda exchanged a look. “Ah, yeah, we were kind of forced to let Nikki know. And then when she found out, we thought it best not to leave Mum in the dark for much longer.”

Vaughn nodded. “Fair enough. Well, I’m chuffed for you both.”

Paige didn’t miss the disingenuous lilt to his tone. Her head snapped around to look at him, but he was smiling, not noticing her scrutiny. She tucked away her curiosity for later when they got a moment alone.

Anthony reached for his bottle of beer and took a swig. “I wish Mum was a little more enthusiastic.”

“Why wouldn’t she be enthusiastic?” Vaughn asked.

Anthony waved his brother’s question away. “Who can tell? You know what she’s like. All I can say is that she better get over it or she’ll find herself missing out on a grandchild.”

Paige flinched. Surely it wasn’t that bad?

“She’ll come around,” Vaughn said.

Belinda straightened taller in her seat. “Of course she will. Maybe she’s a little overwhelmed at this stage. She didn’t expect we had planned for children.”

Vaughn nodded, but he was looking off in the distance, eyes slightly narrowed. He was obviously as baffled about Claire’s negativity as Paige was.

“Well, let’s hope there’s no tension today,” Vaughn said.

“Agreed.”

Belinda placed her hand on Anthony’s forearm. “I’m sure it will be fine. Let’s relax and have a great afternoon.” She chuckled. “And hope it doesn’t end with anyone falling down the stairs this time.”

Paige held up her crossed fingers.

They moved onto simpler topics of conversation before Claire arrived. Claire was vibrant and cheerful when Paige greeted her at the front door. They exchanged their hellos, and, while leading her out the back to join the others, chatted as though the 'gold-digger' incident hadn't even happened.

When Paige opened the door to Nikki, who was standing next to Matt and her two tall sons on the other side, she almost gasped. Nikki appeared so diminutive, hunched, and had, in the last fortnight, lost some weight.

She didn't want to pry, but she also felt that if she didn't say anything, she might be seen as unsympathetic.

"Is everything okay, Nikki?" she asked as she led them out the back. Matt held a protective arm around his wife.

Nikki waved a dismissive hand. "Me? I'm fine. A little tired. Not sleeping well."

"You poor thing. There's nothing worse."

"I'll be okay."

"Well, go sit down with the others and relax."

"Thanks, Paige," she said with a smile and allowed Matt to lead her through the house towards the back door.

A loud, high-pitched scream sounded from outside.

Evie.

The pain and shock in that sound reverberated through Paige's body. Chills scattered up her back and neck. She bolted through the living room and out the back door. Her attention darted to the lawn. The sprinkler still hissed, water spraying into the air. Evie stood by the sprinkler, bright red blood oozing down her face. Vaughn was almost there. Paige sprinted up the steps, across the wet grass.

Evie's cries were loud and insistent.

"Come here," she said, puffing, as she lifted her from Vaughn's arms. "Let me have

a look."

A long cut ran horizontally under Evie's left eye.

Paige turned to Vaughn. "Can you get me something to stop the blood please?"

He nodded and rushed away.

"What happened, baby?"

"I fell over," Evie managed between sobs. Her shoulders were shuddering. Tears streaked the blood that was already running fast over her soaked skin. Evie's pink swimmers were now stained with blotches of red.

"Let me take a look, darling." But there was too much blood. She turned to see where Vaughn was. He was rushing back with a soft, clean towel. He tenderly held it to the wound for a moment, then lifted it away revealing the damage.

Without all the blood, it wasn't as big as Paige had first thought. Her fear eased. "Do you think she'll need stitches?"

Vaughn dabbed again. Evie howled. It was a small but thick cut. "I don't think so. We'll keep the towel on it for a while and see how she goes.

Paige's throat closed over. Tears pricked the back of her eyes, but she blinked them back, so she didn't frighten Evie. She also didn't want to embarrass herself in front of Vaughn's family.

"It's not so bad," she said to Evie. "Come on, darling. You'll be okay." She shifted her onto her hip and carried her past the wide, concerned gazes. She exhibited what she hoped would pass as a smile. "She'll be fine. I'll just get her settled inside."

Paige didn't wait for responses and marched into the house. Vaughn was a few steps behind her. She carefully placed Evie on the couch and sent Vaughn for a pillow and a towel. She laid the towel over the couch and rested Evie's head back against the pillow. Vaughn lingered nearby, hands moving from his hips, into his pockets, to behind his head, back to his hips.

"I'll be right in here with Evie. Just until she settles down. You go out and keep the others entertained."

"You sure?"

She nodded.

Once Evie stopped crying and was more fascinated with the Peppa Pig cartoon on the TV, Paige scouted for antiseptic and cotton wool. She dabbed the lotion over Evie's cut, leaving yellow discolouration. Blueish bruising and swelling were already coming out, staining Evie's delicate skin.

Claire strode in and her lips slanted into a sympathetic frown. "Hey, how's it all going in here?"

"Evie's calmed down now. I think it was more blood than wound."

Hands on the back of the couch, Claire leaned over to inspect the cut closer. "A friend in my art class has a daughter who is a doctor. Do you want me to take a photo and get her opinion, just to make sure she doesn't need stitches?"

She pushed her palms against her eyes long enough to draw a deep breath, then she nodded at Claire. "That would be wonderful."

Claire smiled and took a photo. After a few presses and pushes, the tell-tale *whoosh* sounded as the message sent. "I'll let you know when she replies."

"Thanks so much. I'll sit with Evie a little while longer until she—" she lowered her voice to a whisper, lest she make Evie suspicious of her plan, "—falls asleep. Then I'll take her to her room and head on out and sit with you all."

"Take your time. I know how difficult it is to see your children hurt. Matt was the worst. Such a sickly child." She shook her head and clicked her tongue. "What that boy put me through when he was little."

"It's tough."

"It sure is. But you're doing a great job."

Paige's smile was warm and full of gratitude. Until now, she had had no one around to tell her that she was a great mother. "Thanks, Claire. That means a lot to me."

With that, Claire left to join the others.

Paige made some lunch for Evie and a drink of milk in her cup that she drank while watching cartoons. Soon enough, her eyelids grew heavier and she finally drifted off to sleep in Paige's arms. Paige carefully lifted her up as she stood, aware of how big and heavy her little girl was getting, and carried her to bed. When tucked in, and the door left open in case Evie called out, Paige snuck down the hall and out the back.

"How's Evie?" Vaughn asked when Paige sat beside him.

A sigh of relief. "She's fine. Looked nastier than it was."

"You have all that to look forward to," Vaughn said to Belinda and Anthony.

They grinned and nodded, but Paige knew well enough that they didn't yet understand, nor would they be able to imagine exactly what they were in for.

Paige hadn't known what love was until she held Evie in her arms. And now that she knew how potent love was, she protected it fiercely. Her love for her daughter was a priority above everything and anything else in her life. That was the order of life—without a doubt. Belinda and Anthony would soon know that too.

"Have you heard from the doctor, Claire?" Paige asked.

Claire nodded. "Yes, I did. Sorry, I meant to come in and tell you, but I got to chatting and forgot. She said it's fine. A Band-Aid should do the trick."

Paige's shoulders relaxed on her long exhalation. "Great. I've dressed the cut already." She leaned forward, clapped her hands together once. "So, who's ready for lunch? I'm sure you're all starving."

The two growing boys were emphatic with their chorused 'Me'.

Paige laughed. "Vaughn, I guess that means we better get this barbeque cranking."

Paige put some music on while Vaughn lit the barbeque. Everyone was laughing and chatting and helping bring out the salads and meats. Paige opened a couple of bottles of wine and left them on the table. “Please, tuck in.”

Claire poured a glass of white wine for those who wanted one. After her scare earlier, Paige was more than happy to destress with a glass or two. Belinda, naturally, stuck to sparkling water.

When the meats were cooked and presented on the table, they dished up mounds of salad, sausages, and potato bake.

“Matt, I was telling Paige earlier of the hell you put me through when you were a boy,” Claire said. She had a drunken lisp already, making the *s* words sound more like *sh*.

Matt kept his expression neutral. “All kids have their moments.”

“You more than the other two.”

“I vaguely remember that,” Anthony said. “I remember you being in hospital a few times.”

Claire pressed her finger and thumb to her forehead as she shook her head. “It’s unbelievably stressful when your children are sick.”

“It sure is,” Nikki agreed.

“It’s life. Kids get sick,” Matt said. “And then they grow up with strong immune systems.”

“Yeah, I’ve hardly known you to be sick at all,” Nikki said. “Maybe a couple of colds here and there.”

“See, that’s the problem,” Anthony said. “People provide too clean environments for their children. They don’t let kids play in the dirt or touch the cat. Immune systems suffer.”

“I obviously have the right idea,” Nikki said with a chuckle. “When my house is messy, my excuse from now on is that I’m trying to develop the boys’ immunities.”

“Those two kids running around the footy field would be the best thing for them,” Anthony said.

Matt nodded. “I agree.”

"I did all those things," Claire said. "You boys were forever playing outside. And believe me, I was too busy to be overly clean. Especially once your father passed away. I mean, Nikki, you agree that my ability to wash clothes isn't as good as it could be."

Paige watched on with curiosity as Nikki flinched but soon recovered with a nervous chuckle and a quick narrow-eyed glance at Matt.

"I think you were just a sickly child, Matt," Claire said. "I'm not sure cleanliness or lack thereof had anything to do with it."

Matt stood. "Anyone else up for a beer?"

Vaughn nodded. "Yeah, mate."

"Grab one for me too, please," Anthony said before skolling the remainder in his bottle.

"I hear you're a lady of leisure now," Anthony said fondly to Nikki. Paige couldn't wait until she knew Vaughn's extended family long enough to be spoken to with such familiarity.

"Yep. Couldn't have come sooner. Frees up a lot of time to do all those things I couldn't fit in while working."

"Like the washing," Claire said. "It must be great to finally be able to keep an orderly house."

Nikki didn't meet Claire's gaze or acknowledge her comment. Paige watched on, wondering what was beneath this interplay.

"It will be great to be home with the kids, I'm sure," Anthony said.

"I am appreciating the time with them. Not that they're enjoying it so much. Less time on the video games now."

Ryan rolled his eyes and Flynn's cheeks burned red.

Nikki rubbed Flynn's back. "There's someone in the house now when they get home—keeps them on track. Flynn will be in his senior year soon."

Matt was back and placed beers in front of his brothers. "It makes everything run a little more smoothly. Less rushing around."

"Good to hear," Anthony said.

"Nikki said you're looking to sell your business, Belinda," Matt said.

Belinda held her crossed fingers up. "Hopefully. With the baby coming, I can't see how I would have the time to keep it. I think Nikki has the right idea being home with her kids. I want the same with this little one," she said, running a hand across her stomach.

"I can understand that," said Paige. "That's why I like working from home. I can be here with Evie. I'm reluctant to get an office space until Evie is at school."

"Not everyone has the option to stay home with their children," Claire said to Belinda. "Finances may dictate the opposite."

"Very true. And that's why I'm hoping to get something part-time. Working from home would be best. Just not sure what opportunities there are for me yet."

"I'd be looking into it soon before you make an irreversible decision like selling your business."

"Mum, we'll take care of it." Anthony's words were blunt and deep.

Claire rolled her eyes as she looked away.

Wanting to dissipate some of that thick tension in the air, Paige stood. "Let me clear some of these dishes away." She set about collecting the plates and carried them inside. Vaughn wasn't far behind with a load of dishes in his hands.

"Bit of friction out there this afternoon," Paige said, lowering the plates into the sink. "Your mum is obviously still worried about their financial situation." As she said the words, she realised that would be why Claire wasn't so enthusiastic about the pregnancy. She could understand that, but she was one to know that raising a child on little money was possible. It just meant making sacrifices.

Vaughn shrugged and placed the dishes on the bench. "It's not her place to intrude."

"I guess that's true." She turned to him, hands on hips. "You seem a little quiet today too."

Again, he shrugged. "I'm okay."

"You've been a bit closed off since you heard about the pregnancy. Does it bother you that Anthony and Belinda are having a baby?"

His spine straightened and his eyes dashed away.

"What is it?" she asked.

"I don't know." He shook his head. "I guess I'm a little jealous."

Her eyes widened. "Jealous?"

"I'm the only one in the family now who doesn't have their own children."

She had been in Vaughn's life for a little over six months, and even though their relationship had zoomed forward at warp speed, children were one topic they hadn't discussed in much detail. "You want us to have a baby?"

"I didn't realise I did until today. But, yeah. I think I do."

She stepped back. "Wow. Okay. Well, that's something we'll definitely have to discuss." No matter how wonderful Vaughn was with Evie, Evie wasn't his blood. It was human nature that he would want to have his own children.

Paige needed to explain first, though, that bearing more children was not going to happen until Vaughn fully committed to their relationship. No way was she going to raise a child all on her own again. She didn't have the benefit of a family to help. She had been a single mum in the fullest sense of the word.

But already, excited flutters were beating in her belly. To admit that he wanted children with her was already a strong sign of commitment. She smiled at him.

Vaughn grinned and looked to the table of guests outside. “Perhaps a conversation for a later time.”

“Definitely.” She swayed closer, lifted onto her tiptoes and kissed him hard on the mouth. “And it’s something we can definitely get into practice for, regardless of what we decide.”

“Hmmm, can we get everyone to leave now?”

“I’d love that,” she said and kissed him again.

“Sorry,” came a female voice.

They both snapped their mouths away from each other. Paige took two quick steps back from Vaughn and glanced over her shoulder to see who had interrupted them.

Belinda.

“No, it’s fine,” Vaughn said.

Belinda’s cheeks were flushed. “I was going to grab another beer for Anthony.”

“No worries. I’ll bring one out,” Vaughn said, already heading to the fridge.

Belinda lowered her gaze, turned and left.

Paige laughed. “Busted.”

“Just a little.”

Vaughn grabbed a bottle of beer from the top shelf and swung the fridge door closed. “Mum’s being okay to you today, isn’t she?”

She nodded. “Fine to me.”

“Good.” He motioned his head towards the backyard. “We better get back out there.”

“I’m right behind you.”

Chapter 23

Claire

The past…

The high school Claire attended was not big by any measure—a few double-storey red brick buildings existing since the turn of the century.

A distinct stuffy scent like timeworn polished timber and dust filled the halls to the main building where Claire attended most of her classes. With the end of the school term approaching, Claire's timetable was full of exams. The most recent of which was for English—Claire's least favourite subject.

For some reason, the rules of grammar confused her. It was all nominalisation, gerunds, and possessive apostrophes, which may have well been a whole new language to her, let alone so-called English.

The final bell for the day chimed and she dawdled down the hall, not in any real rush to meet her sisters. It was Thursday, payday, which meant Dad would be itching to head to the horse track and Mum would be fighting him for food money.

No, she planned to collect Sue and Maggie on her way through and head to the park for an hour or so on the way home. But as she made it past the school office, her English teacher, Mrs Randall, stopped her and asked that she come to talk in the classroom.

Mrs Randall was a short woman with a masculine build. She wore her white hair long, down to her waist.

Claire hoped this wasn't about the English test. Maybe she had failed more than she had anticipated. "I better not, Mrs R, I have to pick up my sisters—"

"It won't take long."

She bit back her sigh and followed Mrs Randall into an empty classroom where her teacher took a seat at the desk and gestured Claire sit in the chair opposite.

"How did you find your test this afternoon?"

Claire inwardly cringed. "Fine."

"How did you go with the grammar aspect?"

"Fine."

Mrs Randall smiled. "Good to hear. And how about things at home, Claire. Is everything well at home?"

Claire hesitated a moment as curiosity crept under her skin. "Fine, thank you."

Mrs Randall leaned forward, resting her ageing hands on the desk, her fingers weaved together. "I have noticed that you have lost quite a deal of weight, and I wanted to make sure that you are getting enough food at home."

Claire sat up taller, now aware of her oversized elbows and knees more than ever. She had managed to grow seven centimetres in the last eighteen months, making her appear gangly and awkward. "We do just well, thanks."

Again, that humouring smile graced Mrs Randall's lips. "Glad to hear that. I was wondering if you would like me to bring an extra sandwich with me, maybe a cheese or Vegemite sandwich, which you may wish to eat." She shrugged. "Or not. I'll leave it in your desk, and you can use your discretion. I'm happy with either decision."

Her stomach rumbled and mouth watered. How much she would love to have a cheese sandwich each day for lunch. "That's not necessary."

"I know, but I'll do it anyway. I make one for myself each day anyway, so it's no extra work on my part. In the meantime, Claire, if you want to talk about anything at all, I'm here."

"Thank you," Claire said, face burning. "Can I go now?"

Mrs Randall gestured towards the door. "Of course. You better not keep your sisters waiting any longer."

Claire maintained a stiff but slow gait until she stepped into the empty hallway. Once the door was shut behind her, she raced along the floorboards and out the front door, gasping in air. Heat steamed her cheeks.

Angry tears filled her eyes, but she wiped them away with the back of her palms. The last thing she needed was schoolfriends seeing her crying. Bad enough that she had to walk home fully aware of how much her body resembled a new foal's—long, gangly with oversized joints.

She collected Sue and Maggie from the front gate, where they waited for her every school day, and made them walk home extra fast.

"What's the matter?" they asked as they struggled to keep up with her.

"Nothing. Mind your own business."

When Claire arrived home, Mum was in the kitchen washing the dishes. Claire sent her sisters out the back to play. Hot tears were burning in her eyes when she asked her mother, "Is there anything to eat?"

Mum turned and shook her head. "Not until dinner."

"Dad down at the track again?"

Mum nodded. Worry lined her forehead. "What's the matter?"

Claire took a step closer, placed her hands on her hips. "What is so wrong with you that you had to marry someone like Dad? Are you so deficient that he was the best you could do? Was it your plan to have children you can't even feed?"

Mum took two hurried steps closer. Claire felt the impact first, the sting second as Mum's palm landed hard across her cheek. "Don't you dare speak to me like that. You have no idea what I go through to try and feed you kids. Your father wasn't always the way he is now. He was a good man once…" She trailed off, looked away.

"Do you know how embarrassing it is to have my teacher ask me why I am so skinny?"

"Who? What did he ask?"

"Mrs Randall. She noticed my weight and asked if I was getting enough food at home."

"Did you tell her?"

"Of course I didn't. Though if they took us away from you, at least we might get fed."

Mum's face twisted in disgust, but there was fear in her widened eyes. "You'd get a whole lot more than fed. Believe me, institutionalised kids suffer in ways you couldn't even begin to understand."

Her mum had grown up in an orphanage, which was something Claire had found out by accident. She had overheard a conversation Mum was having with a childhood friend. When Claire had asked where her mother's parents were and why she'd had to live in an orphanage, Mum had smacked her bottom and sent her to her room for being a stickybeak. She never asked again, and Mum never mentioned it.

Mum pointed to the staircase. "Get up to your room and do not come out until teatime."

Claire groaned. "But that's not fair. I didn't do anything."

"If you ever speak to me the way you did today again, I will tell your father and he can deal with you."

Claire stamped her foot, ran out of the kitchen and up the stairs to her room. Dad may not be around much, but she had been on the end of his discipline—unrestrained smacks across her leg with a leather belt, so hard he drew blood.

When in her bedroom, she sat on her bed and scowled. She looked out the window at the house next door. Marie was with her mother on the back patio drinking tea and eating an afternoon snack.

Claire hated her mother so much. She wanted to be nothing like her when she grew up. She was going to marry a good man. Someone who would give her a good home and a good life, and she would make sure her children never knew what it felt like to hurt with hunger.

Chapter 24

Nikki

Sunday morning, Nikki poured Matt a coffee. They carried their warm mugs outside to the deck to drink in the morning sun.

The deck overlooked their backyard, which was an expansive patch of lawn the size of two football fields. A border of rainforest squared the home off from the distant surrounding properties, leaving them in tranquil seclusion.

They barely heard the neighbours, bar a noisy ride-on lawnmower from time to time, a distant dog bark or kids noisily playing. Otherwise, it was the buzz of insects, carolling of birds and the soft rustle of wind as it found a path through tree branches and grass.

Matt had chosen this property, so the boys had a place to play like he and his brothers had while growing up. Not that Matt had got to experience much of that. Perhaps that was the real reason this house appealed. And going by the motorbikes, tinnie, fishing rods and yabby pumps, he was making up for a lost childhood.

Last night, Nikki managed to sleep deeply for the first time in months—possibly assisted by the bedtime activities Matt initiated. At first, his touch on her skin was abrasive and she resisted, but he was always a determined man, and she was glad her body soon blossomed to his advances.

Afterwards, as she had lain beside him catching her breath, she flinched when she realised she couldn't remember the last time they had made love. Maybe two months, maybe three had passed.

Since they were married fifteen years ago, they had always been intimate a handful of times every month, sometimes more. Except for after the birth of the boys, of course.

Nikki lifted her face to the sunlight flickering over the deck. Mid-morning was the best time of day—the cool night air still hadn't pushed past the tall canopy of trees, preventing the spring sun from heating the day up.

"Stunning day," she said then sipped her coffee. "Oh, shit," she hissed, sitting up straighter. "What's the date?"

"The fifth."

She placed a hand over her chest and sighed. "I have to remember to organise your mum some flowers. The anniversary of your dad's death is only a few weeks away."

He grimaced. "I hadn't forgotten."

"I might sort that out this morning, just so time doesn't get away from me." Lately, her memory had been horrendous. She was usually one to pride herself on an almost perfect ability to remember everything. Matt or the boys could ask her where any object in the house was and she would know. Never had she had to rely on a calendar because she never forgot times and dates for appointments. Even at work, she barely made notes about upcoming jobs.

Not anymore. Important matters were completely erased from her brain.

"Have you heard from your mum since the barbeque?"

Matt's brow furrowed as he shook his head.

Silent treatments from Claire were not an unusual experience, though they still irritated Nikki to no end, especially when the childish treatment was not deserved.

"Have you tried to call her?"

"A couple of times. I left a message."

She cringed recalling the snide remarks at the barbeque. "Maybe I shouldn't have got you to say anything about the washing."

Matt looked at her over the rim of his coffee mug as he sipped at it and shrugged. "A little too late for regrets." He was always so blasé about his mother. No matter if she was raging at him, ignoring him, or guilt-tripping him, he always managed to remain easy-going and unflustered. Nikki was not so great at sealing off her emotions.

"I know. But it felt so big. Like I was going to explode. You have to admit, it's been a lot easier without her coming over. Even this silent treatment is like a holiday."

He chuckled, shook his head. "Only you would see it that way. Come here," he said, resting his coffee mug on the table. He held out his hands.

She smiled and went to him, sitting on his lap. He wrapped his arms around her, and she rested her head against his chest. A deep bodily sigh. She had missed this connection. Once in their marriage, they couldn't stop touching each other—even if only a brush of their hands when they passed or a caress of her shoulder.

Lately, though…

She had to get on top of whatever was going on in her brain before she destroyed this marriage. Matt may not be convinced that mental illnesses were serious, but she was. And she was in the midst of experiencing one, she was certain of it.

"I think I need to get professional help," she whispered.

His body tightened beneath her. "How so?"

"Mental health help. There's something very wrong with me. I had a panic attack the other day. While I was driving—"

"You didn't try to—"

She shook her head. "Nothing like that. But I had to pull over because I was scared I might crash. It was so frightening. I thought I was dying."

"Why didn't you tell me?"

"I don't know. I'm ashamed, I guess. I've always been this strong, capable woman and now I feel like I'm anything but." Her throat closed over as tears misted her eyes. She hated to admit such a thing, not only to herself but to her husband who had fallen in love with her when she was a completely different person.

A deep sigh. "Then organise some help. If you need it, get it."

She nodded. "I need it."

"Then it's settled.'

Chapter 25

Matt

The past…

Matt lifted his hand off the steering wheel and squeezed Nikki's thigh. "Don't be nervous, she'll love you."

"It's a lot of pressure meeting the parents, you know?"

He could understand that; he dreaded meeting Nikki's parents but for different reasons altogether. Nikki had hinted that since she was fifteen when her mother and father divorced, she was, in many ways, left to fend for herself.

Her mother got custody, begrudgingly, and Nikki presumed it was for child-support purposes more than anything else. Her mother was more worried about finding another husband, then, once she landed one, starting a new family with him.

He had boiled with anger when she opened up to him about that. He adored Nikki. In the three months since they'd met, his heart was brimming with love for her. Not in any part of his brain could he grasp how her parents, who proclaimed to have loved her, could emotionally abandon her. You didn't stop being a parent to your teenage daughter because you were selfishly wrapped up in your own life.

After losing his father, he understood the agony of abandonment. He also understood how it felt when the remaining parent overcompensated for a loss none of them could have controlled, let alone chosen. When he finally met Nikki's parents, he was afraid he wouldn't be able to hide his disdain for people who, despite having options, chose that life for their child.

"Of course, there's some pressure," he said. "But Mum's laidback. No big deal."

Nikki's fingertips tapped her bottom lip. "I really want to make a good impression. It's your mother."

"You will. Just be yourself."

They pulled into the long driveway of Matt's childhood home. He had lived here until he finished university at twenty-one and landed himself a graduate engineering position in Caboolture. With his new job located over an hour away, he moved out to reduce the commute time.

Approaching the familiar white frame, the wrap-around veranda, the blackened backdrop of forest under dull lighting from a slice of moon, he realised that the moment he drove away from this house, his life had truly begun. Meeting Nikki had continued that trajectory.

They hadn't been dating for too long, but he was sure she was The One. So sure, he had put an engagement ring on layby last week and planned to ask her to marry him while they holidayed in Vietnam next month.

That was the real reason they were here tonight—he couldn't propose to Nikki before she had met Mum. It didn't feel…honourable.

Matt cut the ignition and his headlights blinked off, casting the house in shadow. They climbed out and crunched across the gravel pathway to the door. The front porch was lit by a pale-yellow globe. Moths flickered above their heads.

He knocked and slung an arm around Nikki's shoulders, and she rested her head against him as they waited.

Footsteps sounded inside, then the door swung open. Mum stood in the entry with an enormous grin. Her dark eyes were bright.

"Hello, so great to see you." She gestured with a sweeping arm they step inside. "Come in, come in."

Nikki glanced at him as they strode through the doorway. There was relief in the upward curl of her lips.

Mum invited them to take a seat on the couch in the living room. Since Matt had left home, the furniture had been completely updated. The old fabric couch he recalled from childhood had been replaced with a Nordic-inspired, pale blue leather one. He liked the change—it pointed to the forward momentum of his own life and separated him from the years he had lived under this roof.

Matt and Nikki sat. "Mum, I'd like to introduce you to my girlfriend. Nikki this is my mother, Claire."

"Lovely to meet you, Claire," Nikki said.

"You too. I've heard so much about you these past few months. It's wonderful to finally put a face to a name. How about I make us all some drinks before I start on dinner? How does that sound?"

"Sounds good to me," Matt said.

"Would you like some help?" Nikki asked.

Mum waved her hand. "No, no. You're my guests tonight. I have it all under control."

Nikki relaxed back against the seat when Mum left the room.

"So far so good?" Matt asked and held his breath.

"She's really lovely."

He blew out his breath and grinned. "I'm glad you think so."

They spoke in hushed tones to each other until Mum came back with glasses of white wine. She took a seat across from them and sipped from her glass, leaving a bright red lipstick ring along the rim.

"So, what do you do, Nikki? Matt said you finished university a few months ago."

"I'm an accountant for a small business services firm in Mooloolaba."

"An accountant." Mum's eyes darted to Matt's. "That will come in handy."

Nikki giggled. "I'm sure it will eventually. I'm learning the ropes at the moment."

Matt bumped his shoulder lightly against hers. "You'll get there. I've been exactly where you are. The real learning starts on the job."

Nikki was the smartest woman he knew, yet modest. A perfectionist perhaps. She expected to be great at something immediately and when she wasn't, she was too hard on herself. He quietly suspected it was a residual mindset leftover from childhood—having to be the unobtrusive teenager, the good girl, the one who didn't get under her mother's feet, lest she withdrew her love even more.

"And do you work, Claire?" Nikki asked.

Mum laughed. "No. I don't have time for that."

"Mum volunteers a lot. Probably too much, I would say," he said with a chuckle.

"Never enough," Claire said. "There's always so many people less fortunate than I am."

Nikki leaned forward, elbows on her knees. "What kind of volunteering?"

"What don't I do?" Mum giggled. "Might be the easier question. I volunteer mostly for women's organisations that prepare sanitary packs for homeless women or clothing for job interviews. That sort of thing."

"Sounds incredibly rewarding."

"It is. But that's not why I do it. These women come from the toughest of circumstances. I do it to help. Plain and simple."

"That's incredibly humbling."

A small smile curled Mum's lips, but she waved away Nikki's compliment. "And then there's the art group I'm a part of. We knit baby booties and beanies, things like that, and donate them to hospitals and such."

Matt grinned at his mother. "We are very lucky to have people like you in the world."

"Thank you, Matt. I knew you were my favourite son for a reason."

They all laughed.

"Come on, let's head through to the kitchen. I have a bit of preparation left. We can have a chat in there. Less formal too."

Matt pressed his hand to Nikki's lower back and led her through to the kitchen. Mum had renovated in here a couple of years ago, once Matt and his brothers had all left home. The entire shape was different, and it always caught him off guard when he visited. He expected to find the closed-in, seventies Laminex benches. Now there were pale, glittery stone benchtops and sleek, two-pack cabinetry.

Matt and Nikki slid onto timber stools that lined the island bench while Mum checked on the sizzling baking tray in the oven. It smelled so good.

"So, what of your parents, Nikki? Do they live locally? I may know them."

"Mum lives at the Sunshine Coast, but she and her husband will be moving to Western Australia for work in the next month. And Dad moved to Coffs Harbour a few years ago."

"Divorced?"

"Um, yeah. They divorced about halfway through my first senior year of school."

"What a terrible time that must have been."

"It wasn't easy, that's for sure." Nikki cleared her throat and shifted on the stool. "My, ah, grades suffered a little because of the stress. It wasn't a fuss-free separation."

"No divorce ever is. However, I'm sure it's much easier than the alternative, which this family was unfortunate enough to suffer."

Nikki frowned, lowered her eyes. "I couldn't even imagine how hard it would be to lose one of my parents."

Matt had told Nikki fairly soon into their relationship that his father had passed away when he was in grade eight. He recalled the deep bodily throb of pain that ripped through him at that time. Life after that was a clouded blur like he barely existed between the moment his dad died and the moment he left home, as though that part of his brain that dealt with the mental trauma had closed itself off, so he could continue coping with existence.

"We can all hope that you don't have to experience that for many years to come," Mum said. She spun and grabbed the tray out of the oven. Roast pork with crunchy crackling, roasted potatoes and pumpkin.

She set about cutting the meat and dishing it onto three round plates.

Nikki inhaled deeply. "Smells delicious, Claire."

"Thank you."

"I have to admit that my mother wasn't much of a cook. Dad prepared most meals."

"I'm very sorry to hear that."

Nikki giggled and Mum's shoulders shook with her chuckle.

"Matt's dad was a horrendous cook. I wouldn't dare let him into the kitchen. It would have only been a matter of time before we all succumbed to food poisoning."

They laughed again and the tension in Matt's chest eased. He hadn't realised how nervous he had been about tonight until that tightness dissipated. But, so far, this meeting was going well. Mum was her usual charming, social self, and Nikki was slotting in perfectly.

He gripped her hand under the counter and squeezed it. She winked at him and grinned.

Dinner was perfection. Delicious homemade gravy made from the pan juices, honeyed carrots with sesame seeds, duck-fat roasted potatoes, cabbage with tasty specks of bacon and heaps of black pepper.

Conversation came easily and, eventually, they were poured a glass of port and retreated to the living room to flip through photo albums.

"You don't have to," Matt said to Nikki, well aware that looking at another's family photos was boring.

"I want to. Truly. I'm excited to see what you looked like as a child. I'd love to see if you take after your father. Was he as handsome as you are?"

Mum swayed past them both and chuckled. "You will find, darling, that all of my three boys got their disarming good looks and height from their mother."

They sat on the lounge, Nikki taking a seat beside Mum. Matt sat across from them. He'd seen the photos before, so he would leave this for the two women he loved to bond over.

His mother showed Nikki baby photos galore. Followed by photos of Matt with his brothers once they were born. Then there was an image of Matt when he was thirteen, confined to his bed, all his hair shaved from his head. Even from a couple of metres away, he jolted when he saw it.

Nikki's brow furrowed as she looked at him. "Were you sick?"

His pulse quickened; he preferred to forget about that time.

"Yes, he had lymphoma," Mum said. "A terrible, terrible time for all of us. And only one year after Robert passed away." She rested her hand over her chest. "I believe he got it from all the stress his poor young body was under."

"But I'm still here," Matt said with a nervous chuckle.

Nikki smiled. "Thank goodness."

"Yes, my darling, you thankfully pulled through it. I could not have lost my husband as well as my son." Her voice cracked. "I simply wouldn't have coped." Mum closed the photo album. "That might do it for tonight," she said with a sniffle and wiped tears from her cheeks.

"Of course. I understand. Losing a loved one is not something easily forgotten," Nikki said, each word soft and full of compassion. "And then cancer…I can't even…thank you for showing me the photos. It was a generous insight into your lives."

Mum smiled warmly. Her eyes were still glossy. "My pleasure."

They finished their port and Matt announced that it was time they headed home. He thanked Mum for a wonderful meal and great company.

Mum walked them to the door and beamed. "It was delightful to meet you, Nikki. We will have to get together more often from here on out."

Nikki nodded. "Definitely. I would like that."

In the car, on the way back to Matt's house, he asked, "So what did you think?"

Nikki leaned closer and kissed his cheek. "She was wonderful."

He released a long breath, his shoulders falling back into place. "I'm so glad you think so."

Chapter 26

Belinda

Belinda had been awake for a while, scrolling through social media on her phone when Anthony rolled over and rubbed his hand across her stomach.

"Good morning, gorgeous," he said in a sleep-addled, croaky voice.

"Good morning."

"How are you feeling?"

She placed her phone on the bedside table and frowned. "A little queasy to tell you the truth." But she wasn't about to whine. She'd take a thousand days of queasiness over a thousand days of not being pregnant.

Anthony sat up and kissed her shoulder. "What do you need to make you feel better? A cup of tea? Some toast with Vegemite?"

She nodded and inwardly smiled at this unexpected attention. "That would be so good."

Fully naked, he rolled out of bed and found a pair of shorts in the dresser before strolling out of the room.

Within five minutes, he was back with a tray of goodies. Toast and tea and a sliced apple. She smiled as he handed her the tray, and she rested it on her lap. "Thank you."

In all their nine years of marriage, not once had Anthony made her breakfast in bed. Nor had she ever eaten breakfast in bed.

Anthony was the rough-around-the-edges tradesman with grease under his fingernails type of person. He was kind-hearted, loyal and loving, but he wasn't doting. Belinda had never encountered doting before now. She didn't expect it. But she had to admit, she loved it.

"Take your time. And if you feel up to it, I thought we might go shopping."

She lowered the toast that was almost at her mouth, and her brows rose. "Shopping?"

"For the baby." His eyes brightened along with his grin. "Window shopping mainly, but we might be able to get a few smaller items already."

Her smile grew. "I'd love that."

"We'll head into Brisbane and make a day of it."

Even better—there was no chance of running into his mother. Claire was not on her list of most-liked people at the moment, not since the *irresponsible* accusation, followed by the public implication that she and Matt couldn't afford to have the baby.

Mostly, though, guilt sat like a sharp stone in her stomach every time she remembered that she still owed Claire a lot of money.

She wished there was a change in fate, so that they could pay Claire back and tell her to butt out. This baby was the most amazing gift Belinda had ever been given; the last thing she needed was Claire's negativity.

"What's the matter?" Anthony asked.

Belinda realised she was frowning while staring at a lump of Vegemite on her toast. She shook her head. "I was just thinking."

"About what?"

"Your mother. I wish we didn't borrow that money from her. I mean, Jesus, Ant, we're sneaking off to Brisbane to shop for baby essentials, so she doesn't catch us doing anything other than paying her back."

"We had no choice."

"I know."

But that was Claire—not one gift was without an attached obligation. Even if that obligation came in the form of guilt, spread on thick.

Maybe it was Belinda's moral compass making her feel guilty. She hated borrowing money. Always had. Her parents were the worst for it. Except they were the type who borrowed and never gave it back, rather moved from one family member or friend to the next. Belinda swore she would never be like that. She wouldn't. As soon as they could, that money would be sent straight back to Claire's account.

"Did you receive word about that tender?" she asked.

Anthony looked away, frowned. "Yeah."

Her heart sunk. "I take it that means you didn't win it?"

"Unfortunately, no. But we're doing okay, Bel. I've put more tenders out for more work. Nothing as big as that job, but enough to see us through."

The shopping centre was hectic, especially finding a park. They were both used to the laidback vibe of the Sunshine Coast. As they strode through the packed halls, weaving in and out of shoppers, Belinda silently cursed Claire again.

They could have easily found what they needed locally. She shook away that burning exasperation and sought gratitude instead, for this was what she had dreamt of for eight tormented years. Before, when she didn't have the comfort of a baby dwelling inside her womb, wandering through shopping centres and buying bits and pieces of baby products was a hollow, soul-destroying activity. Now, it was delightful.

She gripped Anthony's hand, linking her fingers with his. Such a big hand compared to hers, strong and protective. They headed inside a department store. No, this low-cost store wasn't where she had hoped to be buying goods for the baby, but under her current financial circumstances, it was a leap above second-hand.

The soft scented creams, shampoos and powders filled her senses first. She breathed the aroma deeply into her lungs, and it tugged on the maternal strings of her heart. Swells of excitement surged from within. Soon this would be in her home. She would be lifting her own baby, smelling his or her powdery-scented hair. Close cuddles. Cradles. Soft blankets. Milk. Warm baths. She couldn't wait for every part of it. Even the sleepless nights. The crying. She wanted every last second of it.

Her hand impulsively shifted to her belly. Tears welled in her eyes when she looked at Anthony and giggled. "I can't believe this is actually happening."

Anthony smiled and wrapped an arm around her shoulder. He pulled her close and kissed her head. "Get used to it, because it's real."

"I never thought I could be this happy."

"Me either."

They walked through the aisles of stuffed toys and blankets, little baby suits and pyjamas, singlets and towels. Finances dictating, they only bought a packet of neutral-coloured singlets and booties.

"If we buy a small amount every week, by the time the baby is born, we'll have everything," she said.

"And we can always put in a wish list for the larger items and hope friends and family will cover those at the baby shower."

She nodded emphatically. "Good idea."

But being reminded of Ant's family made other unwanted, prickly thoughts arise. A long, uncomfortable zap streaked through her body, settling in her chest.

With a sidelong glance, she looked at her husband and silently prayed that this child was his.

Chapter 27

Paige

Sunday evening, with Evie tucked into bed and sound asleep, Paige cracked open a bottle of shiraz and carried two glasses to the living room. At this time of night, relaxing with Vaughn was an indulgent treat after years of sitting alone.

She sank onto the lounge with a sigh next to Vaughn and poured them both a glass of wine. What a hectic weekend. The family barbeque yesterday, then today was spent on the Sunshine Coast at the beach, followed by hours of walking around the aquarium with Evie.

They settled for takeaway fish and chips for dinner because no one could be bothered lifting a knife. A glass of red would round off the weekend well.

She chimed her glass against Vaughn's. "Cheers." Then she sipped deeply on the peppery vintage. "Anything good on television?"

Vaughn flicked through the icons for something new to watch. But Paige had different plans; she wanted to address the conversation they had yesterday. The conversation where he admitted to wanting children. With her.

The idea had looped in her brain. The prospect both exhilarated and terrified her, but she had proven she was ready to be vulnerable again by moving in with Vaughn. If she wanted this relationship to last and remain a joyful union, she had to be all-in.

"I wanted to talk about what we started yesterday."

His forehead furrowed as he continued to scan through the programs. "What's that?"

She sipped again at her wine, then placed it on the coffee table in front of them. "About having babies."

His finger froze over the remote button, and he turned to look at her. "Oh, that conversation."

She laughed. "I think it warrants a more thorough discussion."

He placed the controller down and turned in his chair, so he was facing her more directly. "I agree."

"So, you would like children?"

He nodded, shrugged. "Sure. I guess."

"What kind of timeframe would you have in mind?"

"A few years."

She smiled again. "And you're certain it's me you want to mother those children?"

A slow grin curved his lips as he nodded. "Definitely."

"You know I had to raise Evie all alone. From pregnancy right on through. I didn't have anyone in the delivery room with me. I didn't have anyone helping with the night feeds, the tantrums, the illnesses. It was all me. I didn't have my mother to help me. Or relatives of any kind."

He reached for her and stroked a hand over her thigh. "I know."

"It was bloody hard."

"I can imagine it would have been."

Vaughn was nodding and using all the right empathetic tones, but he really didn't know what it was like. Not until he had his own children would he understand that Paige's entire focus, from the moment Evie let out her first tremendous bellow, shifted towards one person. Every breath was for this little being who was solely dependent on her.

"I won't have any more babies unless I know there are certain guarantees."

His eyes narrowed and then widened. "Like marriage?"

She hated to be blunt about this, but boundaries and protections were required. "Yes. Marriage."

He leaned in closer and pressed his lips to hers—a lingering kiss. "I would expect nothing less."

She shifted back and held his gaze. Their connection was so strong, her heart blossomed with the heat of it. They had always been in sync from the moment they met. "Perfect. We're on the same page."

Chapter 28

Nikki

Nikki's nerves were next level, so much so, she feared she might flip inside out from the tension tightening her muscles. She had attempted to come up with numerous reasons to cancel this morning's appointment with a psychologist, but no excuse was reasonable enough to risk having another panic attack. Imagine if it happened in public. While she was out shopping or at football with the boys. Or worse, she didn't pull the car over in time and crashed for real.

She sat in the passenger seat next to Matt, looking out as the mossy green blur of rainforest sped by the window. Her appointment was at Mooloolaba, and she didn't trust herself to drive. Not that she had to ask Matt for his support; he had surprised her by taking the day off, so he could be with her every step of the way. Knowing he would be in the waiting room was comforting. She needed to lean on him now more than ever, at least until she could find her own strength again.

Nikki's stomach was knotted by the time a pleasant-looking middle-aged man with a balding head and thick black-rimmed glasses called her name. She glanced at Matt. He offered her the warm but encouraging smile she was hoping for. She stood and straightened her jeans before Dr Puethe led her away, down a long hall.

Nikki took a seat on the edge of a big navy-blue armchair across from Dr Puethe. His chair was brown leather and less imposing, didn't shrink him down as Nikki's seemed to.

She placed her hands on her lap and rubbed her thumb while trying to slow her breathing and appear like a put-together woman rather than the panicked mouse she was inside.

That's what most of this anxiety was—hiding. Hiding the fear behind a mask of a woman who had herself and her life under control—both of which were completely untrue. The hiding exacerbated the nerves.

"Comfortable, Nikki?" Dr Puethe asked with a warm smile.

She rigidly sat back against the armchair and nodded. "Fine. Thanks."

Dr Puethe had a notepad on his lap and a pen in his hand, which he held beside his head, thumb poised on the clicker that he would press every now and then.

"Before we start, I want to let you know that this is a safe environment. I am here to work with you. Everything is confidential unless you give me permission otherwise or on the remote chance my notes are subpoenaed by a court of law. If you have questions, you are more than welcome to ask, and I am happy to give you answers to the best of my ability."

She nodded.

"Now, Nikki, I understand your GP referred you because you've been experiencing some anxiety? Is that right?"

"Um...yes. But I'm not sure if it's anxiety as such..."

He titled his head to the side. "It's greater than that?"

She nodded. "More of a general feeling that I'm not coping with anything."

He made a note, and she watched his pen arc across the page, curiosity tugging at her hand to snatch the notepad and see what he was jotting down.

"I'm going to take a few notes as the session continues. I can share these with you at the end if you wish to see them. Nothing here is off-limits." He finished with a professional smile.

"Okay."

"Have you been experiencing this feeling of not coping for a while?"

She shook her head, nodded. "I guess, but it's escalated lately."

"Is there anything that has changed in your circumstances that you think may have caused the escalation? Marriage stresses? Children? Illness?"

She shook her head.

"Okay. Tell me a little about what it is you find most stressful?"

Images of the tree as she careened towards it flickered in her mind. The impact. Her breath hitched. "Work stresses me. I resigned a couple of weeks ago, yet I still feel flurried."

"What do you do for a job, Nikki?"

"An accountant."

"Okay. And what about your job particularly do you find stressful?"

She frowned. "I find talking to clients stressful. Calling on the phone." She glanced away, her cheeks hot. "I'm scared of making mistakes. Not doing my work quickly enough."

"Okay. And, these are long-term experiences?"

She shook her head. "A few years. I used to be able to muster up the courage regardless. Recently, I find it more difficult. More nerve-wracking. My hands shake. My lips." She lowered her eyes and sighed. What grown woman confessed such things? "It's embarrassing and ridiculous."

"And why do you believe it to be embarrassing and ridiculous?"

"Because I'm thirty-six years old. I should not be afraid of doing my job."

"I see. When you're dealing with clients at work, what kind of thoughts are you experiencing?"

She hesitated a moment as she peered through the lens of time and situated herself back there at the desk, a client across from her. "I was scared that I didn't know enough or that I'd be caught out with a question I didn't have the answer to and look like I was unintelligent or that I didn't know how to perform my job."

"It sounds like you have a lot of thoughts rushing through your mind about what other people think of you in those moments. How does that make you feel?"

"It makes me feel like an imposter. Inadequate. Like I shouldn't be there. And then I'm embarrassed and sad and angry because I don't want to feel like that."

"How about we talk about a specific example of that. Can you recall a particular time at work with a client you found challenging?"

She closed her eyes for as long as it took to draw in a deep breath. The day before she crashed her car. "Yes."

"Tell me about what happened."

"I had an older female client come in. She needed a basic tax return prepared. She had recently been promoted and thought that because she now earned more money, she was entitled to a larger refund. I tried to explain to her that it doesn't work that way and that her employer should only take enough withholding tax no matter how much she earns. Then she wanted to claim expenses that she wasn't entitled to claim.

"The more the interview went on, the more nervous I got. My hands were shaking as I tried to type, and I knew she could see that. She was telling me how some family members and fellow colleagues had recently received big tax refunds, and she was angry because she wasn't getting one. She questioned why she would bother earning so much money if she just had to pay more in tax. In the end, I let her claim meals, even though I knew if she was audited, she wouldn't be allowed the deductions, just so she could get a decent refund and stop whining."

"So what thoughts were you having during that time?"

"That I was weak. I was questioning if I knew what I was doing. I thought she could tell I was nervous and lacked the confidence to be assertive. I was scared of her. Breathless. Twitchy. My lips shook. My voice shook. I was embarrassed."

"Okay." Dr Puethe crossed his legs and shifted in his chair. "What would be so bad if your client did think you were weak?"

Nikki shook her head as all the moments she had felt weak during her career flashed in her mind—the time she had to keep going in and out of an interview to ask other employees for help; the time a client sat in her chair and she meekly took the chair reserved for clients; the time her voice shook when an older client angrily questioned her results. "I'm not sure. I guess she already did think that."

"Why must you appear to be strong for this client?"

"Because I'm meant to be a professional. I'm meant to know what I'm doing."

"And what's so bad if you don't know what you're doing?"

"She was paying money for me to do a good job. I wouldn't want to go to an unconfident accountant. I'd leave feeling like they hadn't got the best result for me."

"And what would be so bad about that?"

"I'd lose my job. I wouldn't be able to be an accountant. I'd be a failure." A deep wave of sadness pooled in her chest and crept up her neck, tightening and heating her throat. That's why she quit, so her employers didn't know she was bad at her job.

"What happened there?"

"I realised why I quit." She swallowed hard; it felt like a jagged plum stone was stuck in her throat. "I didn't want my employers to know that I wasn't a good accountant." Tears brimmed in her eyes as another chain-link connected. "It was why I had a panic attack last week while driving home from my sister-in-law's. I thought I had stuffed up the statements she had me prepare for her business. I didn't want her to think I didn't know what I was doing."

"So, what I'm hearing is that you're experiencing some heavy emotions and thoughts about your ability to do your job and this puts a lot of pressure on you. On a scale of one to ten, how strongly do you believe that you are incapable of fulfilling your accounting duties?"

She shrugged. "To be honest, deep down, I know I'm good at what I do. But I'm not perfect. I know I have the capacity to make mistakes and that is scarier than my belief in my abilities."

Dr Puethe leaned forward and looked Nikki in the eyes. "When did you start believing that making mistakes was bad?"

A memory flashed. A whispered conversation with a friend. She used to prepare Claire's tax returns, earlier on before life became too hectic. Nikki's friend had mentioned she had run into Claire at a café. Claire was there with a few of her friends. Claire had just come back from seeing a new accountant and had received a massive refund.

Nikki knew the technical reasons why that was the case—Claire had only worked half of that financial year. The previous years she had sold off a lot of her investments, so no longer had that income. She had a lot of deductions after repairs she made to her investment property. All reasons an accountant couldn't take credit for. But Claire had told Nikki's friend, along with the other women at the table, that she was grateful to have seen a *proper* accountant and questioned Nikki's abilities with her previous tax returns.

Her stomach twisted. "When my mother-in-law mentioned to a good friend that I had not prepared her tax returns correctly. It was embarrassing because it's difficult to explain to laypersons the reasons why one year someone may be due a good tax refund, when in other years they're not. And most of those reasons have nothing to do with the accountant."

"So, you felt like you had to defend yourself?"

Nikki nodded. "Yes, but I couldn't. And I knew, no matter what I said to Claire, that she would believe her refunds were smaller in the years I prepared her tax returns because of my incompetence. After that, I felt like people saw me as incapable. My mother-in-law has a big mouth, and this is a small town."

Dr Puethe nodded thoughtfully. "What was it about your mother-in-law specifically that made you feel the way you did?"

Nikki frowned, shrugged. "Because I trusted her. And she spoke so horribly about me behind my back."

"You feel like she betrayed your trust with this comment?"

"Yes. I gave birth to her only grandchildren. I'm married to her son. I don't understand how…" She closed her eyes and grimaced, then lifted her head and looked at Dr Puethe. "No, I don't understand *why* she would say that?"

"Yes. That would be difficult to understand. Going back to your work situation, can you give me some reasons to suggest that you *are* good at your job?"

Nikki nodded. "My boss respects me. I have a lot of happy clients. It's not always bad. I know this, yet I'm still so nervous all the time. If I could have a job where I just did the work and didn't have to deal with people or budgets or steep deadlines, I would be much happier."

"Because there would be less chance of *failing* as you called it before."

"Exactly."

"What would be so bad if you did fail?"

Nikki shrugged. "It would feel horrible. I would lose the respect of my peers, my friends, my family."

"Would your peers really be so worried if you failed?"

She sighed. "Well, they wouldn't come after me with pitchforks."

"What would they do?"

She shrugged. "They'd move on. Some may try to help me."

"So, what I'm hearing is that sometimes you experience a mindset where you think your co-workers and family may lose respect for you, but, for them, it probably wouldn't be too much of a big deal. They'd move on."

A small smile flickered. She could see how she tended to make mountains out of molehills. "My family would still love me, and my colleagues would still support me."

"That's a rational outlook and relies less on emotional thinking, don't you think?"

Nikki shrugged. "Sure, I guess."

The session continued down that vein for the next forty-two minutes and when she walked out into the waiting room and looked into her husband's concerned eyes, her shoulders felt lighter and her head less clouded.

She had been able to work with Dr Puethe to change her perspective about her anxiety and see that some of it was caused from emotional thinking leading to a worried or anxious mindset. With this new understanding, Dr Puethe anticipated that her behaviour may become more balanced. For homework, he gave her some strategies to counteract her anxious mindset when it arose, along with breathing exercises to re-train her nervous system.

But something else dwelled inside of her, like a weighted balloon ready to explode. A little voice that continued to chatter in her subconscious, trying to make her doubt herself and the gains she had made in this session.

Intuitively, she understood that when she finally uncovered the source of that voice, she would find the root cause of all this. But the root cause was hidden. By what, she didn't know. But she could guess why. It was hidden because she didn't want to see what it was.

"How did you go?" Matt asked as he slid an arm around her waist and led her out to their car.

"I think I'm in the right place."

He kissed her temple and smiled. "I'm so glad to hear that."

Chapter 29

Belinda

Ten weeks ago…

Belinda smiled and waved to the last customer to leave her store before closing time: A fit middle-aged woman who had bought over four hundred dollars' worth of organic products from protein powders to natural deodorants to moisturisers. Tiny bursts of exhilaration had fizzed beneath Belinda's skin when she had scanned all the items. If only there were dozens of customers like this each day, then financial matters may not be so bad.

She shut the front door, locked it and flipped the Closed sign over. Anthony had been away for the last few days in Mackay and was due home on Sunday afternoon.

Belinda's fingers shook as she scrolled through her contacts for Vaughn's number. She had to reach him before he left the bank; otherwise, it was impossible for him to create a believable excuse to leave his home, especially if his new girlfriend was there.

Vaughn answered the phone. "Hey, Bel. How are ya?"

She smiled, her body tingling to hear his deep voice. She equated that honeyed sound to his touch. Her body was already ripening with anticipation. "I'm good. You busy?"

"Nothing I can't finish later."

She smiled again as heat swamped between her legs. "I'm closing up at the shop if you want to stop in. Ant's out of town. I've got no one to rush home to."

"I'll see you in thirty minutes."

Belinda ended the call and set about finishing the few chores she could tackle while she waited. She was flush and buzzing, her nipples hard and sensitive, brushing against her bra as she swept the floor.

When Vaughn's car pulled up, she had to restrain herself from running out to him and dragging him in by his collar. Instead, she unlocked the door and waited inside.

When he strode in to meet her, a bulge already strained against his pants.

"You been thinking about me?" she asked, then shut the door behind him.

He didn't answer, merely lifted her into his arms, carried her out the back to her office and rested her on the desk between invoices, stock orders and her computer.

He kissed her hard on the mouth and crushed her body against his. Already, she was breathless with desire.

Too soon it was over. It was always too soon to finish, but that's how it was with them, like two bundles of kindle sparking each other until they blazed.

She climbed off the desk, panting, and watched him through a sex-flushed daze as he tucked himself back into his pants and zipped up. His chest was rising and falling with each deep breath.

"I needed that," she said with a smile.

He met her gaze and frowned.

Her spine went rigid. A man frowning after sex was unheard of. "What?"

"I'm moving in with Paige next week."

"The young girlfriend?"

"She's a grown woman with a child."

Shame burned from her barren womb up to her heart. She bit down on her bottom lip, pushed the anger back down. “It’s serious then?”

Vaughn nodded. “I can see a future with her. It’s taken me a long while to get my head around a new relationship, but I think I’m there. I want to be exclusive. And I think for your marriage’s sake, you should do the same with Anthony.”

Of course, these brief interludes with Vaughn never pointed to anything serious. She would never consider ruining her marriage over him, nor did she ever consider demanding or wanting anything more from Vaughn than pleasure.

But this delivered a sharp stinging slap—another rejection for this woman who couldn’t bear children. She swallowed all that shame and pain down deep. “I understand. It was fun while it lasted.”

“You must have known this day was coming.”

She nodded, did her best to hide that her lips were trembling. Her throat was so tight, it ached. “Of course. No big deal. Now go on, you get yourself home to Paige before she starts to wonder where you are.”

He hesitated a moment, eyes narrowed as he studied her, obviously trying to decipher if she was genuinely okay with this end to their affair or inwardly upset.

He managed a smile, but it looked more like a wince. “I’m glad you understand.” He patted his pocket, checking if his car keys were still there, then pointed his thumb at the front door. “I better head off.”

She nodded, smiled. “Sure.”

She didn’t follow him out, instead waited for the front door to close and his car to rumble away before she heaved her computer keyboard into the air and threw it across the room.

Chapter 30

Vaughn

The family barbeque…

Vaughn waited a minute before he casually got up from his chair after Belinda had excused herself to use the bathroom. He went inside without a word and cast a quick glance into the living room. Paige was still sitting on the lounge with Evie. She held her daughter in her arms, rocking her as Evie let out little whimpers.

He strode down the hall. The whooshing sound of a tap running rushed through the pipes behind the walls. He only had to wait half a minute for Belinda to stride out of the bathroom. When she saw him, she stopped, eyes wide.

"Ssh," he whispered with a finger to his lips, gripped her wrist and gently pulled her into the spare bedroom across the hall from the bathroom.

He closed the door behind them and stared for a moment, not entirely sure how to broach this subject.

"What is it?" she asked, brow furrowed. "Has someone found out about us?"

He shook his head hard. "No." He rubbed his jaw, the couple of days of stubble rough against his palm. "I have to know, Bel, if there is any chance this baby could be mine."

Her eyes darted away. When she looked back at his face, she frowned. "Of course not."

His heart hammered. A strange cartoonish shift to his vision as his head went dizzy. He was hoping for a flat-out refusal, but her hesitation spoke volumes. So much could be inferred from that slice of silence. "But there's a possibility?" He held his breath as he awaited her answer.

She shook her head, shrugged. "I don't think so."

From the moment she told him that she was pregnant, he rushed to calculate the dates in his head. They were still having sex up until about a month ago. "We weren't ever careful. You assured me you were not capable of getting pregnant. Yet here you are."

"It was a surprise."

He shifted from foot to foot. "How do you know it's not mine?"

"I don't know that."

He stepped closer, reached out to lay a gentle hand over her stomach. Surely if he was the father, he'd have some kind of biological intuition about it.

She slapped his hand away. "What are you doing?"

"I'm trying to feel the baby."

"It's the size of a kidney bean. You can't feel anything at this stage."

His next exhalation was loud. "Did you use me, Belinda? Did you get me drunk that first night to lure me in, so you could have a baby?"

Belinda glanced away for a moment, then met his gaze head-on. "Of course I bloody didn't. I didn't think I was able to get pregnant. This was an accident. A wonderful accident."

"This little accident could be mine."

"Even if it is, does it really matter? Ant's your brother."

He lowered his head, so his face was closer to hers. "Of course it bloody well matters."

"It will destroy this family if Anthony ever knew. It would break his heart."

Vaughn closed his eyes, shuffled a hand through his hair.

"And Paige. What would she think?" she continued.

"I have Type O negative blood. Just like my dad. Anthony and Matt are A positive like Mum. We better hope that this child isn't born with my blood. For all our sakes."

She shook her head hard. "It's not yours."

He crossed his arms over his chest and pinned her with his stare. "I think you should get an abortion."

The sharp sting of her palm, and the loud crack it made, registered before the realisation that she had slapped him. "I will do no such thing."

He covered his cheek with his hand to stop the throbbing prickle and sighed. "Think about it."

"I won't." Her lips twisted into a scowl. Her eyes narrowed. "I'd kill you before I ever did that."

His brows arched to hear the venom in her voice.

"I mean it. I would kill you. Now get out of my way before people realise we are in here together."

He took a step to the side to let her pass. "I see where I stand."

She spun around to face him. "You don't stand anywhere. It was a fling. It meant nothing. This child is Anthony's. I know it is."

"I hope you're right."

Belinda opened the door and gasped.

When he looked past her frame to see why, he found his mother standing in the hall outside the room.

Mum's eyes shifted focus, back and forth, from Vaughn to Belinda. "What are you two doing?"

Vaughn's heart was in his throat. A frightened fog had filled his brain as he shuffled through believable excuses why he would be alone with Belinda in a bedroom at a family barbeque.

"Vaughn wanted my advice on a birthday present for Paige," Belinda said. "I better get back out there. Ant's probably wondering where I am." And with that, she strode past Mum and headed down the hall.

Mum's dark gaze found him, but she didn't speak. He pulled his shoulders down and forward, bent his knees subtly, trying to make himself smaller, less obvious, as he examined her expression for any sign she had overheard their conversation. Surely, if she had heard what they were saying, there would be some emotion, tic or flutter. But there was nothing.

He exhaled. "Need another drink, Mum?" he asked, putting his arm around her shoulders.

"I'd love one."

They made their way down the hall, but before they headed out the backdoor to join the others, she leaned in closer to his ear and whispered, "I heard everything."

Chapter 31

Paige

Paige had three outfits to create before the weekend. An evening gown for her most regular customer—a local politician. A dress and fascinator worthy of winning fashions on the field for a racehorse owner, who ordered at least six dresses from Paige each year. And a mother-of-the-bride dress for a new customer whose sister worked with Vaughn at the bank.

By ten am, she had created the pattern for the evening gown, cut the fabric, draped it over her clotheshorse and pinned it. But morning tea for her daughter was to take priority for the next half-hour.

"Come on, Evie, let's go get a drink and a snack."

She made Evie a Vegemite sandwich, sliced some apple wedges, opened a little pot of yoghurt and set her at the toddler-sized table and chairs in the kitchen. She fixed her a cup of milk and set about making a strong coffee for herself.

Each time she recalled her delicious conversation with Vaughn, excited flutters filled her belly. She was, no doubt, head over heels for him and the thought of them, one day soon, getting married, made her skin flush.

He was so caring and patient with Evie. He would make a wonderful father. Since their talk, she had allowed the possibility of them becoming a growing family to solidify from a wish into something real.

For many years, life had been one slog after another, starting with her mother when she sat Paige down at fifteen and announced with a tremulous, defeated voice that she had terminal breast cancer. That battle continued for two long years, followed by a deep drenching in grief that seemed to never end while Paige was launched into life all on her own.

The only blessing was Evie. Her saviour. Her sun.

She glanced across at her daughter. She had her sandwich above her, flying it around like an aeroplane. Paige giggled. Evie was the most adorable child to ever grace this planet, and Paige's heart was filled to bursting with love for her.

After a snack, Paige suggested Evie play on her trampoline and swing set to work off some of that three-year-old energy. If her planning worked—which was hardly ever the case—Paige would get a good hour or so in at her sewing machine before she made lunch and put Evie into bed for her daytime nap.

She set the espresso machine to grind and placed a cup under the spouts. As the first fragrant drips hit the bottom of her mug, a knock came at the door.

She stretched her neck from side to side.

Please don't let it be Claire.

Yes, their relationship was back on track, but she couldn't forget the anxiety that initial discord with Claire had created.

She marched out to the foyer and opened the door expecting to see Claire, but, instead, her big, muscled ex stood in the entry. Paige took a rushed step back, shook her head. "What the hell are you doing here?"

Joshua was much more solidly built than she remembered—his football club had obviously been training him hard in the gym. His pale hair was short and styled with wax, and his green eyes took her breath away with their familiarity.

Half of his mouth curled into a smile. “Hi, Paige. It’s been a while.”

“What are you doing here?”

“I believe you have something of mine?”

She narrowed her eyes, shook her head. “What are you talking about? I have nothing of yours?”

“That’s not what a little birdy told me. I believe this possession goes by the name of Evie.” He indicated a toddler’s height. “About this tall. Blonde hair. Her father’s green eyes.”

Every muscle tightened and her heart rate ratcheted. “She’s not yours.”

“I heard differently.”

“Who dat?” came Evie’s voice from behind Paige. Her little hand held Paige’s leg as she stood beside her.

“No one, darling. How about you head back and finish your sandwich.”

Paige’s focus darted back to Joshua. He was appraising Evie with something like wonderment on his face. He knelt down until he was crouching at Evie’s height. “Hi there, Evie.”

Evie twisted her lips nervously and turned her body from side to side. “Hello.”

“Aren’t you the prettiest?”

Evie didn’t say anything but nodded.

Paige bent down and gently pushed Evie towards the house. “Go back to your table, Evie. I’ll be in there very soon.” Evie ran away, and Paige’s shoulders relaxed a fraction.

“She looks like me,” he said.

Paige shrugged. “Doesn’t mean anything.”

His brows squeezed together. “Why the hell, Paige? Why would you hide something like this from me?”

Paige lowered her voice and snarled. “I don’t owe you a thing.”

He patted his chest. “I’m her father. It’s not up to you to decide.”

“I damn well do have the right. You hurt me, remember? What rational woman is going to let her child be around a man like that, father or not?”

Shame blared in his gaze, but it was gone as soon as it had arrived. “That was a stupid mistake. I’m not like that anymore. I haven’t touched drugs for years.”

“I wasn’t going to take that risk. And that’s my right.”

He shook his head. “I’m her father. And I had every right to know that she existed. And I have every right to see my daughter now.”

Adrenalin sparked, her limbs twitched. “No. It wouldn’t be good for her.”

“I’ve seen a lawyer. I know my rights. We can do this through the courts, or we can work something out between us.”

Paige scrambled for some kind of excuse, some reason for her to say no, but she couldn’t find one. In the end, he was Evie’s father. He did have access rights, and it wouldn’t look favourably for Paige to have hidden Evie from him.

“Please don’t do this. We’ve been getting on with our lives.”

He slapped his chest with his palm. “And what about me?”

“You lost your right the moment you laid a finger on me.”

He glanced away, lowered his head, but soon enough he drew his chin higher, straightened those big shoulders back. “It doesn’t work that way. Look, Paige, we do this the easy way or the hard way, but whatever you choose, I will see my daughter. I’m giving you a chance here for us to amicably work together.”

She crossed her arms over her chest, hating that tears were pricking her eyes. "Fine." The single syllable was soft and hollow. "Fine," she repeated, a little louder. "But, please, give me some time to let Evie know who you are. And the first meeting is here with me."

"Mum would like to meet her too."

Paige sighed. "Fine, bring your mum. But it will be short. No more than an hour. We have to think about Evie. We can't overwhelm her."

"I can work with that. So, when?"

"I'm really busy with work at the moment—"

"Don't screw me around—"

"Fine. Next Friday. Midday. You can come over and have lunch with her."

He smiled. "Okay. Next Friday. I'll see you here then." He turned and jogged down a few steps onto the path, but she called out to him.

He stopped and faced her.

"Who told you about Evie?" One of her clients? A friend? Her skin burned with anger over the betrayal.

"Not important."

"It's important to me!"

He touched his nose with his finger and didn't give an answer; instead, he turned and marched down the driveway to his Mustang parked on the road.

She shut the door and leaned her head back against the cool timber. An angry groan raced up her throat and exploded into the silence. She punched the door with her fist. Her perfect little bubble had popped.

When Vaughn arrived home that evening, he found her in the bathroom. She was sitting on the edge of the tub drinking a glass of wine while watching Evie take a bubble bath.

One look at her and Vaughn frowned. "What's the matter?"

"You won't believe who turned up on our doorstep this afternoon."

His brow furrowed. "Who?"

"My ex."

"Joshua?"

She nodded solemnly, drank deeply from her glass. Tears swam in her eyes. "I can't share Evie. Not with him." All these years, she hadn't even been able to put Evie in day-care a couple of days a week, let alone allow someone else custody.

Since the beginning, it had been the two of them. A relationship with Vaughn hadn't changed that. She fit Vaughn in around Evie—they made it work. But Joshua, he was a whole other scenario. She could end up losing Evie for half of every week.

Vaughn sighed as he eased her up from the side of the bath and wrapped her in his arms. "Joshua wants custody?"

She nodded against his chest. "He's already seen a lawyer. I've spent the afternoon on the phone getting advice, and he has all the rights in the world to seek access."

"Damn it! Why now?"

"Because one of my so-called friends has obviously decided to play backstabber and tell him about Evie. This was always going to be a massive deal for Joshua. He's from a big family and he always spoke about having lots of children. All his sisters and brothers have kids. It's the most maternal family I've ever known. He would want Evie to be a part of his life."

Paige had envied Joshua for his family. They represented everything she had ever wanted for herself. Big family dinners every week. Barbeques on the weekend. Cousins who played together and were best friends. Blood was thicker than gold in that house.

Vaughn let her go and she sank back down onto the side of the bath.

"Finish up here. I'll get dinner sorted. We'll have a good chat about it once Evie is in bed."

She nodded, though she knew chatting was not going to make this any easier to accept.

Chapter 32

Matt

The past…

"Good morning, my beautiful wife," Matt whispered against Nikki's neck as he roused from his sleep. The sun was barely a source of light, the shadows leftover from the night still filled all the space in the room.

They had arrived at the Perth hotel late last night after a six-hour flight from the east coast. A gorgeous room with champagne and chocolates was waiting for them, along with a king-sized bed and spa. As of yet, all they had sampled was the bed.

Bliss sparked through his limbs as he arched his body to the shape of Nikki's and soaked in her soft warmth and scent.

"Good morning," she whispered. "You're up early."

"A little." Western Australia was two hours behind Queensland, so his body clock must still be running on Queensland time.

She rolled over to face him. "Lucky me." She kissed him hard and lowered her hand between his thighs.

His phone blared on the bedside table and Nikki flinched.

"Bloody hell. How loud do you need that thing?" she asked with a giggle.

His mobile phone was new. He'd never owned one before, so he hadn't had a chance to familiarise himself with the settings.

He rolled over to turn it off, but the digital number on the screen was his mother's. "It's Mum. I better answer. She probably wants to know if we made it okay. You know what she's like."

"A worrywart. Yes, I know. Answer it before it wakes the entire hotel."

He answered. "Hi, Mum."

"I didn't wake you, did I?"

"No, I was awake."

"I can never get my head around the time difference. What time is it there?"

"Five am."

"That is early. What time did you get in last night?"

"After midnight."

"You must be exhausted. I'll go. I just wanted to make sure you got there okay, and you made it to your hotel. Say hi to Nikki for me, and you both have a great time."

"Okay. Thanks, Mum. I'll talk to you later."

He hung up and rested back against his pillow. He pulled the covers down and climbed on top of Nikki, kissing the delicate column of skin at her neck. "Now, let's get back to what we were doing."

The fourth morning in Perth, Matt's phone woke them at twenty-one minutes past five. The fourth phone call before six am, one received every day of their honeymoon so far.

"Seriously. We're on our honeymoon," Nikki said, wrapping the pillow around her head to block out the noise.

Matt stretched for the phone, brought it to his hear. "Mum, it's five-thirty in the morning."

"I didn't realise. I keep getting the time difference all messed up in my head."

"Please, we got home late last night. We're tired."

"Are you having a good time? I'd hate to spend all that money and time organising your trip for you not to be enjoying yourselves."

"We are having lots of fun. Thank you again."

"My pleasure. I really wanted to give you both something from your father. He would have loved to have known he was doing this for you both."

"And we really appreciate it."

"Is Nikki awake? It feels like I haven't spoken to her for ages. Even though it was a mere five days ago. Put her on for me, will you, so I can say hello."

He pressed his thumb and finger to his forehead and squeezed his eyes shut. "She's still asleep, Mum."

"I highly doubt that. Put her on."

Matt sighed and tapped Nikki's shoulder. He covered the mouthpiece and said, "Mum wants to say hello."

Nikki sat up. Her eyes were bloodshot. A frown slanted her lips. She held her hand out for the phone, so he gave it to her. "Hi, Claire. Good to hear from you," she said with a husky morning voice.

"You too, darl. I'm missing you both so much. I never thought I'd hear myself say that. I really hope you're having a wonderful time." Matt could hear Mum's loud voice despite the phone being pressed to Nikki's ear. Mum assumed that she had to speak three times louder than normal when she was calling a mobile phone.

"We are. It's been a fantastic honeymoon. We've been all over the city. Later on, we're going to drive out to see the vineyards."

"That sounds lovely. The hotel room is nice?"

"More than I could have ever hoped for."

"I'm so glad because it cost me an arm and a leg."

"Thank you so much again."

"And what about your parents, Nikki, did they get you anything nice as a present?"

Nikki met Matt's gaze and grimaced. "Nothing in addition to helping pay for the wedding."

"I see." Even Matt could hear the disdain in Mum's tone. "That's well and truly their prerogative, I guess. Anyway, is Matt there, I'd like to say goodbye to him before I hang up."

"I'll just get him. I'll talk to you later, Claire."

"Yes."

Matt watched Nikki as she shoved the blankets aside and climbed out of bed, heading for the bathroom where the door slammed hard behind her.

He brought the phone to his ear. "We've got a big day ahead of us, so I better go."

"Yes, I've got so much to do, too. No rest for the wicked. What I wouldn't give for an all-expenses-paid holiday. All by myself."

Matt closed his eyes and scrubbed a palm over his jaw. "Yes, it's definitely a wonderful experience."

Finally, Mum ended the call, though her voice still rang in his head. He shouldn't have accepted the honeymoon as a gift. It was too much, too big. But how did you say no to something like that? Especially when it meant so much to her that she could give them a gift on behalf of Dad to celebrate their marriage.

He switched the phone off and threw it into his suitcase. It was their honeymoon and they needed to enjoy it. Mum waking them up every morning was not acceptable.

That wasn't wrong, was it? He shook his head. Of course, it wasn't. It was his bloody honeymoon. His mother wasn't meant to tag along with them, even if only in voice.

When Nikki came out of the bathroom, he pointed to the phone. "It's off, and I'm not turning it back on until we get home."

She managed a smile and nodded. "Good."

Matt was in the shower, hot water streaming around him, while Nikki was leaning over the cabinet, completely naked, applying makeup to her face. Her breasts mesmerised him as she moved back and forward, digging through her makeup case then leaning in to apply it. He was so hard from watching and imagining what he would do to her when he climbed out of the shower. He would take her from behind, while he was still steaming wet from the shower, right in front of that mirror.

He opened his mouth to say something dirty when an urgent knocking sounded on the door.

He shook the water from his face. "What the hell was that?"

Nikki's eyes were wide as she looked out the open bathroom door into the entrance hall. Keys jingled.

The knock came again. "Mr and Mrs Radcliffe, it's management."

"What the hell? I'm in the shower, hang on!" he called out and covered his erection with his hand.

Nikki pulled a white towel from the rail and wrapped it around herself. She shrunk against the counter, out of sight from the door.

Matt shut the shower off, reached for a towel and had it wrapped around his waist as the hotel manager opened the door. He was a very tall and thin man with a balding head.

"Mr Radcliffe. Are you and your wife both okay?" His eyes were wide, his tone filled with worry.

Matt's brow was crinkled. "Of course we're okay." He glanced down to make sure his hard-on wasn't quite so obvious beneath his towel. He brought his arms across his waist and clasped his hands in front of his genitals. "Why the hell are you barging into our room?"

"I'm sorry, but it's my duty-of-care to ensure you are both safe and sound."

"I don't understand. Why do you have the impression that we aren't?"

"Your mother rang the hotel—"

Matt groaned.

"—she was frantic that something had happened to you. She had been trying to get in contact with you for two days and no answer…"

Matt scrubbed a hand through his hair. The damn mobile phone. He should never have bought one. No, he should never have given his mother the phone number. No, he should not have accepted this honeymoon present. He should have said, 'thank you very much, that's very kind, but I've put away enough money to pay for our own honeymoon. In fact, we have booked a trip to Japan, and we will not cancel it, even if your gift is a "so-called" present from Dad'.

"I called the room. No one answered—"

"We were in the shower," Matt barked. He gestured to his wet chest, his mussed dripping hair. He didn't have to hide an erection anymore, it was well and truly deflated. "Obviously, we didn't hear the phone."

"I'm sorry, but she was adamant that something was wrong. She was about to call the police but wanted reassurance first."

"Okay, fine. We're fine, as you can see."

"I'm fine," Nikki called out.

"I'll call my mother to let her know we're safe."

"Thank you, sir. And I apologise again for the intrusion."

Matt waved the manager's apology away and gestured towards the door. "Just go. I'll take it from here."

The manager left and Matt blew out an agitated breath.

Nikki was waiting just inside the bathroom door. "If she was so worried, why didn't she ring the hotel before now? She could have asked to be transferred to the room. Or left a message at the front desk."

He shook his head, lips twisting together. "I have no idea."

He marched to his luggage and scouted through the clothes for his mobile. He turned it on and dialled Mum's number. His muscles twitched.

"Mum," he snapped.

"Matt? Thank God. I thought something had happened to you." Her voice was weak and husky like she had been crying. "I couldn't bear it…" She trailed off.

"Matt. Hi, honey. It's Auntie Sue."

He shook his head. "Auntie Sue?"

"Your mum was out of her mind with worry. She asked me to come and stay with her. She's not in a good way. I think this little scare brought up all the fuss from when your father passed away."

"I didn't even realise."

"Yes, well, I know it's your honeymoon and all, but you really should be more mindful of your mother. You know how much she worries. It's so irresponsible that all this time you were at the hotel and you couldn't give her a call."

"I turned my phone off. I forgot to turn it back on."

"Right, okay. Well, best to keep the phone on from now on for your mother's peace of mind."

"I will. I'll keep it on."

"I'm glad you're both okay, but please, Matt, don't let this happen again. You'll give your mother a bloody heart attack."

"I won't. I'm sorry. Tell Mum I apologise."

Matt said goodbye and ended the call. He sank onto the end of the bed, elbows on his knees and stared at the patterns on the carpet beneath his feet.

Nikki, now dressed in a pair of jeans and a red singlet top, sat beside him. She wrapped an arm around his shoulders.

"I probably shouldn't have turned the phone off. Bit stupid, really," he mumbled.

"You weren't to know she'd overreact like this."

"I guess so. I don't know. I'll keep it on, though."
Nikki nodded. "Yes, probably best."

Chapter 33

Nikki

Nikki sat on the big blue chair across from Dr Puethe for their fifth session. They had worked through many stressful moments in Nikki's life, then they focussed on positive emotions and experiences to remind her it wasn't always like this—something had changed. They had to identify the trigger.

At the end of her last session, Nikki still wasn't sure what was at the root of her mental predicament, but the more she hacked at the encasement that kept whatever lay beneath contained, the more energy it gathered.

With each session, she was becoming more and more confused and filled with the scary belief that she was going mad. Maybe there was some structural disease that was making her regress in so many areas of her life—mainly her confidence and her self-belief.

Dr Puethe tapped his notepad with the tip of his pen. "We are going to try something a little different today. See if we can get to the bottom of all this."

Nikki's stomach lurched, and she shifted in her chair to find a comfortable position. *New* didn't sit well with her. She liked *tried and true* and *done before*.

"I'll take some notes during this session, is that okay with you?"

Nikki nodded, used to, at this stage, the general session patter.

"You can have a copy to take home with you later if you so choose."

Again, she nodded.

Dr Puethe leaned against the back of his chair, crossed a leg. "What I find helpful is if we talk about a specific situation. I would like you to recall a time when you felt particularly overwhelmed. It could be something we've talked about before that you'd like to explore more deeply, or we could look at something else."

She drew a deep breath, readying herself to confront her own mind. "The morning I crashed my car into a tree."

"I want you to close your eyes and lie back against that chair. Think about the emotions you felt that day."

Heat flowered in her chest. A familiar swirl of nerves filled her belly as though she was back there, hands gripping the steering wheel, anticipating spending another day at work. A conflict of emotions. "Anger. Fear," she whispered.

"Good. Feel those emotions inside of you."

Darts of remembered feelings shot through her. Her hands twitched. "Hate." Her eyes flung open. "I'm sorry, I don't know why I said that."

"Nothing is off-limits. Even hate has a place here. I want you to feel that anger, fear and hate."

She closed her eyes and concentrated again on trying to recall those emotions. They bubbled up from deep inside her, thrashed at her insides—hot and sharp, blunt and hard.

"Try and animate that emotion," Dr Puethe said. "Give it form and substance."

Shadows formed behind her eyes, then splotches of colour. Bright red like blood at first. Then dark brown. Fur. Grey fur. A snout. Ears. Red rimming the figure's mouth like it had torn at raw meat dripping with blood.

"A wolf," she whispered as she tried to make sense of this. She looked harder. It wasn't blood around the wolf's mouth; it was lipstick. Blood red lipstick. "Lipstick not blood. The wolf is wearing lipstick."

The dark brown was its eyes. Appraising, calculating. The eyes of a manipulator. A liar. She flinched when she recognised that those dark eyes were familiar.

"The wolf is Claire," she cried out. A wave of emotion welled up from deep in her belly and exploded from her as a sob. "It's Claire." She opened her eyes. Tears flooded her cheeks.

Dr Puethe nodded and blinked in such a way that validated Nikki's massive realisation and acknowledged that her answer was as big and cumbersome as Nikki had felt it was within herself.

He handed her a tissue.

"Thank you," she hiccupped and dabbed at her eyes, but the tears wouldn't cease. Her throat was tight and sore, her nose stuffy. Her eyes burned from the tears. She cried for what felt like hours but could have only been minutes.

And then rage brewed. Visceral, blistering anger.

"She's taken my life away," Nikki managed. "From the moment I met her, she has controlled every part of my life. She planned my whole wedding. Chose where we went on our honeymoon. We've spent every damn Christmas with her. She comes into my house unannounced. She ruins my belongings. She talks about me behind my back. And I do everything I can to appease her, humour her, make sure I haven't lost favour with her." She finally stopped for a breath, realising she was angrily rambling and gesticulating. "I hate her. I hate her so much, I dread anytime we have to spend with her."

She stopped, sucking in heaving breaths. Her hands were shaking.

"What I'm hearing is that you feel your mother-in-law's actions—the way she treats you and the negativity of many of your interactions—impacts on the choices you make in your own life. That they are more to ensure her happiness rather than looking after your own needs."

"Exactly. I don't even know who I am anymore. I was once so confident. So happy." Resentment surged through her veins along with a deep throb of despair. "I can't remember the last time I laughed. I'm always on edge, wondering what she'll do next."

"Okay, let's look at something specific. Can you recall a time when Claire made you feel stressed or anxious?"

"When each of my sons was born. She stayed with me for three weeks at the house. She took over completely as though she was the one who had given birth to my children.

"She brought her own sheets to sleep on—one thousand thread count Egyptian cotton—because mine weren't good enough.

"She scrubs my kitchen sink when I'm not in the room as though I'm some slovenly pig who can't do it myself.

"She nit-picks everything I do, but in a sly way, so it doesn't look like it's me she is talking about.

"Matt and I had to stop telling her what we planned to buy the boys for their birthdays or Christmas because she would sneak out and buy it first and give it to the kids early.

"Every single year, I have to listen to sob stories about why I can't choose to spend Christmas how I want. Six years in a row it was because Claire's mother was dying. Then it was her father. Now it's because she's too lonely without her husband around.

"When we go away on holiday, she rings way too early and every single day.

"Everything we say, we are met with a pessimistic response. We stopped telling her about our plans eventually.

"She wore a long, white lace dress to my wedding and didn't think that was inappropriate at all."

With a rush of regret, Nikki recalled how little she and Matt had been intimate lately and the toll this was taking on them both. "She ruined my honeymoon and now she's trying to destroy my marriage."

And on she went, example after example, right up until the last minute of the session.

"It might be a good place to end there for today," Dr Puethe said. "I would like you to book another appointment with the front desk on your way out, and we can pick up on this in our next session. I would like to discuss ways that you can set boundaries with Claire and perhaps some assertiveness training."

Nikki's throat was dry from talking for so long and so quickly. Her body was limp and aching. She craved her bed, where she could tuck herself up and sleep for a thousand years.

By the time she made it to her car, she was sagging like a deflated ball. She reached into her handbag, grabbed out her mobile phone and checked for missed calls or messages before she started the engine. There was one message.

Matt: I hope your session goes well. Call any time if you want to talk.

Nikki lightly pinched the skin at her throat, over and over again while her leg bounced. Obviously, Claire was a big issue, so much so that over the last few years, Nikki had slowly eroded away until she resembled someone completely unfamiliar.

But Claire was her mother-in-law. How could she ever solve the problem of Claire without ruining her relationship with Matt or ruining Matt's relationship with his mother?

How was she going to look her husband in the eye and admit that she hated his mother?

She needed to talk to someone who knew what she was going through. She scrolled through her contacts for her ex-sister-in-law's number and dialled.

"Hi, Joanne, it's Nikki."

"Nikki. Wow, it's so good to hear from you. It's been a long time."

"It has. Um… do you have time to grab a coffee? I need to talk to you about something, well, someone."

"Sure. Eleven o'clock at The Deck?"

"Sounds good. See you then."

Chapter 34

Belinda

Belinda ended the phone call with her new accountant and sat unmoving at her desk for a long while. A clenching swell of sickness started in her stomach and surged up her throat. She lurched to her feet, raced to the bathroom and vomited until there was nothing left in her belly except for a hollow ache.

She was screwed. No other way to describe her and Anthony's circumstances. Well and truly screwed. When she had enough composure to move, she closed the shop and drove home in a daze.

She rang Anthony once she was inside and sitting down. He didn't answer the first call. Or the second. She paced the living room, intermittently trying his phone again. After the fifth no-answer, she rang the office only to be told he was in a meeting.

"Can you get him to call me as soon as he gets out please?"

She hung up and texted him a message to call her and left a voice message too, to make triple sure he rang her back.

Almost an hour had passed when Belinda's mobile rang. She answered.

"Hey, what's up?" Anthony's voice was frantic. "You feeling okay?"

"I'm fine. The baby's fine."

"What's happening? I've got so many missed calls."

"Our new accountant rang me. Seems our other bastard so-called accountants weren't communicating with us just how much ATO debt we actually have or how aggressively they were chasing us to pay it."

"How could they do that?"

"I asked the same question. Our accountant assumes they didn't pass on the correspondence."

"So how much are we talking about?"

"You might want to sit down."

"I am."

She blew out a long breath, squeezed the bridge of her nose between her thumb and forefinger. "Over fifty thousand dollars."

Silence for three heartbeats. A tic in her jaw.

"So, what was the twenty thousand I just paid for?" he asked with an eerie calmness.

"That was a different account. For GST. Supposedly this account is for income tax."

"What do we do? Did they set up a payment plan?"

"They tried, but the best they could get was for us to pay thirty per cent now and pay the remainder off with a plan."

"Thirty per cent?" His voice boomed down the line, and she had to move the earpiece further away. "What's that? Fifteen thousand dollars?"

"Yep. And then the remainder will be instalments of one thousand dollars per fortnight after."

"We can't do it. It's impossible."

Belinda flopped onto the couch and lowered her face into her hand. "I know. We're screwed."

"We have to liquidate the business. Sell the house. We don't have a choice now."

"And then what?"

"I don't know. I'll find work as a tradesman. You could get a retail job. We'll get by."

"What do we tell everyone?"

"How about we tell them the truth for once? That we're drowning in debt."

Belinda's stomach swirled with anxiety. The bitter shame held over from her childhood blossomed under her skin, made her cheeks hot and heart race. "I can't. I can't do that. There has to be another way."

"We're at the end of the road, Bel. Can't you see that?"

"We can't give up now. To give up means bankruptcy. We lose everything. The house. Our cars. Our businesses. All that we have worked so hard for. We will never be able to come back from that. Our credit rating will be ruined. We're not twenty anymore. It will take years to recover."

"We don't have a bloody choice, Bel! I don't know what else we can do."

"What about another credit card? For fifteen thousand dollars. I'll try for it now. Don't do anything until I've at least tried."

"Fine," the word was said with such resignation and despondency it turned her stomach. "See what you can do. But I need you to start thinking seriously about the other option."

"That's not an option, Ant. I couldn't live with myself. It's humiliating. And I'm not bringing a baby into this world whose parents are…are…failures."

Anthony was silent for a long moment. Her breaths were rushed as she waited for him to speak.

"See what you can do. I better go." And he hung up.

Belinda sat there with tears pricking the back of her eyes. A scream sat in her throat. But neither screams nor tears came. "I need to make this right." She heaved herself onto her feet. She was not going to give up. Not now. She rubbed a gentle palm over her stomach. "I'll make this right," she whispered to her baby.

Within a half hour, she had completed a new online credit card application for thirty thousand dollars. Fifteen to pay the ATO and another fifteen to transfer the balance from another card and give them some reprieve on interest for six months.

Surely, they will have their problems solved by then. Surely, something will come up at Anthony's work.

She rang her real estate agent who confirmed that there had been some enquiries about her business, but no one who was genuinely interested in purchasing it. She was chasing a phantom. No one in their right mind would buy that business in the current climate.

With nothing more to do but wait, she made a cup of ginger tea to quell her swirling nausea. When she finished that, she climbed upstairs, fell onto her bed and rolled into a ball under the blankets. Things had to get better. They had to.

The universe would cut her some slack eventually.

Chapter 35

Paige

Paige carried Evie to the couch and sat her on her lap. All week, she had been considering how to tell a three-year-old that she had a father who wanted to meet her. Did a small child understand what any of that truly meant?

In the end, she decided that as little information as possible was best.

"Hi, baby," she said to Evie with a nervous grin.

Evie smiled.

"Remember I said we were going to have some people come over today for a visit?"

Evie nodded.

"Well, it's going to be a man and his mum."

"Yep."

Paige exhaled noisily. How much understanding was happening behind those big, beautiful green eyes?

"The man is your dad."

Evie squirmed and climbed off her lap. "I go do wee," she said and rushed off to the toilet. End of conversation.

But what more could she expect from a toddler? They didn't understand all the twists and sordid turns of life, nor did they care. It was all about food, baths, cuddles and playtime. As it should be.

"Damn Joshua," she grumbled.

Didn't help that she had her period and her stomach and back were giving her hell, despite taking a couple of paracetamols. It was always the way, the most important moments in life made overly complicated because they occurred when she was in pain and angsty.

Joshua and his mother, Paula, arrived a little before twelve o'clock. When the knock came at the door, her stomach tumbled, amplifying the already over-bloated feeling. That knock was what she had been petrified of from the moment she had discovered she was pregnant four years ago.

Her nightmare had come true.

Vaughn had managed to reassure her somewhat. He highlighted the potential positives of the situation: Evie would be able to have a relationship with her real father—a question and a possible problem that would have arisen sooner or later. And if Joshua had gotten over the initial overwhelming impact of stardom, and was on the straight and narrow, it may be a wonderful situation for Evie.

It would also give them some time to themselves. She understood where Vaughn was coming from, but for her, she had never spent more than two nights away from Evie—she didn't know if handing her over to Joshua was something she could adjust to.

"Come in," Paige said.

Joshua stepped inside. He was dressed immaculately—long grey pants and a tight-fitting, black polo shirt that accentuated his enormous bulk. His hair was combed and styled. He lightly bit his bottom lip and his breaths were long and deep like he was doing his best to hold back tears.

Paula, his mother, smiled as she came in behind Joshua. She kissed Paige's cheek. "Good to see you again."

"You too."

Paige had always respected and liked Paula. She had been a huge comfort when Paige's mother passed. She helped organise the funeral, and, many nights, while Joshua was at training or away for competitions, she had sat up late with her talking about her grief over cups of tea.

When her relationship with Joshua broke down, Paige had mourned for her friendship with Paula. She couldn't bear to have told Paula what her son had done, so she had left their lives without an explanation. The weight of guilt was heavy on her shoulders now as she met her gaze.

Evie was waiting in the living room on the couch. Paige had dressed her in a smart, blue tartan dress and matching blue sandals. Paula gasped and covered her mouth when Evie turned to look at them. Tears flooded her eyes and her bottom lip trembled.

"My, goodness, look at you, gorgeous girl," she cooed. "Hi, I'm your grandma. You can call me GG like my other grandchildren if you like?"

"Come say hello to GG," Paige said, taking Evie's hand and leading her from the couch to where Paula and Joshua stood.

"She looks just like your sister," Paula said to Joshua, nudging him in the ribs.

"Just what I thought." Joshua crouched down. "Hi, darling, I'm your dad." His voice was choked. "It's so lovely to meet you."

"Say hi," Paige said.

Evie looked up at Joshua from under her lashes. "Hello."

"I thought we could go out the back," Paige suggested. "I've made some snacks. We can sit out there and let Evie play on her swings. Let GG and—" she stumbled to use the word *dad,* "—Dad take you outside, and I'll be out soon, okay?"

"I have a sandpit," Evie said, reaching for Joshua's big paw.

"You do, hey? Do you have any trucks?"

Evie nodded. "Yep. Vaughn give me some. And big diggers."

"I like the sound of that."

They followed an excited Evie out the back like two puppy dogs being led on a leash.

Paige headed to the kitchen for a private moment to pull herself together. As she unloaded the platters of cheese, biscuits, vegetable sticks and dips, tears pricked the back of her eyes, but she blinked them away. Her chest throbbed with heat.

As horrible as it was to admit, some part of her had wanted Evie to hate Joshua, but Evie had embraced him with all her inner-charm and openness. Of course, it was best for Evie to like Joshua. Love him even. He was her biological father, after all.

One positive was that Joshua was his old self—the kind man she had fallen in love with rather than the intoxicated snake he had morphed into towards the end of their relationship. That arrogance, the peacocking, he had so proudly portrayed, was gone.

Paige rested her hands against the countertop and breathed in deeply. When more composed, she collected the platters and carried them out the back.

She spread the plates and bowls on the table and ensured they were covered properly so no flies could sneak through any cracks.

She squinted against the midday glare to find Joshua sitting in the sandpit next to Evie. He was using a bulldozer to shovel sand while Evie cranked the arm of an excavator to dig. Their similarities were breathtaking. Same coloured hair. Same eyes.

All the pain of losing her mum, all the heartache when she discovered Joshua had cheated on her, and then the ultimate betrayal when he had flown into a rage and punched her, was seeping to the surface. Everything was wrapped into one and this nostalgia was breath-stealing. She wanted to weep, to howl and let all this angst out.

She trudged up the yard to stand next to Paula and watched, arms crossed over her chest, as Evie and Joshua played together.

"When's her birthday?" Paula asked, not turning from her son and grandchild.

Paige cleared her throat, steadied her voice. "February twenty-seventh."

Paula nodded. "Why didn't you tell us about her, Paige? I don't understand."

Paige glanced at Joshua and found, even after what he did and after all these years, she couldn't form the words that would admit the truth to Paula. Not the full story. It would break Paula's heart. To inflict that on her was so terribly difficult.

"I thought it would be best for all of us if I didn't. Joshua wasn't in a good place. I couldn't see how announcing that I was pregnant would have made anything better."

"It would have changed everything," Joshua said, turning to face them from the sandpit.

"You can say that in hindsight, but you need to see it from my perspective." Her tone was clipped. He had no idea how he would have reacted and neither did she.

"I would have helped you both," Paula said. "You know that, Paige. I would have done everything I could."

She wanted to scream the truth, but her voice remained trapped in her throat. Her desire to defend her position was outweighed by her willingness to protect a mother's love for her son.

Instead, she lifted her hands. "It can't be changed. What's done is done. Let's just please move forward."

"I want custody, Paige. Fifty-fifty," Joshua said. "I've missed three years of my daughter's life. I won't miss anymore."

Paige shook her head. "Let's just relax. It's early days yet. And it's the off-season. You know how hectic it is when the football season starts and you're flying all around the country every weekend."

"My mind is made up. I have rights."

"We have to do what's right for Evie. She's who is important."

"Evie is all I can think about. She needs her father. Her grandmother. Her cousins. My sisters and brothers are so excited to meet her. She will be loved, Paige. Don't fear this. It's a good thing. She will be loved."

Her heart was racing. This all felt unsafe like he was ripping Evie out of her life with no regard whatsoever for everything they had been through together. All the night's she spent breastfeeding. The little illnesses. Toilet training. The books read. The difficult moments. Did he not realise that at all?

"She has a big family dying to meet her," Paula said.

Tears were falling down her cheeks. She quickly wiped them away. "Let's slow down a bit, that's all I'm asking. It's been me and Evie for so long, I need some time to get my head around this."

"You've had three years. I've had five minutes," Joshua said. "No more time."

Paula put a hand on Paige's shoulder. "We're not trying to be hurtful. But Josh is her father."

"I know."

"We are not going to take her away from you. We just want to be a part of Evie's life."

There were no objections she could make about that. None that were rational. "Let's do it outside of the courts then," she said.

Joshua nodded. "I agree."

"A practical but fair agreement."

"Of course," Paula said.

"I'll put some suggestions in writing, email them to you, and you can see what works best for you." That would give her time to calm down and think rationally before making any decisions.

Joshua held her gaze. "Sure."

Soon Evie grew tired of the sandpit and ran to the swing-set to show her two new friends. Paige took a seat and squirmed trying to find a comfortable position while her back was aching, and her stomach felt like it was the size of a basketball. A hormone headache—or perhaps it was a stress headache—throbbed.

She watched them all interact. Their patience with Evie was admirable, but they hadn't experienced all the years of monotony and difficult parenting moments like she had. Then again, Paige would take a million monotonous moments or shopping centre tantrums over no time at all with Evie.

Deep sadness cloaked her. A heavy weight pressed on her shoulders. With the knowledge that Joshua had set himself straight, came a niggly sense of guilt for keeping Evie from him. Was it her right to assume what was best for all of them? With all that she had known back then, it had been a cut and dry decision, but now there were shadows and patches of doubt.

She sat there longer, aching, wanting this day to be over. Eventually, Joshua suggested they give Evie a break from the sun and stop for a drink and something to eat. Joshua helped dish up food for Evie and poured milk into her cup as though he had done it a million times before.

"Thank you," Evie said and pushed a whole biscuit with cheese into her mouth.

Joshua and Paula laughed, then Joshua kissed the top of Evie's head. "My pleasure, darling girl."

Paula leaned over and took Paige's hand. "See, it's okay. We can do this together."

Paige nodded because she didn't have any other choice.

Chapter 36

Nikki

Nikki arrived at the café and scanned the tables for Joanne, finding her seated at a small table near the deck railing. Midday sunlight beamed down but was filtered by a canopy of white canvas umbrellas.

Nikki drew her sunglass from her eyes, shoved them in her handbag and headed over.

Joanne stood and pulled Nikki in for a cuddle. "It's so great to see you again."

"You too, Joanne. It's been much too long. I'm sorry about that."

Joanne waved her apology away. "Don't be. We've both got busy lives."

Nikki took a seat, placed her bag on the spare chair beside her and nervously reached for a menu, even though she always ordered the same thing—a flat white.

"You sounded upset on the phone. Is everything okay?"

Nikki frowned. "Not really. No." She lifted her eyes to meet Joanne's. "I've been seeing a psychologist about some…issues."

Joanne leaned back against her seat, linked her fingers and rested her hands on the tabletop. "I'm sorry to hear that."

"Something came up in my session… I don't mean to pry or be disrespectful, but I remember you saying that one of the reasons you ended your marriage to Vaughn was Claire."

Joanne nodded. No hesitation. "Very much so."

"Why? How? I mean, it's not that I don't believe you. Not at all. But I want to understand what exactly she did and why divorce was your only option."

Joanne looked away. Two creases of tension formed between her brows. "It all began quite subtly. A few lies here. Some interfering there. But then came the gaslighting…"

Nikki flinched. "Gaslighting?"

"I should have recognised it earlier. I had a boyfriend who was the same. He would twist my words and lie until I thought up was down and red was blue. It shouldn't have taken me so long to realise that Claire's actions were identical. That's what gaslighting is—she manipulates your reality for her own means."

Nikki pushed stray strands of hair behind her ears. "I was hoping I would come here today, and you'd convince me that I was wrong about her."

"I wish I could say she was a wonderful person. The type of person she likes people to believe she is—the pillar of society, the one you call on when you need help, but I will only speak from my reality and from a place of truth because, for so long, I couldn't recognize either of those things."

"I came to the same conclusion today in my session. Claire is the source of my issues."

"I wouldn't doubt it for a second. I've been meaning to catch up with you and Belinda to see if you were both okay." She focused on her hands and shook her head. "But for my own sanity, I had to keep away."

"It was that bad?"

Joanne nodded, frowned. "People like Claire are insidious. Only those in her close circle would see what she is truly like, while everyone else is left thinking she's an angel. That's how she works. Everything she does in public is to uphold a certain image, but deep down she laps up conflict like cream on a sundae. It's only now that I have finally put some distance between myself and her that I feel I'm getting my life back."

Nikki shook her head. "I had no idea you'd been dealing with all that."

"That's how Claire liked it. I'm not sure if you've realised it yet, but she played us all off against one another. Less chance we'd talk and finally figure out how horrible she is."

"Did you talk to Vaughn about her?"

"Of course I did. But he didn't get it. All he could see was the image she projected. And then he had this weird fear of ever coming across as angry or violent in front of her, so he would let her get away with so much. I can't blame him for not being able to see Claire for what she is. At the end of the day, she's his mother. I'm sure his blindness is his way of coping."

"Did he try and understand your position, though? See it from your perspective?"

"Sure, he tried. But Claire always had a way to twist what I was saying or doing until I looked petty and ridiculous or like I was the one who had done something wrong. She had this snakelike ability to make me come off looking paranoid and overly emotional." She leaned forward and lowered her voice. "I'm sorry if this is too much information but towards the end, I couldn't even have sex with my own husband because all I could see when I looked at him was his mother." She arched a brow, let it drop again. "That turned out to be the worst move I could have made. He came home ranting and raving, as though denying him sex was the worst crime a wife could commit. All this was after talking to Claire, of course. She had been in his ear. That's when I chose to leave. I couldn't see a way out. And it wasn't worth staying."

"That's unbelievable."

Joanne managed a bitter smile. "I assure you, as crazy as it sounds, it was all very real. I was devastated because this man, who I thought loved me, wouldn't stick up for me. I tried to set boundaries with Claire. I tried to reason with her. But it made everything worse." She shuddered, shook her head. "I'm sorry. It's been a while since I've spoken about all this."

Nikki reached across the table and put her hand on Joanne's. "If it makes you feel any better, I know exactly what you went through. I'm dealing with all that now. I've been dealing with it from the moment I met Claire. And now I'm scared that Matt isn't going to understand."

"Then you take the kids and you run far, far away."

"It's not that easy."

"There's no solution to Claire. Believe me, I know. If Matt doesn't support a clean separation from her, then there's only one other way to save yourself—you leave without him."

"I can't ask him to sever his relationship with his own mother. It doesn't feel right. And neither does packing up the kids and running away." She loved her husband with all her heart. Her boys deserved a full-time father. She didn't want Claire to be the knife that slashed their relationship in half.

And if she did run away, Claire wasn't going to let her go without a fight. She had a right to see her grandchildren. She would whisper in Matt's ear, make him fight for custody. It would be never-ending misery and much more destructive than if she stayed.

"And Claire knows that all too well."

Nikki pressed her hands to her cheeks and shook her head. "Why? Why does she do this? She is hurting her own children."

"I don't know the answer to that. Some people are inherently evil."

Tingles ran up Nikki's spine and along her arms. "You believe she's evil?"

"I know she is."

Chapter 37

Matt

The past...

Matt raced out the backdoor, the screen snapping as it sprang shut behind him, and ran down the steep slope towards the new jump he had been eying off for the last week. Vaughn and Anthony had been working on it every afternoon from the moment they got home from school to the time Mum called them in for dinner.

All week, Matt had been confined to his room, where he sat on the bed looking out the window watching the progress they made. No bedroom today; he was done with it. He didn't care what Mum thought. She'd have to come out and chase him back inside if that's what she wanted.

He sprinted to the lone bike that was lying in the grass. A little rust and mud had gathered on the spokes. But it was a great bike. A BMX, which Mum had insisted he didn't need, but Dad had bought him a year ago before he died.

"Only seems fair that the eldest son gets a bike just like his brothers," he had said, then ruffled Matt's hair. "There you go, son, get out there and give it a spin."

Matt picked up the bike, jumped on and pedalled to the base of the jump.

Anthony smirked at him. "It's the ghost boy, finally allowed to play."

Matt punched Anthony's arm. "Shut up."

Anthony pressed hard on the cotton ball pinned to the inside of Matt's arm with white sticky tape. He'd had another blood test today. He barely felt them anymore, he'd had so many.

"What happened to you?" Anthony asked.

"None of your business. I'm out here to do some jumps, not sit around talking." He'd heard adults say things like that on movies and a burst of manliness puffed his chest.

Vaughn came zipping past them. "So long, suckers!" His feet were moving so fast, Matt could barely see them. He zoomed up the manmade mound of dirt and gravel and flew in the air before landing on the embankment directly opposite. Vaughn yahooed and skidded to a halt at the base of the hill, dust flinging in the air.

"I'm next," Matt said. He rode off to get a run-up and sped along the path Vaughn had just taken. His brothers watched him as he careered up the mound, gained heaps of height and landed. He threw his hand up and roared as he pedalled down the opposite side and skidded to a stop. He was puffing, his legs ached from pedalling, but he buzzed with triumph.

Over the next hour, he didn't stop. He was hot and sweaty. Dirt stuck to his skin. He grazed his knee and elbow from a fall. His hair was damp and dusty. His brothers looked the same, but not one of them could wipe the proud smiles from their faces.

Mum came running down the backyard, screaming out to him and waving her arm in the air. He turned away and jumped on his bike again, peddling as fast as could at the jump. Air, so much air. He was floating far away from her, but too soon he came back down, and she was there, still screaming.

"You were told to go up to your room. Now go. My goodness, Matt, we've been at the doctor's all day."

He finally turned to face her. "But I feel fine. Stop bugging me." He'd heard some boys at school talk like that.

Mum's face dropped into a frown. "I beg your pardon."

"I said stop bugging me. There's nothing wrong with me. I feel fine."

Mum's frown deepened and her eyes watered with tears. "Do you know how this feels for me? To have a child who is sick all the bloody time. You obviously have no idea otherwise you would not be talking to me like that."

His stomach sank, and he blew out a noisy breath "Fine. I'm sorry."

"Now, please, for my sake, go up to your room. You'll have to shower now before you climb into bed."

His body shuddered at the thought of spending all night in bed again. He wanted to run until his lungs burst with the need for air, move his muscles until he ached. He wanted to get dirty and sweaty.

But, instead, he dropped his head and marched up to the house, not daring to look at his brothers. He couldn't cope with their sympathetic frowns on top of his own self-pity.

Once inside, Mum sent him for a quick shower. "Wash your hair while you're in there. Auntie Sue is on her way over. You don't want her to think I don't clean my children."

When he climbed out of the shower, his mother was waiting with a chair by the window. She had a set of hair clippers in her hand. "Take a seat."

He eyed the clippers, shook his head. "What are you doing?"

"Shaving your hair off."

He scrubbed a hand through his thick, dark strands. "But I like my hair. Everyone will tease me at school if I shave it off."

"You're sick, Matt."

"The doctor said I was fine."

"Sit!" Mum screamed. "God, I'm at my limits with all this."

"Fine," he hissed and slouched in the chair. As Mum dragged the buzzing clippers over his head, clumps of hair fell onto the floor around him.

His brothers rode their bikes over the jump as he watched from the window.

Soon enough, every strand of hair was gone. Sharp prickles atop his skull remained. When he stared at his reflection in the mirror after Mum had gone downstairs, a burning achiness filled his throat. Tears swam in his eyes.

Life was a nightmare—an endless parade of doctor visits and bed rest. This pale prickled head was the last straw.

His body arched, shoulders tugging forwards. His head loped downwards towards his chest as he made his way to his bed and climbed into it. He lay there until he could no longer hear his brothers' chatter from the backyard and the sun had sunk behind the trees. He lay there looking at the wall, staring.

Sometime later, a soft knock came at the door. Auntie Sue poked her head into his room. "Hi, darling, mind if I come in?"

"Sure," he said, monotone, but he didn't move.

Auntie Sue sat beside the bed. "Hi, honey, how are you feeling?"

"Fine."

"I bought you a pressie to keep the boredom away. One of those new handheld video game thingies."

He finally rolled over to face her and took the present from her, letting it rest on the bed beside him. "Thanks."

"No worries, darling. You're really rocking that new haircut, I must say."

"Thanks."

When Auntie Sue sniffled, he finally lifted his gaze to her face. Her eyes were bloodshot. She wiped tears from her cheeks and gave him a watery smile. "You be strong, my darling. You'll come out the end of this, I promise you."

He narrowed his eyes, frowned. "I'm not dying, Auntie Sue. I'm fine."

She rubbed a hand over his head. "Of course. That's the best attitude. We will always remain positive."

Chapter 38

Belinda

Marked in the calendar, every year on this day was dinner at Claire's house—a tribute of sorts to her husband. Claire had it catered with little sandwiches, savoury pastries and petite cakes as though replicating a wake.

Belinda had attended the mandatory occasion for a decade, and she hated the entire day. For the first few years, she would go to the sombre event, her heart brimming with sympathy for Anthony and Claire, but it became clear that the three sons had all gotten on with the business of living yet were forced to relive a terrible day over and over again for a woman who liked to splash about in sympathy.

Claire would always get much too drunk and eventually cry and wail about how horrible it was to lose her soul mate, which would be understandable were the tears not so obviously manufactured.

As the night progressed, the attendees would pander to Claire until she was carried up to her bed—yes, carried!—and they would all drive home a little more traumatised than the previous year.

Belinda shuddered. This time, she couldn't even rely on wine to dull her senses. Maybe now that she was pregnant, she could feign a pregnancy-related illness and send Anthony on his own. She could spend the afternoon at home finding perfect pictures of baby rooms for her scrapbook.

But with a twenty-thousand-dollar noose around her neck, not to mention the blank stare Claire had given Belinda and Vaughn after the *baby conversation* at the family barbeque, she was obliged to do what Claire wanted.

Belinda cringed as Anthony drove them to Claire's home. They arrived last, parking behind the various vehicles.

Anthony's aunts travelled each year to attend and would stay at the house for a couple of days before and after the anniversary.

When Anthony's grandparents were still alive, they would arrive early in the morning and stay until Grandma May got an inevitable headache and Grandpa Jack would get angry with her, and then they'd storm off all flustered and upset. In the end, it turned out May had a terminal tumour so huge the doctor's assumed she had it a decade before it eventually killed her. Jack passed soon after from lung cancer, though Belinda suspected his death was due more to guilt.

Belinda brushed a hand over her stomach and sent out a little wish to the universe that this baby didn't get a throwback to those genes. She hoped this baby would only inherit some looks and intelligence from Anthony and then siphon the rest from her.

The living room was congested with familiar faces when Anthony took her hand and led her inside. They found Claire sitting on the single lounge chair at the head of the circle of various couches and seats set up around the expansive room.

Bunches of perfumed flowers were arranged on shelves and side-tables, including the measly bunch Belinda had sent. She had barely a cent for frivolities but wouldn't dare skip sending flowers for today. An enormous colourful bunch that would have cost at least two hundred and fifty dollars overshadowed all the floral arrangements in the room—obviously from Matt and Nikki.

Claire's face crumpled as she heaved herself up from the lounge chair in a painfully slow manner as though she were a fragile piece of glass.

Belinda leaned in and kissed her cheek. "Hi, Claire. My deepest sympathies. How are you holding up?"

Claire held Belinda's shoulders and frowned. "I'm doing as well as could be expected."

"Of course."

Anthony kissed his Mum on both cheeks and wrapped his arms around her. "Hi, Mum."

"Hi, darl. Thanks for coming over. I know you have a lot on your plate."

"I wouldn't miss it."

Belinda looked around for a place where she could settle in, but Anthony's aunties rushed to her before she could find a seat.

"Congratulations, Belinda and Anthony," said Auntie Maggie. "What incredible news. When's the little one due? Take a seat, Belinda, put your feet up. You won't have much longer before you'll be unable to do that, so make the most of it. What can I get you? A cup of tea?"

A well of pride had Belinda's skin flushing. How long she had waited for all this fussing. "I'd love a cup of tea. Thank you so much. I've been so tired today."

"The hormones will do that. But by about four months you should start to feel a bit better," said Auntie Sue.

Belinda rubbed her stomach, even though she wasn't showing one bit yet, nor could she feel the baby. "I sure hope so."

"I had morning sickness and fatigue so bad with all three of my children," Auntie Maggie said. "Right up until the day I delivered them. Horrendous. Such difficult pregnancies."

Belinda strained a smile. “Thankfully, I don’t have it that bad. A little nausea in the mornings, but it soon eases up during the day.”

Vaughn was seated on the opposite couch next to Paige. She could sense his attention and turned to find him watching. “Hi, Vaughn, Paige, how are you both?”

Paige smiled, nodded, though there was something tense about it. Darkened circles discoloured the skin under her eyes.

Belinda glanced around for Evie. “No Evie today?”

Paige passed a look with Vaughn, then shook her head. “She is with her—" she cleared her throat “—father.”

“What? When did this happen?”

“He, ah, stopped in last fortnight, wanting to be a part of Evie’s life. We are looking at a custody arrangement at the moment. Evie is spending the day and night with him to see how she goes being away from me.”

“That must be rough.”

Paige sat up rigidly as tears made her eyes shine. “You could say that.”

Vaughn squeezed her thigh. “Evie will be fine.”

Paige nodded. “Sure she will.”

Belinda’s baby wasn’t born yet, but no man was going to dictate what she did with her own child. She glanced at Vaughn again. His focus flickered from her face, down to her stomach before he looked away.

This baby wasn’t his. And even if it was, he would never know. He would have nothing do with this child. She still bristled at his suggestion she abort it. She’d abort him first.

Belinda leaned in closer to Anthony and rested her head on his shoulder. She noted Nikki and Matt sitting together near Claire. Their boys weren’t here either. Not that she could blame them—teenagers wouldn’t want to be trapped in this stuffy house all day long talking to people about a man they never knew.

Auntie Maggie came back with Belinda's cup of tea. Just in time for Claire to stand and deliver her annual speech about how difficult this day was and how much she wished Robert was still with them.

Tears welled and Claire's voice trembled as she rambled for the next half-hour. She directed everyone's attention to the television screen on the wall at the top end of the living room and pressed play on the old reel of home movies and photographs that she had made into a digital film.

Belinda had seen this film ten times. The first time was lovely—a wonderful glimpse into Anthony's past. She adored seeing him running around as a little boy with his brothers. She loved his big toothy grin and boyish body. But the film went for two and a half hours and after ten years that equated to twenty-three hours of her life she would never get back.

By halfway through this screening, she was barely capable of keeping her eyes open. She swore to herself that next year she was definitely going to stay at home. She would have a newborn—a more than adequate excuse to not attend.

By three-quarters through, she had excused herself to use the bathroom twice, made another cup of tea and had to actively work at keeping her eyelids from closing, lest she fall asleep and have Claire shame her forever.

When the screen finally went black, most of the guests were drunk from drowning their tedium for an insufferable few hours. Just for something to do, they all clambered to assist the caterers when they arrived to lay out platters of food.

As they gorged on cucumber and egg sandwiches, slices of brownie, tea cake and mini quiches, they exchanged stories about Robert. Stories they had all heard before, yet you'd never know it from the efforts taken by everyone here to make it feel as though it was the first time.

When Auntie Sue launched into the anecdote about when she was first introduced to Robert and found it difficult to form sentences because of his rugged good looks, Belinda had to excuse herself before she died of boredom.

In the kitchen, Auntie Maggie was bent over the sink, scrubbing plates, cups and cutlery. She glanced over her shoulder as Belinda strode in. "Hi."

"I needed to stretch my legs."

"That's a polite way of saying it. I'm going to come right out with it—these dishes are more enjoyable than hearing, yet again, how Robert delightfully screwed up his speech at his and Claire's wedding."

Belinda chuckled. From the lisping, it was obvious Maggie was tipsy. She had always liked Maggie because she said exactly what was on her mind. Auntie Sue wasn't quite so open, a little more under Claire's thrall.

"I bet my angel sister won't mention that Robert was married already when they met. Nor how they had to wait a year until the divorce papers went through before they could tie the knot. Worked out well, though, what with her being pregnant with Matt and all."

Belinda's eyes widened. Little sparks of curiosity ignited beneath her skin. "No, she has not mentioned that." And if Anthony knew this, surely he would have told her.

"What I find most difficult is hearing her speak about him as though she worshipped the ground he walked on."

Belinda tried to erase the inquisitiveness from her voice before she betrayed how much she ached for this dirt on her mother-in-law. "And, she didn't?"

Maggie shook her head, lifted a cleaned dish from the soapy water and placed it in the dish rack. "He worshipped her. No doubt about that. But I know she didn't love him. She told me as much herself. She had her heart set on another guy, a schoolfriend, but it didn't work out for some such reason."

"And she told you that?"

"Countless times. Every time she had a little too much to drink. It makes me want to scream at her when I hear her go on and on about Robert like this, but I wouldn't dare do it to my nephews. They did love their father. I'll never forgive Claire for not giving those boys a chance to say goodbye to him."

Belinda's heart was racing. She searched through her memories to find a connection to something Anthony may have said about this, but she found nothing. "Anthony hasn't mentioned that."

"He was probably too young to remember the finer details. But I remember. I remember everything."

Footsteps and chatter echoed along the floor. Belinda spun to find Nikki and Paige walking towards them, talking animatedly to each other.

The echoes of what Maggie had admitted hung like dense dark clouds in the room.

Paige was smiling when they strode into the kitchen—a beautiful, genuine smile. Now that Belinda's envy had subsided, she could admit that she liked this new addition to their family. Paige was a great mother and was kind and welcoming. Belinda found it almost laughable that she was once even remotely jealous of her. Not now that she had everything she had ever wanted nestled safely in her womb.

"Hey," Nikki said, then lowered her voice to a whisper. "Come for a break too, have you?"

Belinda nodded. "I'm counting down the minutes until I can go home."

Nikki pointed to Belinda's stomach. "At least you have an excuse. You can feign exhaustion. No one, not even Claire, can be upset about a newly pregnant woman being tired. Surely."

Belinda winked. "I like your thinking. I'll give it another hour or two, then I think we might head off. If I have to hear one more story about Robert fishing with his sons, I'll scream."

Paige's lips were parted, her eyes narrowed as she looked from Belinda to Nikki.

Belinda gripped Paige's forearm and leaned in closer. "You'll soon understand. Give it another few years yet."

Nikki chuckled as Belinda strode away to join the others.

At dusk, Belinda didn't need to feign exhaustion because she was weary deep down to her bones. It had to be the lack of oxygen in this stuffy house. If only Claire would open a bloody window.

"You okay?" Anthony asked when she sighed and shifted uncomfortably on the chair for the hundredth time.

"I'm really uncomfortable, and I'm tired."

"I think I should get you home to bed."

She nodded. "I think so too."

Anthony put his drink down. He wobbled a little from side to side as he went to his mother. Belinda eavesdropped from across the room on his explanation for leaving. Claire looked past Anthony's shoulder to her. If looks could kill. She turned away, but Claire was on her feet, making her way over, champagne in hand.

"Getting tired, are you?" Her words were polite, but there was almost imperceptible restrained temper beneath each one.

"Yes, and uncomfortable. I've had a bit of a sore back."

Claire's lips curled upwards, all teeth and gums, but her eyes didn't wrinkle or brighten. "Yes, I remember all that. Best to prepare yourself now because it's not going to get any easier."

"Exactly why I want to make this as easy for Bel as possible," Anthony said. "Right from the beginning."

Belinda smiled at her husband, grateful he was supporting her. He must be as eager to leave as she was.

"Well, thanks for stopping in. I really appreciate family on a day like today, even if you aren't able to stay for very long."

Anthony frowned. "You've got Auntie Sue and Maggie to spend the night here with you."

Claire smiled. "Yes. My gorgeous sisters. I really don't know what I'd do without them. Their support means so much to me. I wouldn't have gotten out of bed after Robert died if not for them."

A cringe worked up Belinda's spine. Life was on a repetitive reel, every year the same when it came to Claire.

"Well, best get your wife home," Claire said, giving Anthony a kiss and a cuddle.

Belinda kissed Claire's cheek. "See you later, Claire. I'll give you a call during the week to see how you're going."

Once home, Belinda headed upstairs for a long, warm bath, but she didn't linger too long in her solitude. In her resentment for Claire, it was easy to forget that the memorial dinner was difficult for Anthony, and he had been particularly quiet on the drive home.

After changing into comfy clothes, she searched the house for her husband. She found him in the spare room, sitting on the bed with a chest of photos and small possessions once belonging to his father.

"Everything okay?" she asked from the doorway.

He looked up at her and managed a tight smile. "Yeah, I'm okay."

She took a seat beside him on the bed.

"I think with this baby on the way, I'm starting to see how fickle life is." He frowned and his eyes held such sadness. "Dad will never get to meet his grandbaby."

Belinda rubbed his thigh. "I'm sad about that too."

They flicked through the photos, mostly of Robert and Anthony—at the beach, fishing, on his dad's lap while watching TV.

"He looked like he was a great father," she said.

Anthony sighed. “That’s the thing, Bel, I can hardly remember him. I was ten when he died. I can recall little bits and pieces, but most of my memories are these,” he said, pointing to the ageing memorabilia. “I would hate to know that my child could forget me.” Tears glossed his eyes.

Belinda attempted to swallow down the lump of sympathy sitting in her throat. “You’re alive and healthy. We’ve got a long life ahead of us. Our little family.”

“Not guaranteed,” he whispered.

“No, but I have a hunch, it’s all going to be fine. We’ll make new memories together. The three of us.”

He exhaled a long breath and gave her a watery smile. “I think I drank a little too much there today.”

Belinda laughed. “I think everyone did. And seeing as I was the only sober one, I’m a pretty good authority on that matter.”

Anthony reached for his father’s old notebook. It had work notes—descriptions of materials and little calculations. Some construction drawings too. The pages were yellow and burnished around the edges. It smelled like time and dust.

Anthony fanned through the pages, looking at all the inscriptions inside. He flipped to a page near the back and a card fell out onto the bed. Anthony picked it up. “Dad’s blood donor card. I’ve not seen this before.”

“Well, there you go. Something new for you. Maybe it’s a sign from him to say that your blood is his blood. And that’s his way of always being a part of you.”

Anthony smiled at her. “I like that.”

She shrugged.

He looked again at the card and the smile fell from his face. “AB positive”

“What’s that?”

“Dad’s blood type.”

“They have that on there?”

Anthony nodded, his forehead lining with deep grooves. "It doesn't make sense, though." He turned the card over, then back to the front.

"What doesn't?"

"Mum always said that Dad was O negative like Vaughn."

"And he's not?"

He shook his head and handed her the card. "It says right here that he was AB positive"

She checked the card. It did indeed say AB positive. "What does that mean?"

Anthony stood up quickly from the bed. He paced across the room, fingers raking through his hair. His breathing was heavy.

He stopped mid-stride, turned to face her. "You know, I've always suspected this. Deep in my guts. Like intuition. But I convinced myself I was being ridiculous." He shook his head, sighed. "I don't know. Maybe I didn't want to believe it. But I kind of always suspected that one day I'd find something to prove my suspicions right. It's funny almost…" But his tone was anything but humorous.

"What is?"

"How we try to explain away things that we've seen or known, so we don't have to face reality. Because sometimes reality isn't what we want it to be."

Belinda rubbed the back of her neck. "Honey, I'm not really following."

"When I was a kid before Dad died, I saw Mum with another man."

Belinda gasped. "No."

He nodded emphatically. "My parents had barbeques at home all the time. One night, I saw Mum sneak into a bedroom with our next-door neighbour. I thought it was a game, so I went in there to see what they were up to. She was kissing him. I was too young to understand what it all meant."

"You think your mum had an affair?"

He hesitated for a long moment. "Yes," he said, eventually. "And I don't think Vaughn is Dad's son."

"Jesus Christ." Her head was dizzy. "Maybe the blood type recorded on that card is a mistake. Maybe the technology wasn't so precise back then."

"That would be a massive cock-up to make, especially when patients' lives are at stake."

She squeezed her eyes shut as her veins scorched with fear. She wasn't scared by the revelation itself but what it meant for her if this baby was Vaughn's.

But that was not going to happen. This baby was Anthony's. End of story. Fate wasn't so cruel as to destroy this one chance at happiness. No way.

She swallowed hard. "Your mum is not as innocent as she makes herself out to be."

Anthony's expression twisted with anger. "She has lied to my father and to me and my brothers all this time."

"It would cause too much heartbreak to reveal the truth now, though."

He shook his head. "I wouldn't dare say anything. I would never hurt Vaughn like that. Regardless, he's my brother. This doesn't change anything." He dragged in a deep breath and blew it out. "But it does make me see Mum in a much different way. How could she do that to Dad?"

Belinda shrugged, lowered her gaze to her lap where she brushed away an imaginary bit of fluff. "I don't know."

"How can I look her in the eye again, knowing what she did?"

"You're going to have to because she's your mother. People do things for different reasons. That's life. But she's still your mum."

He sighed, threw the card back onto the bed. "I really did not need to learn this on today of all days."

Chapter 39

Claire

The past…

Men were the simplest of creatures. If not for their ability to beat a woman's skull in, they would not have reigned at all, let alone for so long.

Claire pitied the poor sorry women of the world who hadn't realised the truth yet—men were but puppy dogs, their little floppy cocks sniffing out the next best vulva. It was pitiful. Laughable.

Truly, if she was obsessed with anything, anything at all, as much as some men were with women, she would hang herself. It was dangerous to be so devoted to one cause. It left men vulnerable, too open to manipulation.

Mrs Randall's sandwiches had been a godsend. With food in Claire's stomach each day, her body was nutritionally supported enough to go through puberty. At fifteen, years after all of her girlfriends, her gangly body finally softened and womanised.

The very moment her cup size went from a B to a D, boys started to learn her name. They hovered like crows at a bin on garbage collection day. And from this new, unsolicited attention, she learned about boys—how blinkered they were, but, mostly, how easy they were to manage.

The first lesson happened by accident. An older boy from school, John, asked her to the pictures to watch *Dr Zhivago*. Mum had said John would pay for the evening, not to worry about her empty pockets. But Claire couldn't understand why that would be. They weren't married. They barely spoke to one another. And yet, at the picture theatre, John had handed over money for two tickets and bought her popcorn, a drink and a packet of Jaffas.

All she had done in return was enjoy the movie then let him stick his tongue in her mouth and clumsily fiddle with her breasts in the car when he dropped her home.

Then came Tom, a short and round boy who sweated a lot, but who wore lots of nice smelling deodorants. She got to watch *A Clockwork Orange* at the drive-in with ice-cream and lollies to fill her eternally empty stomach. Her payment was to pull his penis like she would a teat of a cow until a warm sticky fluid projected out from the tip all over her hand and his T-shirt.

Despite her hesitation and the icky feeling in her belly when he pushed her hand into his pants and made her hold the warm, stiff member, it wasn't so terrible, except her arm muscles did get a little tired.

As she got older, her expectations grew. Why give it all away on the first night, when you could go to the town show or the pictures or out for milkshakes multiple times. The longer she drew the foreplay out, the higher the cost for her, which was only fair.

She discovered very soon that some men would do everything within his power if it meant he could stick his penis inside of her. She would laugh when she would climb into her bed later at how incredibly pathetic those boys were. It was like her vagina, this strange, hidden body part she had given very little thought about over the years, was sacred—something to be revered, coveted.

After high school, boys morphed into men. Working men who were able to buy her jewellery, expensive dinners, and take her on extravagant drives to the city where they would pander to her whims.

She had developed a repertoire of sorts—a high-pitched, sweet voice that often bordered on baby talk, along with the right combination of suggestion and restraint.

She would casually allow them to glimpse her breasts as she leaned forward, pretending all the while she had no idea he was ogling her. Or she would casually brush the back of her hand against his penis and all the while pretend no such thing had even happened.

Claire played innocent but hinted that once they were alone, something much more seductive and wilder lurked beneath. They needed to know that their efforts were never wasted on her.

Other women detested her and despised her reputation. But she didn't care what they thought; they were jealous, nasty women who wished they had every man in town wrapped around their little fingers. And it was this reputation that spread, letting potential conquests know that even if it did take a little wooing, she always gave them what they so desperately needed. This exchange meant she got what she had been deprived of for so long—good meals, entertainment and fun.

Every man wanted sex, but older men especially wanted oral sex and liked to use vulgar terms to describe his penis while she drew it into her mouth. Younger men were fumbling and fast.

Married men were a delightful game she loved to play. She relished their pathetic initial attempts at self-control, stumbling and stuttering that they had a wife and children at home. But that only made her try harder, say the delicious words that made every single one of them soon forget that any other woman but Claire existed in the world.

Nothing surpassed the thrill of knowing that she was going to give this man *everything* he had ever wanted, and he would, from that day on, resent his wife for not being the seductive woman he experienced the best night of his life with. Those were the best thoughts. Of being victorious. Sexier. Better. Those were what made her giddy with pleasure.

Eventually, when Claire turned twenty-six, she couldn't count on all her fingers, toes and teeth, the number of lovers she had been with. By then, she knew men, how they ticked, what they liked, what made them defensive, angry, and, most importantly, what they wanted in bed. Not the toned down, boring, mummy-and-daddy sex, but the raw, dirty, gritty fantasies that occupied the dark recesses of a man's mind. Every. Single. One of them.

But she had had her fun. She wanted bigger and better. Now was the time to find a husband. Someone who was the opposite of her loser father. Someone hardworking and stable, who could buy her a beautiful home, dress her in sophisticated clothing and never let her feel hungry again.

She wanted to move to an expensive suburb. Have children. Connect with the other residents. Maybe do some volunteer work. Go on holidays by the beach.

Robert was forty-three when they met. She was working at the Brisbane airport in a retail shop that sold newspapers, books and stationery. He travelled regularly for work and always came to her store. The only minor issue was that he wore a thick gold wedding band.

What started with a smile soon turned into polite conversation. After a month or so, she added a flirtatious edge to her enquires and compliments. "A new haircut. Very handsome." He came in more and more often, his smile a little broader, his replies a little more daring.

Then one afternoon, she hinted her shift was finishing soon. She rolled her neck. "What I wouldn't give for a strong cup of tea."

"I've got an hour before my flight leaves, come join me for a drink."

She met his gaze and offered an expression that said so much more than yes. "Sure, I'd love to."

They sat down for a warm drink each time their schedules allowed it. Soon, he was driving to the airport to see her especially.

Their first kiss was in the misty summer rain as they chatted beside his parked car outside the domestic terminal. He was as good as hers once she pressed herself against him, her thigh sliding to put pressure on his growing member and kissed him with enough tongue to leave him hard as steel and panting for more.

He came to see her three more times that week, despite there being no business trips in his schedule. He was a project manager for a major mining company. Married, but with no children. The way he felt about Claire, he had never felt about anyone else—ravenous, like a fifteen-year-old boy, he had said.

He came to her house next. They spent the evening making love in all the ways she knew his wife wouldn't allow. For Claire to win; she had to be more—younger, sexier, more pleasurable.

Three months was all it took to steal Robert away. The afternoon Claire announced that she was pregnant, he moved in with her. Two weeks later, they were engaged.

Claire would never forgive Robert's ex-wife for her intrusion and interference in those early days. Coming by their house at all hours of the day and night, crying and begging like a deranged lunatic for Robert to come home.

Marge was her name. An unsophisticated name. She had no respect that Claire was pregnant or that she needed a stress-free environment for this baby.

Robert would try his hardest to make Marge see sense and explain that he had moved on, but he was always so sensitive and cautious of hurting her.

One evening when Robert arrived home from work, Marge was waiting out the front in her car. Something she often did. Claire pitied the poor soul, she truly did. Marge, all puffy-eyed and white-faced, crying and pleading, pounced on Robert the moment he started walking up the driveway.

Claire was ill with embarrassment as she watched through the window from inside the house. God knows what the neighbours thought of this pathetic display of irrational behaviour.

Robert was soft and placating as usual, and Claire wanted to explode with anger. She charged outside, right up to Marge and slapped her face as hard as she possibly could.

"How dare you. I'm pregnant. Who the hell do you think you are causing this type of stress on my family?" She slapped her again and again until Robert caught her hand. Big red welts streaked Marge's face. "Get off my property. You're embarrassing me."

Marge was stunned into silence as she held her hand against her cheek. Claire initially assumed her reaction was because she had been slapped quite powerfully, but it was because she had no idea Claire was pregnant.

Claire turned to Robert. "You didn't tell her?"

Robert shook his head, frowned.

Marge's shoulders bounced up and down as tears streamed from her eyes. Then she was sobbing and wailing about her inferior womb or some such nonsense. She even threatened to kill herself.

Claire hoped that she would, but it would be more trouble than what it's worth because Robert would become a boring, old, guilt-ridden sad-sack, and she didn't need that negativity going into their new life together.

Claire pressed a hand to her stomach and gripped Robert's arm. "Darling, I…I don't feel so good." She fluttered her eyelids, swayed on her feet.

Robert threw his arms around her, catching her as she almost fainted.

"I can't take much more of this. It can't be healthy for the baby to have this constant stress."

"She's lying," screamed Marge, eyes red and bulging.

Tears pricked Claire's eyes. "I'm sorry," she said to Robert. "I thought I could rise above all this. But if this baby dies…" she bellowed out a sob. "I couldn't live with myself. I just couldn't."

Robert turned to Marge. "Leave. Now! It's over. Do not come back or I will call the police next time."

"She's lying." A whimper.

"Go. Now!" he roared. With an arm around Claire's shoulder and a hand across her back, Robert helped her slowly back up to the house. She glanced over her shoulder and narrowed her eyes at Marge.

They never did see Marge again after that.

The baby arrived six months later—a gorgeous boy they called Mathew. Once Claire had her figure back, which took no more than six months, she married Robert in the most exquisite ceremony in front of friends and family.

Twelve months later, Robert moved them to a gorgeous little town on the Sunshine Coast Hinterland. A big sprawling property that backed onto a lake and forest. Their house was the biggest on their street.

When Claire fell pregnant with her second child, Robert chose to travel out of the country much less, preferring to be home with his growing family. And Claire remained a devoted wife…mostly.

Really, her infidelity was her friends' fault. They needed a shake-up in their marriages. Claire was sick of hearing how they often turned down their husband's advances. She watched them with disgust as they grew plump around their bellies and dressed like dowdy old women.

Honestly, it was no wonder their husbands all came charging willingly at the first suggestion they follow Claire to the spare room during a family barbeque for a quick and dirty bit of fun. And Claire got to sit beside his wife afterwards over dinner knowing that she had their husband panting and clawing at her mere minutes before.

One night at the horse races, when she was especially daring, she led two of Robert's employees to the carpark and knelt in the shadows beside a car. One thrust into her mouth while the other mounted her like a dog from behind.

When she stumbled back to the marquee and sat again with the oblivious party of people, she loved the feeling of warm semen leaking into her knickers, wetting her thighs and the strong taste of it in her mouth.

The tingly, clenching feeling of superiority was addictive. So, when she had another opportunity, she found her next target, said all the right things until they were conspiring to meet in the carpark, and he was inside her, oblivious that another man's seed had filled her a mere hour before. It was heady. Delicious.

It all proved what Claire had known from the beginning—she was better, she was wanted. No harm done.

Robert was none the wiser. Right up until the day he died, he had no idea that their third son wasn't even his.

Chapter 40

Paige

"I feel sorry for her," Paige said to Vaughn on Monday morning as he was wrapping a tie around his neck and tucking it under his crisp white collar.

"Why?"

"The way Belinda and Nikki were talking at the memorial lunch. They had no sympathy whatsoever.'

Vaughn smiled. "To be fair, it's as boring as sin."

"But he's your father. He was Claire's husband. Your mother is obviously still very hurt by his passing."

"Of course she is."

"Where's the respect?"

Vaughn shrugged. "I guess they've had longer to come to grips with it all. It's new to you."

"Well, I'm going to invite Claire for breakfast with Evie and me this morning. Maybe we'll go to the park afterwards too."

Vaughn kissed her lips. "That sounds like a wonderful idea. I'm sure Mum will love you asking her along."

"Good. And I think Evie needs to know Claire as a grandmother figure. Particularly if we are going to have children in our future."

Vaughn smiled. "That makes a lot of sense."

"Do Belinda and Nikki ever do anything with your mother?"

Vaughn looked to the side in thought. "Not anymore."

"Don't you find that weird? They're family."

"You do what feels right for you, let Belinda and Nikki handle themselves."

"I can't handle their lack of empathy."

Vaughn studied her face. "It upset you, didn't it?"

Paige nodded as a decade-old lump burnt up her throat. "I miss my mum so damn much, it hurts every single day. I would hate if anyone reduced my grief to something to be mocked. My mother deserves more than that and so does your dad."

He kissed her lips. "You're gorgeous, have I ever told you that? The kindest, most beautiful heart."

She sighed. "I know the pain of losing a loved one."

He wrapped his arms around her waist, and she rested her head against his chest. "I know. Me too, sweetheart." His soothing voice and big frame mollified her. She had never known that a man could do that.

How long she had needed Vaughn in her life. Now that she had him, she never wanted to let him go. With him, she had everything she had ever desired—a big extended family, a father figure for Evie, financial stability, and a future they could look forward to.

With Evie buckled into the backseat of the car, Paige pulled into Claire's driveway and drove up to the house. The house was tucked away a distance from the road. Borders of tall pines afforded privacy from the neighbours.

She left Evie in her seat with the air conditioner running while she jogged to the front door, too reluctant to use the car horn to announce her arrival this soon in her and Claire's relationship.

Claire answered the door in a knee-length skirt that showed off her flattering calves and gorgeous strappy sandals. She wore a flowy button-up T-shirt with cut-outs over the shoulders. Her hair was pulled into a high ponytail, the tail curled into a long blonde ringlet.

Claire pressed her hands to her knees and grinned. "Look at the darling sitting like a big girl in the back seat."

"She's so excited. We don't get out much for treats like this because I'm usually too busy during the week."

"Downtime is vital. Especially in this day and age."

Claire whipped her phone out of her oversized brown leather purse. "Let me take a photo. That smile on her face is adorable." She took a couple of photos then climbed into the car alongside Paige.

"So where are we headed?" Claire asked, her red lipstick accentuating her overly brightened white teeth.

"I thought we'd head to The Deck. They do great eggs Benedict there."

"Perfect."

They arrived a few minutes later. Tourists were packed into seats—always the same as the weather heated up. A chattering hum filled the air. A table was free on the back deck, so they rushed to it and took a seat.

"How did Evie go at her father's over the weekend?" Claire asked as she perused the menu.

"She really enjoyed herself. Joshua has lots of nieces and nephews and cousins' children who are all around Evie's age. They came over to meet her, and they had heaps of fun playing together."

"That might be exactly what she needs. I'm sure it's lovely to be home with her every day, but kids do get to an age where they need interaction with other children, so they can learn social skills."

Paige nodded. "I do take her to swimming classes and mothers' group days, so she can socialise, but it is different when it's blood relatives. The bond is stronger."

"As they say, blood is thicker than water."

"I still wish he wasn't involved," she said with a sigh. "But it's not as bad as I had imagined it would be." She had been petrified Evie would get hurt or scared or that Joshua would steal her away and never bring her home. But that wasn't the case. Their night together was uneventful, and Evie was in perfect health and happiness when Joshua drove her home yesterday.

"Joshua has changed. I can tell he isn't that same man he was when our relationship was ending. If he were the same, then I think we'd be having an entirely different conversation right now."

Claire's smile was tight. "It's always difficult when parents separate. That's why it's so important to have children with the right man. A responsible man. And make sure you get a ring on your finger first."

Paige laughed at Claire's naivety. "It's not always so easy to tell, unfortunately. But I did say to Vaughn that we won't be having children until he fully commits."

Claire's eyes raised from the menu. "So, you've been discussing children?"

Paige grinned as renewed excitement stormed through her veins. "He has said that he'd like to start a family."

"Wonderful." Claire lowered her focus and frowned. "I really hope Belinda and Anthony come through unscathed."

"Come through what?" Paige asked.

Claire waved her hand as if to say, 'It's no big deal'. "They're having marriage troubles. That's inevitable when finances aren't great. Anthony admitted that he was going to end their relationship." Her voice lowered to a whisper as she said, "But then he found out Belinda was pregnant, so he's trapped in the relationship now."

Paige gasped. "That's so sad. They seem so loving. It's hard to imagine they would be having troubles."

"Only the strongest make it in this day and age. The moment it gets tough, it's too easy to end the marriage. I tell you now, in my day, we didn't back down so quickly. We stuck through it, even the bad times. Robert was not perfect, but I certainly wouldn't have gotten divorced. And then there are all these women having babies before they're even married. They wonder why it all goes pear-shaped. Pregnancy traps never work in the long run."

Claire had to be speaking in generalities, not to Paige's own circumstances. "It's certainly a different time."

"In my day, I wouldn't have dared even open my legs to a man before the marriage certificate was signed, sealed and framed. I'm proud to say I was a virgin when I met Robert. No chance of so-called *accidental*," she said, using air quotations, "pregnancies."

"Yes, well, abstinence is the best protection." *As the old Puritans say.*

"And I've not been with a man since Robert. I've got all I need. My days are done with having my individualism eroded by relationships."

"Fair enough. Whatever makes you happy."

"Exactly."

The waiter arrived at their table. Paige ordered Evie a child's serving of pancakes, eggs Benedict for herself and Claire chose the Bircher muesli.

"I'm trying to watch my weight," Claire said when the waiter left. "It's very important we women look our best."

Paige shifted in her seat and didn't offer a reply, merely gave an awkward humouring smile. She detested weight-related conversation, especially as she wasn't petite.

"You'll have to be careful with Evie. It starts early."

Paige bit her tongue. She detested talk of weight around her daughter and particularly if it was directed at Evie.

Paige pulled on her earring. "It was a lovely day on Sunday. It's wonderful that all the family still gather so many years after Robert's passing to celebrate his life."

"It really is. They understand how difficult it is for me, so I appreciate their support when I'm most fragile."

Paige nodded sombrely. "It must help ease the burden. My Mum's anniversary is next month. For too many years it's been a burden I've shouldered alone—"

"Yes, both my parents have passed. It's the natural order of things."

"Sure, but it came too soon for me. Seventeen, in my final year of school, no other family—"

"It's never the right time to lose a parent."

Paige blinked, cleared her throat. Why would Claire not allow her to share her own experiences and afford her some empathy? "Your sisters were so lovely. Do they live close?"

"Sue lives in Brisbane. Maggie is in Port Douglas."

"Not too far away then."

"Far enough to have escaped helping care for my father before he passed. I handled the lion's share. Honestly, it was so bad, in the end, I was praying for him to die."

All the breath was stolen from Paige's lungs. She understood how hard it was to be the sole carer of a dying parent. She had, too, in those last horrendous days, wished for death to find her mother, but that was because Mum's physical pain was so great. She couldn't lie on the bed without the soft sheets scratching at her sensitive skin until she cried out in her morphine-induced sleep.

"It must have been a difficult time."

"It was terrible," Claire said. "Truly horrible. My life stopped. I couldn't go on holiday or move if I wanted to because Dad preferred me to be his carer. Never stopped Sue or Maggie taking their families on holidays. They'd head off for weeks at a time whenever they pleased. Never mind about me being stuck here looking after Dad. Sure, Sue and Maggie came to see Dad whenever it suited them or after I'd whined for long enough, but it would have been much easier if the load was shared equally."

"Your father lived with you?"

"For a little while, but it was just too hard. So, we sold his home and used the funds to put him in a nursing home. He needed that extra level of care."

"Yes, of course."

A gloominess descended over Paige as she recalled her own experiences. Mum's last wish was to die peacefully at home, but the pain was so great that Paige made the difficult decision to put her in palliative care in the local hospital.

Mum had only lasted three days once that decision was made. She swallowed the solid lump of guilt in her throat and sent out a prayer to Mum to please forgive her for not being strong enough to cope.

How long ago that felt now. How young Paige was. After shouldering her mother's slow demise, the days, weeks and months of debilitating grief afterwards, then raising a child on her own, she felt a hundred years old.

"Some people are born to bear the greatest burdens," Claire said. "Seems I'm one of them."

Paige nodded and frowned with sympathy, but it was superficial. The empathy she held for Claire was waning. Her perspective of Belinda and Nikki's attitudes on Sunday took a sharp shift. If they had been dealing with this obvious martyr for years, it's no wonder their sympathy was depleted.

"I've enrolled Evie in school. She'll be going to the local pre-school here in Montville."

"And how will that work with your custody arrangement? Will she attend another school for a number of days per week closer to Joshua?"

Paige blanched. She hadn't thought about that. Her fifty-fifty arrangement with Joshua worked well while Evie wasn't in school, but what would happen next year?

"I'll have to raise this with Joshua."

"Seems you will. He might ask that you move closer to him."

"I could ask that he move closer to me..." She stopped herself as her anger flared. Was this what Claire wanted? To provoke her?

Of course not.

She breathed in deeply. *Calm down.* She was reading too much into it. It wasn't Claire's fault this was a sensitive issue for Paige.

She fought to find something neutral to speak about. Thankfully, the waiter interrupted them with their meals. Evie's was placed in front of her and received big smiles. Paige's eggs Benedict looked and smelled delicious.

When the waiter strode away, Claire said, "This looks pathetic. Two spoonfuls of muesli. I would have been better off making it myself at home. These pretentious cafés want people to starve and charge a fortune for the privilege."

Paige's cheeks flushed. "Maybe you can ask for some more?"

"I would be mortified." She pushed the bowl away. "I don't even want to eat this now. I'm disgusted."

"Would you like half of mine? There's plenty here."

"No, I wouldn't dare take food out of your mouth. You eat it. I'll just drink my coffee."

Paige cringed as Claire crossed her arms and watched her and Evie eat their meals. She was ill with responsibility that Claire was going hungry. When they had finished, she offered to pay for Claire's meal too.

"Don't be silly. I wouldn't dare ask you to pay for me."

Up at the counter, Claire let loose a loud tirade of disappointment at the small teenage boy, who was, Paige soon found out, working his first shift. Claire stormed outside, leaving Paige by herself as she paid for her own meals.

She frowned at the boy whose hands were now shaking as he took her card. "I am so incredibly sorry about that. Please don't take it personally. That woman is what you would call a sour-faced bitch."

The boy's lips tugged up at the corners when she said that.

"Who a bitch?" Evie called out.

"No one, darling. You don't say words like that."

"Bitch," Evie yelled.

The boy smiled a little more.

"Try and enjoy the rest of your day. You're doing a wonderful job."

She met Claire on the sidewalk and begrudgingly said, "I was going to take Evie to the local park if you'd like to come with us."

Claire's eyes brightened at the suggestion, which made Paige turn back to the restaurant and wonder if she imagined the whole horrible morning.

"That sounds wonderful. I have nowhere else I need to be."

The park was located near the centre of town, across from the main carpark and bus stop. They strolled down the hill in the mid-morning sunlight. Paige held tightly to Evie's hand as she skipped beside her. Claire stood tall, her posture perfect, as she walked.

People bustled past them, mostly couples of all ages who were likely here on a romantic getaway. Cars cruised up and down the main street, passing gift shops and eateries that lined either side of the road.

Paige let go of Evie's hand as they made it to the grassed park, bordered by trees. Branches extended long and proud over the play area providing a reprieve from the summer sun.

"We should have grabbed a takeaway coffee," Paige said as she strode across the thick grass towards Evie who was climbing up a ladder to slip down a short slide.

"I'll run across the road and grab one," Claire suggested.

'You don't mind?"

"Not one bit."

Claire headed off and was back five minutes later with two lattes in takeaway cups. The conversation was easy going as they watched Evie play on the playground equipment. Other parents arrived with their children who climbed and ran around with Evie. The park was soon filled with delightful childish chuckles and voices. Maybe the space and sunshine catapulted Claire out of whatever mood she had slipped into at the restaurant.

Paige got to talking with another mother, which allowed Claire some time to spend with Evie—pushing her on the swings, helping her climb the ladders and navigate the wobbly bridges.

Paige's head snapped around when Evie's scream echoed across the park followed by her yelling out for her. Claire led Evie out from behind the slide. Evie was crying, tears rolling down her cheeks, as they made their way over.

"She hurt her arm," Claire said. "Nothing too bad."

An inevitable mishap, which was prone to happen with small children at parks. Paige held her arms out. "Come here, darling. Where did you hurt it?"

Evie pointed to her upper right arm.

"Here, let me kiss it better." She kissed Evie's arm, up and down with quick comical kisses until her tears ceased. "She sounds like she might be a little tired," Paige said to Claire.

"I not tired," Evie barked and weaselled her way out of Paige's grip.

"Oh, you aren't tired yet?" she asked with a knowing giggle.

Evie shook her head and ran towards the playground again. Worked every time. The sore arm was soon forgotten.

Claire took a seat beside Paige, and they watched Evie play for a little longer before Paige decided time was up. She had work to do back at home. With luck, Evie would have a daytime nap giving Paige some solid uninterrupted time to sew.

With as much resistance, screeching and tears as possible, Paige eventually convinced Evie to leave the playground and head back to the car.

Paige's cheeks were flushed, and she was sweaty and exasperated by the time she buckled a too-rigid-to-bend-at-the-waist Evie into her car seat. She almost caught Evie's inner-thigh in the buckle, she was so flustered.

Of all the days Evie chose to chuck a tantrum, it was in front of Claire. Claire didn't say anything about it, but she rushed from the car and waved goodbye on the run when Paige dropped her off out the front of her house.

Of course, Evie fell asleep in the car on the way home, which put Paige's chances at slim of her daughter having a daytime nap at home. Paige tried her hardest to carefully unbuckle the seatbelt and gently carry Evie into her bed. She managed to lay her down without her waking.

Paige crept out to her sewing room and got to work, knowing too well that this small block of sleep was fragile and may only last a few minutes. A little over two hours went by before Evie woke. She was bright and alert when she ran into the sewing room and into Paige's arms. "Good afternoon my gorgeous girl. Did you have a good sleep?"

Evie nodded.

"Excellent. And Mummy got lots of work done. You want some lunch?" Her own stomach rumbled. "Because I certainly do."

She fixed them both some lunch, then Paige worked sporadically until Vaughn came through the door a little before six that evening.

"Hey, I thought I'd find you both in here," he said with a grin.

She stood, stretched her neck from side to side before rushing to him for a kiss. It was a foreign feeling to be watching the clock, waiting in anticipation for Vaughn to finish work for no other reason than because she wanted to spend time with him. "Hi. How was your day?"

"Hectic, which is great. Certainly not complaining about that. But, more importantly, how was yours? How did you go with Mum this morning?"

Paige smiled, shrugged. “Breakfast was strange. But our trip to the park was really nice.”

“Strange how?”

Paige wrinkled her nose. “I’m not entirely sure. She seemed combative. And then her meal wasn’t what she anticipated, so she didn’t end up eating. I felt guilty about choosing The Deck. But later, at the park, she seemed perfectly fine.”

“Mum can be pretty fussy when it comes to food. She likes to tell everyone that she eats everything, but it’s far from true.”

“I wish I knew that titbit earlier. I would have asked that she suggest a place.”

“Babe, honestly—” he rubbed her arms “—you don’t have to try so hard. Just be yourself. Relationships are about give and take. It’s the same with Mum. She may not have liked the café this morning, but there will be future chances.”

Paige sighed. “Very true.”

“At the end of the day, all that really matters is how you and I feel about each other. That has nothing to do with Mum, okay?”

Paige nodded. “Yep.”

After dinner, Paige urged Evie into the bathroom. She ran the bathwater while she undressed her. Evie jumped up and down, leaning over the edge of the bath, eager to get in, so she could play with her toys.

When the water was at a nice level and safe temperature, Paige lifted her daughter up but placed her back down on the ground when she noticed the bruises on her upper arm.

“Oh, my gosh, Evie. Your arm. Is this the arm you hurt today?”

Evie looked at her arm and Paige could see it pained her to lift it. “Claire hurt it.”

“Claire hurt your arm?”

Evie nodded.

"How? How did she hurt it?"

Evie demonstrated on Paige's forearm by squeezing it as tightly as she could.

All the blood drained from Paige's face and burst hot into her stomach. "That's not very nice of Claire."

Evie shook her head. "It hurt lots."

She lifted Evie up with more care this time and lowered her into the bath. "There you go, darling, you just relax." She marched to the door. "Come take a look at this," she yelled to Vaughn, trying to keep the rising panic from her voice so as not to scare her daughter. "Show Vaughn your arm, Evie."

Evie held her arm up but winced as she lifted it.

"Bruises?" Vaughn asked.

Paige nodded. "She said your mother did it."

He shook his head. Two lines of tension sat between his brows. "Mum? Couldn't be. When?"

"At the park today, Claire was watching Evie. Evie started to cry and said her arm was sore. I didn't think it was so bad until I took her shirt off and saw these bruises."

"I'm pretty sure Mum wouldn't have done this. There has to be an explanation."

"She showed me how she did it." She re-enacted Evie's explanation, squeezing hard on Vaughn's arm. "Evie is too little to make something like this up."

"Maybe it was an accident. Like she nearly fell, and Mum had to grip her tightly. This isn't something I could see Mum doing. Especially not on purpose. It had to have been an accident. Surely you can't think—"

Paige sighed, closed her eyes as she squeezed the bridge of her nose. "I don't know what to think."

"Ask Mum. I'm sure there's an explanation."

Paige took a photo of Evie's arm and attached it to a message.

PAIGE: *Hi, Claire. I just went to bath Evie and found this bruising.*

CLAIRE: *The poor darl. That looks very sore.*

PAIGE: *How did it happen?*

CLAIRE: *She ran into the ladder of the slide.*

PAIGE: *Evie told me you squeezed her arm.*

CLAIRE: *Evie is obviously telling a tall tale.*

PAIGE: *It looks exactly like fingerprints.*

CLAIRE: *It does a bit, doesn't it? I'm sure she'll be fine in a few days. Just give her a little paracetamol.*

Paige growled and shoved the phone back in her pocket. "She won't admit it."

Vaughn frowned. "Maybe she has nothing to admit, Paige." He shook his head, turned and strode out of the bathroom.

Paige's legs were shaky. She sat on the edge of the bath and stroked Evie's back as she played with her toys.

Had she overreacted? Placed blame unfairly?

No, it was her right as a mother to understand how her daughter was hurt. The last thing she wanted was someone purposefully hurting Evie.

Chapter 41

Nikki

All weekend, the words *I hate your mother* had been pinned to the forefront of Nikki's thoughts. They had sat in her throat like glue, but she couldn't speak of them. Not when it was Matt's Dad's memorial weekend. It felt immoral, lacking.

The last thing she wanted was a repeat of what happened between Vaughn and Joanne. If her marriage was to survive this, she needed Matt on her side. And that required tact and precision.

When Matt left for work Monday morning, she drew her first full breath. She didn't have to bite her tongue while he wasn't at home. Nikki spent the day cleaning the house more thoroughly than she ever had in her life. She would never have predicted that she would become a stress cleaner. Maybe it was due in part to all this extra time on her hands now that she wasn't working.

When her boys got home from school that afternoon, even they commented on the pristine state of the place. She didn't have to ask them to put their backpacks, shoes and dirty socks away—seemed the shiny surfaces propelled them to maintain the gleam.

Ryan came running down the stairs with his new phone. Claire had bought both boys a mobile phone, along with a cheap call and data plan, and had given them to Matt to bring home for them after the memorial dinner. Nikki wanted to object because the boys already had mobile phones, but Claire had insisted it was a gift from their grandfather. It didn't seem right to reject such a gift on that day.

"Mum?" Ryan called out.

"In here." She was in the kitchen wiping above the fridge where it always gathered a greasy layer of dust.

"I've got this weird photo on my phone."

"What kind of photo?" she said pushing higher onto her tiptoes to reach to the back.

"Of some kid. I don't know where it came from."

"You've probably just forgotten taking it."

"He's got a chain over him."

Nikki lowered onto flat feet and turned to him, holding out her hand. "Let me have a look."

On the screen was a boy on a bed. He wore board shorts and a T-shirt. He faced away from the camera and appeared to be sleeping. Across his waist was a thick chain.

"What the hell?"

"Who is it?" Ryan asked.

Nikki shook her head. A hot tingly sensation was soaring through her veins. This picture was off. "And you have no idea where it came from?"

He shook his head.

"Can photos just randomly appear on your phone?"

He shrugged. "Maybe. If my phone was hacked it probably could."

"Bloody hell. It looks like this boy's been chained up."

"I know."

"Send it to Dad and ask him what he thinks."

Ryan quickly shot the picture off to Matt. Meanwhile, Nikki grabbed her phone from the bench and dialled his number.

"Did you get that picture?" she asked when he answered.

"Yeah, what is that?"

"That was on Ryan's phone."

"It's dated today," Ryan said loud enough for Matt to hear through the phone piece.

"He has no idea where it came from."

"It looks sick," Matt said. "Maybe you should take it down to the police station. Some boy could be being held captive somewhere."

"The police? Is that a bit drastic? We probably should do a little research first. Maybe it's a virus that's going around."

"Look into it. But if we can't find out where it's come from, I think we have an obligation to tell the police."

Nikki sighed. "Okay. Maybe you can do that when you get home."

"See what you can find out. I'll talk to you when I get there."

She said goodbye and hung up.

"Go check Flynn's phone. You are both on the same plan. Maybe it has something to do with that."

Ryan ran upstairs to check with his brother. Their footsteps pounded as they both ran down the stairs. "It's not on Flynn's phone," Ryan said. "Only mine. I don't understand."

"Give Grandma a call. See if the phone's been refurbished. The picture might have been left over from the previous owner."

Ryan dialled Claire and put her on speakerphone. "Hi, Grandma."

"Hi, darl. How are you? How was your day at school?"

"Good. Hey, Gran, I just want to know if my phone is refurbished?"

"Not that I'm aware of. Why's that?"

"I got a weird photo of a boy on it."

"What? Show me," she said, voice rising an octave.

He clicked with fast fingers well versed with technology and sent the photo.

A moment of silence, some rustling, then, “That’s disgusting.”

“I know. Mum thought that maybe it had something to do with the plan I’m on or maybe the phone was refurbished.”

“Well, you can tell your mother that if she thinks I have anything to do with this photo then I’m appalled.” Pure acid dripped from every syllable. Her tone was murderous. Each word pounded Nikki like a blunt hammer. Her pulse rampaged. Ryan looked at her with widened eyes.

“As if I would have something to do with a photo like this. I’ve never been more offended in my entire life.” And Claire hung up.

The three of them stood silently in the kitchen.

“Why did you make me ring her?” Ryan asked.

“I’m sorry, I should have called myself. I didn’t think she would react like that.”

Nikki spun and reached for her phone again and quickly dialled Claire’s number to explain, but the call went straight to message bank. She tried another three times, but she couldn’t get through.

She was shaking. Had she just inadvertently accused her mother-in-law of chaining a boy up?

She shook her head. Of course bloody not.

Anger rushed hot through her veins. Here she was again, thinking she was the one in the wrong. Not this time. No way. Her intentions were clean. Ryan had asked a simple question, so Nikki could understand where this photo had come from before she wasted a police officer’s time.

“Do you boys have homework?” Her tone was clipped. She winced, hating herself for directing her anger at her children.

“I do,” said Flynn.

“Good, go and start that. What about you, Ryan?”

He shook his head.

"Well, you take the rubbish out and wheel the bins up to the kerb."

He nodded and moped away.

She tried one more time to call Claire, but there was no answer.

Nikki, hands still shaking, returned to cleaning the fridge. Her movements were frenetic. When done, she started on the cupboards and handles, polishing them until they shone, and she was breathless.

When her phone rang, she jumped and clambered for it. It was Matt.

"What the bloody hell is going on?" he growled.

"Why? What do you mean?"

"Anthony called, followed closely by Auntie Sue. Supposedly you accused Mum of paedophilia?"

"For Christ's sake. Are you serious? Claire rang your brother and auntie about this?" Her anger was raging now. The injustice this woman inflicted upon Nikki was beyond her comprehension.

"What happened? You didn't accuse her of putting that picture on the phone, did you?"

"Of course I bloody well didn't. Who the hell do you take me for? I had Ryan ask her if the phone was refurbished in case the photo was left on there from the previous owner. She went off her head at him. Screamed like a banshee. Then she didn't answer my calls when I tried to call her to explain. But of course, I couldn't get through because she was too busy telling the whole damn town about it!"

She was breathless, vibrating. Too many times, she had had to deal with her words being twisted. How effortlessly Claire could take Nikki's reality and turn it into something so sordid. Nikki barely knew what was real and what wasn't anymore.

"How did you ask her exactly?"

Tears sprang to her eyes. Her own husband was doubting her now.

Had Ryan phrased his question in a way that accused Claire of paedophilia? She pressed her hand to her head, slid her palm down her face. *I'm going insane*. "Matt, I'm at my wit's end. I'm losing my mind here. Your mother is sick."

"Oh, please," he scoffed

"Take a look at what she does to us! What she has always done to us!"

"I'm not going to discuss this over the phone. I'll talk to you when I get home."

Nikki ended the call and stood there, hands on hips, trying to catch her breath. Tears rolled onto her cheeks. She was sick and tired of this.

If Claire wasn't in their life, everything would be ordinary. How much Nikki craved ordinary. She was fed up with the in-fighting. The twisted conversations. The blabbering to the family about everything Nikki did or didn't do.

Needing an escape, if only for fifteen minutes, she climbed the stairs to the bathroom. Each limb was a dead weight. Dealing with this for fifteen years was taking its toll. She was done. Joanne was right; there was no escape.

Once the bath was filled, she undressed and climbed in, her aching muscles hugged by the water's warmth. Tears rushed down her cheeks as she sobbed into the echoing silence.

She slowly immersed her ears, cheeks, nose, under the water and squeezed her eyes shut. No noise, only a consuming warmth and darkness. How much she wanted to stay here.

She held her breath, letting the warmth fill every crack and fissure. Little bubbles popped and fizzed as air trickled from her nose.

Her lungs were burning, but she ignored the sensation. When her diaphragm contracted, a painful cramping, she stayed. Another contraction, harder, longer. Again. Again. She stayed. Again.

She yearned for the escape of remaining under that surface forever, not breathing ever again.

She burst from the water, gasping for breath, and sat upright, both hands clawing the side of the bath. A full bodily shudder wracked her. Her limbs trembled; her lips. She heaved in each breath. Her eyes were wide as she stared at the tiled wall.

Water from her hair, sluiced down her skin, *drip, drip,* dripping into the bathwater. She pressed her palms against her eyes, shook her head. So close. So close to sinking into oblivion as though that was her only escape from Claire.

How tilted that thought was. How disconnected from reality. She drew her hands from her eyes and cocked her head to the side as she began seeing things from a new perspective.

Images flashed like bright lights behind her eyes of launching at Claire, wrapping her fingers tightly around her neck, her thumb on her throat, and squeezing as hard as she could. Her muscles tightened, her breathing hardened as she choked her mother-in-law…

Nikki shook her head. Blinked.

What the hell is wrong with me?

She stayed there until the water grew too cool to bear, then slowly dried herself off using the edge of the bath for support and dressed into her pyjamas. She stood at the closed door, her forehead leaning against the cool timber while she gathered her wits. Then, when she couldn't stay locked away in the bathroom for any longer, she strode downstairs to face her husband.

Matt was home and talking with the boys in the living room, one on either side of him. All three heads turned to look at her when she entered the room. Her eyes would be red raw from crying and her wet hair hanging limply around her face.

Ryan held the phone up, showing the picture of the boy. “Turns out I took a screenshot of a YouTube video. It’s not a bad picture after all.” His voice was small and apologetic, and she wanted to tell him that it was okay, that none of this was his fault, but she hadn’t the energy.

She focused on Matt. “You need to do something about your mother.” The words were monotone, apathetic. Her shoulders were hunched.

“Boys, head on up to your rooms for a moment while your mother and I talk.”

The boys, without any whining, scampered away. Matt had that way with them—an assertiveness they didn’t question.

“What do you expect me to do about her?”

She shook her head. “I don’t know. I don’t care. But it’s her or me. And I mean that.”

“She’s my mother.”

She slapped a hand to her chest and pulled at her pyjama top. “And I’m your wife.” Emotion sat heavy beneath that fact. “It’s your choice.”

Matt sighed and reached for his mobile. He dialled a number and waited.

“Hi, Mum,” he said. “Yes, don’t worry, I’ve been informed about what happened. And if you believe Nikki accused you of paedophilia then maybe it’s time you go and seek some professional help. No, Mum, you listen to me. You’re not to come near Nikki. You are not to call her. You are not to visit here. Every conversation, message, or piece of gossip goes through me. You can be disgusted all you like, but this is how it must be. And stop telling the family about our private matters. I’ve already had a phone call from Auntie Sue and Anthony today. I’m a grown adult, not a sick little boy who needs his mother taletelling about everything that happens. Fine. I will. Bye.”

Matt hung up. Anger blazed in his gaze until his eyes met Nikki's and they softened with something akin to sympathy. Only then did she realise his anger hadn't been directed at her. He was as frustrated with his mother as she was.

Relief spread along her arms and tingled down her neck. "Thank you," she whispered. "You don't know how much that means to me."

She stared at her husband for a long moment as he held out his arms and beckoned she come sit with him. She did, curling up beside him and resting her head on his chest. He stroked her hair but didn't speak.

"Thank you," she said again.

Unlike poor Joanne, perhaps Nikki's husband had her back after all.

Chapter 42

Anthony

Anthony finished work a little before six and raced to his mother's house while there was still sunlight. He had to fly out early in the morning to check on a job he had running in Newcastle and would be away until Sunday. The last thing he would feel like doing when he arrived back home was mowing Mum's lawn, so that left tonight to get it done.

He had almost said no when she had called him. He had wanted to suggest she organise a student who needed the money to do it for her. Hell, if he had a spare hundred dollars, he would have organised one for her.

But he couldn't say no because he owed her money. And in some twisted way, he knew that was why she had asked him. She had her sick voice on when she had called—soft and husky and she ended every sentence with *darl*. It made him cringe, but he was the dutiful son, and he would mow her lawn. That's how it worked. That's how it had always worked.

When he arrived at the house, he let himself in.

A door creaked upstairs, footsteps. "Is that you, darl?" came her sick voice.

"Yeah, Mum. I'm going to get straight into this lawn. I've got an early flight tomorrow morning. I still need to pack."

"Can't Belinda do that for you? I'm sure it wouldn't hurt her."

Her voice was getting louder as she descended the stairs. The house was dim in the encroaching twilight.

"She works too, Mum. She's probably not even home yet. She does her accounts on Thursday nights."

Mum was dressed in her dressing gown and walking very slowly in her slippers. Her hair was this way and that. Much different to the composed woman she usually showed to the world.

She pressed a hand to her back and breathed past her teeth. "I wouldn't have got you over, but I've gone and hurt my back."

"How did you do that?"

"I don't know. Stress, most likely. After being accused of paedophilia, I thought that was the worst that could happen. And then Matt called and told me that Nikki wants nothing to do with me or this family again."

Anthony baulked. "What? He said that?"

Mum nodded, then winced. Obviously, the small movement was too much for her. She was lisping, most likely bombed up on the various prescription drugs she kept in her medicine container. Just how she managed to get them was beyond him. He didn't want to know.

Beneath the anger he had held since learning of her infidelity, sympathy unfurled. What a horrible thing for Nikki to do. "What happened? Why doesn't she want anything to do with us?"

"She's obviously losing her mind. How she could even think that I would keep a photo of a boy chained up is beyond me. And then she blames me for getting upset over it. How else am I meant to react? How would you feel to be accused of something like that?"

He frowned. "I would be upset."

"Exactly. I can't make heads nor tails of it. First, she crashes her car on purpose. The last I heard she was seeing a psychologist. A lot of good that's doing her. Matt hasn't even called to see how I am. All week, not one word. Is he pushing me out of his life too because of Nikki?" Tears filled her eyes, but she blinked them away. "Anyway, thanks for coming over to the mow the lawn. I really appreciate it."

"It's okay, Mum. I'll head out to the shed and get started. You relax."

"Thanks, darl."

By the time Anthony finished, the house was solidly masked in night. He parked the ride-on lawnmower back in the shed and cleaned his shoes on the mat at the back door. Under the gauzy light spilling from the globe overhead, he checked his phone. He puffed out a breath to see a few missed calls from Belinda. He had forgotten to tell her where he was. Before heading inside to say goodnight to Mum, he phoned Belinda to let her know he was on his way home.

In his car, halfway down the range, he launched a call to Matt via his car's Bluetooth.

"Hey, Ant." Matt's words were blunt, deep.

"You got a minute to talk?"

"Sure."

"I just come from Mum's—"

"I don't want to hear it," Matt said.

"Hang on, give me a chance here. I want to understand what's going on."

"Do you honestly think Nikki would accuse Mum of paedophilia? Honestly? Think logically about it."

Anthony sighed. "No, I don't. But she showed me the photo. It was all kinds of messed up."

"The photo was. The conversation about the photo wasn't. Nikki even had Ryan make the call, that's how innocent the question was. All Ryan asked was if the phone

Mum gave him was refurbished. Then Mum completely twisted it and jumped into some long tirade."

"Well, that's not what she told me."

"No, she wouldn't have. Because it wouldn't suit her story." A frustrated exhalation. "Look, Ant, Nikki is over it. She needs a break. I told Mum to go through me if she needs anything."

"Why would Mum make something like that up?"

"You tell me why! I don't know. She has a screw loose."

"That's what she's saying about Nikki. Said she's seeing a psychologist and she purposefully crashed her car."

Matt growled. "Yes, true, but it's not because she has a loose screw."

"Well, it all sounds a bit like he-said she-said. I'm not sure what to believe."

"I don't care what you believe because this doesn't concern you."

"When I hear Nikki wants nothing to do with our family, it does concern me."

"Nikki never said that. She wants a break from Mum. Not the whole family." Matt's words were loud and angry.

"I'm just relaying what I heard, don't shoot the messenger."

"I'm going. I'll talk to you later." And Matt hung up.

Anthony gripped the steering wheel more tightly as he navigated through the darkness. One thing his family was never short of was controversy. Sometimes he wished he and Belinda could pack up and move to the backend of nowhere where no one would ever find them. A new start. No baggage.

Chapter 43

Belinda

Anthony arrived home covered in dust and smelling like petrol. His eyes were a little bloodshot, his stance droopy. Belinda sent him for a shower while she finished making their dinner of spaghetti bolognaise. Cheap mince. Cheap pasta. And could be eaten as leftovers for days.

As she was dishing up, Anthony strode into the kitchen sniffing the rich tomato aromas. "I'm starving."

"Good, because I've made heaps. I forgot you were going away tomorrow, so there's no way I'm going to eat all the leftovers myself."

"Don't remind me. The last thing I want to do is leave you for five days."

She pressed a hand to his shoulder and kissed his cheek. "Can you stay? Send someone else?"

Since discovering she was pregnant, one thing had been going right and that was their relationship. Sex had been amazing. Anthony was loving and warm in all the ways she needed. When they had been at their worst, she would count down the weeks and days until he left, but now she truly wanted him to stay.

He smiled but shook his head. "It's all booked. I'm not wasting that kind of money."

"I understand."

Belinda dished them both a bowl of spaghetti and layered bolognaise on top. They carried it into the living room to eat from their lap on the couch.

"Your mum rang me today," she said.

Anthony rolled his eyes. "Christ, more drama. I just got off the phone from Matt about it."

"So, she told you about Paige?"

He narrowed his eyes. "No. What about Paige?"

"Supposedly she accused your mother of hurting Evie's arm when they were at the park."

"What? How?"

"Evie had bruising on her arm that looked like fingerprints. Paige asked Claire if she had done it."

"What is wrong with everyone at the moment? Mum's far from perfect, we know that—"

Belinda nodded emphatically.

"—but she's clearly doesn't go around hurting children."

She shovelled a forkful of spaghetti into her mouth and chewed. "You know, I was starting to believe that Paige was a lovely person, but maybe she's just as bonkers as Joanne was. Vaughn can certainly pick them."

"I'm about ready to throw my hands up with all of them. Is family really worth all this bullshit?"

"Our little family will be worth it," she said. And she knew it, deep down, they would have a wonderful family. Maybe even another child or two if it happened naturally. She had heard stories of fertility springing to life once the first birth takes place. No pushing it, of course. She was blessed to be having one.

"Maybe this trip away is looking better and better."

Belinda laughed. "Lucky you. Don't worry about your poor pregnant wife. She'll shoulder the storm for you."

His expression grew serious. "Not your storm to shoulder. Don't get involved. You need to be looking after your own well-being." He reached for her and lifted her shirt to expose her belly. He gently traced his fingers along her skin. The skin on his thick fingers was rough, but he touched her gently. "This baby is who's important."

"I know."

"I mean it, Bel. You're the most important person in the world right now. Not some stupid concocted family drama."

"It really is never-ending, isn't it?"

He slid his hand from her stomach, and she lowered her shirt. "And here we were thinking we had problems."

Belinda laughed. "Exactly. So, how's your spaghetti?"

He winked. "Delicious."

"Good."

Chapter 44

Paige

A knock came at the door early Thursday morning. Vaughn had left for work twenty minutes ago and Paige wasn't yet out of her pyjamas. She eyed the breakfast dishes lining the bench and Evie munching away on her Weet Bix at her little table and chairs in the corner of the kitchen.

The heavy knock came again. Paige looked through the window on the way to the entry. In the driveway was an executive black car.

Who the hell could this be?

She opened the door. A man and a woman dressed in professional clothing stood on the doorstep.

"Paige Johnson?"

Paige straightened her sleep-mussed hair with her hand and nodded. "Yes."

"I'm Bridget and this is Paul. We are child safety officers from the Department of Child Safety."

Paige's heart thudded one strong bass beat in her chest.

They both lifted their identification cards that hung around their necks. She glanced at the photos on the card and back to their faces.

"We are here because we were given information that your child, Evie Johnson, may be experiencing physical harm in the home. We would like to assess your home and talk with you and Evie."

"What? I don't understand. What's happened?"

Bridget handed her a pamphlet titled *When Child Safety Officers Visit Your Home*. "This outlines the general process today and your rights as a parent. We would like to sit down with you and discuss this further. We will first talk with Evie and do an assessment of your home. Can we come in and get started?"

Paige stepped to the side and gestured they come in. "I don't understand why this is even necessary. Who would even say such a thing?"

"We are unable to divulge who has issued the complaint."

She shook her head, trying to cast off the confusion. "I would never hurt my daughter. Ever."

"That's what we are here to determine. It's vital when a complaint is made that we act to ensure Evie's safety. Where is your daughter?" Bridget asked.

"She's eating breakfast."

In the kitchen, Paige pointed to Evie. "See, she's perfectly fine."

Evie was spooning Weet-Bix into her mouth and casually looked to the intruders without the faintest idea of the magnitude of this home call.

"Thank you. I will talk with Evie now. Paul would like you to show him around the house, then we will all sit down for a conversation."

"I can't believe this," she said, rubbing her face. "I can't believe someone would accuse me of hurting my daughter."

Bridget looked at her. "Evie is three-years-old, is that correct?"

Tears were pooling in Paige's eyes. Her breaths were hard to drag in. "Yes. She turns four next February."

"Thank you."

"Can you show me Evie's bedroom?" Paul asked.

Paige looked back at Evie who was still eating her breakfast. Bridget sat on the small chair opposite her and smiled warmly.

"Evie's room please?" Paul asked.

Paige pointed towards the hall. "Up here." She led him to Evie's pink room filled with fluffy pillows and stuffed toys. She leaned against the door frame for support, watching as Paul inspected the room, opening drawers and cupboards.

"I'm sorry, I haven't had time to clean up in here today. We're not even out of our pyjamas." Tears wet her cheeks and she wiped them away. Why hadn't she got into a better routine of dressing promptly in the mornings?

When Paul was done, she showed him to her and Vaughn's bedroom. He repeated his assessment with a cursory glance around the room. "You live here with your partner?"

Paige nodded. "Vaughn Radcliffe. Evie and I moved in a few months ago."

"No other adults or siblings?"

Paige shook her head. "Just the three of us."

"We would like to talk with Vaughn too."

"Now?" she asked.

"If you can arrange it."

"I can call him. See if he can come home."

"That would be helpful."

She strode into the kitchen and called Vaughn. He answered quickly.

"Hi, um, you need to come home…" that was all she got out before she burst into tears.

"What's the matter? Are you okay? Is Evie okay?"

"I have the Department of Child Safety here inspecting the house. Someone reported that I've been harming Evie."

"What the fuck?" Vaughn roared.

"They are doing an assessment of the home, but they would like to talk to you too. Can you come home?"

"I'll be there in twenty minutes."

Paige hung up, turned to watch Bridget as she spoke with Evie. Evie was giggling, which offered her a margin of relief. "Can you show me where your toys are?" Bridget asked. Evie pushed her chair back and ran into the sewing room to her play corner.

Paige slid onto a stool, her weak legs unable to hold her up anymore. Her tears wouldn't slow. But mostly she was vibrating—anger and betrayal coursing through her system.

"Does Evie attend day-care?"

Paige jumped at the sound of Paul's voice. She spun to find him standing beside her, iPad in hand. "No."

"Is she cared for by anyone else?"

She shook her head. "Just me. Oh, her father. Recently, though. She's only had a weekend with him so far."

Bridget came back in, Evie in tow. "Paige, I would like to inspect a reported injury. Paul will assist, but I will need you to help with clothing."

Paige's heart dropped into her stomach. She didn't need to be told that Bridget was referring to Evie's arm.

"Maybe we can do it here at Evie's table, so she is comfortable."

Paige nodded as she joined them at the table setting.

"Could you please remove Evie's shirt, so I can see her right upper arm."

Tears sprang to Paige's eyes as she unbuttoned Evie's pyjama top and peeled it off. Big yellow and blue bruises still blossomed on Evie's delicate white skin. Bridget inspected the injury closer. Paul took notes.

"Thank you. You can put her top back on."

Paige dressed Evie again, her fingers shaking as she tied the buttons back up.

"Is there an activity to occupy Evie while we have a chat?"

"I…I can put her cartoons on."

"Peppa Pig," Evie said, running to her play corner.

Paige followed and turned a marathon of Peppa on. "You sit here while I talk to the people, okay? Do you want juice?"

Evie nodded, not looking from the television screen.

Paige quickly made a juice in Evie's cup and handed it to her. She breathed in deeply, steadied her voice and mustered a tremulous smile. "I won't be long. If you want something, I'm in the dining room, okay?"

"Okay, Mummy."

As she crossed the distance back to the kitchen, fear was tightening all her muscles, making each step stiff. These people could take her daughter away.

Paige sat with Bridget and Paul who were waiting at the dining table, paperwork spread out before them. They ran through names and dates of birth for Paige, Evie and Vaughn.

"Do you have any support available to you, Paige? Someone or an organisation you can turn to for help if needed?"

Paige could hardly think. Her lips were trembling. "Friends. My partner."

"What about your parents?"

"My mum passed away ten years ago. I don't have a father."

"Are there any stressors in your life at the moment?"

She shook her head. "Nothing unusual. Except maybe Evie's biological father who has come back into the picture. We are working out a custody arrangement. That's been a little stressful for me because I've been Evie's sole parent since she was born."

"Have you been diagnosed with any mental illnesses?"

Again, she shook her head.

"What does a normal day look like in the Johnson household?"

"I'm the full carer of Evie. Well, I was. That will be changing, as I said. I work from home. I'm a clothes designer. Evie plays with her toys while I work. We'll stop regularly for snacks and meals. Some days we go for swimming lessons. Other times we might go to the park…" She trailed off when she realised that it couldn't be Joshua who reported Paige to Child Safety because he didn't know about Evie's bruised arm.

The only people who knew were Vaughn and Claire. Her stomach sank. Could Claire have done this?

"Who made the complaint?" she asked, more forcefully this time.

"Under the Child Safety Act, we are not at liberty to disclose the complainant."

Paige blew out a long breath, ran her fingers through her hair. "Anyone who knows me well will tell you that I would never hurt Evie."

Bridget nodded, managed a tight smile. "We have had a number of complaints with photographic evidence provided." Bridget placed a picture on the table of Evie when she cut her eye on the sprinkler. "This is one incident. Can you tell me about this please?"

She swallowed. "We had a family barbeque. Evie was playing under the sprinkler. She slipped over and her face hit the sprinkler arm, cutting her cheek. I tended to her. Gave her paracetamol. Got advice from a doctor that she didn't need stitches, so I dressed the cut myself."

"Was there alcohol at this barbeque?"

Her heart stuttered. "Yes. But I hadn't had any at that stage."

"Did you see her have the accident?"

"No, I was inside when it happened, but I got to her within seconds."

"Was there anyone nearby?"

"Vaughn and his family were sitting on the outdoor setting, metres from her."

"Do you have the name of the doctor you saw after this injury? We would like to talk to them too."

She shook her head. “I don’t know her name. She was the daughter of my mother-in-law’s friend. Claire took a picture and sent it to her. You would have to ask Claire…” She trailed off, wondering if this was the real reason Claire took the picture.

Another image was laid on the table. Evie in the car on her own out the front of Claire’s house.

“Can you tell me about this?”

Paige lowered her face into her hands and growled. “I can’t believe this.”

“What can’t you believe?”

She pointed to the image. “Evie was in the car on her own for no more than thirty seconds. I left the car running. The air con was on. The house is private and a good distance from the road. All I did was leave her in there while I walked to my mother-in-law’s front door. We were heading out for breakfast. The three of us.”

“Do you leave your daughter in the car under other circumstances?”

“Never. That was the first time. She was in my sight the entire time.”

Another image was placed onto the table. The picture Paige had sent to Claire the other night while bathing Evie. The big dark bruises stood out on Evie’s fragile skin.

“Can you tell me about this?”

An angry scream sat in the back of her throat. She was going to strangle Claire for this. She could barely draw in a breath as betrayal stung her. The deepest, most treacherous betrayal she had ever experienced in her life. Did Claire want her to lose custody of her daughter?

“Is everything okay?”

Paige stood up, hands on the back of her head, elbows out wide. “No, it’s not. The only other person who has this image is my mother-in-law.” She marched to the bench and grabbed her phone. She brought it back, scrolled through her messages until she found the ones she sent to Claire.

"Here. Read that. That's what happened. I went to the park. Claire was helping Evie on the swings. Evie was hurt. I didn't think it was a big deal until later that night when I was bathing her and saw these bruises that looked like fingerprints. Evie told me that Claire had done it. She showed me how Claire had squeezed her arm. I didn't do any of this. I take good care of my daughter. Always. She is, and always has been, my priority. I would die first rather than see her hurt."

Vaughn pushed through the front door and rushed into the dining room, frowning. An undercurrent of anger sat beneath his greetings to Paul and Bridget. He kissed Paige's cheek before taking a seat beside her. He reached under the table to hold her hand, but she moved it out his grasp.

The officers ran through similar questions with Vaughn and asked him to respond to the photos. No doubt that he was drawing the same conclusion about Claire.

They spoke about Evie's milestones, discussed parenting methods and both Vaughn and Paige's perceptions and feelings about Evie.

Paige exhaled a long breath when Bridget started gathering all her papers together. "I think we have what we need. We are required to talk with extended relatives and various caregivers, like Evie's doctor and the like. She doesn't attend school or day-care, so we won't need to inform anyone in that regard. Thanks for your cooperation this morning. I know this is not an easy process. We may call you in for another interview, but it's unlikely. Otherwise, we will be in contact with you soon regarding our findings."

"What could be the outcome of this?" Paige asked.

"We will need to work through all the information before we can give an answer to that. I don't want to speculate on the outcome at this point."

Paige sighed, her shoulders slumped.

"We can show ourselves out," Paul said, and they left.

When the front door clicked closed behind them, Paige collapsed onto the chair, head in her hands. For a long moment, she dragged in deep breaths. Vaughn rubbed her back until she wriggled free of his touch.

She lifted her head and looked him in the eye. "Your mother is responsible for this," she said with such restrained rage, her chest ached.

"I can't see her doing this."

She got to her feet. "I could lose my daughter!"

"You won't lose her."

"You saw the pictures, Vaughn."

"I know."

"No one else but your mother has those pictures."

He didn't answer.

Paige snatched her phone off the table and with shaking hands, dialled Claire.

Claire answered after a few rings. "Hi, darl, how are you going?"

"I'll tell you how I'm going!" she screamed. "I just had a surprise visit from Child Safety. They had photos. Photos that are in your possession."

"I'm not sure what you're talking about. Child Safety? I don't understand." Her voice was so calm it slid through Paige's veins like splinters of glass.

"You can't deny this. I know it was you. I know it. How dare you!" Her hands were vibrating, chest hot.

"You're getting a little wound up, darl."

"I could lose my daughter! Do you understand what you've done? Why? Why would you do this? What have I ever done to you?"

"Darl, look, you really need to calm down. I don't deserve this kind of abuse."

"Abuse? You just called The Department of Child Safety on me. You want to talk about abuse!" She was screaming, her whole head shaking as each word flew from her mouth.

"My goodness, Paige. Maybe you do have some kind of anger issues. I'm sure Joshua would be interested to hear about this harassment. It might help his cause all the more."

Alarm broke through Paige's rage. Tingles spread over her face and down the back of her neck. All the pieces clicked into place.

Claire was who told Joshua about Evie in the first place. She had to be very careful with what she said or did around this woman.

Air rushed from her lungs and she fought for her next inhalation. Claire was sick. Twisted. Evil. Paige had underestimated this woman.

She hung up and turned to Vaughn. "I need to leave."

"You're not leaving. This is *our* house."

"I'm going to stay in a hotel tonight, but I'll be looking for a place for me and Evie to live."

"What? What about us?"

"As long as that vile woman you call Mother is around, there is no *us*." She rushed to her bedroom to pack a bag of necessities for Evie and herself. "I need somewhere safe. Claire hurt my daughter and now she's trying to have her taken from me. Who knows what else she's capable of?"

"You can't be serious. Please, let us talk this through rationally. Maybe I can go talk to Mum."

She shook her head fast. She could no longer risk being anywhere near Claire, not when her daughter's safety was at stake. "Evie is my main responsibility. Unless you can get rid of your mother, there won't ever be an *us*! Do you understand that, Vaughn? Evie comes first. Always. And she isn't safe."

With two bags packed, she bundled Evie in her arms and loaded up her car. She couldn't look at Vaughn's dejection, his sombre eyes, lest she changed her mind. She loved him, but she didn't love him as much as she loved her daughter.

Forty minutes later, she had found a hotel, booked in, parked, and lugged Evie and her baggage to their room. A queen-sized bed filled the centre of the room. From the window, there was a view of the ocean that glittered under the afternoon sunlight. It was too vast and beautiful when contrasted with her suffocating inner turmoil.

"We stay here?" Evie asked.

"Yep, just you and me. We will have a little holiday. How does that sound?"

Evie jumped up and down and clapped. "Good." She ran through the small room, opening cupboards and poking her head into the bathroom. She climbed onto a chair and sat before a desk. Fiddled with the pens and information booklets.

"Do you want to have a shower?"

Evie nodded and ran to the bathroom. Paige wanted some semblance of privacy when she made a call to Joshua.

She undressed Evie and turned on the taps until the water was warm. She grabbed a few of Evie's toys she had packed in her bag and placed them on the tiled floor in the shower. Evie could play in there until her fingers pruned.

With Evie happily contained, Paige dialled Joshua's number.

"Hi, be quick, I'm just about to head into the gym," Joshua said when he answered.

She stood at the window and looked out over the ocean. "I'll take as long as I need." Her tone was venomous.

"I assume you had some visitors today?"

"So, you do know. What the hell are you playing at? Saying that I hurt Evie? You know I wouldn't."

"I don't know that, Paige. What I do know is that you hid my daughter from me for three years. And then I get pictures of her being left in a car during the day, a swollen eye and handprints on her arm. It broke my heart to see Evie like that."

"That's bullshit. If you had have acted like a grown-up and asked me, you would have learnt that there were perfectly reasonable explanations. Children hurt themselves. You should know that. You've got enough nieces and nephews. They're always getting scrapes and bruises. It doesn't mean they are getting abused. I'm sick to my absolute stomach here. What the hell are you trying to do—take Evie from me?" Her voice cracked, despite her best efforts to remain steady.

Silence for a long moment, then a sigh. "I was doing what I thought was best. When you get contacted by a close relative who is scared for a child's safety, it makes you sit up and listen."

"You need to tell me the truth. Was it Claire who contacted you about Evie."

"Yes."

"And she sent you those photos?"

"Yes."

"And you believed her? A woman you barely know. Over me. After everything we've been through." Tears flooded her eyes, her words wobbled.

"I believed her because why else would a woman go to such lengths to help a little girl and put her own relationship with her son at risk if she didn't think Evie was in danger?"

"I have never laid a hand on Evie."

"It's in the hands of Child Safety now. Let's wait to hear what they say. And I've seen a lawyer about gaining full custody of Evie too."

"What? No. We agreed to a fifty-fifty arrangement. That's not fair. You can't do this to me. Or to Evie."

"Claire was generous enough to remind me that Evie starts pre-school next year. It was never going to work with you and Evie living so far away. This way she'll be able to attend a decent private school. She'll get the best of everything."

"You can't do that. I won't let you."

"It's out of my hands. Look, Paige, I have to go. I'll talk to you later."

"Wait…" But he hung up.

She let the phone drop to the carpet beneath her feet. Her world was falling apart. The only person she lived for, darling Evie, was going to be stolen from her.

Chapter 45

Nikki

Nikki was dressed in her bra and knickers, rushing between her bedroom and bathroom, attempting to dress before her next psychologist appointment when her phone rang. She snatched her mobile from her dresser. Paige's name flashed on the screen.

She answered, "Hi, Paige."

"Hi, Nikki, I hope I'm not interrupting anything."

Nikki looked to her outfit of jeans and a T-shirt laid out on her bed. "No. What's up?"

A silence, then a muffled cry. "I didn't know who else to turn to. I need to talk to somebody who may understand."

Nikki's stomach twisted. "Sure. What is it?"

"It's Claire. She has done a very bad thing. I'm scared, Nikki. I'm scared of what she might be capable of." Fear sat behind every trembling word.

Nikki blew out a long breath. An eerie high-pitched squeal sounded inside her head. "Oh, God, what happened?"

Paige told her about her ex-boyfriend coming back into her life, his quest to get custody, and the assessment by The Department of Child Safety. Claire had masterminded it all.

"I should be surprised," Nikki said, pacing across the bedroom. "I really should, but I'm not. Not one bit." She checked her watch—half an hour left before her appointment. Nikki realised then that sitting in a chair talking to a stranger about Claire wasn't going to fix the problem. She needed to speak with her sisters-in-law. She needed them all on the same side working together to get to the bottom of how much damage their mother-in-law was wreaking.

"I think you, me, and Belinda are long overdue for a talk. Let me call Belinda and we'll arrange a place to get together."

"Thank you so much, Nikki. I appreciate this. I really do. I didn't know where else to turn."

"You're not alone, okay? I know exactly how you feel. And I'm guessing that Belinda does too."

After a phone call, it was decided they meet at Belinda's home. Belinda would arrange a temp to cover her shop for the afternoon and Nikki would cancel her psychologist's appointment.

When Nikki arrived forty-five minutes later at her sister-in-law's home, Belinda opened the door looking beautifully flushed and radiant.

"Pregnancy definitely suits you," Nikki said.

A smile stretched across Belinda's mouth. "Thank you. It certainly feels that way. Come in. Paige is already here."

Nikki followed Belinda through her echoing house. Despite being sisters-in-law for so many years, she hardly ever visited her home. Maybe once a year. With her new insight, she wondered if Claire's meddling had a lot to do with that. Keep them all separate, so they couldn't talk about the true perpetrator.

"Coffee?" Belinda asked as they marched down the hall to the spacious kitchen filled with top-end appliances, a butler's pantry and loads of bench space.

"Thanks."

Paige was sitting on a stool at the breakfast bar. She was drawn, pale and her eyes had that beady, scattered look. If anyone went after Nikki's children like Claire was doing to Paige, she would be murderous. Nikki didn't like confrontation, but when it came to protecting her children, no one stood in her way.

"Hi, Paige."

"Hi."

"Where's Evie?"

"I dropped her at a friend's place to spend the day."

Nikki nodded. "Of course. It's too grown-up to talk about such things in front of a child."

"Exactly. And even though she doesn't understand it all, she still sees me upset and that's not good for her. We had a restless night last night."

"I can imagine you would."

Belinda was watching them as she filled the jug and set it to boil.

"Have you had a chance to tell Belinda what happened?"

"Not yet."

Nikki faced Belinda and frowned. "Wait until you hear this."

"Do I need to be sitting first?" Belinda asked.

Paige shook her head. "No, but I need to be."

As Belinda poured coffees, Paige told her all that she had shared with Nikki on the phone earlier. As they went out onto the patio and sat at the outdoor setting, Paige continued talking, stopping intermittently when she was overcome with tears.

"It was Claire. She was the only other person on this planet who had those photos." Paige's face crumpled with regret. "I found it strange that she was taking a photo of Evie in the car that morning we went to the park, but I stupidly believed it was innocent."

"Her ability to twist things is abnormal," Nikki said. "It's just like what happened with me recently." She told them about the picture on Ryan's phone and how their innocent query was twisted to be an accusation of paedophilia. That was just one example of hundreds over the years.

Belinda gasped. “Are you serious? Is that what happened?”

Nikki nodded. “Why, what version of the story were you told?”

“A very different one that made you—” Belinda winced, apology shaping her eyes, “—look insane.”

“Can’t you see it? Claire is playing us,” Nikki said. “She’s pitting us against each other. Honestly, I don’t know why I didn’t notice it before now. The things she has said about both of you…” She trailed off.

“Like what?” Belinda asked.

Nikki’s tone was rueful as she said, “You’re demanding and insisted on buying a big home. Well above your budget. A home you can no longer afford. You’re terrible with money and are in financial trouble, so much so that you borrowed money off Claire, then asked her to also pay a restaurant bill. And she said you’re too irresponsible to be having a baby.”

Belinda’s lips parted, her eyes were wide. “She said all that?”

Both Paige and Nikki nodded.

“More recently she said that you and Anthony were having marriage troubles,” Paige said. “She told me all about the financial problems as well.”

“What has she said about me?” Nikki asked.

“That you crashed your car on purpose,” Belinda said.

Paige nodded. “I heard that too. And that you’re seeing a psychologist.”

Belinda leaned forward and ran her finger along the rim of her coffee mug. “Anthony told me you accused Claire of paedophilia. I also heard the psychologist story.”

Nikki shook her head. “Wow.”

“Oh, and that your house is always dirty because you’re too lazy to clean it,” Belinda said.

Paige nodded in such a way that showed she had received that gossip too.

Nikki rolled her eyes, blew out an exasperated breath. The stories were not exactly lies, but Claire had delivered the gossip in such a way that the recipient saw what Claire wanted them to see.

"What about me?" Paige asked, though there was hesitation in her voice.

"Claire told me that you accused her of calling you a gold-digger," Nikki said.

"Yep, I heard that one too," Belinda said. "And that you accused Claire of hurting Evie, which, unfortunately, she has."

Silence fell over them then at that stark realisation: Claire had physically hurt a three-year-old child. This was big, huge…

"It makes me wonder if she's hurt my children," Nikki said.

"She won't be coming near my baby. I'll make sure of that. I don't care if I owe her twenty thousand dollars or not. She can sue me."

Nikki glanced from Paige to Belinda. "What the bloody hell have we been dealing with all these years? How did our husbands make it through their childhoods unscathed?"

They shook their heads.

"She's not who she makes out to be," Nikki said. "Behind that veneer, she's abominable."

"At the memorial dinner, Auntie Maggie told me that Robert was married already when Claire fell pregnant with Matt," Belinda admitted. "They had to wait until the divorce went through before they could marry each other."

"Are you serious?" Paige shrieked, nose crinkling. She crossed her arms over her chest. "I had to sit through a frigging lecture the other morning about how women who get pregnant before having a ring on their finger are basically trapping their partners and shouldn't feel shocked when the relationship ends."

Nikki clicked her tongue. "Typical."

"And that's not the least of it," Belinda said.

Paige turned her focus to Belinda, her head tilted to the side. "How so?"

"Anthony discovered that Claire had an affair. We even have proof."

"Proof? What proof?" Nikki asked.

Belinda explained about the blood donor card that slipped out from between one of Robert's old workbooks and how his blood type was different to Vaughn's.

Paige gasped. Her eyes opened wider. "So, Vaughn isn't Robert's son?"

Belinda shook her head. "Can't possibly be."

"What about Matt and Anthony? Are they Robert's?" Nikki asked.

Belinda shrugged. "They have Claire's blood type, but I guess we'll never know definitively without a DNA test. There could be a chance. If she's had one affair, it may be possible that she's had others."

"What a two-faced lying, cheating, conniving bitch," Paige hissed from between gritted teeth. "I'm sorry, but she is. Poor Vaughn."

"You can't tell him," Belinda said quickly. "Anthony doesn't want to cause any trouble."

"He has a right to know."

"Please don't. Anthony will know that I've let it slip. I promised him I'd keep it to myself."

Paige huffed out a breath. "Fine, it's not like we're together anymore anyway."

"What?" Belinda asked.

"We're over. I can't risk Evie being around Claire. And he's obviously not willing to walk away from his mother. He's proven that in the past with Joanne. He happily let his marriage fall apart rather than stand up to Claire."

"A lot of good standing up to her does," Nikki said. "It makes her dig her heels in. After the picture incident, I got Matt to call her and tell her to keep out of my life. She's obviously started her black propaganda campaign since then, not to mention giving Matt the silent treatment. She usually calls him every day. But this week, nothing."

"Don't even get me started about her silent treatments," Belinda scoffed. "Like we really bloody care if she's not ringing us at six o'clock every morning. I always hope the silent treatment will go on forever."

"So, it's not just us?" Nikki asked with a grin.

"Obviously not."

"We're all violins," Paige said.

Belinda and Nikki nodded. "Looks like it."

Paige pressed her palms to the table and leaned forward. "So, the question is—what do we do about her?"

That was one question Nikki didn't have an answer to, short of leaving her husband.

"We can't be expected to end our relationships just to get away from her," Belinda said.

"But can we expect our husbands to shun their mother?"

Belinda shrugged. "Maybe we do. This isn't a minor situation. It's not a petty case of three women who are upset with their mother-in-law. Claire is actively trying to harm us. She hurt Evie, an innocent little girl, for Christ's sake."

Nikki shuddered. Belinda was right—Claire was trying to harm them, and she was succeeding. She may not be leaving physical bruises on Nikki and her sisters-in-law, but the emotional turmoil she inflicted was worse than any broken bone. Not only that, she was getting worse. When did this end?

"Recently, my psychologist and I unearthed the root cause of why I've felt so out of control lately," Nikki said. "It's Claire. Right from the beginning, she's been controlling every aspect of my life to such an extent and for so long that I'm not me anymore." Images flashed in Nikki's mind of Claire's wolfish features and her blood-red lipstick. "We can't let her get away with this"

"But what could we do?" Belinda asked. "It's not like we can have her arrested. Technically, she can do what she damn well pleases. No law enforcement is going to take seriously claims that our mother-in-law is making our lives hell. Half the world's population of mothers-in-law would be behind bars if that were the case."

"Claire is no ordinary beast," Nikki said.

"*We* know that," Belinda said.

Nikki recalled all the times she tried to tell her own mother about Claire and the resistance she was given. As though admitting that one mother-in-law was evil implicated every other mother out there. No in-law wanted to be framed negatively or seen in a harsh light, but this was bigger than that. Claire was destroying marriages, hurting children and stealing sanity.

"Do we move?" Nikki asked.

"That might be an option for you, but Anthony and I have our businesses here. And—" she lowered her gaze, a sheepish tilt to her head, "—as you well know, thanks to Claire's blabbering mouth, we aren't financially capable at this stage."

"And why should we have to?" Nikki asked. "It would mean uprooting my children from school. Matt would have to find another job. And I'd have to sell my home."

"Exactly," Paige said.

"Maybe we can see if Matt and Anthony can tell her to butt out?" Belinda suggested.

"You've seen how well that could turn out," Paige said. "Vaughn barely tried yesterday. He just let me walk away." Her eyes glossed, but she blinked quickly to stem the tears. "He hasn't even tried to call me."

"You love him still," Belinda said. Not a question but a statement.

Paige nodded and a sob hiccupped from her. "Of course I do. That doesn't stop because his mother is a psycho. I still want to be with him, but I can't take the risk."

Nikki placed a comforting hand on Paige's shoulder. "You're doing the right thing. Evie is your biggest concern at the moment."

Paige lowered her face in her hands and moaned such a mournful cry. "What if I lose her? I won't be able to live without her. I can't. She's my whole world."

A lump formed in Nikki's throat. "You're not going to lose her. You're a great mum. The Department of Child Safety would've been able to see that. Surely."

Belinda's eyes were glossing with sympathy.

Paige lifted her face, wiped at her cheeks with her shirt. "I really hope so. And I hope the courts see it that way too."

"This is so messed up," Belinda said. She placed her cup on the tabletop, tea sloshing over the rim.

"I've been on my own for ten years—" Paige's voice was tremulous, "—just when I think my life is finally complete with Vaughn and Evie and meeting all of you, Claire comes along and strips it all away. She's depraved. I wish she'd get hit by a car. I know that sounds horrible, but, honestly, she deserves it. After everything that evil bitch has put me through, it's the kindest thing to say."

"I'm hoping her house implodes during a storm and washes her down to the river where she drowns under a pile of debris," Belinda said.

Nikki chuckled. "Or her heart gets so cold and stony that it finally stops beating, and we all get some peace at last."

"That's it then. It's obvious," Paige said with a watery smile. "We have to murder her."

Belinda grinned. "Exactly. We can poison her champagne at the next memorial dinner. At least we won't have to sit through that family movie again."

"I can't possibly wait another year," Nikki said. "I reckon we lace her air conditioner with mould spores. She always goes on and on about how toxic black mould is. And no one would even know."

Paige burst out laughing. "That's fantastic."

"Such a Nikki kind of murder," Belinda said with a giggle.

Nikki beamed. "You can tell I've been plotting this in my fantasies for a long while. I have it all planned out. I buy some spores from the dark web. I use my key to get into her house while she's at her art class. I sprinkle the spores along the spongey filter in her air- conditioner above her bed. Spray it with a little warm water to create a nice moist living environment. Then when the weather heats up, which it's starting to now, Claire turns her air conditioner on, and she's breathing those spores in all night long."

Belinda rocked back in her chair, face tilted skyward as she cried with laughter. "That's a perfect plan. I could actually see that working."

"Me too," said Paige. Her smile fell away and she drew her lips into a straight line as she looked from Belinda to Nikki. "You know, we could get away with that. Who in their right mind would ever suspect that someone has intentionally planted mould at Claire's house?"

Silence for a long moment before Belinda leaned forward, elbows on the table. "You're not serious?"

"I think I am." Paige's voice was higher pitched, emphatic. "I hate her that much for what she has done to me. To all of us. I'm not over-exaggerating right now. I would gladly watch her body lowered into the ground."

"Jesus, Paige. That's a bit much," Belinda said with a nervous chuckle.

"Is it, though?" Paige gestured towards Nikki. "Think of it this way—you'll get your sanity back. Your life. Just you, Matt and the boys, happy again. And Belinda, I think you might stand to gain the most. Claire's got money, right? Anthony would inherit that. You could pay off your debt. You'd be free again."

Belinda looked out over the glistening canal. "That would be so fantastic. I'm not going to lie. It's been hell trying to live day to day." She turned back. "But I'm not going to kill my mother-in-law in order to get it. I'm not a murderer. No way."

"I don't think it could be labelled murder," Nikki said. "More like self-defence. We'd be doing ourselves and our families a huge favour." Her heart was racing. Adrenalin was sparking in her veins.

Paige nodded. "I agree. Claire is evil. Obviously psychotic. I don't think she'll stop until all our lives are destroyed."

Nikki recalled sliding under the warm bath water and never wanting to come back to the surface, happy to sink into the darkness, because, for that split second, she believed that leaving her loving husband and beautiful boys behind was better than living another moment more with Claire in her life.

But why kill herself when the problem was Claire?

"I considered suicide this week," she blurted through an aching throat. Tears sprung to her eyes.

"What? No," Belinda said, shaking her head, eyes crinkled with sympathy.

"For so long I've tried to hide how bad it is, but I refuse to any longer. We need to fight back. Otherwise, I'm not sure how much longer I can last."

"But by murdering her?" Belinda asked.

"We've reached the point where it's her or it's us. As time goes on, Claire is getting worse. I spoke to Joanne last week. Nearly eighteen months since her divorce and only now is she beginning to feel herself again. She said there is nothing you can do to stop people like Claire. And I know that's true. Whenever I fight back or try to set boundaries, Claire hits back fifteen times harder. Why should we break our families apart because of her? And now she's hurting three-year-old children. This has to be stopped before someone…dies." She swallowed hard. "I'm with Paige. I reckon we do it. If we plan it carefully, really cover our tracks, no one will ever know."

"But we might slip up." Belinda covered her stomach with her hand. "I'm about to have a baby. I'm not going to give birth behind bars. You will all lose your kids because you'll be in gaol. For a long time. For years."

Paige and Nikki exchanged a glance, a glance that said they were fed up and fearless. Desperate measures.

"I'm so certain I can do this without getting caught, that I'm willing to take the risk," Nikki said.

Belinda threw her hands up. "I'm not. No way. I don't care what the two of you do, but I'm not getting involved."

"It has to be unanimous or it doesn't happen."

"It's a no from me," Belinda said.

Nikki nodded. "That's fair enough. We've all got a lot to lose if it goes wrong."

"But we also have so much to gain if it goes right," Paige added.

"I already own Bitcoin," Nikki said. "I know how to access the dark web. Matt and I did a tonne of research, so I could stay a step ahead of my kids in case they were ever curious."

Belinda smiled and shook her head as though that didn't surprise her one bit.

"But we all have to be involved. Where one goes, so do all the others," Paige said.

"I'm not going to kill my mother-in-law," Belinda shouted.

"Okay. Okay. We can't force you." Nikki focused on her lap, picked a small ball of fluff from her jeans. She lifted her head, looked Belinda in the eyes. "But if you change your mind, I'm a phone call away."

Chapter 46

Vaughn

Vaughn's head was thick with pressure. Each pulse of blood throbbed in his temples. His mouth was dry and furry from the bottle of scotch he attacked last night.

He had lived on his own for nine months before he met Paige but never had his house felt so big nor empty. The silence ached all through his bones. His heart was torn. Big gaping fissures remained where he stored his love for Paige and Evie.

He wasn't a perfect man—no, in his grief, he had allowed his pain to make him do things he regretted so much. Belinda especially. He shouldn't have been so weak as to fall for her. Paige deserved more and so did his brother.

He ached to think that Belinda's baby could be his and that he would never know the truth. The only thing that got him through was Paige and Evie. His love for them both soothed that discontent.

But now Paige was gone too, and the agony of his existence was so loud it deafened him. He had attempted to blunt his misery with scotch until he had passed out on the couch.

He slowly sat up, opened his eyes and squinted against the mid-morning sunlight blasting through the front windows. His shoulders, arms and neck ached like they had been loaded with cement.

He pressed his face into his hands. How could his mother have done such a terrible thing to the woman he loved? There had to be another explanation. There had to be.

Spurred into action, he showered and brushed his teeth and tongue vigorously to scrape away last night's mistake. He dressed, then skolled down two Beroccas followed by paracetamols.

He climbed into his car and headed towards his mother's house. His stomach was stirring with nerves when he arrived at his childhood home. He was anxious about what he was going to hear. He couldn't believe his mother would call The Department of Child Safety on Paige, but he also couldn't come up with another possible explanation. She was the only one who had those photos.

He knocked on the front door and Mum answered it after a few moments.

"Hi, Mum," he said.

"Hi, darl, how are you? You don't look so well. Come inside and I'll make you a cup of coffee and some toast."

He followed her to the kitchen and took a seat at the small dining table. He glanced out the windows that overlooked the sprawling backyard. So many childhood memories were made here. Not all easy; it was tough after Dad died. He didn't remember too much about that time except for how his body never seemed to stop aching each time he had thought about his father.

"Paige left me," he said, voice unexpectedly quivering. He was pretty good at hiding his emotions but not today.

Mum's lips parted as her hand flung to her chest. "What? When did this happen?"

"Yesterday."

After a moment, she said, "I think that might be the best outcome for you both."

He met his mum's gaze. He had to ask her outright about Evie. A big part of him had resisted this conflict—the part that intuited Mum would divulge her knowledge of his affair with Belinda if he dared to confront her.

But he could no longer allow these games to go on, not when children were getting hurt. He had let Joanne down by doing nothing; he couldn't do the same to Paige, regardless of the cost to him.

"Did you hurt Evie?"

Her mouth fell open. "Of course I bloody well didn't. I disregarded Paige's text the other night thinking she was upset and would soon come to her senses, but now you."

Vaughn shrugged, sighed. "What about The Department of Child Safety? Did you send them those pictures?"

Mum shook her head, pressed a hand to her hip. "Vaughn, I did not send anyone any pictures. The only pictures being sent were from Paige. Honestly, the way she abused me over the phone, it scared me. I locked up the house, afraid for my safety."

"Seriously? We're talking about a five-foot-nothing young woman. Don't go blowing it all out of proportion."

"You obviously didn't hear the way she screamed at me. I have never copped that kind of abuse from anyone in my entire life. I was shaken. I'm getting older, Vaughn, I can't handle that kind of thing. It makes my nerves bad."

Vaughn rubbed his jaw with his palm. Three days of stubble scratched his hand. "I don't know what to believe anymore."

"I know who you should be believing and it's not that psychopath who hurts her own child. That cut under Evie's eye was alarming, you must admit."

He looked sidelong at his mother. "Evie fell onto the sprinkler."

"That's what Paige wants you to believe. It didn't look like a sprinkler cut to me. It looked as though she'd been punched, the way it swelled and her skin split open."

Vaughn furrowed his brow. Was this conversation really happening? “We were both there, Mum. We know exactly what happened. Evie fell onto the sprinkler.”

Mum shrugged. “That’s what Paige wants you to believe.”

He brushed a hand through his hair. “So, you didn’t complain to Child Safety?”

“I did no such thing.”

“Did you send the photos to Joshua?”

“No, I didn’t.”

“You were the only one who had those photos. There was no one else.”

Again, she shrugged, as calm as the sea on a bright sunny day. Yet inside Vaughn was in so much turmoil his hands were shaking.

“Can you be certain Paige didn’t send those pictures to someone else?” Mum asked. “Maybe she sent them to Joshua? Maybe it’s some gold-digging plan she has with Joshua against you. She is a lot younger. And you’re well set up with your own house. She moved in quite quickly, don’t you think?”

He shook his head, mouth gaping. How had he not seen this before? The way she twisted everything, flipped it on its head and turned the victim into the perpetrator.

Memories of arguments with Joanne flashed in his mind. She had been telling the truth about his mother. Guilt swamped his bloodstream and wrenched in his guts. She had pleaded with him, gave him ultimatums, desperate for him to see her point of view, but he couldn’t. Not when his mother was in the other ear, whispering her lies.

“You’re insane,” he said, shock and suspicion loud in his tone.

“Paige is insane. Look what she’s doing. She’s turning you against me now too. I don’t know what I did to deserve this. I did my best to be a good mother to you and your brothers. I had to do it all my own once your father died. I tried hard to give you everything you needed."

"Paige is not doing anything but trying to understand why you're hurting her."

"Listen to what you're saying. It doesn't make sense. She has brainwashed you to work against me. She is trying to take you away from this family. Can't you see? Nikki's already succeeded with Matt. He's no longer speaking to me. And now you." She pressed fingers to her temples as she shook her head. "I don't know what I did to deserve this. People always said that I would be shunned by my sons. Girls are loyal, but sons are very different. I did everything to make Paige feel settled with our family..."

He jerked backwards in his seat remembering that exact line coming out of his mother's mouth when he had come to see her about Joanne. *I did everything to make Joanne a part of our family*. He remembered those same sentiments with his girlfriend before that. *I tried my hardest to make her feel like she was part of this family.*

Had she always done this? Had she destroyed all his relationships?

He stood up.

Her eyes widened and she scurried back towards the sink, hands up in fear. "Don't hurt me!"

His lips twisted. "I wasn't going to hurt you. I was standing up to leave—"

"Get away from me," she screamed. "Get out, Vaughn. Get out. You're violent. Angry. You always have been. You frighten me. You're not a good person. You're a lying cheater and you're a horrible son."

Vaughn watched his mother. He was frozen to the spot. When he could make his body work, he shook his head, turned away from the cowering woman and left.

Chapter 47

Belinda

Once Belinda's sisters-in-law left a little after lunchtime, she convinced herself that she had fabricated the entire conversation. Surely, they couldn't have concocted a plot to murder their mother-in-law.

She scooted around clearing away cups and dishes and ran the vacuum over the carpet, all the while laughing to herself at the absurdity of the morning.

"Murder Claire," she mumbled, then giggled. "They couldn't have been serious."

Her phone blasted in the silence, and she raced to answer it. It would be Anthony calling her from Newcastle. But when Claire's name flashed on the screen, she almost dropped the phone. Her conscience, despite outright rejecting the murder plot, had her convinced that the mere conversation made her a criminal.

She contemplated not answering, but it kept blasting away with Claire's name flashing. She quickly brought her phone to her ear. "Um, Hi, Claire. How are you?"

"Hi, darl. I wasn't sure if you would be home or not."

Belinda clenched her teeth to hear Claire's overly polite sick voice. Her spine rigidly straightened. "I'm at home. I organised a temp to cover the store."

"Can you afford that? Considering."

Belinda rolled her eyes and suppressed the groan that sat in the back of her throat. "Not really, but I can't handle everything singlehandedly all the time."

"No, I suppose not."

"Is there something I can help you with?" Belinda asked. Her patience had run out after the previous barb.

"I've been trying to get onto Anthony, but he's probably very busy with work."

Again, Belinda rolled her eyes, not missing what was left unsaid: *as opposed to you sitting around at home fiddling your thumbs all morning*. "He would be, yes."

"I guess I better tell you then, just so you have some forewarning."

She stood very still. "Tell me what?"

"I'm going to need the twenty thousand dollars back as soon as possible. The stock market has taken a dive and I've received a margin call."

"A margin call? What's that?"

"Basically, it means I don't have enough money to cover the loan repayments I need to make on my investments. All very convoluted."

Belinda swallowed, but her mouth was too dry. "When would you need it by?"

"Immediately. I don't have that kind of cash sitting around. And I don't want to sell off more investments while the stocks are priced so low. I'd be going backwards."

"Right. Okay. And there is no other option?"

"None whatsoever."

Silence for a long moment as Belinda fought to find a solution to this, but every which way she looked at it, there was nothing. She had exhausted the very last of her available credit applying for a credit card, which she barely managed to get and had to concede to a lower amount than she had hoped for.

"We don't have twenty-thousand dollars, Claire. That's why we borrowed it off you in the first place. You said we could pay you back when we were capable." Her words were fast, filled with panic.

"I feel terrible. I hate putting this pressure on you both. It's the last thing I wanted to do. But I have no choice. I'm so sorry. I'm the worst. I really am. I've been in bed for two days in such a dark place because I knew I had to make this call." Her tone was laden with self-deprecation and apology. If Belinda had any less experience with this woman, she would be consumed with guilt and sympathy for her.

But Belinda knew better now. After her talk with her sisters-in-law this morning, she could see this reaction was a long-recurring pattern of behaviour.

"I don't know what to say. If we had it, I'd transfer you the money this minute. But we don't. The only option I have left is to go bankrupt. Then you definitely won't see the money. Ever."

"Oh, I see," Claire said with a seething tone, no trace of apology remaining. "So, you never planned to pay me back in the first place? At least I know where I stand now. I was trying to do the right thing, but perhaps I should be selfish next time. You know all about being selfish, don't you, Belinda? I wonder if your devoted husband would like to know about the ways you and Vaughn love to be selfish together behind his back."

All the blood rushed from Belinda's face. *Claire knows about the affair*. She swallowed hard as fear scuttled through her. "There's no need for that, Claire," she placated with a nervous chuckle. "Of course we plan to pay you back. We need some time, that's all. Forcing us right now to find it is impossible. I can't get blood from a stone."

"Better try and come up with something then, my dear, or that perfect bubble you try and convince yourself you live in might burst."

Belinda squeezed her eyes closed. "Look, let me speak with Anthony. Maybe he can sell off a truck at work or something." Although, he was already on a skeleton supply of equipment. But there was no other way out of this.

"Okay, darl, yes, that would be great if you could talk to Anthony." Claire's voice was sickly sweet again. Belinda shook her head, confused now if she had imagined the earlier threats or not. "But let me know as soon as you can please."

"Um…yes, of course. I'll talk to you soon."

When Belinda ended the call, she arched her head back and screamed. She knew Claire would do this to her. From the very beginning, she knew one day that this would end up costing her. It always did. Always. Nothing was ever given without it costing her ten times more in return.

And now that she had confirmation that Claire knew about the affair, it complicated matters so much more. If Anthony ever found out—their marriage was over. She placed a hand over her stomach and groaned. No, he could never know about Vaughn. Ever.

She called Anthony, but his phone rang out, so she left a message, though struggled to keep the fearful tremble from her voice. "Hi, Ant, can you give me a call as soon as you get this please."

She sank to the carpet, legs crossed beneath her. This circus was never going to end. And, after that phone call from Claire, she was certain circumstances were only going to get worse. Much worse.

They were in too much trouble, too deep. Bankruptcy was the only remaining solution. But if she didn't pay her mother-in-law back, Claire would tell Anthony about the affair. Then where would she be?

She scrubbed her face with her hands and groaned. Her body was throbbing. Each joint ached as the realisation she was about to lose everything pummelled her. All this stress could not be good for the baby, yet, she couldn't make it go away.

Nikki was right today about one thing—a big, fat inheritance would be a godsend. Claire had a stack of money. Her house was worth over a million dollars. Belinda had inadvertently stumbled across Claire's investment statements and knew that the balance of her portfolio was over three million dollars.

Belinda imagined how it would feel to inherit a million dollars. She and Ant would be able to pay off their debts and nearly all the mortgage. They could decorate the baby's room just like all those nurseries she had pasted into her scrapbook.

She imagined what life would be like without Claire in it. She smiled. Afterall, dead mothers-in-law couldn't spill marriage-ending secrets, could they?

The desire for that life burned up from within, lighting her with hope unlike anything else she had experienced in the past five years. Soon, it was all she could see—the relief, the joy. She would have her life back. She would keep her marriage intact.

She reached for her phone, in a daze, like she was floating above her body, and dialled Nikki.

"I'm in," was all she said when Nikki answered.

"I'll let Paige know."

Belinda sat there on the carpet for a long moment swallowing down her rising guilt. She wasn't a bad person. She had to do what was right for this growing family. Claire had no right to blackmail her. She had brought this upon herself.

She jumped when her phone rang again. Anthony's name filled the screen.

"Hey, babe, what's up? Everything okay?" he asked.

She closed her eyes and steadied her voice. "Yeah, everything's fine. I'm missing you."

"I miss you too. Every time I go away. But I have a surprise."

"You do?"

"We've finished earlier than anticipated, so I'm going to catch a flight home in about an hour. I should be back by five."

"You want me to pick you up from the airport?"

"I'd love it if you could."

"Send me your flight schedule and time and I'll meet you there."

"I can't wait to see you."

"Me too." And she really meant it. Hope was flourishing. Hope for their future. The future they were always meant to have—happy, loving, stable.

"I better give Mum a call back. I've had five missed calls from her."

Belinda's heart thumped hard. "No, no. That's fine. Don't worry about calling her back. I've spoken to her already. She didn't realise you were working away. She just wanted to know where you left the lawnmower because she has someone coming around to service it."

"Where the hell would she think I left the lawnmower? The same place it's been since I was a kid. I'm certain that woman uses any excuse to call a hundred times a day."

"Tell me about it," Belinda said.

Chapter 48

Paige

"I believe you," were the first words Vaughn spoke when Paige answered his call. "I believe you."

Relief flourished. Goosebumps fanned over her skin. She sank onto the bed and squeezed her forehead with her finger and thumb.

"I couldn't see it before, but I did today. I went to see Mum…she's lost her mind. I believe you."

A small whimper escaped Paige's throat. "Thank you."

"Where are you? I need to see you. I miss you so much."

She squeezed her eyes closed. "I miss you too."

"I'll do everything to make it right, Paige. Everything. Mum has destroyed every relationship I've had, and I didn't even realise. Until this morning." His words were strangled with grief; her heart sang with sympathy for him. No matter what Claire had done, this was not Vaughn's fault. He was as much a victim as she was. Probably even more so because he had to deal with Claire all his life.

She gave him the name of the hotel she was staying at and waited for him.

After a phone call from Nikki earlier, letting Paige know that Belinda was willing to move ahead with their murder plot, she had wanted some time to gather her thoughts, so she kept Evie with her friend for a little longer than planned.

When Vaughn arrived, she rode the elevator to the foyer. She spotted him from across the room and ran to him, throwing her arms around his big, protective body.

He enclosed her in his arms, pulled her tightly against him and kissed her. “Don’t ever leave me again.” The faintest scent of alcohol hung around him. He was dishevelled, crumpled.

“Rough night?” she asked.

“Don’t even ask.’

They headed up to her room and sat on the end of the bed beside one another.

She reached for his hand and peered into his hazel eyes. A sadness had dulled their usual shine. “What made you believe me?”

Vaughn told her of his visit to Claire that morning. Her head spun as he recounted the horrendous details. Never had she met someone like Claire who underhandedly but deliberately made her children’s lives chaos.

Vaughn lowered his gaze and sighed. “All these little fragments of my life are piecing together. You know, I grew up believing I was an angry person. A violent person. I would get into spats at school, then when I was a young man, out on the town, I’d fight with other men. But then one day, I stopped. I stopped because I realised I wasn’t angry or vicious. Fighting distressed me. But I had been told by Mum all my life that I was that person. When you hear something enough times, you believe it.” He groaned, rubbed the back of his neck. “What kind of messed up childhood did I have?”

She held his shoulder. “It doesn’t matter. You came to know who you truly are, regardless.”

“I can’t distinguish what was real and what wasn’t. Was Matt ever sick? You know, he had lymphoma when he was thirteen. One night, he crept into my and Anthony’s room. He was hysterical, blubbering and shaking. He tried to convince us he wasn’t sick. That the doctor had said he was fine. He said Mum was making it all up." Vaughn lifted his head, looked into Paige's eyes. "I thought he was trying to make us feel better, so we didn't worry. But what if he was telling the truth?"

Paige gasped and threw her hand over her mouth. "You've got to be kidding."

He shook his head. "I wish I was. He was always sick. Always stuck in his room watching us from the window."

"When all along it was your Mum saying he was sick, so she could get attention."

"Or she was making him sick? I really hope it isn't true, but after today, I don't know anymore." He shook his head, looked away. So softly, that she could barely hear it, he said, "Poor Matt. So many years of his life, wasted."

"And yet he seems like he's doing okay now."

He faced her again. "He changed so much once he left home for work. Nothing like the child he was."

"Because your mum couldn't influence him anymore."

"Exactly."

"I'm mortified, Vaughn. Absolutely mortified."

"I don't know how to deal with all this."

"Give it a couple of weeks. You're shocked. Give yourself some time to come up with a rational plan about how we go forward."

"We?" he asked, hope in his eyes. "There's an *us* again?"

She smiled, nodded. "We're too right for one another to give up on what we have."

"Will you come home?"

Warmth blossomed in her chest because a *home* with Vaughn and Evie was all she had ever wanted. "On one condition. Claire doesn't step foot on our property."

"Deal. I'm going to organise a locksmith to change the front lock, and I'll get security screens installed on all the windows."

She leaned in, kissed his lips, and whispered. "Thank you."

"I'll do whatever it takes to have you back where you belong and keep you and Evie safe."

A deep clenching in her guts as she recalled her conversation with Joshua. "I rang Joshua yesterday. He's seen a lawyer and is seeking full custody."

"How could he possibly get full custody?"

"Under normal circumstances, he wouldn't. But if they think I'm putting Evie in danger, I'll lose custody."

"But it's not true."

She pressed a palm to her chest. "You know that, and I know that. But the courts may see it differently. We have no idea what kind of stories Claire has spun about Evie's injuries. But we do know how convincing she is."

He rolled his head back and groaned as he looked up to the ceiling. "What do we do?"

She shrugged and blinked back tears as all her fear crept up her limbs and settled in her chest. "Hope that Child Safety can see that I love my daughter very much and would never hurt her. And hope that the courts are fair."

"That's not good enough. I'm not counting on *hope*. We need action." He held out his hand. "Pass me your phone, please."

"What? Why?"

"Just pass it here. I've let too many people down in my life by doing nothing. No more. It's time I start taking care of you—in all the ways that count. Otherwise, we lose."

She tentatively gave him her phone. He scrolled through her contacts and hit dial. When he clicked it onto speakerphone, the bleeping ringtone blared in the silent hotel room.

"Hi, Paige," Joshua said.

"It's Vaughn. Paige's partner."

"What do you want?"

"I want to ask you a serious question that demands an honest answer."

"What is it?"

"Do you believe, deep in your heart, that Paige would ever intentionally hurt her daughter?"

"Mate, I don't have to listen to this—"

"You're trying to take a daughter away from her mother, so, yes, you do have to listen. And you need to, for once in your life, think about someone other than yourself. Because you're going to hurt two beautiful, loving people—one of those people being your daughter. So, I repeat, do you believe Paige would intentionally hurt Evie?"

"I don't know."

"Honestly?"

"I'm being honest. Why would your mother throw her under the bus if it weren't true?"

"My mother isn't the kind-hearted woman she makes herself out to be."

"Well, as the biological father of Evie, unlike you, I'm not going to take that risk."

"Bullshit!" Vaughn barked. "This is, and always has been, about you. So let me tell you a little bit that I know about you. One night you slammed your fist into your pregnant girlfriend's face so hard and so violently that you broke her cheekbone—"

"I don't have to listen to this shit—"

"Man-up to what you've done. You broke your girlfriend's face. She had to go to the hospital on her own because you were bombed out of your brain. If you expect any young woman to go running back to her abuser rather than run as far as she can in the opposite direction, so she can provide a safe home for her and her child, then you're a moron."

"Get fucked. Don't pretend to know what my life is like."

"I don't care about you or your life. I care about Paige and Evie. But I will tell you this—if you want to play this custody game, we will play it too. There's a full report at the hospital about what you did to Paige. We got access to it, including photos and police statements. I am one click away from emailing this to a reporter. You may have gotten away with domestic violence in the past, but nowadays, society, especially the media, looks down on thug football players who beat their pregnant girlfriends. I suspect you might lose your job. How do you like the sound of that?"

Silence. "Don't blackmail me."

"It's not blackmail. Not one bit. Just the truth finally coming out."

"I'm not like that anymore."

"That doesn't matter in the end. Trial by media doesn't play by any rules."

Joshua blew out a long breath. "What do you want?"

"Drop the custody battle. I'm not going to get in the way of you having a role in Evie's life, but it will be on Paige's terms and what works best for Evie. If I were you, I'd be trying to make it up to the two of them, rather than screwing them both over again. You can start by paying child support. Or did you forget about that side of your responsibility? And how about you apologise to Paige when you talk to her next. That would be a good start."

A low rumble from Joshua. Paige met Vaughn's gaze. Her stomach was flipping. After what felt like a long minute, Joshua finally said, "Fine. I'll drop the custody claim. But I can't stop Child Safety; it's in their hands now."

Vaughn squeezed his eyes shut, then opened them. "Let's just hope that they can see through your bullshit accusations. Because if they don't, I'm hitting send on the email. You don't get to falsely complain that someone is abusive and yet get away with what you did. No way."

Vaughn hung up and laid the phone on the bed beside them.

Paige's breaths were rushed. Her eyes glossed as a modicum of weight lifted from her shoulders. A small smile flittered at the corners of her mouth. "I think that may have worked."

"I hope so. Let's wait and see if his actions match his words."

Paige crossed her fingers and held them up. "I'm hoping with every part of me."

"Me too."

"Thank you so much, Vaughn. I mean it, you don't understand how much I value your support."

He kissed her lips. "That's what I promise to do from now on. I'm sorry I let you down."

"It's not your fault." She took his hand in hers and stared at their entwined fingers. "Um, Vaughn, I think there's something I need to tell you. Something I found out that might be difficult for you to hear."

Vaughn's brow crumpled.

"I saw Belinda this morning. I needed someone to talk to."

Vaughn nodded quickly. "Okay."

"I promised not to say anything, but I think after all the lies and twisted half-truths, it's better you know the facts."

"Tell me," he said, impatience thick in his words.

"Anthony found an old blood donor card that belonged to your father. The blood type recorded on the card is not the same as your blood type."

Vaughn wheezed, lifted his hands onto his head and stood up. "What? I don't understand?"

"The donor card had Type AB positive listed for Robert. Supposedly yours is different."

Vaughn squeezed his eyes shut, shuffled his hands through his hair, then looked down at her. "I'm O negative."

"And no one else in your family has that blood type?"

"I was told Dad did."

"Anthony has a memory of seeing your mother kissing another man at a barbeque when he was younger. He thinks that this man might be your real father."

"What the hell, Paige?"

"I know. I'm sorry. I wasn't going to say anything. But I think the truth needs to come out. There are too many falsehoods. I don't know which way is up."

Vaughn collapsed onto the bed beside her, elbows on knees, and stared at the carpet beneath his feet. She rubbed his back but stayed silent, giving him the mental space needed to work through this enormous revelation.

"How could she?" he finally asked, lifting his head to look at her. His eyes were wet with tears. "How could she hide this from me all this time?"

Paige shook her head. "I can't answer that."

He lowered his face into his hands. "Who is my father then?"

"I don't know."

"All this time. I had not one clue," he groaned. "Fuck this."

"I'm sorry," Paige said. "I'm so sorry."

Chapter 49

Nikki

Belinda stood in Nikki's doorway, twitchy and alert, the pallor of her face noticeable in the morning summer sunlight.

"It's here," Belinda said.

It had taken four days from start to finish for their delivery of *Stachybotrys chartarum* to arrive. Nikki ordered and paid for it, Belinda set up an anonymous post office box where it could be delivered, and Paige sought out the face masks and utensils they would need when planting the toxic mould.

Nikki had researched in books at the library—no traceable Google searches that way—that Claire, with her asthma, childhood exposure to toxic mould, and her allergy, was highly susceptible to the mycotoxins that this kind of mould produced.

The microscopic spores could be inhaled or ingested and could even pass through the skin. Placing them in Claire's bedroom air conditioner would ensure these mycotoxins would find their way into her system.

Nikki's stomach swirled and punched—all their plotting over the past week was no longer a pipedream but a reality.

They had ensured the majority of their contact with each other was face-to-face. Limited phone calls. With the types of metadata that telecommunication companies kept, it was too great a risk. If anything went wrong, they didn't need the evidence pointing to any of them. Paige had bought her masks from two different stores in rural areas where it was less likely there were any cameras.

"Come in," Nikki said, nerves already flourishing, making her fingers jittery. "I'll give Paige a call. How long do we have until art class?"

"One hour," Belinda said. "That will give us at least two hours to get it done. And if Claire has lunch after her class, then even longer."

"We can't count on lunch. We'll aim to get to her house by ten-thirty and be out in fifteen minutes max."

Nikki sent a text to Paige.

NIKKI: *Hi, Paige. Do you have any lemons I can use for this tart I'm baking?*

PAIGE: *I do. Will be there soon.*

"Have you opened the package?" Nikki asked.

Belinda shook her head.

"Good. I don't want you exposing yourself—not while you're pregnant. We'll wait for Paige to get here. Do you want a cup of tea?"

"I couldn't possibly." Belinda shook her hands in front of her. "I'm so nervous."

"Come into the living room. We'll sit there while we wait."

It didn't take long for Paige to arrive. When Nikki opened the door and saw the two misshapen lemons in Paige's hands, she chuckled—nervous delirium of some kind. Paige's mouth lifted at the corners as she held up the lemons and shook them about. They both cracked up laughing until tears were rolling down their cheeks and Nikki had to cross her legs lest she wet herself.

"Quickly. Come inside," Nikki managed through giggles.

Paige wiped the tears from her cheeks and followed Nikki to the living room, intermittently laughing all the way.

They had met at Nikki's home, and sometimes at Belinda's, nearly every day to discuss their plans. Nothing was written down, but each point was soldered into their memories through repetition.

"We have the package," Nikki said as she took a seat.

The smile fell from Paige's face. She placed the lemons on the coffee table and took a seat next to Belinda. Her noisy exhale was notably tremulous.

"Today's the day. I think we get it over and done with," Nikki said.

Paige nodded, movements quick and sharp.

"What I want you both to do…" Nikki looked each of them in the eye "…is to really contemplate what we're about to do here. Claire will die. With her allergy and past exposure, it's likely that she will fall ill first with pneumonia or some other lung complaint, but it should take her out in a matter of days, maybe a week."

Belinda wiped her mouth; her fingers were trembling. "I have changed my mind so many times this past week. But I need to think about my baby and the future of my family. They are what is most important. Claire is doing everything she can to ruin me and Ant. Purely out of spite. As difficult as today will be, living with Claire is harder. I just want to get it over with."

Paige swallowed hard as she lightly pinched her throat. "I will never forgive Claire for what she has done to me. Ever. Every time I think about losing Evie, the hatred and anger I feel for Claire makes me shake. I haven't deserved any of this and neither has my daughter. If Claire could do this to Evie, who knows what rights she will believe she has over future babies that share her biology. I'm not taking any risks because she is rotten. Evil, right down to her marrow."

Nikki blew out a long breath. Her neck was tense; her stomach a knot of nerves. Every part of her was screaming to back out. Nightmares had rocked her these last few nights. She had awoken, amidst early morning shadows, terrified, sweating and trembling.

But no matter how much her conscience and body tried to warn her of the immorality of murder, of how momentous and wrong it was, her mind was set because for Nikki, with her mental decline, it was a matter of life or death—her own or Claire's. "I want my life back. The quicker the better."

"I guess that means we're all in," Belinda said. Her words were hollow, full of doubt.

Paige nodded. "I guess so."

They had made their decision, prepared for it, now they had to carry through with it, no matter how hard that would be.

"So, you've got care covered for Evie?" Nikki asked Paige.

"Yes, I feigned a migraine and my friend came around and picked her up for the day."

"Great."

"I arranged a temp to cover the shop," Belinda added. "All organised on that front."

"Good. Both my boys are at school. Matt is at work," Nikki said. "You've brought a change of clothes?"

Paige nodded.

"I'll go get the masks, and we'll see what we've got inside that package."

Nikki ran downstairs into the sub-level garage. She had hidden the two masks away in a barely used cupboard inside a plastic box she kept for miscellaneous tools.

When she opened the cupboard door, the masks were now hanging from a hook on the side of the cupboard. Matt must have found them, though he hadn't mentioned anything to her. But why would he? The masks were only incriminating because she knew that a crime would be committed while wearing them.

She rushed back upstairs. “Come on, Paige, we’ll do this in the mudroom.”

Masks donned, they enclosed themselves in the backroom, pulled on some latex gloves and safety goggles. Nikki carefully unwrapped the package, disposing of the brown wrapping paper into a garbage bag.

She opened the box with unsteady hands and found two translucent petri dishes, both sealed and sitting in a balloon of bubble wrap. The outskirts of her vision were dreamlike, shadowed by the fear shooting through her bloodstream. She practiced calm, deep breaths, in and out.

With Paige’s help, she lifted out the dishes and placed them separately into clear Ziplock bags, then closed them off. Inside the first dish was a gelatinous culture, discoloured with brown-black splotches of mould, like someone had flicked blobs of paint onto a canvas. The second dish was filled with a grey powdery substance—dry mould.

Nikki had anticipated breaches to the containers or some other type of trickery considering she had bought it off the dark web, but what she observed was highly professional. It sent a chill down her neck and back to know that these dark operations existed undercover to normal society.

The cultured mould should continue to thrive if conditions were kept right; however, if the dried mould didn’t find something to attach to in a warm, moist environment, it would soon die. They had to plant it in Claire’s home today.

Nikki disposed of the box into the garbage bag. She and Paige peeled off their gloves and tossed them in too. She tied off the bag and tucked it inside an empty sealable plastic tub, which they would use to store all of today’s waste, before closing the lid.

They washed their hands in the laundry tub, rinsed their goggles and dried them with a paper towel, then carried the Ziplock bags to show Belinda.

Belinda took a step back, eyes wide when she saw them. "So, this is it?"

Nikki trembled, a long wrack from her ankles to her head, as she checked the clock on the wall. Her mouth was bone dry. "I'll go change my clothes, then it's time to go."

With Nikki in the passenger seat and Paige in the back, Belinda drove into town and soon enough they were about to pass the detached brick building where Claire attended her art classes. Nikki and Paige both ducked out of sight.

"Her car is there," Belinda reported.

A little farther up the road, they pulled into a large carpark that was already filled with tourists' cars. Belinda parked but kept the engine rumbling. "Keep your mobiles on vibrate. I'll call if need be. Otherwise, let me know when you are both on your way back."

Belinda climbed out and Nikki shifted along to the driver's seat. They waited for Belinda to make it to the café across the road. When she sat on the deck, she would have a perfect vision of the art building. If Claire was, for any reason, to leave her art class, Belinda would know.

Belinda's job was to keep a lookout and to text if there was any unusual movement. With Claire's house an eight-minute drive from the centre of town, that would give Nikki and Paige more than enough time to clear the house and drive away in the opposite direction.

With Belinda out of sight, Nikki drove out of the carpark. In exactly eight minutes, they arrived at Claire's property. She parked down the long driveway as close as they could to the house. Shady trees offered some privacy from neighbours and the road.

Nikki cut the engine. Paige collected the precisely packed backpack at her feet, slung it over her shoulder, and they climbed out of the car and walked as casually as they could towards the front door.

Nikki retrieved the key from her pocket, pushed it into the lock and they went inside. The familiar scent of Claire's home rushed at them—subtle perfume, the strong scent of bleach, leather and timber. That smell was so reminiscent of Claire it was as though she was here, her dark eyes watching them.

Nikki's calmness slid away for a moment as her legs jellied. She had an overwhelming urge to vomit. Paige's face was pale. Her eyes watered.

"We can back out. It's not too late," she whispered through quivering lips.

Paige was quiet for a long while as she scanned the room and passed Nikki the bag. "This was always going to be hard." Nikki could barely recognise Paige's voice—weak, low, unsure. "But we have to keep going."

Nikki closed her eyes, waited until her breathing had calmed. She had to focus on each of her tasks and ignore everything else if she was going to get through this.

Task one: she slid her shoes off, kept her socks on. Task two: she started towards the stairs while Paige closed and locked the front door.

Task three: "Anyone home?" she called out.

She waited, holding her breath.

No one answered. The silence was thick, overwhelming. Nikki's heart was racing. One after the other, Nikki leading the way, they tiptoed up the stairs and headed down the long hallway and into Claire's room. Paige checked all the rooms as she followed, in case an unexpected visitor was there.

In Claire's bedroom, Nikki unpacked what they needed: two petri dishes, cotton tips, a spray bottle filled with warm water, garbage bags, gloves, masks, and goggles.

"All clear," Paige said as she joined Nikki again at the foot of Claire's bed. Everything was laid out in order on the floor. They put on their masks, gloves and goggles as quickly as they could.

Paige collected the first petri dish, while Nikki went to the head of the bed and stood onto it. The mattress sank under her weight, and she wobbled slightly before righting herself. Her heart was in her throat, her blood pulsed in her ears. She didn't dare imagine Claire slowly dying on the bed as she breathed in murderous spores.

She steadied herself, then lifted open the casing of the wall-mounted air conditioner. It was pristine inside—no dust and definitely no mould. Claire was meticulous when it came to mould proofing her home, thus the reason it always smelled like bleach.

Paige opened the Ziplock bag, lifted the top casing of the petri dish and handed it to Nikki along with a clean cotton tip. Nikki swept the cotton tip across the mould, digging out a gelatinous swab, then wiped it onto the fibrous filter pads. She lifted the tab that opened when the air conditioner was running and wiped the mould onto a few of the fan blades.

She handed the petri dish back to Paige and was given the powdery dry mould. She sprinkled a dusting along the rim of the air conditioner so that when it opened, the fan would blow the spores into the room.

She crouched on all fours, reached her hand behind the head of the bed and sprinkled more of the dust along the carpet. With the spray bottle in hand, Paige stretched a hand under the bed and sprayed the dusty carpet with warm water, hoping to provide the mould with the perfect environment to thrive.

Nikki climbed off the bed and disposed of everything she had used today into the garbage bag. Paige followed her lead while Nikki set about straightening the bed, smoothing the creases in the coverlet and realigning the pillows just right.

When downstairs, they stood in the entrance hall and removed their clothes, gloves, goggles and mask, pushing them into a garbage bag. They changed into clean clothes, then strode outside the house, making sure the door was locked behind them.

Nikki gasped at the fresh air as though she hadn't taken a breath the whole time she was inside. She scanned the driveway, the road, the neighbour's home—no one was visible.

She went to the boot, shoved the garbage bags, backpack, all their clothes and gear into the plastic tub, sealed the lid, then climbed into the driver's seat. Within a moment, they were back on the road and heading towards the café.

Paige sent the pre-arranged coded text to Belinda.

PAIGE: *Want to grab a coffee?*

Paige read the reply to Nikki.

BELINDA: *Sure. Meet you soon.*

Back at the carpark, Belinda strode stiffly to meet them, climbed into the back seat and they set off.

No one was able to speak until the last of the rubbish had been tossed out of the car, including the big plastic tub, down the steepest, most treacherous part of the range. It landed tens of metres below amidst thick vines and trees, unreachable by anyone.

Nikki's knuckles were white as they gripped the steering wheel. Little convulsions wracked her body from time to time. She blinked back tears and suppressed the overwhelming desire to sob and scream.

Paige turned to her, then to Belinda through the rear-view mirror. "We really did it." There was a tight, hoarseness to her voice.

"The hard part is over," Belinda said. "I honestly thought I was going to have a heart attack while waiting. I kept imagining someone catching you both."

Nikki shook her head. "No problems."

"We checked the room before we left, didn't we?" Paige asked.

"Three times, thoroughly. We left nothing behind."

"And I locked the door?"

"I checked it," Nikki said. "It was locked."

"And Claire stayed where she was the entire time," Belinda said. "We're clear."

"We're clear," Paige repeated with a sharp nod and a long exhalation.

"We don't have to do anything else but be there for our husbands," Nikki said. "And then we're free."

"We're free," Belinda said breathlessly. "We're free."

Chapter 50

Belinda

Belinda arrived home a little after lunchtime. Her adrenalin had finally slowed. Her mouth was dry and judging by the headache pounding at her temples, she was dehydrated. Her hands shook and her stomach was painfully hollow. All morning, she hadn't been able to handle the thought of anything in her stomach.

She headed to the kitchen for a big drink of water and some lunch. Anthony was at the sink, dressed in his work uniform. She yelped with fright.

He smiled at her reaction.

"You scared the hell out of me. I wasn't expecting you home."

He pressed a palm to his forehead. "Got a massive headache. I need to have some paracetamol and a sleep."

"That's no good," she managed, steadying herself.

"How come you're home?" he asked.

"Same thing. A headache. I hope it's not a virus going around."

He shrugged. "I think it's stress."

"Why? What's happening?"

His shoulders slouched on his long exhale. "I'm always on the back foot. At work. With our finances. I need a day away from it all."

In the ten years Anthony had owned his business, Belinda had barely known him to take a day off. "Go have a lie-down. I'll come up soon. I think I need a nap as well."

When he was out of the kitchen, she used the time to gather her thoughts. She made a toasted sandwich and refilled her water bottle. She sipped on the water while her sandwich cooked, a strong bready scent making her stomach groan with hunger.

Flashes of imagined scenes kept flickering through her mind: Nikki and Paige in the house with their masks, goggles and gloves; Claire, pale and unmoving on the floor, eyes ghostly grey as they stared at nothing. She shuddered and forced the thoughts away.

It was more than apparent that their circumstances were taking a toll on Anthony. She wanted to rush upstairs and tell him not to worry—soon it would all be okay. They had some heartache to get through, but then when the inheritance came, they would be able to look forward and start fresh. All this exhausting clambering to survive, day after day, would be over. But she couldn't. This was something she would never be able to confess. Not to Anthony. Not to anyone. But that was okay. What she did today was a burden she was willing to endure because the outcome would be worth it.

After lunch, she dragged her weary body upstairs to join Anthony. He was resting on the bed, dressed only in a pair of shorts.

"Mum rang me this morning," he said when she climbed onto the bed beside him.

Her heart stuttered in her chest so hard she thought he'd be able to hear the pounding. She drew a breath in, steadied her voice. "Yes?"

"I don't understand what she was going on about. She assumed I was selling a work asset to pay her back the twenty grand. Something about a margin call. Said you knew all about it and was going to handle it."

Her heart crept up her throat. She looked up to the ceiling. "I don't know anything about that."

"That's what I told her. News to me. She sounded upset. I said there was no way I could sell anything at work. We're already bare-bones as it is."

"So bizarre. Why would she even ask such a thing?"

He shrugged. "God knows. Like I need that extra pressure."

Belinda rolled onto her side and wrapped an arm around him. She nestled her head on his shoulder. "So, what did you tell her?"

"I told her that she had no right to go back on our agreement and put us under so much pressure. I was frustrated because I thought she had bothered you with it. We can't be stressing you out, not while you're pregnant."

She cuddled in closer, wrapping a thigh over his. "Exactly. I'm glad you stood up to her."

A weary grumble in his chest. "Yes, well, experience tells me it won't be the end of it."

But it would be the end of it, Belinda thought as she snuggled against the heat of his body. It would be ended permanently. As she drifted off to sleep, she willed time to hurry. The sooner Claire was buried, the better off they would all be.

Chapter 51

Claire

The weather was disgusting with humidity through the roof. Claire wasn't able to handle Queensland's extreme summer temperatures as much as she could when younger, but she abhorred the cold much more, so it was something she chose to put up with.

After art class, she skipped her usual lunch date. The day was too stuffy. Not a breath of air rustled the tree branches. Besides, she had recorded a great movie last night that she was itching to get back to.

Her next-door neighbour, Macie, was skipping across the driveway after a black and white chequered ball when Claire pulled into her yard. She obviously had the grandkids again for the day, something Macie gloated endlessly about. Claire would smile and nod but quietly think that she'd rather get her eyes plucked out than look after grandkids every day.

Her child-rearing days were over. She had earned a break. If not now at sixty-five, then when? She'd be too old to enjoy herself another ten or twenty years down the track.

Claire contemplated driving past Macie, up to the garage and closing the door on her before she could say anything, but that's not what neighbours did. So, she stopped beside Macie and smiled as she wound down her window. "Good afternoon. Looks like you've got the little ones to keep you on your toes again today."

Macie grinned. "Yeah, I've got Jack today. So that means outdoor ball games to keep him occupied."

She looked past Macie through a gap in the pines into her front yard where four-year-old Jack was waiting for his grandmother to return. It took her breath away sometimes how much this boy looked like Vaughn. She was glad Robert wasn't still around to see the similarities.

"How are you, Macie?"

"I'm well. Ruby is pregnant again, so I'm clucky as hell."

"Congratulations. So that's her…"

"Third baby," Macie finished for her.

"So wonderful. I'm chomping at the bit for Anthony and Belinda to have their baby."

"I bet you're hoping for a girl after three boys of your own, then two grand-boys," Macie said.

"Yes and no. I'll be happy as long the baby is healthy."

"Of course," Macie said nodding emphatically. "I saw your daughter-in-law here earlier today, but I was busy so I couldn't come over and say hello."

Claire's brow furrowed. "Really? Which one?"

"Nikki, along with a younger woman. I've seen her here a couple of times with Vaughn."

"Today?"

Macie looked at her watch. "Yeah, about an hour or so ago, I guess."

Claire shrugged. "Who knows? Be nice if they stopped in to clean up for me."

"Wouldn't that be lovely? A little bit of payback for all the help you give them."

"Exactly. But wishful thinking on my part."

Macie rolled her eyes. "Always is. They want everything for nothing."

"So true. Not like our generation, that's for sure."

"Grandma," Jack called. "Throw me the ball."

Macie glanced away, then turned to Claire with an apologetic grin. "I better get back to it."

"Of course. I'll talk to you later."

Claire raised the window again and drove into the garage. She went inside and looked around the house. What would Nikki have wanted? She was having one of her annual hissy fits and apparently not speaking to Claire right now.

"Yeah, right," Claire scoffed. "Until she wants me for something."

She put her bag on the bench and scrounged inside for her mobile phone. She called Matt.

"Hi," Matt said.

"Hi, darl, how are you?"

"I'm okay."

"I was just talking to Macie next door. She said Nikki stopped around here earlier today. Any idea what for?"

"I don't know. Maybe she wanted to call a truce."

"Surely, though, she knows by now I have art class on a Tuesday."

"Look, Mum, I'm not certain. I'm sure if it's important, she'll call you."

"Very true. So how are you going? I haven't heard from you for weeks."

Deep male voices sounded in the background.

"I'm just about to head in to see a client. So, I better go. I'll give you a call later."

Claire bit down her anger. "Oh, okay. Talk soon."

She hung up with an aggressive press of the button. The way her sons always rushed to get off the phone to her was so damn rude.

Claire quickly changed into more comfortable clothing and hurried to the living room, a bottle of ice-cold white wine and a clean glass in her hand. She settled on the couch in front of the television and flicked on her recorded movie.

Chapter 52

Paige

Paige threw herself into her work to distract from her jittery impatience. Every phone call, she jumped. Every visitor, whether that be a pre-arranged appointment or a parcel delivery, her heart raced. If she kept busy, then she didn't have to think about what she had done and what was yet to come—Claire's eventual death.

Halfway through sewing a hem on a long evening gown, her phone buzzed, and she flinched. A private number. She answered it, her pulse thrumming when the woman on the other end of the line introduced herself as Bridget from The Department of Child Safety.

"Hi, Bridget," she said, then swallowed the dread in her throat.

"I wanted to give you a call to let you know that we have closed your case."

Paige jumped to her feet, started pacing across her sewing room. "What does that mean?"

"We found no evidence that you are harming or neglecting Evie. The case is closed."

Paige fell to the floor on her knees. Air streamed from her lungs. "Thank God."

"We knew the moment we walked into your house and spoke to you that nothing was there, but when we receive that type of complaint, we have to follow up."

‘I understand. Thank you for letting me know.”

“Have a good day.”

“Yes, you too.”

Paige crouched there for a long while as tears streamed down her face. Eventually, she dragged herself from the floor and wiped her eyes. She raced up the hall to Evie’s room and poked her head inside to watch her beautiful daughter sleeping. Relief begged her to run in, gather Evie into her arms and give her the biggest cuddle, but she let her sleep.

Back in her sewing room, she rang Vaughn.

“Hi, sweetheart, how are you?”

“I’m doing really well.” Her smile flourished in her tone.

“Really? Why, what happened?”

“Child Safety rang me saying that they’ve closed the case,” she squealed. “They couldn’t find any signs of abuse.”

“I knew they’d be able to see what a great mum you are.”

“I’m so relieved, I can’t stop crying happy tears.”

“We’ll have to celebrate tonight. We’ll go out for dinner. The three of us.”

“That sounds perfect.”

“No word from Joshua yet?” he asked.

“Not a peep. I’m not going to go out of my way to contact him. And I hope he doesn’t ever contact me again.”

“Now that’s a thought,” Vaughn said with a chuckle.

She wanted to gloat and say Claire was not as clever as she presumed herself to be. But deep down, Paige held tightly to the knowingness that Claire would soon get her comeuppance.

Chapter 53

Claire

Claire startled awake when her own snore interrupted her deep unconsciousness. She slowly sat up. The lights were bright overhead. The television was blaring—some unknown late-night show.

Two empty bottles of wine sat on the coffee table beside a lipstick-stained wineglass. Her mind whirled around her. Her body was numb. Tomorrow she would have a raging headache and an aching body. That was the reason she only drank every second night these days. It took so long to recover, and the hangovers were much worse than when she was younger.

She dreaded dragging her heavy body up the stairs. Maybe it was time to sell this place and downsize to a single level home. Or she could turn the library into her bedroom—that would be easier. *Or I can bloody well drink less.*

Swaying slightly as she stood, she waited until she was steady before she headed upstairs, gripping the handrail tightly and trudging up each step. Her shirt clung to her back by sweat. Beads of perspiration covered her forehead. Summer this year was going to be a killer.

When in her room, she undressed, having to sit on the end of the bed to take off her pants and knickers lest she fall over and hurt herself again. She crawled along the bed, digging down under the covers before kicking them off.

She laid there, naked, a little cooler, but tonight would be a night the air conditioner was a must. She grabbed the remote from the wall and pressed the start button. The air conditioner whirred and then gusted. A fine layer of dust shot out and covered her face and bed.

"Jesus Christ," she hissed, wiping her face and dusting off her bed with her palm. She had only cleaned that bloody thing a few days ago. How could it possibly be dusty already? She was fastidious with her cleaning. Especially equipment or places in her house that could easily grow mould. It only took two weeks for mould to find a home and start flourishing.

But by the time she finished that thought, her eyes closed, and unconsciousness was creeping up on her.

I'll wipe it out again tomorrow, she thought before sleep found her.

Chapter 54

Matt

The past…

"Mum's going to head out again," Auntie Maggie said. "And I will be looking after you three."

Matt rolled his eyes. "I'm twelve-years-old. I'm old enough to look after myself."

Auntie Maggie laughed and ruffled his hair. "Boys are always the same. Too big for your boots."

"I'm exactly the right size for my shoes," he said. "And I don't own boots."

Mum marched past him, wrapping her coat around herself, and headed out the door. "I'll see you later."

When the door clicked closed behind her, he shook his head. Mum hadn't collected him and his brothers from school today; the next-door neighbour, Macie, met them at the school gates instead. She wouldn't say why.

"What's going on? Has Mum got a new job?"

Auntie Maggie bent at the waist and rested her hands on her knees as she addressed him. "Your mum needs to be with your father."

His brow furrowed. "Why? What's Dad doing?"

Auntie Maggie shifted from one foot to the other, narrowed her eyes. "You don't know?"

"Know what?"

"Matt, your father is badly hurt. He's in hospital."

Matt flinched. Auntie Maggie's words were like a kick to his chest. "Dad's hurt?" He lowered his eyes, heart beating faster. "What's wrong with him?"

"Has your mother told you nothing?" she asked.

He shook his head. "I don't know anything." Panic was rising. What could have happened that was so bad his mother had kept it hidden from him?

"He fell off scaffolding at work."

"From up high?"

She nodded, frowned. "Three storeys."

Matt understood that was high enough to kill a person. "Is he dead?" he whispered, words struggling to escape his tightening throat.

Auntie Maggie rubbed her forehead and wiped the tear that rolled onto her cheek. "No. But it doesn't look good."

His lips trembled. Dad was going to die. Urgency rocketed through him. "I want to go see him. I want to go see him now."

"Your mother wants you to stay here."

"No," he yelled. "That's not fair. I want to see my dad."

"I know. I know, sweetie. But your mum knows best."

"Why didn't she tell me? I don't understand. I want to go to the hospital. Can you take me there?"

She shook her head. "I'm going to do what your mother wants."

Tears streamed down his cheeks. He found it hard to breathe. "That's not fair."

Auntie Maggie rested her hands on his shoulders. "You need to understand that this is very hard on your mother at the moment. She needs a little breathing room, okay? Can you understand that? This is a terribly difficult time."

Matt closed his eyes and sighed. All he could understand were the emotions storming through him: fear and sadness and an impatience unlike any he had ever experienced.

Every twitching fibre was urging him to get to that hospital in case he never saw his father again.

"Now go on up and have your shower and get into your pyjamas," Auntie Maggie said. "Dinner will be ready soon."

He groaned and stamped his foot but reluctantly did as he was told.

Tomorrow he would beg Mum to take him to see Dad. He would buckle himself into the car and refuse to move until she agreed. At the hospital, he would be quiet. He would give Mum space. He would stand at the back of the room like a statue.

Matt jolted awake. Voices downstairs. He must have dozed because when he looked at his alarm clock, it was past twelve am.

Mum was home. He snuck out of bed and crept to the top of the stairs. The room smelled of cigarettes and alcohol.

"Where the hell have you been?" Auntie Maggie asked Mum.

Mum swayed and had to catch herself on the wall.

"Out."

"The hospital called. They couldn't tell me anything because I'm not Robert's next-of-kin. It was important. Are you listening to me?"

Mum looked at her sister. "Yes, yes, I'm listening." Her words were uneven, long and lispy.

"Have you spoken to the hospital?"

"Not yet. Everything will be fine, Maggie. You can go home now. Thanks for looking after the boys."

"Do you want me to stay? In case it's bad news?" she asked.

Mum shook her head. "It's fine. Go home, okay? Go home."

"Ring me. Doesn't matter what time. Ring me."

"Of course. Thank you. I really wouldn't cope without you here."

Auntie Maggie kissed her cheek and left. The long arc of light cast by her car's headlights blasted Matt's eyes through the front windows and he had to squint until it was dim again.

Mum swayed to the phone on the telephone table and dialled a number.

"Hi, yes, this is Claire Radcliffe. I was informed you rang earlier regarding my husband, Robert. Oh, okay, so he passed a couple of hours ago. That's very disappointing to hear. No, there's really nothing I can do at this stage. I'll come in tomorrow morning."

Mum haphazardly replaced the receiver and headed for the kitchen, her shoulder brushing one wall before bouncing off another.

Matt sat at the top of the stairs holding his breath. A painful squeezing in his chest. Aching, burning and pinching in his throat.

Mum ambled back out, a glass of water in her hand. She started up the stairs and stopped when she spied him on the landing.

She frowned and sighed. "What are you doing up?"

"Is Dad dead?" he asked, body squeezing as he wished with all his heart that he had misunderstood the phone call.

"Yes, Dad died tonight."

Matt burst into tears as his grief and shock tore his heart down the middle. "No. I didn't get to see him. I didn't get to say goodbye," he wailed.

His mum was beside him now. "Calm down or you'll wake up your brothers."

He tried to stop, but he couldn't. Each cry was like a hiccup. "I didn't get to say goodbye. Dad. Dad!" he yelled.

Mum gripped him by the shoulders and pushed him towards his room. "For goodness sake, Matt. Get into bloody bed now."

He ran to his room, jumped on his bed and pulled the blankets over his head. It was a hot night, but he couldn't stop shivering.

His throat throbbed from crying. His heart was on fire, filling his ribcage with hot, achy heat. But he couldn't stop. Dad was dead. All he could think about was never again seeing his crinkled blue eyes, his proud smiling face or his big, callused hands.

How would he be able to get through tomorrow knowing Dad was no longer here? Or the next day? Or the next?

A trembling started in his jaw, moved to his neck, and wracked down to his hands and legs. A shuddering sob bellowed in the steamy darkness from under his blanket. He would get no comfort tonight, of that he was sure, no matter how much his trembling body needed it.

Tomorrow, he would make sure he was the one to tell his little brothers about what had happened. He would be kind and careful with his words. He would let them cry and he would answer their questions, then he would hold them both in his arms for as long as they needed.

Chapter 55

Nikki

Saturday morning, Nikki tightened the belt of her satin dressing gown around her waist as she ambled downstairs, still bleary-eyed from a night of little sleep. Matt, dressed only in a pair of shorts, was clanging and banging around in the kitchen, noisily tossing plates into the dishwasher and shoving dirty cutlery from last night's dinner into the basket.

"Those boys are lazy. We shouldn't have to ask them to get up and do the dishes once we've finished dinner."

She nodded. "I agree. But that point never sinks in, no matter how many times I tell them."

"Flynn, Ryan!" Matt yelled.

Footsteps came scurrying down the stairs, then slowed as the boys got to the kitchen.

"Dishes. Now," he yelled when the kids came in, both shirtless, dressed only in boxer shorts. Too hot for much else. "You are to do them without being asked, every night! Do you hear me? If you don't, I'll be taking your game console and throwing it out the window."

The boys nodded, knowing well enough to keep their mouths closed. They rushed in beside Matt and set about loading the remaining dirty dishes into the dishwasher.

"And wipe the benches down, please," Nikki added.

She followed behind Matt out onto the back deck. The early morning sun was already sweltering.

She took a seat beside him. "What's the matter?"

He shook his head, pointed back inside to the kitchen. "I'm sick of them doing nothing around the house."

"What's really the matter?"

He glanced away as he sighed. "I just had a call from Mum. She's getting sick."

Nikki flinched. It had been four days since they had planted the mould and no word until now had come through about Claire's health. "What, like a cold or something?"

"Most likely. She thinks it might be a chest infection. I told her to go to the doctor, but you know how she likes to embellish matters for a little sympathy. It frustrates me because I never know if what she is telling me is the truth. The number of times she has said she was sick and then it turns out to be nothing."

"Hmm," Nikki said, afraid of her voice.

"It pisses me off. I'm over dealing with her, to be honest."

Nikki's eyes widened. This was the most open Matt had ever been about his relationship with his mother. When around Claire, Matt always closed himself down—became a man of few words—as though his emotions were cordoned off.

"Why? What's brought all this on?"

"I got up this morning to look for a safety certificate I need for work on Monday. I came across that old picture of me, Mum and Dad. You know the one where Dad is carrying me on his shoulders and we're looking at each other laughing?"

Nikki nodded.

"Dad and I were laughing, and Mum was staring at Dad as though she wanted to stick a knife in him."

She had often thought about getting the photo retouched to remove Claire because it would otherwise be a gorgeous photo. A real expression of loving fatherhood. "She is very skilled at death stares."

He chuckled sardonically. "I hadn't noticed that look on her face before. I think with all that is going on with you lately, I've been seeing my past a little differently."

Nikki sat back, crossed her arms over her chest. "Like what?"

"So many moments. But, mostly, the night Dad died."

He had never offered too many details about that time in his life. She had always presumed it was too difficult for him to talk about.

Curiosity ignited like a glowing ember, yet a part of her didn't want to know. She had been worn down by Claire over the years, and she was at a tipping point, but she had to be a support for Matt until they had seen this through to the end.

"Tell me," she urged.

"When Dad had his accident, she didn't tell us he was hurt. I found out from Auntie Maggie. The night he passed away, Mum had gone out. I thought she went to the hospital to see Dad, but she came home early in the morning smelling of alcohol and cigarettes."

He told her of the cold phone call Claire had made to the hospital when she was informed of Robert's passing. The punch came, though, when he mentioned her lack of sympathy for Matt.

"She went to her room and closed the door. I was left alone, shivering in my bed all night without any comfort, not a kind word, not even a cuddle."

Tears filled Nikki's eyes to learn that her husband had to endure a moment like that. She wanted to reach back into his past and be that comfort he needed as a twelve-year-old boy. "It breaks my heart that you had to go through that."

He frowned, pointed to her. "See, that's the right reaction. Warmth. Compassion. I don't think I ever got that from Mum my entire life unless we were in public or she somehow benefited from it."

"Doesn't surprise me."

"But I can't help thinking…I don't know." He shook his head. "Maybe I'm creating false memories."

"No, tell me. What do you think?"

"I think she purposefully didn't tell me or my brothers that Dad was dying because she didn't want us to say goodbye. She wanted to punish Dad for no other reason than because she could."

Nikki gasped. "That's horrible. That's—"

"Evil," Matt finished for her, meeting her gaze.

Nikki nodded. "It really is."

"After Dad died, it was all about Mum. How upset she was. How hard it was to cope with three boys on her own. How sick I always was and if only Dad was still around to shoulder the burden. And all the time, I kept replaying that night in my head and knew every word that was coming out of her mouth was a complete fabrication."

"She can't be that cold-hearted, though, can she?"

Matt shrugged. "I honestly don't know what to believe." He looked away for a silent moment. When he faced Nikki again, he said, "I'm so sorry." Each word was weighted with deep and genuine apology.

"For what?"

"For not recognising what Mum was like earlier. Maybe I could have helped you more." He hung his head.

She pushed her chair back, stood, and went to him. She sat on his lap. "The last thing anyone wants to see is that their mother is a covert narcissist hell-bent on destroying everyone's life for her own sick pleasure."

He sighed, wrapped his arms around her body protectively. "I feel like we've lost who we were as a husband and wife over the years. I'm sorry about that."

She shook her head, kissed his cheek. "Don't be. Let's just move forward together from here. Let's show Claire that she will never come between us. Our love is stronger than she is."

He kissed the top of her head. "I don't know what I'd do without you."

"Nor me without you."

"I love you so much," he whispered in her ear. He cuddled her closer to him and she could feel his heart beating hard in his chest.

This man was her whole life. She would do anything for him. And at this point, she had not one regret about the lengths she had taken.

Not long now, she told herself silently. Not long now and Claire would no longer be a problem.

Chapter 56

Belinda

Belinda's stomach was a knotted jumble of nerves since Anthony had called to say Claire visited her doctor about asthma and flu symptoms, only for her to have an asthma attack in the doctor's office. An ambulance was called, and she was transported to hospital.

"I better go see her," Anthony had said. "Just in case."

"I can't leave the shop. I don't have any backup today." They still needed to pay the bills, regardless of what state his mother was is in. She resented that Anthony had to take time off work; she hadn't factored that in when making plans to kill Claire. "I'll visit her with you tonight," she suggested. Despite how she felt about Claire, she was Anthony's mum and Belinda had to play the supportive wife until this was all over and done with.

"Yeah, probably a good idea. She'll be wondering why you haven't visited otherwise."

Belinda rolled her eyes. It always came down to that—not heartfelt empathy or concern, but that they might be seen as doing wrong in Claire's eyes.

"Give me a call as soon as you know what's going on, okay? Keep me up to date."

"I will. I'll call you soon."

Belinda hung up and rushed to attend the customers that were browsing the store. Adrenalin was blasting through her veins. She had been well aware that their plot would end with Claire's death, but now that the reality was slamming her hard in the face, anxiety was growing.

She breathed deeply in through her nose and out through her mouth, trying to manage the adrenalin dump, so she could speak to her customers without looking like a nervous fool. When she had finally dealt with them, she rushed out to the backroom to call Nikki.

"Claire's in hospital. She had an asthma attack this morning," she blurted when Nikki answered, each word delivered with so much speed each syllable rolled into one.

"Yes, Matt called to tell me."

'Are you going to visit her?"

A short moment of silence. "I had Matt tell her never to speak to me again. It would be disingenuous to see her now. Matt will finish work early and head up there this afternoon."

'I'll go up there tonight. I better make an appearance."

"Makes sense that you do."

"I'll give Paige a call to make sure she's been updated."

Belinda ended the call and dialled Paige.

"Hi, Paige. I'm not sure if you've heard or not, but Claire has been taken to hospital with asthma."

Paige gasped. "I didn't know. I wonder if Vaughn knows yet. Oh, he's trying to call me now. I'll give you a call back."

Belinda headed out onto the main shop floor to dust shelves and rearrange misplaced products. Within a couple of minutes, her phone rang.

"Hi, Paige."

"Vaughn just called to tell me," Paige said.

"Is he heading to the hospital?"

"After everything that happened this week, he's reluctant. Very reluctant. He hasn't decided yet."

"Will you go with him if he decides he wants to visit Claire?" Belinda asked.

"No way. If I ever have to see that woman's face again, it'll be too soon."

Belinda chuckled—a nervous burst of sound. "Understandable after everything she has put you both through."

"If Vaughn wants to see her, I won't hold it against him. But I will not be stepping foot in the hospital room."

"Nikki's not going either. I told Anthony that I'll go to the hospital with him tonight if he wants."

"That makes sense. One of us should go. Keep me posted on her condition."

"I will. I'll talk to you later."

Belinda sighed. This was really happening. Claire was dying.

Her stomach contracted. She dropped the dusting rag and bolted to the back room, barely making it to the bathroom with her head over the toilet bowl before she vomited. Her hands were trembling as she wiped her mouth with toilet paper.

She had to get it together. The finish line was so close; she had to make it through until then.

Chapter 57

Anthony

A nurse directed Anthony to the room his mother was being treated. He marched down the long linoleum hallway, watching for the numbers pinned above each door. He glanced into the rooms, seeing patients in pale blue gowns lying atop steel-framed beds.

When he arrived at the right number and headed inside, he startled at his mother's appearance as she rested in a seated position on a lone bed. She was shrunken and frail. Clear tubing wrapped around her ears and under her nose, pushing oxygen into both nostrils.

A doctor and a nurse were standing beside the bed.

"Hi, son," Mum said taking a deep breath before and after each word. She had suffered mild asthma her entire life, but Anthony had never seen her like this. Her chest wheezed with each breath. Her lips were a little blue.

He kissed her forehead. "Hi, Mum."

"You're Claire's son?" The doctor asked.

"Yes, I'm Anthony Radcliffe," he said, shaking the doctor's hand.

"You're listed as next-of-kin along with your brothers. I'd like to discuss treatment with you."

Anthony looked again to Mum who nodded.

"Claire arrived this morning. She suffered a life-threatening asthma attack. We treated her in the ED with oxygen and nebulized salbutamol, then transferred her to a ward to receive higher-level care. She has had an IV of magnesium sulphate and continuous nebulisation, but her condition wasn't resolving, so we have started systemic corticosteroids. We are seeing improvements now. But as her oxygen saturation is low and carbon dioxide is elevated, she could be at risk of respiratory failure, so I'd like to keep her in for treatment at least overnight but possibly longer."

Anthony frowned. "Will she be okay?"

The doctor nodded. "With continued treatment, we should see rapid improvement over the next twenty-four to forty-eight hours."

Anthony sighed with relief. "Okay good."

"So, it's a bit of waiting game now. Oxygen saturation is starting to normalise again, but we will certainly be keeping a close eye on her." The doctor smiled at Claire. "I'll come back in in a little while to check how you're going."

Claire nodded. "Thank you."

The doctor gave a sympathetic smile before he strode out of the room along with the nurse, leaving Anthony alone with his mother.

"What happened?" Anthony asked.

"Couldn't breathe." Exhale. "Went to the doctor." Inhale.

Anthony patted her arm. "Don't worry about talking. You just concentrate on getting oxygen into those lungs. When you're feeling a little better, you can tell me all about it."

"Belinda?" Mum asked.

Anthony hid his guilt behind an impartial expression. "She's feeling under the weather too, but she's going to come up this afternoon to see how you're going. I hope you're feeling a little better by then."

"You're better off." Exhale. "Without her."

Anthony twitched. "Please, Mum, let's not do this now. I love her. She's a good person."

"So you think."

"What does that mean?"

Mum said nothing, just stared at him, and he stared back. Even beneath the tubing and pale face, her brown eyes glazed with mischief. But he wasn't in any frame of mind to play games. To be perfectly honest, he was shattered, the weariness seeping deep down to his bones.

For the past few years, he had held the weight of his childless marriage, their strangling debt and the responsibility for his employees' livelihoods on his shoulders, but his legs and back were weakening. The load was teetering, and he was petrified it would fall and shatter around him.

No more games, no more controversy. No more. He was about to be a father. He just wanted a simple life.

Chapter 58

Vaughn

When Vaughn arrived at Mum's room, she was sound asleep. He sat on the chair beside her bed. Her face was so familiar—the woman who had raised him. And yet, watching her rested form and placid face, he wondered if he really knew her at all.

It was a disconcerting realisation that the woman he believed to have known more than anyone else had an inner world, an entire life, secrets and desires discordant to what she projected to the world.

After an hour or so, when he stood to leave, she woke up with a start.

He hunched his shoulders, bent his knees a little, trying to shrink himself down like he always had. But he recognised it now—his wanting to be soft for her, unobtrusive, gentle. He stretched himself taller, no longer willing to change himself because she had chosen to see him as someone he wasn't.

"Hi, Mum," he said, leaning over the bed and kissing her cheek. She didn't flinch or cower like he had anticipated.

He took the seat beside her again. "How are you feeling?"

Her chest rattled with each breath. "Not great," she whispered. Her words were airy, soft and small. He had never used hose last two words to describe his mother before.

"So, the doctor wants to keep you in for a couple of days?"

Mum nodded.

He smiled nervously. "Well, it's best to do what the doctor orders.

He watched her for a long moment until she looked away and closed her eyes. His sympathy for this obviously frail woman was present but hidden beneath a stack of accumulated resentment. He ached to hear her side of the story if only to ease the burden of mystery.

Before he even knew what he was saying, he asked in a calm, soft voice, "Were you unfaithful to Dad?"

Her eyes opened slowly, and she looked at him, but she didn't answer.

"Were you?" A harsh whisper.

No answer. She shifted her gaze, stared up at the ceiling. This wasn't the time or the place, but he couldn't walk away today without some acknowledgement of the truth.

"I know Robert wasn't my biological father. We don't have the same blood type. Did he know?"

Again, that silent stare.

"Mum, answer me. I just want to know the truth."

"Men who live." Inhale. "In glass houses." Exhale. "Shouldn't throw stones."

He shook his head. "Is he my father or not? It's a simple question."

"A question Belinda's baby may soon be asking."

He stood, leaned over the bed so his face was close to hers. "You're a vile, evil woman."

A small smile flittered at the edges of her lips. As he glared at his mother, all that fury she had told him he had possessed his whole life sparked inside of him like a raging fire.

Chapter 59

Paige

Paige waited in the living room, the phone by her side. The sun had dipped and shifted away hours ago. Evie was asleep. The television was on but silent. Vaughn had raced to the hospital when all three brothers were called with word that Claire's condition had taken an unexpected turn and her time was soon up.

Paige couldn't move, couldn't do anything until she knew what was happening with Claire. A part of her wanted it all to be over, and yet she wished she could take it back. Imagining death was nothing like confronting the reality of it. The reality of death was massive, unable to be sidestepped or reduced. She had been through such a moment when her own mother passed away.

Ahead of them all were the tremors that rocked in the hours, days and months that followed death. When those tremors subsided, only then could life go on. She would eventually be okay, that was the truth. And Claire would be gone—another truth. She had to hold tight to those simple blessings.

Her phone blared in the silent room; she flinched. Her heart raced when Vaughn's name flickered on the screen.

Breathless, she answered. "Hi, Vaughn—"

"She's passed," he whispered, voice low and gravelly like the words were squeezing from the tightest opening.

"About five minutes ago. It was peaceful." She could hear it, the resignation, relief, finality and momentousness.

A long exhalation. "I'm really sorry."

A shuddered breath inward. "I'll be home in an hour."

"I'll be here."

Paige let the phone fall onto the couch beside her.

Claire was dead. Tears squeezed from the corners of her eyes onto her cheeks.

Chapter 60

Nikki

Nikki kept her head down as she strode onto the deck of the café. She looked up only long enough to find Paige and Belinda were already there sitting at a table in the corner. They both wore dark sunglasses. Their clothes were shades of black.

She glanced at her own dark-coloured attire; no one would pull a bright shade of T-shirt from their cupboard the day after murdering their mother-in-law.

Nikki waved quickly at her sisters-in-law as she approached. They waved back. But no smiles. No, they weren't so heartless that they were going to sit here this morning gloating and grinning. The enormity of their actions would be worn like a heavy cloak around their shoulders.

She sat down and gave a sharp exhalation. Belinda reached across the table and put her hand on hers. Paige placed hers on top.

"It's over," Belinda said.

Nikki pursed her lips, squeezed her eyes shut. "It's over."

Paige lifted her hand when the waiter arrived. Belinda followed. They ordered strong coffees.

When the waiter left, Nikki hunched against the backrest. "How were Vaughn and Anthony this morning?"

Paige shrugged. “Sad. Conflicted. Vaughn’s relationship with Claire had eroded these past few weeks. I’m not sure he knows how to feel, to be honest.”

“Time will help,” Belinda assured.

Paige nodded.

“I heard Anthony crying in the shower,” Belinda said. “He’s fairly broken. I think that’s the hard part—watching our men grieve.”

Nikki’s eyes glistened with tears, but she blinked them back. Her chest was hot and achy. “Matt’s been quiet. He doesn’t want to talk. He hasn’t wanted to talk all week.”

“That might be how he deals with loss—retreats into himself,” Paige suggested.

She sighed. “I guess so. Honestly, he had me wondering if he somehow discovered what I’d done. He’s so smart. Maybe he can see through my act. It’s been tough to play the sympathetic wife when I’m ten shades of guilty.”

Belinda leaned forward, lowered the volume of her voice. “There’s no way he could know. We covered our tracks. No one knows anything. Not even the doctors suspect any kind of foul play. As far as everyone is concerned, this was a horrible accident. A time bomb waiting to go off, considering Claire’s predisposition to mould.”

She hoped they were right, but there was niggling doubt in the back of her mind. She knew her husband inside and out. All his tells. But she had never seen him retreat like this in all their years of marriage. Then again, he hadn’t lost anyone as close to him as a parent during that time.

“We will be okay, won’t we?” Paige asked.

Nikki nodded. “Of course we will.”

“This was never going to feel exhilarating,” Belinda added.

“What we did was right and necessary,” Nikki said. “This was the best solution for all of us. We can be the families we always intended to be. Live the lives we had planned for ourselves."

"But we have to promise not to become complacent and fall back into our old ways," Belinda said. "We need to be a family from here on out. A close family. I've got this baby on the way. I want her aunts and uncles to have a big role in his or her life."

"I've always wanted a family," Paige said with a bashful smile. "I've gone much too long without anyone. And over these past few weeks, even under the circumstances, I have got to know you both enough that I can call you my sisters."

Nikki smiled. This was how it was always meant to be. "I couldn't agree more. This is the greater good. We always knew this part was going to be hard, but we've got so much to look forward to."

"We have to remember that Claire was evil. It was her or us," Paige said.

"Exactly," Belinda said. "Now all we have to do is get through the funeral then the future is ours."

Nikki didn't hang around too long with her sisters-in-law. She wanted to get back to Matt, conscious that she had left him and the kids alone so soon after Claire's passing. But she had to talk with Belinda and Paige to get all her thoughts out of her head.

For the past couple of weeks, she had felt like a balloon slowly filling to bursting point with pressure. Last night, that pressure had eased, but she needed to spew out her worries this morning with people she trusted.

Their bond was so strong now. Paige was right, they had become more than sisters-in-law but, rather, sisters. She could feel it as they chatted there this morning and linked their hands. You didn't commit such an act with another person and not break through social barriers. They had stripped each other back to bare bones. Seen one another's skeletons. Nikki would carry that in her heart forever.

The boys were having the day off school. The shock of their grandmother's sudden death impacted them hard. When she saw their solemn faces, she kissed and cuddled them both. No one escaped learning about death. In time, they would be fine. Life would continue for them all.

Matt was on the deck drinking coffee.

"Hi," she said when she joined him. "How are you feeling this morning?" Sympathy strangled her words. Real sympathy. Despite how she felt about Claire, she did care deeply for her husband, and to know that he was hurting, made her hurt too.

He managed a half-grimace, half-smile. "I'm okay. Did you get some comfort from Belinda and Paige?"

"Yeah, I did."

"Good." Then he looked away.

Her heart sank. *Does he know? Does he know what I've done?* "Did you…um…want another coffee?"

He swirled the remaining contents in his mug and shook his head. "I'm fine, thanks."

"Okay, well, I'm going to make myself one."

He nodded.

Her breaths were hard to draw in as she walked back inside the house. In all the scenarios she had planned with Paige and Belinda about if police ever got involved or if a doctor suspected foul play, she never, foolishly, considered what would happen if one of their husbands found out.

Chapter 61

Belinda

Belinda had dressed into a knee-length black dress with short sleeves. Too hot for more coverage when the Queensland weather was in full force. Temperatures today would reach the mid-thirties.

Outside her bedroom window, the sky overhead was big and blue, interrupted only by white feathery clouds. Much too beautiful a day for a funeral, but at least it was better than wind and rain.

Anthony came up from behind her and slung his arms around her middle. She nestled against his hard chest while he smoothed his palms over her stomach. It seemed overnight her belly had formed a small but noticeable baby bump. This little baby inside her was thriving with life, even while its parents had to stare at death today.

"I love you," Anthony whispered in her ear.

She smiled, something that had been hard to naturally construct over the past week as they made plans for the funeral and swam through the thickness of Anthony's grief.

"I love you too." She spun to face him. "I know today is going to be hard, but I'm here for you however you need me, okay?"

He swallowed hard but nodded. "Thank you."

They arrived at the cemetery located a little way outside of Montville on an expansive lush lawn surrounded by trees. Birds carolled. Bees and little grass insects buzzed and flickered as they strode to a small tent fixed with rows of chairs set amidst tombstones.

Matt and Nikki were already waiting nearby. Matt had to be sweltering in this heat, dressed in long black slacks, a metallic grey long-sleeved shirt and tie. Nikki wore a dark blue dress and comfortable flats—eternally, her no-nonsense, practical style.

Not long after that, Vaughn and Paige arrived. Evie was dressed in a black dress with a red ribbon tied around the waist. Vaughn looked a little drawn. His eyes were bloodshot. Never had she seen a man frown so deeply.

Vaughn stood beside his brothers. His pale hair, tanned skin and hazel eyes were an obvious contrast to Anthony and Matt's features and dark colouring. She was amazed that she hadn't seen the truth before.

Would her baby look like Vaughn? Anxiety squeezed like tight fists all through her body. No, there was no space for that kind of worrying today. With Claire now gone, Anthony would never know about her affair and this baby would be born his; she was certain of it.

Claire's sisters and their families arrived next, followed by friends and extended family members Belinda didn't know too well. They all stopped and offered condolences before taking their seats.

Too soon, it was time to start. The men strode away only to march back, sweat beading on their brow as they carried the weighty timber casket on their shoulders from the hearse to the gathering.

Belinda followed her sisters-in-law to the front row of chairs leaving a space between them for their husbands. She reached across and held their hands, a sign of comradery, of sisterhood.

Exquisitely mournful songs played as the casket was set by the pallbearers onto a trolley over the rectangular hole bordered by synthetic green grass. Anthony sat beside her. He was breathing heavy.

Photos of Claire and her family flashed on the projector. Belinda couldn't bring herself to look at Claire's face. Anthony and Vaughn each read heartfelt poems that spoke of reuniting and eternal love, while Matt delivered a no-nonsense eulogy. After the priest finished the funeral mass, the casket was slowly lowered into the ground where Claire would lay to rest in a plot beside Robert.

Belinda blew out a long breath when she could no longer see the human-sized box. Claire was now underground. She was never coming back.

People gathered around her, kissing her cheek, cuddling her, whispering their heartfelt condolences, but she was floating through the motions, being propelled from person to person without thought, only reaction.

Their closeness was cloying. Too hot. Too much. Belinda's mind whirled around her. She gripped Anthony's arm. "I don't feel so good," she managed before her head swam and bent until there was nothing more than blackness.

When she woke, she was on her back, warm blades of grass prickling her. Auntie Sue was fanning her face with the funeral program. The image of Claire on the cover was centimetres from Belinda's face. Claire's steely eyes stared at her from the pages.

"Get her away," she shouted, slapping the small booklet aside.

An ambulance sounded in the distance. Someone offered her a drink of water. Anthony kneeled beside her. "Give her some room, please," he yelled.

"It's so hot," she whispered, tongue thick. She tried to sit up, but Anthony gently pushed her shoulder downward.

"Just relax. Don't go moving."

Nervous chatter. Wet, bloodshot eyes. So many faces. And then two paramedics pushed through the throng and assessed her with assertive questions.

They helped her onto the gurney and wheeled her into the back of the ambulance. Anthony jumped in too, taking a seat beside her.

He tenderly stroked her hair from her forehead. “Everything will be fine, Bel, I promise.”

She rested back against the pillow, placed a loving hand on her stomach, and whispered the only prayer she had ever made in her life, “Please, please, please let my baby be okay.”

Chapter 62

Paige

No official wake was planned. God knows Vaughn and his family had been through enough replica wakes to last them a lifetime. Instead, they organised a spread of catered nibbles to be eaten in an undercover area at the cemetery. Standing room only.

The summer sun sweltered outside. Humidity left a slick coating of sweat on Paige's arms, chest and legs. She weaved through mourners with heat-flushed faces. They held napkins topped with assorted cakes and sandwiches in one hand and a hot beverage in the other.

Evie was restless, clinging to her leg, which only made Paige sweat more as she picked out foods Evie would enjoy and handed them to her.

"Try not to spill it on the floor or your dress, okay?"

Evie nodded and bit into a piece of chocolate cake.

Getting ready this morning reminded her so much of her mother's funeral. Everything was shimmery like she was seeing the world underwater. When she was handed the funeral program earlier with Claire's smiling face, she couldn't look her in the eyes. It was as though that dark gaze knew what she had done.

Then Belinda had fainted and since then, Paige's mind had been heavy with worry that Belinda's baby could be harmed or worse…dead.

Paige could live with killing Claire, but if the side-effect of their plan was to harm Belinda's baby—she could never live with that. She would never ever forgive herself.

Nikki rushed over, her blue sandals shuffling on the cement floor, holding up her phone. Her cheeks were pink, and the roots of her hair wet with perspiration.

"I just heard from Anthony," Nikki said, gripping Paige's arm. "The baby is fine. Belinda is fine. She hadn't eaten today and was a little dehydrated, but nothing too serious. They've got her on a drip and some oxygen, but all is good."

Paige leaned over, hands on her knees and exhaled. Tears blurred her eyes. "Thank God."

"I know. I know," Nikki said, rubbing Paige's back.

"I just want this day to be over."

"Me too. People are starting to clear out now. So not too much longer."

Vaughn spotted her from across the room where he had been chatting with his cousins. He marched over, eased Paige upright and wrapped his arms around her. "You okay?"

She nodded. "I'm relieved that Belinda and her baby are okay."

"You heard from them?"

Nikki nodded. "They're both doing fine. They will go home after she's been given fluids."

"Understandable."

"I better go tell Matt," Nikki said and hurried away.

"We'll head home soon," Vaughn said. "I'm exhausted. This has been the hardest day of my life."

She kissed his cheek. "Evie's getting restless too. It's the heat. All of us in this small stuffy area without any air-conditioning… Let me know when you want to leave, and we'll head home."

Tomorrow, she said to herself. Tomorrow is a new day and when I get there, this horrible day will be over.

Chapter 63

Matt

Two days before Claire's death...

Today, Matt's mother looked like a completely different person from the woman he had visited in hospital yesterday.

She was sitting up in her bed. Colour had returned to her face. The rattle in her chest had died down, though she was still a little breathless.

"Wow. Is this the right hospital room?" he said with a smile.

The doctor at her bedside smiled too. "Claire has made marked improvements as predicted."

Matt kissed Mum's cheek. "Good to see you're doing so much better."

"You and me both," the doctor said. "Looks as though Claire has gotten through the worst of it. Oxygen saturation is back to normal. We're continuing with treatment, so I would ask that Claire remains admitted for another day. We'll reassess tomorrow."

Matt nodded. "Sure."

"We've spoken a little about potential triggers as this was such an out-of-character, severe asthma attack, so we ran a few tests. It appears that Claire has been exposed to *Stachybotrys Chartarum*."

Matt frowned, shook his head.

"It's toxic black mould. Claire mentioned an allergy, which would explain her life-threatening reaction yesterday. There is no chance of re-exposure while she remains here in hospital, so we expect that Claire's condition will continue to improve." He turned to Claire. "I'll catch up with you again this afternoon."

"Thanks, Doctor."

Matt took a seat. "Black mould, really? Even with how fastidious you are."

Claire sighed a husky wheeze. "I need you to check something for me. The air conditioner. I cleaned it with bleach, including the filter, and then a few days later, I had dust spray out everywhere when I turned it on. Just check it for me please."

He nodded. "No worries. I'll head to your place once I leave here."

"And please can you get me some toiletries and pyjamas. And my makeup. I feel like a haggard old dog," she said, covering her face with her hands.

He laughed. "Surely you can allow yourself to dress down a little while you're in hospital."

"This is the worst place to do that, what with all the rich, handsome doctors walking the halls."

Matt chuckled. "Some things never change."

When Matt finished at the hospital, he headed home. He recalled seeing face masks a couple of weeks ago. He could wear one as a precaution when he was at Mum's. Not that he was at any great risk. He and his brothers had been tested for allergies, but they didn't come back positive for black mould. That was his mother's burden to carry.

He parked in his garage and kept the engine running as he climbed out and searched through the cupboards where he stored all the tools and equipment he'd collected over the last twenty years.

He reached to the side for a mask, but they weren't there. They weren't in the box he had originally found them in either. Someone else must have got their hands on them—maybe one of the boys re-enacting some dystopian fallout.

He grabbed a pair of safety glasses from a drawer and jumped back into his car. When he arrived at Mum's, he parked and headed inside, taking the stairs two at a time to her room.

As he eased his shoes off, he eyed the air conditioner mounted on the wall above her bed. Mum would kill him if he left great dirty footprints on her coverlet.

He slid his safety glasses on and covered his mouth and nose with his shirt as he stood on the bed and opened the air conditioner tab. Small black globs were on the filter. Along the rim of the air conditioner were dusty grey specks. He leaned in closer. Definitely mould, but it was set in a jelly-like substance. It wasn't growing on the air conditioner, but it looked like it had been placed in there.

Tingles fanned along his arms and neck and his heart thudded hard. He jumped off the bed onto the carpet. Disconnected memories spun together until they formed a recognisable chain. The gas masks. The phone call from Mum to say that Nikki, despite avoiding Mum, was seen at her house during the day. Now this mould.

"Fuck!"

Has Nikki done this?

He climbed up onto the bed and looked closer at the smears in the air conditioner. There was no denying that the mould was placed in almost even margins along the length of the filters. The mould was not growing on the actual air conditioner surface, which was impossible.

He groaned as he recalled the hawkish, beady look in Mum's eyes and the urgency in her voice when she asked him to check.

Mum knew. She knew that Nikki had done this.

Was life so hard for Nikki that she would hurt his mother? Or worse, kill her? His body sank under the weight of understanding. His own wife had reached such a low place that she was carrying out haphazard plots to kill her mother-in-law.

He sat on the bed, his breathing unsteady. What the hell was he going to do about this?

Chapter 64

Nikki

Nikki arrived home from the funeral mid-afternoon. Despite the heat and lack of seats, attendees had been content to stand around talking, eating and drinking cups of tea for hours.

Desperate to get out of her uncomfortable clothes, she headed up to her bedroom, lifting her dress over her head and sighing when she unclipped her bra and tossed it onto the bed.

Matt came in, waggling his tie. "I know the feeling." With two quick moves, he loosened the knot, slid the tie off and started unbuttoning his shirt. Those four words from Matt made up a total of ten words he had spoken to her today.

At the funeral and wake, he had been chatty with the attendees and extended family. He had delivered his eulogy with heartfelt emotion. But when it came to opening up to Nikki, Matt locked himself away.

She ruffled through her drawers, found a singlet and threw it on. In search of a comfortable pair of shorts, she reached up to the top shelf inside her walk-in-robe. She pulled her favourite shorts down, but as she did, a makeup pouch dropped to the floor at her feet.

Nikki stared at the dark purple purse on the carpet. She narrowed her eyes as she picked it up from the floor and held it out. “Why do you have your mum’s makeup purse?”

It seemed an innocuous thing—he could have brought it home from the hospital with him along with her other possessions and placed it in the cupboard for safekeeping—but her intuition was screaming a different story. Her husband was black-and-white, and this reeked of grey. He would have left it in the open on the dining table or in the kitchen but not hiding among their clothes.

Matt looked at her then and sighed so deeply it was as though it was the first exhalation he had taken since his mother’s death. His neck loosened. His eyelids drooped a little. She could see now that he had been holding onto so much stress and it all had to do with this makeup purse.

“Today was hell,” he said. “I didn’t think I was going to get through it.”

“It was a very difficult day,” she said cautiously.

He sat on the end of their bed, the mattress sinking under his weight, and lowered his face into his hands. He rocked his head from side to side and groaned.

She placed the makeup pouch on her dressing table and took a seat beside him. She was much too conscious that he still hadn’t answered her question, and yet she was afraid to ask it again.

He sat up straighter and turned his face to her. His lips were drawn into a frown. “I know what you did, Nikki,” he said in a low, measured voice. No malice. Just fact.

A bolt of fright, her heart thumped, but she stopped herself from flinching. “What’s that?”

“The mould. The air conditioner.”

She stood up, breaths coming faster. “I…I don’t know what you’re talking about.”

He patted the space beside him. “Sit back down. It’s time we had a talk.”

Chapter 65

Matt

Two days before Claire's death...

Matt sat on his mother's bed. His jaw was tight, shoulders drawn upward from the weight of realisation.

His wife had tried to kill his mother. The words kept bouncing through his brain. Betrayal almost rocked him off balance.

"Nikki, what the hell were you thinking?"

He tried to reconcile this new understanding of his wife with the woman he had married all those years ago. She was so happy and carefree. The mother of his children. She was maternal and loving to their boys.

Her face filled his mind, her beautiful smile, the way her lips gently parted when they made love. He felt her warm arm around him, the weight of her body as she sat on his lap. She was his whole life; the glue to their family.

Then he saw the slow but inevitable downward turn of her lips. The times she ground her teeth, grinned and bore the almost imperceptible abuse. And he stood by and watched his wife fade away and be replaced by the nervous, disillusioned woman she had become.

And he did nothing because he had refused to see what was really happening. He had managed to compartmentalise his past—a defence mechanism, perhaps—so that when he looked at his mother, he didn't see what she truly was. It was the only way he survived his childhood. But he had forgotten to take those defences down. The moment he was out on his own, he should have torn them apart. But he hadn't and Nikki bore the brunt of that. He had failed the only woman he had ever loved.

Fear scuttled through him like the agitated feet of cockroaches. If his mother knew what Nikki had done, she wouldn't hesitate to destroy her. Exactly how, he couldn't predict. That was one thing he had never managed to accomplish—understanding his mother's mind. He had no idea why she did what she did or what she would do next.

Blackmail. Shaming. Law enforcement?

Nikki couldn't take any more. If she was resorting to murder, she had not only hit her limits but had annihilated them on the way down. Her wherewithal was fading.

He recalled the day they were married and the hope that lived in his heart. He recalled his love for her and his deepest promise to love and protect her forever. He had meant every vow he had spoken.

He remembered all the times as a child when he was confined to his bed, lonely and confused. So much wasted life. With the walls in his mind now crumbling, he saw everything for what it was—a light had been switched on and illuminated his hellish existence.

He was never sick. He was Mum's little sympathy generator, the pin-pricked, drug-addled kid she could show off to anyone who would listen, so she could get her narcissistic supply. But Mum's needs were insatiable; there would never be enough to supply her.

After Matt moved out of home, he slowly got his strength back. Mum knew he wouldn't play the willing victim she needed him to be. When Nikki came on the scene, Mum moved her target and did it with such subtlety, he hadn't noticed. Different game, different victim, same result.

If he didn't end this now, Mum would not only have been responsible for stealing his childhood but the best years of his and Nikki's adulthood too. And what about his children—were they sitting ducks? Or was she already manipulating them too?

Anger curled through his veins. His jaw clenched tight until his teeth ground.

Matt raced into Mum's ensuite bathroom and opened the cupboard and the drawers under the sink. He found her lipsticks. His mother was so vain. So incapable of showing her true face that she wouldn't dare go a day without makeup and certainly not lipstick. It was killing her to be barefaced at that hospital in front of so many people.

He grabbed three lipsticks, rushed back into the bedroom and climbed on the bed. He uncapped the first lipstick, wound it up, and gently wiped it over the live mould. He capped it again and did the same with the other three. He jumped off the bed, paced to the drawers in the ensuite and pulled out some makeup brushes.

His breaths were coming hard as adrenalin coursed through him. His hands were shaking. He feathered the brushes along the dry dust, turned them on their end and patted the tops, so the fine particles dropped to the root of the hairs.

He lunged off the bed, found a makeup pouch and thrust the mould-tainted lipstick and brushes inside along with other makeup his mum might use, then zipped it up. He put the pouch aside and raced down the stairs, two at a time, to the kitchen.

Under the sink was bleach. In a drawer was a cloth. He bounded back upstairs, poured a little bleach on the cloth and wiped the air conditioner down as thoroughly as possible until there was no trace of mould left. He rubbed at the rim to dissolve any fingerprints he may have left behind.

Systematically, he did what he could to hide Nikki's evidence as well as his own—vacuumed the carpet, stripped the bed and shook Mum's coverlet and sheets outside, before carefully restoring everything to how it was when he arrived.

By the time he was finished, he was sweating, panting. He gathered Mum's toiletries, collected a couple of nighties and underwear, picked up the makeup pouch and packed them all in an overnight case.

He wasn't someone who lied often. Of course, there were those small social situations where they were necessary but lying never sat right with him. Today, though, when he arrived at the hospital, he was going to have to put on one hell of a show.

Matt strode down the long hospital hallway, his shoes squeaking on the linoleum, overnight bag in one hand, keys in the other.

Mum was alone when he made it to her room.

She looked up at him and grinned as though he was the most loved child on Earth. He knew differently—his mother's love was only ever conditional.

"How did you go?" she asked.

Now that he had given himself permission to observe reality, he could see so much more—the shiftiness, the quick darting of Mum's eyes, the strain to keep that mask in place.

"I got you everything you should need. Some nighties. Your toiletries. A few bits and pieces of makeup."

"Lipstick?" she asked urgently.

"Yeah, I threw three in there. Didn't check the colours." He placed the overnight bag beside the bed. "I'll just leave it all here for you."

"Thank you. It's so wonderful for you to take good care of me like this. Without your father around, I know it's a burden to be lumped with the responsibility of looking after your mother—"

"No burden at all."

She ran her fingers along the sheets, straightening them as they sat across her lap. She kept her eyes focused downwards. "And what about the air conditioner?"

He controlled his facial expressions, his breathing. "There was a big dirty moth in there. But I got it out. Might explain the dust. As for mould, I couldn't see anything. It looked clean to me."

Mum grimaced. "It doesn't make sense."

"Would you like me to organise someone who knows what they're actually looking for to come in and do some air tests. The last thing we need is you getting home and being re-exposed. While you're in here, we can nip it in the bud. Mould could be festering behind a wall for all we know."

She nodded. "That's a good idea. Do that. But I want to see the report."

He smiled, reached over and squeezed her hand. "Of course. I'm just glad you're okay."

"You and me both."

Chapter 66

Nikki

Nikki's blood was whooshing in her ears. Her heart was in her throat. Matt stood and walked to the door, shutting it quietly. She watched him, barely breathing.

He sat down beside her again, the weight of him pulling her closer until their thighs touched. Her mind was blank as she waited.

Nikki couldn't speak as her husband explained how he had put two and two together after a conversation with Claire. He recounted his trip to Claire's house where he discovered the mould and then the steps taken to ensure his mother was reinfected. Soon after that, Claire relapsed and eventually died from complications.

Her lips were parted, eyes unable to leave Matt's face. "You did that? To your own mother."

He frowned, lowered his focus to his lap. When he met her gaze again, he told her about his childhood—the truth of it. How Claire had made him sick and kept him in his room, only to be paraded to her friends and sisters for sympathy. He told Nikki all he could remember now that he had allowed himself to see Claire for who she truly was—a monster.

"But mostly," he said. "I did what I did to protect you. Nikki, she knew what you had done."

She flinched. "How?"

He explained about the phone call Claire had made, asking why Nikki had gone around to her house, and how she felt the dry mould burst from the air conditioner, knowing she had cleaned it days before.

"She would have destroyed us," he said. "This was never going to end. I had to make a choice. And I hate that I had to make that choice, but, in the end, I chose you. I chose *us*."

Her heart was a bullet train in her chest. Her pulse gushed in her ears.

He drew her hand into his, entwined their fingers. "I have never loved anyone, and I know I will never love anyone else, more than I do you. As your husband, it's my duty, no—" he slapped his palm on his chest "—my obligation to keep you safe. I stood for too long on the sidelines pretending that this hell she put us through wasn't happening. But I couldn't stand by any longer. I had to step up and do the only thing I could do."

Her next breath was a shudder. "To kill Claire."

He nodded sombrely. "I'm not proud of it. I've been a wreck trying to come to grips with it this past week. But to finally know that her body is in the ground, I feel…relieved."

Nikki pointed to the makeup pouch. "That's the lipstick?"

He nodded.

"You need to get rid of it."

"I know. I'm going to light the barbeque tonight and make sure it burns to ashes."

Nikki sat there for a long moment, unsure of what to think. Her husband had confessed to being a murderer, and yet she wasn't afraid. After all, when her own survival was pushed to the limits that dormant darkness had arisen within her too. Perhaps it existed within everyone, coded into our DNA, but, like the mould that killed Claire, it needed the right environment to grow and flourish.

Nikki and Matt had had their backs to the wall for far too long, and instead of cowering any longer, they chose to fight. But mostly, they had chosen each other.

Love swelled from deep inside her belly, filled her heart, making it pump double-time with fiery blood.

"I need to say this, so you know who you're going to bed with tonight," he said.

She nodded, awaiting his admission.

"I'm sad. And I don't ever want to be put in this situation again. But I don't regret it. I don't. I watched that coffin lower into the ground today and I almost forgot where I was. It wasn't like Dad's funeral where I could barely see from the grief. It was as though a lightness had spread over me. Like all my life Mum had weighed me down and now I'm free. I'm not proud to admit that, but it's the truth."

She pressed her palm to his thigh and squeezed it gently. "I know how you feel."

"It's just you and me now," he said and so much hope and relief shaped each syllable. "You don't have to worry about her anymore."

Nikki smiled, leaned in and kissed her husband's lips. He had saved her this week in so many ways. She didn't love him any less for what he had done. No, she loved him more.

Epilogue

Belinda

Belinda had to wait months for the inheritance to be finalised, but she didn't stress or worry because the money was inevitable. She happily watched overdue payments slide, knowing they would soon be taken care of.

The chunk of cash that eventually landed in her account was larger than she had imagined. She was able to pay off the mortgage and all credit card debt.

Belinda wasn't so blinded by her new-found freedom that she missed the life-lesson in all this. She and Anthony vowed never to splurge unnecessarily again—after she had finished decorating the baby's room, of course.

In April, Belinda delivered a healthy baby boy. Thad James Radcliffe. A long, painful and difficult labour. Thad was born eight pounds two, had Anthony's nose and hair colouring, and, most importantly, his blood type.

Belinda didn't sell her business. She hired an assistant soon after Claire's death and trained her to step into the manager role once Thad was born. At this stage, Belinda didn't have any plans to rush back to her organic shop, preferring the morning baby cuddles, mothers' group gossip, and the blissful, perfect day-to-day monotony of motherhood.

Anthony was doing well. His I-am-a-provider instincts went into overdrive the moment he held his baby boy in his arms. Since then, he had taken a no-prisoners attitude with his business and was winning big-ticket jobs.

Their marriage was stronger than ever. Right now, from inside their baby bubble, they were not inclined to try for another child. Thad was all they had ever wanted, and they both knew it was difficult to improve on perfect.

Belinda didn't think about Claire much. There were frightful nightmares initially, but they soon petered away. Life was moving forward as life always seemed to do.

Paige

Life was blasting towards the future at full pace for Paige. With the brakes Claire put on her relationship with Vaughn now severed, momentum carried her forward.

Vaughn proposed in April. They would have a small marriage ceremony next month. The whole family was invited. Vaughn suggested she go off contraception now before the big event, so they could put all their practice into baby-making action on their honeymoon. Beautiful, delightful explosions of happiness filled her every time she thought about becoming a mum again.

Joshua had called Paige soon after Claire's funeral to apologise for all the stress he had inflicted on her. He agreed to every second weekend with Evie and half of every school holiday period. To date, she had not had to hit send on their tell-all email.

Evie was thriving with her new situation and falling in love with both her fathers. She was eagerly awaiting a baby sister or brother and was loving pre-school.

Nikki

Nikki never went back to see her psychologist. No need now that the reason for her turmoil was six feet underground.

The nervousness that once riddled her body was slowly leaving, though it sometimes raised its head in high-stress situations. After a couple of phone calls and a face-to-face meeting with her old boss, she managed to get her job back. Since starting two months ago, not once had she thought about crashing her car. Without all that free time on her hands, her house went back to being messy, but she didn't care one bit.

Matt, like he always did, got on with the function of living. He had done what had to be done and had moved on. She admired that in him. Always had.

A flame had lit their marriage on fire. So much laughter, happiness and lovemaking filled the walls of her home, just like when they first met each other so many years ago at the pub. Who would have known that murder could be considered romantic? But Nikki couldn't think of any greater declaration of love or commitment one could make.

Since Claire's death, the extended family had remained close. They held barbeques and went out to restaurants together. Anthony and Vaughn often watched Ryan and Flynn play football and attended school events.

But it was with her sisters-in-law that the magic existed. They called each other all the time, met for coffee, went to the movies. Paige had said it right that sombre morning: They were not just sisters-in-law but sisters now.

She never did tell them about what Matt had done, and she never would. There was no need. That part of their lives was over. All the sheep were safe at last from the big bad wolf.

More from the author

Thanks for reading *The Perfect Family.*
I hope you enjoyed it.

If you'd like to know more about me, my books, or to connect with me online, you can visit my webpage www.jacquieunderdown.com

Reviews can help readers find books, and I am grateful for all honest reviews. Thank you for taking the time to let others know what you've read, and what you thought.

If you liked this book, here are my other books:

Women's fiction/family saga

The Secrets Mothers Keep
The Perfect Family

Contemporary small-town romance

Wattle Valley Series
Catch Me a Cowboy
Meet Me in the Middle

Brothers of the Vine Series

Bittersweet
The Sweetest Secret
Sweet from the Vine

Mercy Island Series

Pieces of Me
One Hot Christmas
Only Ever You

Fantasy/Paranormal/Magical-realism romance

The Book of Spells and Such
After Life
Out of Time

Transcendent Series

Beautiful Illusion
The Paler Shade of Autumn
Unstitched
Beyond Coincidence

The Secrets Mothers Keep

One Family. Three generations. A common goal to unite them. A lifetime of secrets to divide them. But could uncovering the truth be the only way that this family can finally heal?

Three generations of women find their way back home to Tasmania. They embark on a project together to renovate the family manor and convert it into a bed and breakfast.

After a tumultuous life of pain and betrayal, Mary swore she'd never let anyone hurt her or her family again. But in order to keep her word, she must guard a secret she swore to keep fifty years earlier.

But with the family now under the one roof, and the past tampered with, the foundations of this secret are shaken.

Mary always believed that hiding the truth was protecting the family, but when all is exposed, she finds that by keeping her secret, she was the one hurting them all.

Made in the USA
Monee, IL
02 July 2020

35629602R00231